Maureen (handwritten)

The Minerva
Book of Short Stories 2

Giles Gordon was born in Edinburgh in 1940. He is the
author of six novels and three collections of stories. He has
edited a dozen collections of short stories, including
Modern Short Stories 1940–1980, *English Short Stories 1900
to the Present* (both Everyman) and *Shakespeare Stories*. He
has compiled a bibliography for the British Council of *The
British Twentieth Century Short Story*. He works in London
as a literary agent.

David Hughes was born in Hampshire in 1930. His better
known novels include *The Major*, *The Man Who Invented
Tomorrow*, *The Pork Butcher*, for which he won the W.H.
Smith Literary Award in 1985 and which was recently
filmed as *Souvenir* starring Christopher Plummer, and *But
for Bunter*. He is currently the fiction reviewer for the
Mail on Sunday.

Also by Giles Gordon and David Hughes
available in Minerva

The Minerva Book of Short Stories 1

The Minerva
Book of Short Stories 2

EDITED BY GILES GORDON
AND DAVID HUGHES

Minerva

A Minerva Paperback

THE MINERVA BOOK OF SHORT STORIES 2

First published in Great Britain 1989
as *Best Short Stories 1989* by William Heinemann Ltd
This Minerva edition published 1990
by Mandarin Paperbacks
Michelin House, 81 Fulham Road, London SW3 6RB

Minerva is an imprint of the Octopus Publishing Group

This collection, together with the introduction and notes,
copyright © Giles Gordon and David Hughes 1989

A CIP catalogue record for this book
is available from the British Library
ISBN 0 7493 9085 9

Printed in Great Britain
by Cox and Wyman Ltd, Reading

Contents

Introduction

This is the second collection of short stories published by Heinemann as *Best Short Stories* to be brought out in paperback. It was our fourth annual selection of short stories in English by writers not American and contains, for the first time, more than twenty stories. As the list of contributors suggests, 1988 was something of a vintage year for the publication of stories, not least by newspapers.

The *Observer,* for instance, printed during the summer twelve stories in as many weeks by leading novelists and short-story writers, all but two of whom were British. Moreover, in a year which saw a proliferation of newsprint as various papers added new sections, one obvious and gratifying solution to the search for copy was the publication of fiction.

The weeklies – the *Spectator, News Statesman & Society,* the *Listener* – published the occasional story (all three printed fiction in their Christmas issues) and we reproduce two of them in these pages.

Perhaps it should be noted that some 'commissioned' stories are less good than the author at his or her best (though not, we trust, any we have chosen). Of course it is pleasing for a writer to be asked to create for a series, perhaps, such as 'summer reading' or for Christmas – and to be paid a considerably higher fee than a literary magazine could manage. Any professional should be able to turn a hand to such requests and fulfil them competently. But the fact is that the best mostly arise from compulsion and urge; a writer being unmoved by his material is often a sad and ridiculous spectacle. Newspapers might do better to offer their admired writers *carte blanche* rather than commission on a specific theme or for a particular occasion.

We read as widely as usual in literary journals and in the women's magazines which make a point of giving space to good fiction, as well as in the *New Yorker*, which keeps the wolf from a number of our most distinguished doors.

As so often, the *London Magazine* and *Ambit* are back with splendid stories, as are *Panurge* and *Granta*: we might wish in passing that the last-named would represent the best of new British writing as handsomely as it treats the more established younger Americans. The *Critical Quarterly* enters for the first time. With Maureen Duffy as fiction editor it is including a number of fine stories in each issue. We are conscious that our year's selection is more narrowly 'British' than in previous years. We see no significance in this.

Our range might have been even wider had we allowed ourselves to select from four interesting anthologies published during 1988. They are to be welcomed for showing that once again publishers are positively regarding the short story as no poor relation of the novel but a nursery for new writers – and for not such new writers too – whose passion is for short fiction. Three of these collections, as it happens, contain stories by authors we have included in previous volumes of this series. Sceptre published *20 Under 30*, original stories by the best of British young and new. Bloomsbury's *Soho Square* was packed with sixteen stories and is to be an annual from that burgeoning firm. Pandora's *Storia* will appear twice a year; the first issue from this women's press printed eighteen stories. Finally *Northern Stories 1988* (Littlewood Press, Todmorden, Lancashire) brought out the twenty-four stories judged best in their competition. The winning story is by David Almond, editor of *Panurge*.

As we have suggested before, no single reader is likely to enjoy all the stories in this book equally. It both satisfies and amuses us as selectors that, in assessing earlier hardback volumes, reviewers invariably single out different stories as their favourites. That's what 'best' means, no more nor less than that.

Giles Gordon and David Hughes

The Secret
History of World War 3

J. G. BALLARD

NOW THAT WORLD War 3 has safely ended, I feel free to comment on two remarkable aspects of the whole terrifying affair. The first is that this long-dreaded nuclear confrontation, which was widely expected to erase all life from our planet, in fact lasted barely four minutes. This will surprise many of those reading the present document, but World War 3 took place on January 27, 1995, between 6:47 and 6:51 p.m. Eastern Standard Time. The entire duration of hostilities, from President Reagan's formal declaration of war, to the launch of five sea-based nuclear missiles (three American and two Russian), to the first peace-feelers and the armistice agreed by the President and First Secretary Gorbachov, lasted no more than 245 seconds. World War 3 was over almost before anyone realised that it had begun.

The other extraordinary feature of World War 3 is that I am virtually the only person to know that it ever occurred. It may seem strange that a suburban paediatrician living in Arlington, a few miles west of Washington D.C., should alone be aware of this unique historical event. After all, the news of every downward step in the deepening political crisis, the ailing President's declaration of war and the following nuclear exchange, was openly broadcast on nationwide television. World War 3 was not a secret, but people's minds were addressed to more important matters. In their obsessive concern for the health of their political leadership, they were miraculously able to ignore a far greater threat to their own well-being.

Of course, strictly speaking, I was not the only person to have witnessed World War 3. A small number of senior military personnel in the Nato and Warsaw Pact high commands, as well as President Reagan, Secretary Gorbachov and their aides, and the submarine officers who decrypted the nuclear launch codes and sent the missiles on their way (into unpopulated areas of Alaska and eastern Siberia), were well aware that war had been declared, and a cease-fire agreed four minutes later. But I have yet to meet a member of the ordinary public who has heard of World War 3. Whenever I refer to the war people stare at me with incredulity. Several parents have withdrawn their children from the paediatric clinic, obviously concerned for my mental stability. Only yesterday one mother to whom I casually mentioned the war later telephoned my wife to express her anxieties. But Susan, like everyone else, has forgotten the war, even though I have played video-recordings to her of the ABC, NBC and CNN newscasts on January 27 which actually announce that World War 3 has begun.

That I alone happened to learn of the war I put down to the curious character of the Reagan third term. It is no exaggeration to say that the United States, and much of the western world, had deeply missed this amiable old actor who retired to California in 1989 after the inauguration of his luckless successor. The multiplication of the world's problems — the renewed energy crises, the second Iran/Iraq conflict, the destabilisation of the Soviet Union's Asiatic republics, the unnerving alliance in the USA between Islam and militant feminism – all prompted an intense nostalgia for the Reagan years. There was an immense affectionate memory of his gaffes and little in-competencies, his fondness (shared by those who elected him) for watching TV in his pyjamas rather than attending to more important matters, his confusion of reality with the half-remembered movies of his youth.

Tourists congregated in their hundreds outside the gates of the Reagans' retirement home in Santa Barbara, and occasionally the former President would totter out to pose on the porch. There, prompted by a still soignée Nancy, he would utter some amiable generality that brought tears to his listeners' eyes, and lifted both their hearts and stock markets around the world. As his successor's term in office drew to its unhappy close, the necessary constitutional amendment was swiftly passed through both Houses of Congress, with the express purpose of seeing that Reagan could enjoy his third term in the White House.

In February 1993, after the first uncontested Presidential election in the history of the United States, more than a million people turned out to cheer his inaugural drive through the streets of Washington, while the rest of the world watched on television. If the cathode eye could weep, it did so then.

Nonetheless, a few doubts remained, as the great political crises of the world stubbornly refused to be banished even by the aged President's ingratiating grin. The Iran/Iraq war threatened to embroil Turkey and Afghanistan. In defiance of the Kremlin, the Baltic republics of the USSR were forming armed militias. Yves Saint Laurent had designed the first chador for the power-dressing Islamicised feminists in the fashionable offices of Manhattan, London and Paris. Could even the Reagan presidency cope with a world so askew?

Along with my fellow-physicians who had watched the President on television, I seriously doubted it. At this time, in the summer of 1994, Ronald Reagan was a man of 83, showing all the signs of advancing senility. Like many old men, he enjoyed a few minutes each day of modest lucidity, during which he might utter some gnomic remark, and then lapse into a glassy twilight. His eyes were now too blurred to read the teleprompter, but his White House staff took advantage of the hearing aid he had always worn to insert a small microphone, so that he was able to recite his speeches by repeating like a child whatever he heard in his ear-piece. The pauses were edited out by the TV networks, but the hazards of remote control were revealed when the President, addressing the Catholic Mothers of America, startled the massed ranks of blue-rinsed ladies by suddenly repeating a studio engineer's aside: 'Shift your ass, I gotta take a leak.'

Watching this robotic figure with his eerie smiles and goofy grins, a few people began to ask if the President was brain-dead, or even alive at all. To reassure the nervous American public, unsettled by a falling stock market and by the news of armed insurrection in the Ukraine, the White House physicians began to release a series of regular reports on the President's health. A team of specialists at the Walter Reed Hospital assured the nation that he enjoyed the robust physique and mental alertness of a man fifteen years his junior. Precise details of Reagan's blood-pressure, his white and red cell counts, pulse and respiration were broadcast on TV and had an immediately calming effect. On the following day the world's stock markets showed a memorable lift, interest rates fell and Secretary Gorbachov was able to announce that the Ukrainian separatists had moderated their demands.

Taking advantage of the unsuspected political asset represented by the President's bodily functions, the White House staff decided to issue their medical bulletins on a weekly basis. Not only did Wall Street respond positively, but opinion polls showed a strong recovery by the Republican Party as a whole. By the time of the mid-term Congressional elections, the medical reports were issued daily, and successful Republican candidates swept to control of both House and Senate thanks to an eve-of-poll bulletin on the regularity of the Presidential bowels.

From then on the American public was treated to a continuous stream of information on the President's health. Successive newscasts throughout the day would carry updates on the side-effects of a slight chill or the circulatory benefits of a dip in the White House pool. I well remember watching the news on Christmas Eve as my wife prepared our evening meal, and noticing that details of the President's health occupied five of the six leading news items.

'So his blood sugar is a little down,' Susan remarked as she laid the festival table. 'Good news for Quaker Oats and Pepsi.'

'Really? Is there a connection, for heaven's sake?'

'Much more than you realise.' She sat beside me on the sofa, pepper-mill in hand. 'We'll have to wait for his latest urinalysis. It could be crucial.'

'Dear, what's happening on the Pakistan border could be crucial, Gorbachov has threatened a pre-emptive strike against the rebel enclaves. The US has treaty obligations, theoretically war could –'

'Sh . . .' Susan tapped my knee with the pepper-mill. 'They've just run an Eysenck Personality Inventory – the old boy's scored full marks on emotional resonance and ability to relate. Results corrected for age, whatever that means.'

'It means he's practically a basket case.' I was about to change channels, hoping for some news of the world's real troublespots, but a curious pattern had appeared along the bottom of the screen, some kind of Christmas decoration I assumed, a line of stylised holly leaves. The rhythmic wave stabbed softly from left to right, accompanied by the soothing and nostalgic strains of 'White Christmas'.

'Good God . . .' Susan whispered in awe. 'It's Ronnie's

5

pulse. Did you hear the announcer? "Transmitted live from the Heart of the Presidency".'

This was only the beginning. During the next few weeks, thanks to the miracle of modern radio-telemetry, the nation's TV screens became a scoreboard registering every detail of the President's physical and mental functions. His brave, if tremulous heartbeat drew its trace along the lower edge of the screen, while above it newscasters expanded on his daily physical routines, on the 28 feet he had walked in the rose garden, the calorie count of his modest lunches, the results of his latest brain-scan, read-outs of his kidney, liver and lung function. In addition, there was a daunting sequence of personality and IQ tests, all designed to reassure the American public that the man at the helm of the free world was more than equal to the daunting tasks that faced him across the Oval Office desk.

For all practical purposes, as I tried to explain to Susan, the President was scarcely more than a corpse wired for sound. I and my colleagues at the paediatric clinic were well aware of the old man's ordeal in submitting to this battery of tests. However, the White House staff knew that the American public was almost mesmerised by the spectacle of the President's heart-beat. The trace now ran below all other programmes, accompanying sit-coms, basketball matches and old World War 2 movies. Uncannily, its quickening beat would sometimes match the audience's own emotional responses, indicating that the President himself was watching the same war films, including those in which he himself had appeared.

To complete the identification of President, audience and TV screen — a consummation of which his political advisers had dreamed for so long — the White House staff arranged for further layers of information to be transmitted. Soon a third of the nation's TV screens was occupied by print-outs of heartbeat, blood pressure and EEG readings.

Controversy briefly erupted when it became clear that delta waves predominated, confirming the long-held belief that the President was asleep for most of the day. However, the audiences were thrilled to know when Mr Reagan moved into REM sleep, the dream-time of the nation coinciding with that of its chief executive.

Untouched by this endless barrage of medical information, events in the real world continued down their perilous road. I bought every newspaper I could find, but their pages were dominated by graphic displays of the Reagan health bulletins and by expository articles outlining the significance of his liver enzyme functions and the slightest rise or fall in the concentration of the Presidential urine. Tucked away on the back pages I found a few brief references to civil war in the Asiatic republics of the Soviet Union, an attempted pro-Russian putsch in Pakistan, the Chinese invasion of Nepal, the mobilisation of Nato and Warsaw Pact reserves, the reinforcement of the US 5th and 7th Fleets.

But these ominous events, and the threat of a Third World War, had the ill luck to coincide with a slight down-turn in the President's health. First reported on January 20, this trivial cold caught by Reagan from a visiting grandchild drove all other news from the television screens. An army of reporters and film crews camped outside the White House, while a task force of specialists from the greatest research institutions in the land appeared in relays on every channel, interpreting the stream of medical data.

Like a hundred million Americans, Susan spent the next week sitting by the TV set, eyes following the print-out of the Reagan heartbeat.

'It's still only a cold,' I reassured her when I returned from the clinic on January 27. 'What's the latest from Pakistan? There's a rumour that the Soviets have dropped paratroops into Karachi. The Delta force is moving from Subik Bay . . .'

'Not now!' She waved me aside, turning up the volume as an anchorman began yet another bulletin.

'. . . here's an update on our report of two minutes ago. Good news on the President's CAT scan. There are no abnormal variations in the size or shape of the President's ventricles. Light rain is forecast for the D.C. area tonight, and the 8th Air Cavalry have exchanged fire with Soviet border patrols north of Kabul. We'll be back after the break with a report on the significance of that left temporal lobe spike . . .'

'For God's sake, there's no significance.' I took the remote control unit from Susan's clenched hand and began to hunt the channels. 'What about the Russian Baltic Fleet? The Kremlin is putting counter-pressure on Nato's northern flank. The US has to respond . . .'

By luck, I caught a leading network newscaster concluding a bulletin. He beamed confidently at the audience, his glamorous co-presenter smiling in anticipation.

'. . . as of 5:05 Eastern Standard Time we can report that Mr Reagan's inter-cranial pressure is satisfactory. All motor and cognitive functions are normal for a man of the President's age. Repeat, motor and cognitive functions are normal. Now, here's a newsflash that's just reached us. At 2:35 local time President Reagan completed a satisfactory bowel motion.' The newscaster turned to his co-presenter. 'Barbara, I believe you have similar good news on Nancy?'

'Thank you, Dan,' she cut in smoothly. 'Yes, just one hour later, at 3:35 local time, Nancy completed her very own bowel motion, her second for the day, so it's all happening in the First Family.' She glanced at a slip of paper pushed across her desk. 'The traffic in Pennsylvania Avenue is seizing up again, while F-16s of the 6th Fleet have shot down seven MiG 29s over the Bering Strait. The President's blood pressure is 100 over 60. The ECG records a slight left-hand tremor . . .'

'A tremor of the left hand . . .' Susan repeated, clenching her fists. 'Surely that's serious?'

I tapped the channel changer. 'It could be. Perhaps he's thinking about having to press the nuclear button. Or else –'

An even more frightening possibility had occurred to me. I plunged through the medley of competing news bulletins, hoping to distract Susan as I glanced at the evening sky over Washington. The Soviet deep-water fleet patrolled 400 miles from the eastern coast of the United States. Soon mushroom clouds could be rising above the Pentagon.

'. . . mild pituitary dysfunction is reported, and the President's physicians have expressed a modest level of concern. Repeat, a modest level of concern. The President convened the National Security Council some thirty minutes ago. SAC headquarters in Omaha, Nebraska, report all B-52 attack squadrons airborne. Now, I've just been handed a late bulletin from the White House Oncology Unit. A benign skin tumour was biopsied at 4:15 Washington time . . .'

'. . . the President's physicians have again expressed their concern over Mr Reagan's calcified arteries and hardened cardiac valves. Hurricane Clara is now expected to bypass Puerto Rico, and the President has invoked the Emergency War Powers Act. After the break we'll have more expert analysis of Mr Reagan's retrograde amnesia. Remember, this condition can point to suspected Korsakoff syndrome . . .'

'. . . psychomotor seizures, a distorted sense of time, colour changes and dizziness. Mr Reagan also reports an increased awareness of noxious odours. Other late news – blizzards cover the mid-west, and a state of war now exists between the United States and the Soviet Union. Stay tuned to this channel for a complete update on the President's brain metabolism . . .'

'We're at war,' I said to Susan, and put my arms around

her shoulders. But she was pointing to the erratic heart trace on the screen. Had the President suffered a brain storm and launched an all-out nuclear attack on the Russians? Were the incessant medical bulletins a clever camouflage to shield a volatile TV audience from the consequences of a desperate response to a national emergency? It would take only minutes for the Russian missiles to reach Washington, and I stared at the placid winter sky. Holding Susan in my arms, I listened to the cacophony of medical bulletins until, some four minutes later, I heard:

'. . . the President's physicians report dilated pupils and convulsive tremor, but neurochemical support systems are functioning adequately. The President's brain metabolism reveals glucose production. Scattered snow-showers are forecast overnight, and a cessation of hostilities has been agreed between the US and the USSR. After the break – the latest expert comment on that attack of Presidential flatulence. And why Nancy's left eyelid needed a tuck . . .'

I switched off the set and sat back in the strange silence. A small helicopter was crossing the grey sky over Washington. Almost as an afterthought, I said to Susan: 'By the way, World War 3 has just ended.'

Of course, Susan had no idea that the war had ever begun, a common failure among the public at large, as I realised over the next few weeks. Most people had only a vague recollection of the unrest in the Middle East. The news that nuclear bombs had landed in the deserted mountains of Alaska and eastern Siberia was lost in the torrent of medical reports that covered President Reagan's recovery from his cold.

In the second week of February 1995 I watched him on television as he presided over an American Legion ceremony on the White House lawn. His aged, ivory face was set in its familiar amiable grin, his eyes unfocused as he stood supported by two aides, the ever-watchful First Lady standing in her steely way beside him. Somewhere beneath the bulky black overcoat the radio-telemetry sensors transmitted the live print-outs of pulse, respiration and blood pressure that we could see on our screens. I guessed that the President, too, had forgotten that he had recently launched the Third World War. After all, no one had been killed, and in the public's mind the only possible casualty of those perilous hours had been Mr Reagan himself as he struggled to survive his cold.

Meanwhile, the world was a safer place. The brief nuclear exchange had served its warning to the quarrelling factions around the planet. The secessionist movements in the Soviet Union had disbanded themselves, while elsewhere invading armies withdrew behind their frontiers. I could almost believe that World War 3 had been contrived by the Kremlin and the White House staff as a peacemaking device, and that the Reagan cold had been a diversionary trap into which the TV networks and newspapers had unwittingly plunged.

In tribute to the President's recuperative powers, the liner traces of his vital functions still notched their way across our TV screens. As he saluted the assembled veterans of the American Legion, I sensed the audience's collective pulse beating faster when the old actor's heart responded to the stirring sight of these marching men.

Then, among the Medal of Honour holders, I noticed a dishevelled young man in an ill-fitting uniform, out of step with his older companions. He pushed through the marching files as he drew a pistol from his tunic. There was a flurry of confusion while aides grappled with each other around the podium. The cameras swerved to catch the young man darting towards the President. Shots sounded above the wavering strains of the band. In the panic of uniformed men the President seemed to fall into the First Lady's arms and was swiftly borne away.

Searching the print-outs below the TV screen, I saw at once that the President's blood pressure had collapsed. The

11

erratic pulse had levelled out into an unbroken horizontal line, and all respiratory function had ceased. It was only ten minutes later, as news was released of an unsuccessful assassination attempt, that the traces resumed their confident signatures.

Had the President died, perhaps for a second time? Had he, in a strict sense, ever lived during his third term of office? Will some animated spectre of himself, reconstituted from the medical print-outs that still parade across our TV screens, go on to yet further terms, unleashing Fourth and Fifth World Wars, whose secret histories will expire within the interstices of our television schedules, forever lost within the ultimate urinalysis, the last great biopsy in the sky?

A Letter to Our Son

PETER CAREY

BEFORE I HAVE finished writing this, the story of how you were born, I will be forty-four years old and the events and feelings which make up the story will be at least eight months old. You are lying in the next room in a cotton jump-suit. You have five teeth. You cannot walk. You do not seem interested in crawling. You are sound asleep.

I have put off writing this so long that, now the time is here, I do not want to write it. I cannot think. Laziness. Wooden shutters over the memory. Nothing comes, no pictures, no feelings, but the architecture of the hospital at Camperdown.

You were born in the King George V Hospital in Missenden Road, Camperdown, a building that won an award for its architecture. It was opened during the Second World War, but its post-Bauhaus modern style has its roots in that time before the First World War, with an optimism about the technological future that we may never have again.

I liked this building. I liked its smooth, rounded, shiny corners. I liked its wide stairs. I liked the huge sash-windows, even the big blue-and-white checked tiles: when

I remember this building there is sunshine splashed across those tiles, but there were times when it seemed that other memories might triumph and it would be remembered for the harshness of its neon lights and emptiness of the corridors.

A week before you were born, I sat with your mother in a four-bed ward on the eleventh floor of this building. In this ward she received blood transfusions from plum-red plastic bags suspended on rickety stainless steel stands. The blood did not always flow smoothly. The bags had to be fiddled with, the stand had to be raised, lowered, have its drip-rate increased, decreased, inspected by the sister who had been a political prisoner in Chile, by the sister from the Solomon Islands, by others I don't remember. The blood entered your mother through a needle in her forearm. When the vein collapsed, a new one had to be found. This was caused by a kind of bruising called 'tissuing'. We soon knew all about tissuing. It made her arm hurt like hell.

She was bright-eyed and animated as always, but her lips had a slight blue tinge and her skin had a tight, translucent quality.

She was in this room on the west because her blood appeared to be dying. Some thought the blood was killing itself. This is what we all feared, none more than me, for when I heard her blood-count was so low, the first thing I thought (stop that thought, cut it off, bury it) was cancer.

This did not necessarily have a lot to do with Alison, but with me, and how I had grown up, with a mother who was preoccupied with cancer and who, going into surgery for suspected breast cancer, begged the doctor to 'cut them both off'. When my mother's friend Enid Tanner boasted of her hard stomach muscles, my mother envisaged a growth. When her father complained of a sore elbow, my mother threatened the old man: 'All right, we'll take you up to Doctor Campbell and she'll cut it off.' When I was ten, my mother's brother got cancer and they cut his leg off right up near the hip and took photographs of him, naked, one-legged, to show other doctors the success of the operation.

When I heard your mother's blood-count was low, I was my mother's son. I thought: cancer.

I remembered what Alison had told me of that great tragedy of her grandparents' life, how their son (her uncle) had leukaemia, how her grandfather then bought him the car (a Ford Prefect? a Morris Minor?) he had hitherto refused him, how the dying boy had driven for miles and miles, hours and hours while his cells attacked each other.

I tried to stop this thought, to cut it off. It grew again, like a thistle whose root has not been removed and must grow again, every time, stronger and stronger.

The best haematological unit in Australia was on hand to deal with the problem. They worked in the hospital across the road, the Royal Prince Alfred. They were friendly and efficient. They were not at all like I had imagined big hospital specialists to be. They took blood samples, but the blood did not tell them enough. They returned to take marrow from your mother's bones. They brought a big needle with them that would give you the horrors if you could see the size of it.

The doctor's speciality was leukaemia, but he said to us: 'We don't think it's anything really nasty.' Thus 'nasty' became a code for cancer.

They diagnosed megnoblastic anaemia which, although we did not realise it, is the condition of the blood and not the disease itself.

Walking back through the streets in Shimbashi in Tokyo, your mother once told me that a fortune-teller had told her she would die young. It was for this reason – or so I remembered – that she took such care of her health. At the time she told me this, we had not known each other very long. It was July. We had fallen in love in May. We were still stumbling over each other's feelings in the dark. I took this secret of your mother's lightly, not thinking about the weight it must carry, what it might mean to talk about it. I hurt her; we fought, in the street by the Shimbashi railway station, in a street with shop windows advertising cosmetic surgery, in the Dai-Ichi Hotel in the Ginza district of Tokyo, Japan.

When they took the bone marrow from your mother's spine, I held her hand. The needle had a cruel diameter, was less a needle than an instrument for removing a plug. She was very brave. Her wrists seemed too thin, her skin too white and shiny, her eyes too big and bright. She held my hand because of pain. I held hers because I loved her, because I could not think of living if I did not have her. I thought of what she had told me in Tokyo. I wished there was a God I could pray to.

I flew to Canberra on 7 May 1984. It was my forty-first birthday. I had injured my back and should have been lying flat on a board. I had come from a life with a woman which had reached, for both of us, a state of chronic unhappiness. I will tell you the truth: I was on that aeroplane to Canberra because I hoped I might fall in love. This made me a dangerous person.

There was a playwrights' conference in Canberra. I hoped there would be a woman there who would love me as I would love her. This was a fantasy I had had before, getting on aeroplanes to foreign cities, riding in taxis towards hotels in Melbourne, in Adelaide, in Brisbane. I do not mean that I was thinking about sex, or an affair, but that I was looking for someone to spend my life with. Also – and I swear I have not invented this after the fact – I had a vision of your mother's neck.

I hardly knew her. I met her once at a dinner when I hardly noticed her. I met her a second time when I saw, in a meeting room, the back of her neck. We spoke that time, but I was argumentative and I did not think of her in what I can only call 'that way'.

16

And yet as the aeroplane came down to land in Canberra, I saw your mother's neck, and thought: maybe Alison Summers will be there. She was the dramaturge at the Nimrod Theatre. It was a playwrights' conference. She should be there.

And she was. And we fell in love. And we stayed up till four in the morning every morning talking. And there were other men, everywhere, in love with her. I didn't know about the other men. I knew only that I was in love as I had not been since I was eighteen years old. I wanted to marry Alison Summers, and at the end of the first night we had been out together when I walked her to the door of her room, and we had, for the first time, ever so lightly, kissed on the lips – and also, I must tell you, for it was delectable and wonderful, I kissed your mother on her long, beautiful neck – and when we had kissed and patted the air between us and said 'all right' a number of times, and I had walked back to my room where I had, because of my back injury, a thin mattress lying flat on the floor, and when I was in this bed, I said, aloud, to the empty room: 'I am going to live with Alison.'

And I went to sleep so happy I must have been smiling.

She did not know what I told the room. And it was three or four days before I could see her again, three or four days before we could go out together, spend time alone, and I could tell her what I thought.

I had come to Canberra wanting to fall in love. Now I was in love. Who was I in love with? I hardly knew, and yet I knew exactly. I did not even realise how beautiful she was. I found that out later. At the beginning I recognised something more potent than beauty: it was a force, a life, an energy. She had such life in her face, in her eyes – those eyes which you inherited – most of all. It was this I loved, this which I recognised so that I could say – having kissed her so lightly – I will live with Alison. And I know that I was right.

It was a conference. We were behaving like men and women do at conferences, having affairs. We would not be so sleazy. After four nights staying up talking till four a.m. we had still not made love. I would creep back to my room, to my mattress on the floor. We talked about everything. Your mother liked me, but I cannot tell you how long it took her to fall in love with me. But I know we were discussing marriages and babies when we had not even been to bed together. That came early one morning when I returned to her room after three hours' sleep. We had not planned to make love there at the conference but there we were, lying on the bed, kissing, and then we were making love, and you were not conceived then, of course, and yet from that time we never ceased thinking of you and when, later in Sydney, we had to learn to adjust to each other's needs, and when we argued, which we did often then, it was you more than anything that kept us together. We wanted you so badly. We loved you before we saw you. We loved you as we made you, in bed in another room, at Lovett Bay.

When your mother came to the eleventh floor of the King George V Hospital, you were almost ready to be born. Every day the sisters came and smeared jelly on your mother's tight, bulging stomach and then stuck a flat little octopus-type sucker to it and listened to the noises you made.

You sounded like soldiers marching on a bridge.

You sounded like short-wave radio.

You sounded like the inside of the sea.

We did not know if you were a boy or a girl, but we called you Sam anyway. When you kicked or turned we said: 'Sam's doing his exercises.' We said silly things.

When we heard how low Alison's blood-count was, I phoned the obstetrician to see if you were OK. She said there was no need to worry. She said you had your own blood-supply. She said that as long as the mother's count was above six there was no need to worry.

Your mother's count was 6.2. This was very close. I kept worrying that you had been hurt in some way. I could not share this worry for to share it would only be to make it worse. Also I recognise that I have made a whole career out of making my anxieties get up and walk around, not only in my own mind, but in the minds of readers. I went to see a naturopath once. We talked about negative emotions – fear and anger. I said to him: 'But I *use* my anger and my fear.' I talked about these emotions as if they were chisels and hammers.

This alarmed him considerably.

Your mother is not like this. When the haematologists saw how she looked, they said: 'Our feeling is that you don't have anything nasty.' They topped her up with blood until her count was twelve and although they had not located the source of her anaemia, they sent her home.

A few days later her count was down to just over six.

It seemed as if there was a silent civil war inside her veins and arteries. The number of casualties was appalling.

I think we both got frightened then. I remember coming home to Louisa Road. I remember worrying that I would cry. I remember embracing your mother – and you too, for you were a great bulge between us. I must not cry. I must support her.

I made a meal. It was a salade niçoise. The electric lights, in memory, were all ten watts, sapped by misery. I could barely eat. I think we may have watched a funny film on videotape. We repacked the bag that had been unpacked so short a time before. It now seemed likely that your birth was to be induced. If your mother was sick she could not be looked after properly with you inside her. She would be given one more blood transfusion, and then the induction would begin. And that is how your birthday would be on September thirteenth.

*

Two nights before your birthday I sat with Alison in the four-bed ward, the one facing east, towards Missenden Road. The curtains were drawn around us. I sat on the bed and held her hand. The blood continued its slow viscous drip from the plum-red bag along the clear plastic tube and into her arm. The obstetrician was with us. She stood at the head of the bed, a kind, intelligent woman in her early thirties. We talked about Alison's blood. We asked her what she thought this mystery could be. Really what we wanted was to be told that everything was OK. There was a look on Alison's face when she asked. I cannot describe it, but it was not a face seeking medical 'facts'.

The obstetrician went through all the things that were not wrong with your mother's blood. She did not have a vitamin B deficiency. She did not have a folic acid deficiency. There was no iron deficiency. She did not have any of the common (and easily fixable) anaemias of pregnancy. So what could it be? we asked, really only wishing to be assured it was nothing 'nasty'.

'Well,' said the obstetrician, 'at this stage you cannot rule out cancer.'

I watched your mother's face. Nothing in her expression showed what she must feel. There was a slight colouring of her cheeks. She nodded. She asked a question or two. She held my hand, but there was no tight squeezing.

The obstetrician asked Alison if she was going to be 'all right'. Alison said she would be 'all right'. But when the obstetrician left she left the curtains drawn.

The obstetrician's statement was not of course categorical and not everyone who has cancer dies, but Alison was, at that instant, confronting the thing that we fear most. When the doctor said those words, it was like a dream or a nightmare. I heard them said. And yet they were not said. They could not be said. And when we hugged each other – when the doctor had gone – we pressed our bodies together as we always had before, and if there were tears on our cheeks, there had been tears on our cheeks before. I kissed your mother's eyes. Her hair was wet with her tears. I smoothed her hair on her forehead. My own eyes were swimming. She said: 'All right, how are we going to get through all this?'

Now you know her, you know how much like her that is. She is not going to be a victim of anything.

'We'll decide it's going to be OK,' she said, 'that's all.'

And we dried our eyes.

But that night, when she was alone in her bed, waiting for the sleeping pill to work, she thought: If I die, I'll at least have made this little baby.

When I left your mother I appeared dry-eyed and positive, but my disguise was a frail shell of a thing and it cracked on the stairs and my grief and rage came spilling out in gulps. The halls of the hospital gleamed with polish and vinyl and fluorescent light. The flower-seller on the ground floor had locked up his shop. The foyer was empty. The whisker-shadowed man in admissions was watching television. In Missenden Road two boys in jeans and sand-shoes conducted separate conversations in separate phone booths. Death was not touching them. They turned their backs to each other. One of them – a red-head with a tattoo on his forearm – laughed.

In Missenden Road there were taxis NOT FOR HIRE speeding towards other destinations.

In Missenden Road the bright white lights above the zebra crossings became a luminous sea inside my eyes. Car lights turned into necklaces and ribbons. I was crying, thinking it is not for me to cry: crying is a poison, a negative force; everything will be all right; but I was weeping as if huge balloons of air had to be released from inside my guts. I walked normally. My grief was invisible. A man rushed past me, carrying roses wrapped in cellophane. I got into my car. The floor was littered with car-park tickets from all the previous days of blood transfusions, tests, test results, admission etc. I drove out of the car-park. I talked aloud.

I told the night I loved Alison Summers. I love you, I love you, you will not die. There were red lights at the Parramatta Road. I sat there, howling, unroadworthy. I love you.

The day after tomorrow there will be a baby. Will the baby have a mother? What would we do if we knew Alison was dying? What would we do so Sam would know his mother? Would we make a videotape? Would we hire a camera? Would we set it up and act for you? Would we talk to you with smiling faces, showing you how we were together, how we loved each other? How could we? How could we think of these things?

I was a prisoner in a nightmare driving down Ross Street in Glebe. I passed the Afrikan restaurant where your mother and I ate after first coming to live in Balmain.

All my life I have waited for this woman. This cannot happen.

I thought: Why would it *not* happen? Every day people are tortured, killed, bombed. Every day babies starve. Every day there is pain and grief, enough to make you howl to the moon forever. Why should we be exempt, I thought, from the pain of life?

What would I do with a baby? How would I look after it? Day after day, minute after minute, by myself. I would be a sad man, forever, marked by the loss of this woman. I would love the baby. I would care for it. I would see, in its features, every day, the face of the woman I had loved more than any other.

When I think of this time, it seems as if it's two in the morning, but it was not. It was ten o'clock at night. I drove home through a landscape of grotesque imaginings.

The house was empty and echoing.

In the nursery everything was waiting for you, all the things we had got for 'the baby'. We had read so many books about babies, been to classes where we learned about how babies are born, but we still did not understand the purpose of all the little clothes we had folded in the drawers. We did not know which was a swaddle and which was a sheet. We could not have selected the clothes to dress you in.

I drank coffee. I drank wine. I set out to telephone Kathy Lette, Alison's best friend, so she would have this 'news' before she spoke to your mother the next day. I say 'set out' because each time I began to dial, I thought: I am not going to do this properly. I hung up. I did deep breathing. I calmed myself. I telephoned. Kim Williams, Kathy's husband, answered and said Kathy was not home yet. I thought: She must know. I told Kim, and as I told him the weeping came with it. I could hear myself. I could imagine Kim listening to me. I would sound frightening, grotesque, and less in control than I was. When I had finished frightening him, I went to bed and slept.

I do not remember the next day, only that we were bright and determined. Kathy hugged Alison and wept. I hugged Kathy and wept. There were isolated incidents. We were 'handling it'. And, besides, you were coming on the next day. You were life, getting stronger and stronger.

I had practical things to worry about. For instance: the bag. The bag was to hold all the things for the labour ward. There was a list for the contents of the bag and these contents were all purchased and ready, but still I must bring them to the hospital early the next morning. I checked the bag. I placed things where I would not forget them. You wouldn't believe the things we had. We had a cassette-player and a tape with soothing music. We had rosemary and lavender oil so I could massage your mother and relax her between contractions. I had a thermos to fill with blocks of frozen orange juice. There were special cold packs to relieve the pain of a backache labour. There were paper pants – your arrival, after all, was not to happen without a great deal of mess. There were socks, because your mother's feet would almost certainly get very cold. I packed all these things, and there was something in the process of this packing which helped overcome my fears and made me concentrate on you, our little baby, already so loved although we did not know your face, had seen no more of you than the ghostly blue image thrown up by the ultrasound in the midst of whose shifting perspectives we had seen your little hand move. ('He waved to us.')

On the morning of the day of your birth I woke early. It was only just light. I had notes stuck on the fridge and laid out on the table. I made coffee and poured it into a thermos. I made the bagel sandwiches your mother and I had planned months before – my lunch. I filled the bagels with a fiery Polish sausage and cheese and gherkins. For your mother, I filled a spray-bottle with Evian water.

It was a Saturday morning and bright and sunny and I knew you would be born but I did not know what it would be like. I drove along Ross Street in Glebe ignorant of the important things I would know that night. I wore grey stretchy trousers and a black shirt which would later be marked by the white juices of your birth. I was excited, but less than you might imagine. I parked at the hospital as I had parked on all those other occasions. I carried the bags up to the eleventh floor. They were heavy.

Alison was in her bed. She looked calm and beautiful. When we kissed, her lips were soft and tender. She said: 'This time tomorrow we'll have a little baby.'

In our conversation, we used the diminutive a lot. You were always spoken of as 'little', as indeed you must really have been, but we would say 'little' hand, 'little' feet, 'little' baby, and this evoked all our powerful feelings about you.

This term ('little') is so loaded that writers are wary of using it. It is cute, sentimental, 'easy'. All of sentient life seems programmed to respond to 'little'. If you watch grown dogs with a pup, a pup they have never seen, they are immediately patient and gentle, even solicitous, with it. If you had watched your mother and father holding up a tiny terry-towelling jump-suit in a department store, you would have seen their faces change as they celebrated your 'littleness' while, at the same time, making fun of their own responses – they were aware of acting in a way they would have previously thought of as saccharine.

And yet we were not aware of the torrents of emotion your 'littleness' would unleash in us, and by the end of September thirteenth we would think it was nothing other than the meaning of life itself.

When I arrived at the hospital with the heavy bags of cassette-players and rosemary oil, I saw a dark-bearded, neat man in a suit sitting out by the landing. This was the hypnotherapist who had arrived to help you come into the world. He was serious, impatient, eager to start. He wanted to start in the pathology ward, but in the end he helped carry the cassette-player, thermoses, sandwiches, massage oil, sponges, paper pants, apple juice, frozen orange blocks, rolling pin, cold packs, and even water down to the labour ward where – on a stainless steel stand eight feet high – the sisters were already hanging the bag of Oxytocin which would ensure this day was your birthday.

It was a pretty room, by the taste of the time. As I write it is still that time, and I still think it pretty. All the surfaces were hospital surfaces – easy to clean – laminexes, vinyls, materials with a hard shininess, but with colours that were soft pinks and blues and an effect that was unexpectedly pleasant, even sophisticated.

The bed was one of those complicated stainless steel machines which seems so cold and impersonal until you realise all the clever things it can do. In the wall there were sockets with labels like 'Oxygen'. The cupboards were filled with paper-wrapped sterile 'objects'. There was, in short, a seriousness about the room, and when we plugged in the cassette-player we took care to make sure we were not using a socket that might be required for something more important.

The hypnotherapist left me to handle the unpacking of the bags. He explained his business to the obstetrician. She told him that eight hours would be a good, fast labour. The hypnotherapist said he and Alison were aiming for three. I don't know what the doctor thought, but I thought there was not a hope in hell.

When the Oxytocin drip had been put into my darling's arm, when the water-clear hormone was entering her veins, one drip every ten seconds (you could hear the machine click when a drip was released), when these pure chemical messages were being delivered to her body, the hypnotherapist attempted to send other messages of a less easily assayable quality.

I tell you the truth: I did not care for this hypnotherapist, this pushy, over-eager fellow taking up all this room in the labour ward. He sat on the right-hand side of the bed. I sat on the left. He made me feel useless. He said: 'You are going to have a good labour, a fast labour, a fast labour like the one you have already visualised.' Your mother's eyes were closed. She had such large, soft lids, such tender and vulnerable coverings of skin. Inside the pink light of the womb, your eyelids were the same. Did you hear the messages your mother was sending to her body and to you? The hypnotherapist said: 'After just three hours you are going to deliver a baby, a good, strong, healthy baby. It will be an easy birth, an effortless birth. It will last three hours and you will not tear.' On the door the sisters had tacked a sign reading: QUIET PLEASE. HYPNOTHERAPY IN PROGRESS. 'You are going to be so relaxed, and in a moment you are going to be even more relaxed, more relaxed than you have ever been before. You are feeling yourself going deeper and deeper and when you come to you will be in a state of waking hypnosis and you will respond to the trigger-words Peter will give you during your labour, words which will make you, once again, so relaxed.'

My trigger-words were to be 'Breathe' and 'Relax'.

The hypnotherapist gave me his phone number and asked me to call when you were born. But for the moment you had not felt the effects of the Oxytocin on your world and you could not yet have suspected the adventures the day would have in store for you.

You still sounded like the ocean, like soldiers marching across a bridge, like short-wave radio.

On Tuesday nights through the previous winter we had gone to classes in a building where the lifts were always sticking. We had walked up the stairs to a room where pregnant women and their partners had rehearsed birth with dolls, had watched hours of videotapes of exhausted women in labour. We had practised all the different sorts of breathing. We had learned of the different positions for giving birth: the squat, the supported squat, the squat supported by a seated partner. We knew the positions for first and second stage, for a backache labour, and so on, and so on. We learned birth was a complicated, exhausting and difficult process. We worried we would forget how to breathe. And yet now the time was here we both felt confident, even though nothing would be like it had been in the birth classes. Your mother was connected to the Oxytocin drip which meant she could not get up and walk around. It meant it was difficult for her to 'belly dance' or do most of the things we had spent so many evenings learning about.

In the classes they tell you that the contractions will start far apart, that you should go to hospital only when they are ten minutes apart: short bursts of pain, but long rests in between. During this period your mother could expect to walk around, to listen to music, to enjoy a massage. However, your birth was not to be like this. This was not because of you. It was because of the Oxytocin. It had a fast, intense effect, like a double Scotch when you're expecting a beer. There were not to be any ten-minute rests, and from the time the labour started it was, almost immediately, fast and furious, with a one-minute contraction followed by no more than two minutes of rest.

If there had been time to be frightened, I think I would have been frightened. Your mother was in the grip of pains she could not escape from. She squatted on a bean bag. It was as if her insides were all tangled, and tugged in a battle to the death. Blood ran from her. Fluid like egg-white. I did not know what anything was. I was a man who had wandered onto a battlefield. The blood was bright with oxygen. I wiped your mother's brow. She panted. *Huh-huh-huh-huh*. I ministered to her with sponge and water. I could not take her pain for her. I could do nothing but measure the duration of the pain. I had a little red stop-watch you will one day find abandoned in a dusty drawer. (Later your mother asked me what I had felt during labour. I thought only: I must count the seconds of the contraction; I must help Alison breathe, now, now, now; I must get that sponge – there is time to make the water in the sponge cool – now I can remove that bowl and cover it. Perhaps I can reach the bottle of Evian water. God, I'm so *thirsty*. What did I think during the labour? I thought: When this contraction is over I will get to that Evian bottle.)

Somewhere in the middle of this, in these three hours in this room whose only view was a blank screen of frosted glass, I helped your mother climb onto the bed. She was on all fours. In this position she could reach the gas mask. It was nitrous oxide, laughing gas. It did not stop the pain, but it made it less important. For the gas to work your mother had to anticipate the contraction, breathing in gas before it arrived. The sister came and showed me how I could feel the contraction coming with my hand. But I couldn't. We used the stop-watch, but the contractions were not regularly spaced, and sometimes we anticipated them and sometimes not. When we did not get it right, your mother took the full brunt of the pain. She had her face close to the mattress. I sat on the chair beside. My face was close to hers. I held the watch where she could see it. I held her wrist. I can still see the red of her face, the wideness of her eyes as they bulged at the enormous *size* of the pains that racked her.

Sisters came and went. They had to see how wide the cervix was. At first it was only two centimetres, not nearly enough room for you to come out. An hour later they announced it was four centimetres. It had to get to nine centimetres before we could even think of you being born. There had to be room for your head (which we had been told was big – well, we were told wrong, weren't we?) and your shoulders to slip through. It felt to your mother that this labour would go on for eight or twelve or twenty hours. That she should endure this intensity of pain for this time was unthinkable. It was like running a hundred-metre race which was stretching to ten miles. She wanted an epidural – a pain blocker.

But when the sister heard this she said: 'Oh do try to hang on. You're doing *so* well.'

I went to the sister, like a shop steward.

I said: 'My wife wants an epidural, so can you please arrange it?'

The sister agreed to fetch the anaesthetist, but there was between us – I admit it now – a silent conspiracy: for although I had pressed the point and she had agreed it was your mother's right, we both believed (I, for my part, on her advice) that if your mother could endure a little longer she could have the birth she wanted – without an epidural.

The anaesthetist came and went. The pain was at its worst. A midwife came and inspected your mother. She said: 'Ten centimetres.'

She said: 'Your baby is about to be born.'

We kissed, your mother and I. We kissed with soft, passionate lips as we did the day we lay on a bed at Lovett Bay and conceived you. That day the grass outside the window was a brilliant green beneath the vibrant petals of fallen jacaranda.

Outside the penumbra of our consciousness trolleys were wheeled. Sterile bags were cut open. The contractions did not stop, of course.

The obstetrician had not arrived. She was in a car, driving fast towards the hospital.

I heard a midwife say: 'Who can deliver in this position?' (It was still unusual, as I learned at that instant, for women to deliver their babies on all fours.)

Someone left the room. Someone entered. Your mother was pressing the gas mask so hard against her face it was making deep indentations on her skin. Her eyes bulged huge.

Someone said: 'Well get her, otherwise I'll have to deliver it myself.'

The door opened. Bushfire came in.

Bushfire was aboriginal. She was about fifty years old. She was compact and tactiturn like a farmer. She had a face that folded in on itself and let out its feelings slowly, selectively. It was a face to trust, and trust especially at this moment when I looked up to see Bushfire coming through the door in a green gown. She came in a rush, her hands out to have gloves put on.

There was another contraction. I heard the latex snap around Bushfire's wrists. She said: 'There it is. I can see your baby's head.' It was you. The tip of you, the top of you. You were a new country, a planet, a star seen for the first time. I was not looking at Bushfire. I was looking at your mother. She was all alight with love and pain.

'Push,' said Bushfire.

Your mother pushed. It was you she was pushing, you that put that look of luminous love on her face, you that made the veins on her forehead bulge and her skin go red.

Then – it seems such a short time later – Bushfire said: 'Your baby's head is born.'

And then, so quickly in retrospect, but one can no more recall it accurately than one can recall exactly how one made love on a bed when the jacaranda petals were lying like jewels on the grass outside. Soon. Soon we heard you. Soon you slipped out of your mother. Soon you came slithering out not having hurt her, not even having grazed her. You slipped out, as slippery as a little fish, and we heard you cry. Your cry was so much lighter and thinner than I might have expected. I do not mean that it was weak or frail, but that your first cry had a timbre unlike anything I had expected. The joy we felt. Your mother and I kissed again, at that moment.

'My little baby,' she said. We were crying with happiness. 'My little baby.'

I turned to look. I saw you. Skin. Blue-white, shiny-wet.

I said: 'It's a boy.'

'Look at me,' your mother said, meaning: stay with me, be with me, the pain is not over yet, do not leave me now. I turned to her. I kissed her. I was crying, just crying with happiness that you were there.

The room you were born in was quiet, not full of noise and clattering. This is how we wanted it for you. So you could come into the world gently and that you should – as you were now – be put onto your mother's stomach. They wrapped you up. I said: 'Couldn't he feel his mother's skin?' They unwrapped you so you could have your skin against hers.

And there you were. It was you. You had a face, the face we had never known. You were so calm. You did not cry or fret. You had big eyes like your mother's. And yet when I looked at you first I saw not your mother and me, but your two grandfathers, your mother's father, my father; and, as my father, whom I loved a great deal, had died the year before, I was moved to see that here, in you, he was alive.

Look at the photographs in the album that we took at this time. Look at your mother and how alive she is, how clear her eyes are, how all the red pain has just slipped off her face and left the unmistakable visage of a young woman in love.

We bathed you (I don't know whether this was before or after) in warm water and you accepted this gravely, swimming instinctively.

I held you (I think this must be before), and you were warm and slippery. You had not been bathed when I held you. The obstetrician gave you to me so she could examine your mother. She said: 'Here.'

I held you against me. I knew then that your mother would not die. I thought: 'It's fine, it's all right.' I held you against my breast. You smelled of love-making.

'Tis Pity She's a Whore

ANGELA CARTER

THERE WAS A rancher who had two children, a son and then a daughter. A while after that, his wife died and was buried under two sticks nailed together to make a cross because there was not time, yet, to carve a stone.

Did she die of the loneliness of the prairies? Or was it anguish that killed her, anguish, and nostalgia for the close, warm neighbourly life she had left behind her when she came to this emptiness? Neither. She died of the pressure of that vast sky, that weighed down upon her and crushed her lungs until she could not breathe any more, as if the prairies were the bedrock of an ocean in which she drowned.

She told her boy: 'Look after your sister.' He, blond,

Note: John Ford: 1586–circa 1639. English dramatist of the Jacobean period. His tragedy, *'Tis Pity She's a Whore*, was published in 1633. 'Deep in a dump John Ford alone was got/With folded arms and melancholy hat.' (*Choice Drollery*, 1656.)

John Ford: 1895–1973. American film-maker. Filmography includes: *Stagecoach* (1939); *My Darling Clementine* (1946); *She Wore a Yellow Ribbon* (1949). 'My name is John Ford. I make Westerns.' (*John Ford*, Andrew Sinclair, New York 1979.)

solemn, little; he and Death sat with her in the room of logs her husband split to build. Death, with high cheek-bones, wore his hair in braids. His invisible presence in the cabin mocked the existence of the cabin. The round-eyed boy clutched his mother's dry hand. The girl was younger.

Then the mother lay with the prairies and all that careless sky upon her breast, and the children lived in their father's house. So they grew up. In his spare time, the rancher chiselled at a rock: 'Beloved wife of . . . mother of . . .' beneath the space at the top he had left for his own name.

America begins and ends in the cold and solitude. Up here, she pillows her head upon the Arctic snow. Down there, she dips her feet in the chilly waters of the South Atlantic, home of the perpetually restless albatross. America, with her torso of a woman at the time of this story, a woman with an hour-glass waist, a waist laced so tightly it snapped in two, and we put a belt of water there. America, with your child-bearing hips and your crotch of jungle, your swelling bosom of a nursing mother and your cold head, your cold head.

Its central paradox resides in this: that the top half doesn't know what the bottom half is doing. When I say the two children of the prairie, suckled on those green breasts, were the pure children of the continent, you know at once that they were *norteamericanos*, or I would not speak of them in the English language, which was their language, the language that silences the babble of this continent's multitude of tongues.

Blond children with broad, freckled faces, the boy in dungarees and the little girl in gingham and sun-bonnet. In the old play, one John Ford called them Giovanni and Annabella; the other John Ford, in the movie, might call them Johnny and Annie-Belle.

*

34

Annie-Belle will bake bread, tramp the linen clean and cook the beans and bacon; this lily of the West had not spare time enough to pause and consider the lilies of the field, who never do a hand's turn. No sir. A woman's work is never done and she became a woman early.

The gaunt paterfamilias would drive them into town to church on Sundays with the black Bible on his knee wherein their names and dates of birth were inscribed. In the buggy, his shy, big-boned, tow-headed son in best, dark, Sunday clothes, and Annie-Belle, at thirteen, fourteen, increasingly astonished at and rendered shy by her own lonely flowering. Fifteen. How pretty she was growing! They came to pray in God's house that, like their own, was built of split logs. Annie-Belle kept her eyes down; she was a good girl. They were good children. The widower drank, sometimes, but not much. They grew up in silence, in the enormous silence of the empty land, the silence that swallowed up the Saturday-night fiddler's tune, mocked the rare laughter at weddings and christenings, echoed, a vast margin, around the sermons of the preacher.

Silence and space and an unimaginable freedom which they dare not imagine.

Since his wife died, the rancher spoke rarely. They lived far out of town. He had no time for barn-raisings and church suppers. If she had lived, everything would have been different, but he occupied his spare moments in chiselling the gravestone. They did not celebrate Thanksgiving for he had nothing for which to give thanks. It was a hard life.

The Minister's wife made sure Annie-Belle knew a thing or two when she judged it about the time the girl's bleeding started. The Minister's wife, in a vague, pastoral way, thought about a husband for Annie-Belle, a wife for Johnny. 'Out there, in that little house on the prairie, so lonesome ... Nobody for those young folks to talk to 'cept cows, cows, cows.'

★

What did the girl think? In summer, of the heat, and how to keep flies out of the butter; in winter, of the cold. I do not know what else she thought. Perhaps, as young girls do, she thought that a stranger would come to town and take her away to the city and so on, but, since her imagination began and ended with her experience, the farm, work, the seasons, I think she did not think so far, as if she knew already she was the object of her own desire for, in the bright light of the New World, nothing is obscure. But when they were children, all they knew was they loved each other just as surely a brother or a sister should.

She washed her hair in a tub. She washed her long, yellow hair. She was fifteen. It was spring. She washed her hair. It was the first time that year. She sat on the porch to dry her hair, she sat in the rocking-chair which her mother selected from the Sears Roebuck catalogue, where her father would never sit, now. She propped a bit of mirror on the porch railing. It caught the sun and flashed. She combed out her wet hair in the mirror. There seemed to be an awful lot of it, tangling up the comb. She wore only her petticoat, the men were off with the cattle, nobody to see her pale shoulders except that Johnny came back. The horse threw him, he knocked his head against a stone. Giddy, he came back to the house, leading his pony, and she was busy untangling her hair and did not see him, nor have a chance to cover herself.

'Why, Johnny, I declare –'

Imagine an orchestra behind them: the frame-house, the porch, the rocking-chair endlessly rocking, like a cradle, the white petticoat with eyelet lace, her water-darkened hair hanging on her shoulders and little trickles running down between her shallow breasts, the young man leading the limping pony, and, inexhaustible as light, around them the tender land.

The 'Love Theme' swells and rises. She jumps up to tend him. The jogged mirror falls.

'Seven years' bad luck –'

In the fragments of the mirror, they kneel to see their round, blond, innocent faces that, superimposed upon one another, would fit at every feature, their faces, all at once the same face, the face that never existed until now, the pure face of America.

EXTERIOR. PRAIRIE. DAY.

LONG SHOT: Farmhouse.

CLOSE UP: Petticoat falling on to porch of farm-house.

Wisconsin, Ohio, Iowa, Missouri, Kansas, Minnesota, Nebraska, the Dakotas, Wyoming, Montana ... Oh, those enormous territories! That green vastness, in which anything is possible.

EXTERIOR. PRAIRIE. DAY.

CLOSE UP: Johnny and Annie-Belle kiss.
'Love Theme' up.
Dissolve.

No. It wasn't like that! Not in the least like that.

He put out his hand and touched her wet hair. He was giddy.

ANNABELLA: Methinks you are not well.

GIOVANNI: Here's none but you and I. I think you love me, sister.

ANNABELLA: Yes, you know I do.

And they thought, then, that they should kill themselves, together now, before they did it; they remembered tumbling together in infancy, how their mother laughed to see their kisses, their embraces, when they were too young to know they should not do it, yet even in their loneliness on the enormous plain they knew they must not do it ... do what? How did they know what to do? From watching the

37

cows with the bull, the bitch with the dog, the hen with the cock. They were country children. Turning from the mirror, each saw the other's face as if it were their own.

Music plays.
GIOVANNI: Let not this music be a dream, ye gods.
　　For pity's sake, I beg you!
　　[*She kneels.*]

ANNABELLA: On my knees,
　　Brother, even by our mother's dust, I charge you
　　Do not betray me to your mirth or hate.
　　Love me, or kill me, brother.
　　[*He kneels.*]

GIOVANNI: On my knees,
　　Sister, even by our mother's dust, I charge you
　　Do not betray me to your mirth or hate.
　　Love me, or kill me, sister.

> EXTERIOR. FARMHOUSE PORCH. DAY.
> Upset water-tub, spilling over discarded petti-
> 　　coat.
> Empty rocking-chair, rocking, rocking.

It is the boy – or young man, rather – who is the most mysterious to me. The eagerness with which he embraces his fate. I imagine him mute or well-nigh mute; he is the silent type, his voice creaks with disuse. He turns the soil, he breaks the wills of the beautiful horses, he milks the cows, he works the land, he toils and sweats. His work consists of the vague, undistinguished 'work' of such folks in the movies. No cowboy, he, roaming the plains. Where the father took root, so has the son, in the soil that was never before broken until now.

　　And I imagine him with an intelligence nourished only by the black book of the father, and hence cruelly circumscribed, yet dense with allusion, seeing himself as a kind of Adam and she his unavoidable and irreplaceable Eve, the unique companion of the wilderness, although by their toil he knows they do not live in Eden and of the precise nature of the forbidden thing he remains in doubt.

Was it bliss for her too? Or was there more of love than pleasure in it? 'Look after your sister.' But it was she who looked after him as soon as she knew how and pleasured him in the same spirit as she fed him.

GIOVANNI: I am lost forever.

Lost in the green wastes, where the pioneers were lost. Death with his high cheek-bones and his braided hair helped Annie-Belle take off her clothes. She closed her eyes so that she could not see her own nakedness. Death showed her how to touch him and him her. There is more to it than farmyard ways.

> INTERIOR. MINISTER'S HOUSE. DAY.
> Dinner-table. Minister's wife dishing portions from a pot for her husband and her son.

> MINISTER'S WIFE: T'ain't right, just ain't right, those two out there, growing up like savages, never seeing nobody.

> MINISTER'S SON: She's terribly pretty, Mama.

> The Minister's wife and the Minister turn to look at the young man. He blushes slowly but comprehensively.

The rancher knew nothing. He worked. He kept the iron core of grief within him rustless. He looked forward to his solitary, once-monthly drunk, alone on the porch, and on those nights they took a chance and slept together in the log cabin under the patchwork quilt made in the 'log cabin' pattern by their mother. Each time they lay down there together, as if she obeyed a voice that came out of the quilt telling her to put the light out, she would extinguish the candle-flame between her fingertips. All around them, the tactility of the dark.

She pondered the irreversibility of defloration. According to what the Minister's wife said, she had lost everything and was a lost girl. And yet this change did not seem to have changed her. She turned to the only one she loved, and the desolating space around them diminished to that of the soft grave their bodies dented in the long grass by the creek. When winter came, they made quick, dangerous love among the lowing beasts in the barn. The snow melted and all was green enough to blind you and there was a vinegarish smell from the rising of the sharp juices of spring. The birds came back.

A dusk bird went chink-chink-chink like a single blow on the stone xylophone of the Chinese classical orchestra.

> EXTERIOR. FARMHOUSE PORCH. DAY.
> Annie-Belle, in apron, comes out on home-stead porch; strikes metal triangle.
>
> ANNIE-BELLE: Dinner's ready!
>
> INTERIOR. FARMHOUSE. NIGHT.
> Supper-table. Annie-Belle serves beans. None for herself.
>
> JOHNNY: Annie-Belle, you're not eating any-thing tonight.
>
> ANNIE-BELLE: Can't rightly fancy anything tonight.

The dusk bird went chink-chink-chink with the sound of a chisel on a gravestone.

He wanted to run away with her, west, further west, to Utah, to California where they could live as man and wife, but she said: What about father? He's lost enough already.

When she said that, she put on, not his face, but that of their mother, and he knew in his bones the child inside her would part them.

The Minister's son, in his Sunday coat, came courting Annie-Belle. He is the second lead, you know in advance, from his tentative manner and mild eyes; he cannot long survive in this prairie scenario. He came courting Annie-Belle, although his mother wanted him to go to college. What will you do at college with a young wife? said his mother. But he put away his books; he took the buggy to go out and visit her. She was hanging washing out on the line.

Sound of the wind buffeting the sheets, the very sound of loneliness.

SORANZO: Have you not the will to love?

ANNABELLA: Not you.

SORANZO: Who, then?

ANNABELLA: That's as the fates infer.

She lowered her head and drew her foot back and forth in the dust. Her breasts hurt, she felt queasy.

> EXTERIOR. PRAIRIE. DAY.
> Johnny and Annie-Belle walking on the prairie.
>
> ANNIE-BELLE: I think he likes me, Johnny.
>
> Pan blue sky, with clouds. Johnny and Annie-Belle, dwarfed by the landscape, hand in hand, heads bowed. Their hands slowly part.
>
> Now they walk with gradually increasing distance between them.

The light, the unexhausted light of North America that, filtered through celluloid, will become the light by which we see America looking at itself.

Correction: will become the light by which we see *North* America looking at itself.

EXTERIOR. FARMHOUSE PORCH. DAY.
Row of bottles on a fence.
Bang, bang, bang. Johnny shoots the bottles one by one.
Annie-Belle on porch, washing dishes in a tub.
Tears run down her face.

EXTERIOR. FARMHOUSE PORCH. DAY.
Father on porch, feet up on railing, glass and bottle to hand.
Sun going down over prairie.
Bang, bang, bang.

FATHER'S POINT OF VIEW: Johnny shooting bottles off the fence.

Clink of father's bottle against glass.

EXTERIOR. FARMHOUSE. DAY.
Minister's son rides along track in long shot.
Bang, bang, bang.

Annie-Belle, clean dress, tidy hair, red eyes, comes out of house on to porch. Clink of father's bottle against glass.

EXTERIOR. FARMHOUSE. DAY.
Minister's son tethers horse. He has brushed his Sunday coat. In his hand, a posy of flowers – cottage roses, sweet-briar, daisies.
Annie-Belle smiles, takes posy.

ANNIE–BELLE: Oh! [*Holds up pricked forefinger; blood drops on to a daisy.*]

MINISTER'S SON: Let me . . . [*Takes her hand. Kisses the little wound.*] . . . make it better.

Bang. Bang. Bang.
Clink of bottle on glass.

CLOSE-UP: Annie-Belle, smiling, breathing in
the scent from her posy.

And, perhaps, had it been possible, she would have learned
to love the Minister's gentle son before she married him,
but, not only was it impossible, she also carried within her
the child that meant she must be married quickly.

INTERIOR. CHURCH. DAY.
Harmonium. Father and Johnny by the altar.
Johnny white, strained; father stoical. Minister's wife thin-lipped, furious. Minister's son
and Annie-Belle, in simple white cotton
wedding-dress, join hands.

MINISTER: Do you take this woman . . .

CLOSE-UP: Minister's son's hand slipping
wedding-ring on to Annie-Belle's finger.

INTERIOR. BARN. NIGHT.
Fiddle and banjo old-time music.
Vigorous square dance going on; bride and
groom lead.

Father at table, glass in hand.
Johnny, beside him, reaching for bottle.

Bride and groom come together at end of
dance; groom kisses bride's cheek. She
laughs.

CLOSE-UP: Annie-Belle looking shyly up at
the Minister's son.
The dance parts them again; as Annie-Belle
is handed down the row of men, she staggers
and faints.

43

Consternation.

Minister's son and Johnny both run towards her.

Johnny lifts her up in his arms, her head on his shoulder. Eyes opening. Minister's son reaches out for her. Johnny lets him take hold of her.

She gazes after Johnny beseechingly as he disappears among the crowd.

Silence swallowed up the music of the fiddle and the banjo; Death with his hair in braids spread out the sheets on the marriage bed.

> INTERIOR. MINISTER'S HOUSE. BEDROOM. NIGHT.
> Annie-Belle in bed, in a white night-gown, clutching the pillow, weeping. Minister's son, bare back, sitting on side of bed with his back to camera, head in hands.

In the morning, her new mother-in-law heard her vomiting into the chamber-pot and, in spite of her son's protests, stripped Annie-Belle and subjected her to a midwife's inspection. She judged her three months gone, or more. She dragged the girl round the room by the hair, slapped her, punched her, kicked her, but Annie-Belle would not tell the father's name, only promised, swore on the grave of her dead mother, that she would be a good girl in future. The young bridegroom was too bewildered by this turn of events to have an opinion about it; only, to his vague surprise, he knew he still loved the girl although she carried another man's child.

'Bitch! Whore!' said the Minister's wife and struck Annie-Belle a blow across the mouth that started her nose bleeding.

'Now, stop that, mother,' said the gentle son. 'Can't you see she ain't well?'

The terrible day drew to its end. The mother-in-law would have thrown Annie-Belle out on the street, but the boy pleaded for her, and the Minister, praying for guidance, found himself opening the Bible at the parable of the woman taken in adultery, and meditated well upon it. Only tell me the name of the father, her young husband said to Annie-Belle.

'Better you don't know it,' she said. Then she lied: 'He's gone now; gone out west.'

'Was it –' naming one or two.

'You never knew him. He came by the ranch on his way out west.'

Then she burst out crying, again, and he took her in his arms.

'It will be all over town,' said the mother-in-law. 'That girl made a fool of you.'

She slammed the dishes on the table and would have made the girl eat out the back door, but the young husband laid her a place at table with his own hands and led her in and sat her down in spite of his mother's black looks. They bowed their heads for grace. Surely, the Minister thought, seeing his boy cut bread for Annie-Belle and lay it on her plate, my son is a saint. He began to fear for him.

'I won't do anything unless you want,' her husband said in the dark after the candle went out.

The straw with which the mattress was stuffed rustled beneath her as she turned away from him.

INTERIOR. FARMHOUSE KITCHEN. NIGHT.
Johnny comes in from outside, looks at father asleep in rocking-chair.
Picks up some discarded garment of Annie-Belle's from the back of a chair, buries face in it.

45

Shoulders shake.
Opens cupboard, takes out bottle.
Uncorks with teeth. Drinks.
Bottle in hand, goes out on porch.

EXTERIOR. PRAIRIE. NIGHT.
JOHNNY'S POINT OF VIEW: Moon rising over
prairie; the vast, the elegiac plain.
'Landscape Theme' rises.

INTERIOR. MINISTER'S SON'S ROOM. NIGHT.
Annie-Belle and Minister's son in bed. Moonlight through curtains. Both lie there, open-
eyed. Rustle of mattress.

ANNIE-BELLE: You awake?

Minister's son moves away from her.

ANNIE-BELLE: Reckon I never properly
knowed no young man before . . .

MINISTER'S SON: What about —

ANNIE-BELLE: [*shrugging the question off*]
Oh . . .

Minister's son moves towards her.

For she did not consider her brother in this new category
of 'young men'; he was herself. So she and her husband
slept in one another's arms, that night, although they did
nothing else for she was scared it might harm the baby and
he was so full of pain and glory it was scarcely to be borne,
it was already enough, or too much, holding her tight, in
his terrible innocence.

It was not so much that she was pliant. Only, fearing the
worst, it turned out that the worst had already happened; her
sin found her out, or, rather, she found out she had sinned only
when he offered his forgiveness, and, from her repentance, a
new Annie-Belle sprang up, for whom the past did not exist.

She would have said to him: it did not signify, my darling; I only did it with my brother, we were alone together under the vast sky that made us scared and so we clung together and what happened, happened. But she knew she must not say that, the most natural thing of all was just precisely the one she must not acknowledge. To lie down on the prairie with a passing stranger was one thing. To lie down with her father's son was another. So she kept silent. And when she looked at her husband, she saw, not herself, but someone who might, in time, grow even more precious.

The next night, in spite of the baby, they did it, and his mother wanted to murder her and refused to get the breakfast for this prostitute, but Annie-Belle served them, put on an apron, cut the ham and cooked it, then scrubbed the floor with such humility, such evidence of gratitude that the older woman kept her mouth shut, her narrow lips tight as a trap but she kept them shut for if there was one thing she feared, it was the atrocious gentleness of her menfolk. And. So.

Johnny came to the town, hungering after her; the gates of Paradise slammed shut in his face. He haunted the backyard of the Minister's house, hid in the sweet-briar, watched the candle in their room go out and still he could not imagine it, that she might do it with another man. But. She did.

At the store, all gossip ceased when she came in; all eyes turned towards her. The old men chewing tobacco spat brown streams when she walked past. The women's faces veiled with disapproval. She was so young, so unaccustomed to people. They talked, her husband and she; they would go, just go, out west, still further, west as far as the place where the ocean starts again, perhaps. With his schooling, he could get some clerking job or other. She would bear her child and he would love it. Then she would bear *their* children.

47

Yes, she said. We shall do that, she said.

> EXTERIOR. FARMHOUSE. DAY.
> Annie-Belle drives up in trap.
> Johnny comes out on porch, in shirt-sleeves, bottle in hand
> Takes her reins. But she doesn't get down from the trap.

ANNIE-BELLE: Where's Daddy?

Johnny gestures towards the prairie.

ANNIE-BELLE: [*not looking at Johnny*] Got something to tell him.

CLOSE-UP: Johnny.

JOHNNY: Ain't you got nothing to tell me?

CLOSE-UP: Annie-Belle.

ANNIE-BELLE: Reckon I ain't.

CLOSE-UP: Johnny.

JOHNNY: Get down and visit a while, at least.

CLOSE-UP: Annie-Belle.

ANNIE-BELLE: Can't hardly spare the time.

CLOSE-UP: Johnny and Annie-Belle.

JOHNNY: Got to scurry back, get your husband's dinner, is that it?

ANNIE-BELLE: Johnny ... why haven't you come to church since I got married. Johnny?

Johnny shrugs, turns away.

EXTERIOR. FARMHOUSE. DAY.

Annie-Belle gets down from trap, follows Johnny towards farmhouse.

ANNIE-BELLE: Oh, Johnny, you *knowed* we did wrong.

Johnny walks towards farmhouse.

ANNIE-BELLE: I count myself fortunate to have found forgiveness.

JOHNNY: What are you going to tell Daddy?

ANNIE-BELLE: I'm going out west.

GIOVANNI: What, chang'd so soon! hath your new sprightly lord
Found out a trick in night-games more than we
Could know in our simplicity? – Ha! is't so?
Or does the fit come on you, to prove treacherous
To your past vows and oaths?

ANNABELLA: Why should you jest
At my calamity.

EXTERIOR. FARMHOUSE. DAY.

JOHNNY: Out west?

Annie-Belle nods.

JOHNNY: By yourself?

Annie-Belle shakes her head.

JOHNNY: With him?

Annie-Belle nods.
Johnny puts hand on porch rail, bends forward, hiding his face.

ANNIE-BELLE: It is for the best.

She puts her hand on his shoulder. He reaches

49

out for her. She extricates herself. His hand, holding bottle; contents of bottle run out on grass.

ANNIE-BELLE: It was wrong, what we did.

JOHNNY: What about . . .

ANNIE-BELLE: It shouldn't ever have been made, poor little thing. You won't never see it. Forget everything. You'll find yourself a woman, you'll marry.

Johnny reaches out and clasps her roughly to him.

No, she said: never. No. And fought and bit and scratched: never! It's wrong. It's a sin. But, worse than that, she said: I don't want to, and she meant it, she knew she must not or else her new life, that lay before her, now, with the radiant simplicity of a child's drawing of a house, would be utterly destroyed. So she got free of him and ran to the buggy and drove back lickety-split to town, beating the pony round the head with the whip.

Accompanied by a black trunk like a coffin, the Minister and his wife drove with them to a railhead such as you have often seen on the movies – the same telegraph office, the same water-tower, the same old man with the green eye-shade selling tickets. Autumn was coming on. Annie-Belle could no longer conceal her pregnancy, out it stuck; her mother-in-law could not speak to her directly but addressed remarks through the Minister, who compensated for his wife's contempt by showing Annie-Belle all the honour due to a repentant sinner.

She wore a yellow ribbon. Her hair was long and yellow. The repentant harlot has the surprised look of a pregnant virgin.

She is pale. The pregnancy does not go well. She vomits

all morning. She bleeds a little. Her husband holds her hand tight. Her father came last night to say goodbye to her; he looks older. He does not take care of himself. That Johnny did not come set the tongues wagging; the gossip is, he refuses to set eyes on his sister in her disgrace. That seems the only thing to explain his attitude. All know he takes no interest in girls himself.

'Bless you, children,' says the Minister. With that troubling air of incipient sainthood, the young husband settles his wife down on the trunk and tucks a rug round her legs, for a snappy wind drives dust down the railroad track and the hills are October mauve and brown. In the distance, the train whistle blows, that haunting sound, blowing across endless distance, the sound that underlines the distance.

EXTERIOR. FARMHOUSE. DAY.
Johnny mounts horse. Slings rifle over shoulder.
Kicks horse's sides.

EXTERIOR. RAILROAD. DAY.
Train whistle. Burst of smoke.
Engine pulling train across prairie.

EXTERIOR. PRAIRIE. DAY.
Johnny galloping down track.

EXTERIOR. RAILROAD. DAY.
CLOSE-UP: Train wheels turning.

EXTERIOR. PRAIRIE. DAY.
Hooves churning dust.

EXTERIOR. STATION. DAY.

MINISTER'S WIFE: Now, you take care of yourself, you hear? And – [but she can't bring herself to say it]

51

> MINISTER: Be sure to tell us about the baby
>   as soon as it comes.

> CLOSE-UP: Annie-Belle smiling gratefully.
> Train whistle.

And see them, now, as if posing for the photographer, the young man and the pregnant woman, sitting on a trunk, waiting to be transported onwards, away, elsewhere, she with the future in her belly.

> EXTERIOR. STATION. DAY.
> Station-master comes out of ticket-office.

> STATION-MASTER: Here she comes!

> LONG-SHOT: Engine appearing round bend.

> EXTERIOR. STATION. DAY.
> Johnny tethers his horse.

> ANNIE-BELLE: Why, Johnny, you've come to
>   say goodbye after all!

> CLOSE-UP: Johnny, wracked with emotion.

> JOHNNY: He shan't have you. He'll never
>   have you. Here's where you belong, with
>   me. Out here.

> GIOVANNI: Thus die, and die by me, and by my hand!
>   Revenge is mine; honour doth love command!

> ANNABELLA: Oh, brother, by your hand!

> EXTERIOR. STATION. DAY.

> ANNIE-BELLE: Don't shoot — think of the
>   baby! Don't —

> MINISTER'S SON: Oh, my God —

> Bang, bang, bang.

Thinking to protect his wife, the young husband threw his arms around her and so he died, by a split second, before the second bullet pierced her and both fell to the ground as the engine wheezed to a halt and passengers came tumbling off to see what Wild West antics were being played out while the parents stood and stared and did not believe, did not believe.

Seeing some life left in his sister, Johnny sank to his knees beside her and her eyes opened up and, perhaps, she saw him, for she said:

ANNABELLA: Brother, unkind, unkind . . .

So that Death would be well-satisfied, Johnny then put the barrel of the rifle into his mouth and pulled the trigger.

> EXTERIOR. STATION. DAY.
> Crane shot, the three bodies, the Minister comforting his wife, the passengers crowding off the train in order to look at the catastrophe.
>
> The 'Love Theme' rises over a pan of the prairie under the vast sky, the green breast of the continent, the earth, beloved, cruel, unkind.

Note: The Old World John Ford made Giovanni cut out Annabella's heart and carry it on stage; the stage direction reads: *Enter Giovanni, with a heart upon his dagger*. The New World John Ford would have no means of representing this scene on celluloid, although it is irresistibly reminiscent of the ritual tortures practised by the Indians who lived here before.

Card Trick with Hearts

ADRIAN DANNATT

IN HER BEDROOM she'd collected all the postcards, ever since she'd first become intrigued by an uncle's red fire-engine on her eleventh birthday. She kept them in a large yellow envelope.

On Sundays, when certain of no post, she would pour the contents on to the floor, slithering round her knees like the sea, where she knelt on the carpet, a flood of past fragments, of memory and happiness.

There was an intimate connection between the images and the sender, cyphers of their personalities rather than just the casual choice of an afternoon. She could remember who had sent which cards without having to turn them over.

The Eiffel Tower was her sister, aged sixteen, on her first trip to Paris. The Bonnard nude was her father, just before he left her mother, on a trip to Zurich from which he now rarely returned. She didn't have to turn the pastel arrangement of bath, wallpaper and water, to read the words, scrawled doubtless in the artificial airport-night: 'Whatever happens, I still love you very much.' Hardly words to cheer a teenage girl at breakfast, especially on the morning of her Latin 'O' level. Exactly the unthinking selfishness her mother found so impossible.

The comic picture of three kittens, presumably in deliberately bad taste, represented her first proper boyfriend.

When she looked at the fluffy trinity, the horrible mock-silk background, his voice became part of it, that self-contented, pompous tone of a young man about to go up to university.

Sometimes when they had lain together (rarely essaying anything more advanced than dutiful fumbles) she could tell he was imagining all the prospects that would open to him in the bawdy cloisters of further education.

She also had a laughing donkey which repulsed her almost as much as the smug message on the back: 'In memory of all the laughter of that summer.' From her memory most of the laughter had been occasioned by what he termed her 'gaucherie'. She'd found the word enchanting, like some patisserie delicacy, until looking it up in the dictionary.

He'd tailed off with an uncharacteristically tasteful picture of a college doorway, as though this visual refinement was part of his increased maturity. She only had to glance at the stone archway to recall his callous manner and nasty set of undergraduate friends.

Only postcards had the right exotic flavour, a slither of some hot and distant country dropping to her mat amongst the English rain. The drama of that simple cross to mark the spot at which they stayed, knowing where people were, not just the town or country, but the precise window over the cerise sea.

She opened letters immediately and quickly scanned their contents. They were always formal, pompous, too long and burdened by expensive stationery. Even if, as they rarely had been, they were declarations of passion they remained grave and unexciting.

She liked the challenge of the cryptic postcard, the need to communicate in code before the public eye. Letters were too permissive, within their envelopes you could speak at length on whatever you wished. Letters were like the self-indulgence of a first novel. Postcards were the haikus of a wise old writer.

She'd come downstairs to breakfast and glance at the doormat with a fatalistic casualness. If there were only dull envelopes, or no mail at all, she had to fight the urge to go back upstairs to bed.

The possibilities of blazing Seychelles or snowy Prague were her only incentives to rise each morning, the delicious, half-heard creak of the letter-box.

She took the postcards into the kitchen and propped them on the toast rack. She looked at them, trying to establish who had sent them and their mood at the time. Only after she'd finished breakfast and cleared the table would she turn them over and read the messages.

At the office she imagined her correspondents, so distant, so tangible. She pictured the sun-blind moment at which they'd decided to send her a card. Perhaps after too many retsinas on a dusky harbour or after they'd showered, stepping into the tropical sunlight in thick hotel towels, thinking of her, briefly, genuinely.

She kept the cards for exactly a week from the day they arrived on her mantelpiece beside the Art Deco clock and jar of dried flowers. She looked at them, as a row of others' travels, a sequence of tiny kindnesses, each memory of her that had prompted them added slowly to become the sum total of the world's love for her.

She would turn from the streaming window and remind herself, with South American stadiums, aerial perspectives of Sienna, peasants playing poverty to the camera, that she was loved, was remembered, for a fraction of the world's time, all over the planet.

She was happy to let others do her travelling for her. Her secret passport was filled with the blurred ink of a thousand cards, these franked pages turned her flat to a jungle of artificial colours, a forest chattering with stamps, undergrowth of biro marks, horizon of lurid sunset-sands.

A week over, she put them in the yellow envelope.

Justin had become the regular provider. Every day another postcard arrived, and she would know it was him from the rectangle of sky, the touristic lilt. They kept a straight geographic pattern, a sequence from the journey across America, the stopping-places of that trail from San Francisco to New York, the drifting, migratory desires that country had been founded on.

She found America particularly satisfying. It had never been amongst her most popular places, her friends tended to avoid it, preferring more esoteric pleasures.

The cards seemed typical of Justin; all the promise and novelty that he had suggested to her, were borne out by the new varieties of stamps and the richness of the colour reproduction.

Justin had been working as a waiter when she'd met him, handing out hamburgers to finance his journey to the States, a cherished ambition. She was impressed by the suitability of his job, the quintessential Americanness of the burgers and the very Americanness of his proposed trip. The restaurant was proud of its yankee flavour, its menu even featured a sequence of postcards from various American towns, surrounding the list of chilli specials. They'd fallen into chat over the extent of the concept 'medium-rare' and he, beguiled no doubt by her precise humour, her mature smile, had set off in pursuit of her, like the cowboys featured elsewhere on the menu, chasing Indians.

It had started with phone calls, those hopeless substitute postcards, all the brevity with none of the colour, asking her out to films and cheap restaurants. She enjoyed the way he laughed at what she said, as though he was her apprentice in the craft of happy living.

He was brown even in winter and with the perfect degree of musculature provided by carrying plates all day. He behaved protectively, respectfully towards her, as if she was a maiden aunt that he incidentally found attractive. He stroked her hair in the cinema and looked at her profile intensely until she was forced to turn full-face to him, partly from the magnetism of his gaze and partly because she was embarrassed by her left profile.

He sent her flowers and an unexpected postcard, as though he'd guessed her secret pleasure. It was a reproduction of a Pop painting in the Tate that was in itself a parody of postcards, of America, of Romance. His handwriting was lean and amused, a turquoise slant spelling out those fatuous three words that he was too embarrassed ever to speak.

Eventually they spent an early evening in bed at her flat, falling over each other in greed, hammering at their bodies as though such wet violence was final proof of compatibility.

And then they saw each other every afternoon or night when his shifts allowed; talking, collecting together their pasts, presenting them in neat sections, instalments of a flawless, giant anecdote. They showed each side of their worlds, like a prism slowly rotated in the hand, letting each other see the sadness, excitement, the hatred and lusts.

She was satisfied with his company, his daily visits took the place of her cards, he seemed to be a degree nearer the ideal of love they had represented. She tried to keep that word 'love' simply as a description of another town or hotel: 'We simply love Vienna,' 'You'd love the swimming-pool here.'

But often she might think of him, of his brownness, his emptiness, whilst at work, doodling his name by the telephone.

In time he'd served enough burgers and fries, dished up enough of the American culinary dream on its giant-size platter, to afford the reality. They were full of affection but nothing as strong as his lust for that continent, a consoling daydream still with him from his childhood.

She cried a little on the tube-ride back from Heathrow,

depressed by the rows of suburban houses, by having come so close to the dream of travel, the metal palace of escape and exile, the tannoy poetry of foreign cities.

The first card was from the Golden Gate Bridge. She'd prolonged the pleasure of reading it for so long that she was almost late for work. She took it with her, aware that it rested next to her heart by the nature of her jacket pocket.

San Francisco was lost in a blur of heat, the magnificent iron structure looped out of the mist like a prehistoric animal. The franking was a loud sprawl, an eagle on waves of print, it had all the authority and brashness of the country, she imagined the franking-machine making the loud beat of California.

His Los Angeles was a strip of freeway, a mesh of connecting tracks, a sprawl of junctions, like a heart built from concrete and tarmac veins. She gauged his feelings not by his words or any amateur cartography, but by the pictures he chose to send her.

Phoenix was nothing but a bus station with the name lit up in neon and a sliver of Greyhound bus. Predictably he had written a few lines of the song 'By the Time I Get to Phoenix', as well as recounting a minor adventure with a negro grandmother.

El Paso was a comic Mexican in the straw-halo of his sombrero. It spoke of the grotty border scenery, the poverty, and he sent his love, this time serenaded by a row of crosses, lopsided graves of murdered wetbacks.

She kept them together, segregated from the ordinary friendship of the other postcards, tied them in the expected pink ribbon, rereading them to trace any weakening in the pattern of his scribbled affections.

The towns and vistas went by, shards of the mosaic of American travel, sometimes parodying the clichés, a 3-D Elvis grinning from Memphis, sometimes obviously enraptured by the myth itself.

As an intrigued, futile gesture she had gone to the

American Tourist Board, after he'd sent her a weathered shack near New Orleans asking her to come out and join him.

But she knew very well that she could never join him. If she went to him she would lose the pleasure of his cards. Instead she kept track of him on a map given to her by the Tourist Board. She followed him in her imagination, tracing fingers down the cartographic veins, spending her time comforted by his journey, the images of spinning wheels, Greyhound buses and the dust of frontiers.

The expectation of his arrival each morning, spread out flat on the mat, his streets and sunsets, his gallery of cowboys and stars, was enough to turn her life into something like an adventure, an internal emigration that left her shell alone in the office.

She sensed danger with his Twin Towers, forking the entrance to a pink-eveninged Manhattan.

She had always expected him to stay in America. Working in a downtown bookmart, or with transatlantic irony, serving beef and Yorkshire pudding in a pastiche English restaurant.

She had assumed that his cards would get less frequent, he would understand the power of the ocean's vastness against the weakness of human closeness. She waited for the cards to die away with anticipation, a vindication of her pessimism. But his cards had continued to arrive each day, each day with words of love.

New York became sinister, she began to imagine it was on the west coast of Britain rather than the east coast of America, it seemed terribly near. It would be easy for him to step over to London, it was less a journey than a fairytale wish.

He sent her the Guggenheim, an apple-peeling of concrete, to keep the World Trade Centre company:

'Must come back to London, to see you above all. You've been with me all the way, I need you even more. See you very soon, all my love.'

She put it next to the teapot, annoyed. He'd broken the rules of the postcard-game with his blatant message. It was devoid of any subtlety, it lacked the charm of the usual postcard clichés, it was like a pass from a drunken man.

Two days later she found what she'd been dreading, sprawled fat and white on the floor, a letter with a London postmark. She hesitated before opening it, only examined the numerous pages cursorily. He'd become a letter. He'd become rambling, ill-formed, a spew of sensations and sentimentality, he had fatally lost the picturesque, given up the short, delirious moment for the duties of long labour.

She refused to join the melodramatic scenario that every letter begs for, she didn't tear it to shreds, weep over the pages, she had no desire to re-read it.

She put it in the bin along with the other junk, shopping-mall adverts, cheap offers of photographic development.

That lunch-hour she went to the second-hand shop and bought the treat she'd long promised herself.

In the evening the telephone rang. She put down the postcard she was reading and waited patiently. The phone wouldn't stop so she picked it up, listened to a few of his words, then left it off the hook.

She returned to her card, put it down and chose another from the vast heap around her.

Flowers, castles, sepia infantrymen and zeppelins, a thousand forgotten messages stretching from the Zulu War to the Abdication crisis, tales of honeymoons and peaceful holidays, shards of yellowing love; a pile of ghost-talk, a mountain of small memories and brief passions for her to choose from.

The Bad Boy

BERLIE DOHERTY

THERE'S A STRANGE man who lives down the valley from us.
My mother calls him the bad boy but I believe he's been a
man for many years now. But I know he's bad because he
never goes to Mass, not even at Christmas. For all that, I
like him. He has a gypsy face and black hair that curls like
a child's, and his beard is always just about to grow. His
voice is husky with too much smoking and drinking, and
when he talks to you one of his eyes turns slowly, casually,
towards the other. I don't know how he does it, but it
fascinates me. He's pretty slow. His father goes out fishing,
and sometimes he goes out with him, and sometimes he
just sits on the rocks by the slipway waiting to haul the
boats back in. And sometimes you see him following the
tide out if he's in the mood for cockling with the gangs.

My mother was the first to notice that he was interested
in Geraldine.

The first sign was when he cycled home with her one
night from the hospital. I saw them coming up the lane
together and thought nothing of it, because when Geraldine
swerved in at our gate he cycled straight on past, with
neither of them looking at the other; but my mother stood

62

up from her gardening, and thought everything. She watched while Geraldine pulled off her bicycle clips. She liked to wear a pair of Michael's old corduroys for cycling in the winter; she would tuck her skirt down inside them, not noticing how it made them bulge.

My mother followed her into the kitchen. Geraldine was red-cheeked with the cycling, and still breathless when I came in. My mother took both her cold hands in her own and shouted at her.

'That Larry's a bad boy. You know that, don't you?'

Poor Geraldine didn't know whether to nod her head or shake it. She rolled her eyes mysteriously. I could see the pressure of my mother's fingers, and kept well out of it. Besides, I was puzzled and curious.

'Tomorrow, you stay at the hospital till your father comes for you. D'you hear?'

'You'll ask me first,' my father said. 'I'm not acting chauffeur every five minutes.'

My mother didn't leave go of Geraldine's hands, nor did she look at my father, but said with a cold quiet that chilled me, 'No man is interested in Geraldine. If this Larry's interested in her, then it's for only one thing.' When she finally let go of Geraldine's hands they had the white stripes of her fingers pressed in them, and the tiny moon-cuts of her nails.

During the family prayers that evening Geraldine received a special mention. 'Let her not be led into temptation,' my mother whispered fervently. 'In her heart she's still a child. Let her always be a child in Your eyes.'

I peeped up. My father was tying his shoe-laces, ready to jog down the lane and meet Uncle Rory for a Saturday drink. Terence, clean in his pyjamas, was yawning. My mother had her eyes shut tight and Geraldine had hers wide open. She beamed round at us all through her fingers.

'She's nearly thirty,' my father reminded my mother when she hung the rosary beads back up.

'She's a child,' my mother asserted. 'And always will be. Look at her now, won't you.'

Geraldine was brushing my hair. She had always done this for me at night, and I loved her to do it. She was the only one who had the patience to get all the tangles out. She sat back on her heels to admire the job when she'd finished, and tonight, for the first time ever, handed me the brush and leaned forward till her head was on my lap. I stroked her thin, greasy strands with the brush. I could see her pink scalp.

'Poor Geraldine,' I said, not meaning to. She rolled her head sideways to peer up at me through her fringe.

'Poor, poor, poor,' she murmured. She laughed, sucking the dribble on her wet lips. 'Poor Dendine.'

'You can't even say your own name,' I said. 'You should have had an easy name, like Anne.'

'Lie Kan,' she echoed. 'Kan.'

My Aunt Bridget had come bustling in from the cold for an hour's company and a quiet drop of Irish while Rory was out drinking.

'How's the old woman?' my mother asked her. 'Poor thing.'

'The old woman is knitting dishcloths,' Aunt Bridget said, sliding her coat over the back of a chair inside out to catch the fire's warmth, 'in the old people's home, and loving it. Who'd have thought!' She eased her shoes off and stretched her legs out to the hearth, wriggling her grey old toes. 'We went to see her this afternoon, and there was a new girl in the next bed to her who was giving her visitor the devil of a time. "Take me home, Katie, take me away home," she'd say to the poor woman. "I will Mam, you'll go back home as soon as you're well enough." "That means never," the old woman said, "cos ye've selt me home. Let God take me, or send me to hell, that's the only home waiting for me." Well, the daughter was up to here with it, and I was near crying myself, and that's the truth, and Rory's mother pipes up, the shrill old bird,

"Shush your ranting, woman," she says, "or there'll be no tiddleywinks tonight." And the woman did shut up, that's what took me. Tiddleywinks, when there's her whole life on display there, her house and home gone, and nothing in sight for her but a full stop. Is this what we're reduced to, good strong willing creatures that we are, Kathleen?'

My mother filled her glass and sighed.

Geraldine stood up and pulled me out of my chair for bed. We cleaned our teeth in the cracked bowl together, taking it in turns to spit out the fizz of paste. Hers always had a touch of blood in it, because she brushed her gums too hard. She seemed to fall asleep before I was in bed, but during the night I heard her lumbering round the room, and I sat up, surprised to see her fully dressed and pulling on her thick socks.

'Geraldine, where are you going?' I asked her. 'It's too early for Mass.'

She looked dismayed, caught out in mischief, and then decided that she hadn't heard me. She crept out of the room as though I was still fast asleep, and made every step creak on her cautious way downstairs. I heard the whine of the front door, and ran to the window to see her jogging down the lane in her wellies.

My mother and father seemed to be a heaving bundle rocking in their sleep. I didn't know how to disturb them. I went back into my room and dressed quickly, keeping my night-clothes on underneath. My mother whimpered across the landing; my father moaned. I paused again at their open door, and daren't speak out. 'Geraldine's gone,' I whispered. The bundle gasped some kind of pain. I ran away from it and out into the bitter cold of the night. The tide must have turned, changing the wind with it. I ran down the hill in the direction Geraldine had taken, and it wasn't long before I saw her squat figure stumbling on in front of me.

'Geraldine!' I shouted. 'Wait for me!'

She half-turned, changed her mind, and lunged off the

lane into the shadowed trees. I could hear her plunging through the undergrowth. 'Please wait, Geraldine!' I shouted. I could hear her laughing as I ran alongside her path, too frightened myself to follow her into the blackness, and afraid of leaving her there alone.

Then I saw Larry waiting at the far end of the lane for her, and I realised what it was all about. He ducked his head when he saw me, in that familiar mocking servile way he has, and I felt betrayed. Geraldine lumbered up behind me, panting from the race, and laughing. Larry nodded to her.

'So you've brought your sister, have you?'

'We'll go back now, Geraldine,' I said. 'She has to go'.

'Does she now?' He held his hand out and Geraldine stepped forward shyly and took it, and I like a fool hung back while they climbed over the stile at the side of the lane and went down into the fields. I stood with my hands over my face thinking of my sin at the communion rails and of my mother and father rocking in their bed, and somewhere out on the dark sea the gulls taunted me with their grieving laughter. Feeling like a traitor myself I moved slowly to the stile and leaned on it, and there they were, picking their way slowly down the field-track towards the beach. I climbed over and slithered down the track after them, and as soon as they were lost in the shadows of the bay I started to run, dry in my throat with thrill.

But they were not in the bay, hiding together in the silksand by the rocks. I saw them heading out across the wet mud-flats in a silver track of moonlight, Geraldine stumpy and slow and slurping the mud with her wellingtons, and Larry easing her out of the sticky slime. He was carrying a bucket. I kicked off my shoes and plunged in after them, letting the soft cool mud ooze up between my toes, and the brown water trickle after it. When I reached them Larry and Geraldine were squatting in the mud by a little channel dug into it, and he was whispering to her as if she was a child.

'This is where you find them, in the slurry-slime. You'll watch out for them spitting-off. There, look.'

He pointed to a froth of brown bubbles and eased his hand into the mud. When he brought it out again he had a cockle in his palm. Geraldine laughed and held out her hands for it.

'There,' he said, pleased. 'Now wash it in the channel and drop it in my pail.'

She swilled the shell again and again in the water, intent on her task, her lips pursing together, her wellingtons sloshing quietly as she swayed.

'We'll have the tide back in at this rate,' he told her. 'Drop it in the pail, and look for another.'

She did as she was told, reluctant to let go of the tight-frilled white shell in her palm, letting her fingers linger in the murky pail water.

'Look.' He pointed. With a gasp of pleasure Geraldine reached out to the spittle and drove her fingers down. She brought them up slowly, as though the mud made them heavy, as though it would drag her down and she would wallow there. Her fingers sucked at last out of the slime and came out pale and silky in the moonlight, and she kept her fist clasped over her find so he had to lean forward and gently prise open her hand, finger by finger, stroking the mud off each languorously, till he eased his own fingers into her hollowed palm and crooked out the white shell and held it between his lips and hers; in all that time that seemed like infinity he never took his eyes off hers, nor did she look away from him.

'Geraldine,' I said, uneasy, locked out, and she laughed and broke her look away from his and dived her hand again and again into the mud, scooping and swilling, scooping and swilling, so the mud spattered her arms and her face with the frenzy of her movements, and the cockle-shells clattered into the pail like the chipped bones of ancient men. And suddenly she'd had enough.

She put her hands out onto his shoulders to heave herself

up, and steadied herself against him as he stood up too. The light was changing, streaked pink and lemon like the little button shells I used to collect as a child. Larry's bucket was heavy, and he leaned slightly to one side as they half-slid like skiers through the slime till they reached their own scooped steps in the cushions of moist banks by the shore. I followed them, and it wasn't until I sat on a stone to rub the sparkling dry sand off my feet and slip my shoes back on that they acknowledged me. In all that time it had been as though they hadn't noticed me at all, and I was an eavesdropper in a deep and intimate conversation. Now Larry dumped the pail onto the sands and still without looking at me, held out his arm for me to join them.

'You go back up with your sister,' he told Geraldine. 'And get yourself clean and dry for work.'

As I approached them he cupped her face gently in his big muddy hands. 'Enjoy it?'

She laughed up at him, and he turned away from her, picked up his pail, and stumped off over the sands to the slipway sheds. We hurried back home. I had a thousand thoughts whirling in my head, yet I was aware of a calm kind of stillness about Geraldine that I'd never known before, even in the way she walked, and in her soft and steady breathing; in the white silver silk of her face in the early light, and in the kind warmth of her eyes. How I would have wished to know that peace in her again.

We slipped as quiet as cats into the house, and up to bed, and lay muddy and silent between our sheets till my mother's shout would give us leave to fill up the cracked bowl and wash away our crime. The next night my father met her on the way back from work, and although she came home on her bicycle he drove behind her, and she rode into the yard and came inside without saying anything. I was sitting doing my homework at the kitchen table and she came and sat by me and pulled my maths books over towards her, poring over the lovely patterns of numbers as though she could understand it all, or as if it was a book of stories that said something to her. After night prayers my mother locked the house doors on the inside, which she had never done before, and let us see her doing it. She took the key upstairs with her. Geraldine bit her lip and tried to turn the door handle, first to the front door which goes out to the yard and the lane, and then the back door where the wellingtons and raincoats are kept, and as though it was a puzzle to be solved she tried the windows too, and the doors again, and again.

Nobody said anything, that day or ever. I didn't dare to share her sorrow with her, though I stood by her the nights she opened our bedroom window and leaned out, and out again, as though leaning out would bring her so much nearer to the wet silk-soft of the cocklebeds and to Larry's fond laughter. But whether she ever saw him again I never knew, or daren't ask her. My father or my mother, or sometimes Uncle Rory, would see her to and from work as though she was an infant starting school, and she closed herself up away from it all, even from me. Child as I was, I saw her as a woman of mystery and sorrow, and that gave her, poor simple thing, a kind of dignity for me.

And then, in the freakish spring tides of the equinox, four members of the cockle-gang were swept out to sea, and one of them was Larry. It was the first time an accident of this sort had happened in our village. One of the bodies was never found ever, and must be rocking now, jammed by a fist perhaps, between boulders deep below the sea, and turning to bone. And two of the others, a husband and wife, were found together nestled up in a sandbank pool the next morning when the tide had gone quiet. They were found by the rest of the cockle-gang who'd gone out searching for them, and it's said they were crouched together and cupped in each other's embrace, and that it was quite a lovely thing to see in the shallow green water in early sunlight, and that they were difficult to separate.

There seemed to be a kind of grim satisfaction that it had happened like this, and the cocklers finding them in this way went silent and prayed for their souls, and some would have left them there, sanctified in their marriage bed, but it was felt in the end that it would have been a startling thing for children to come by unawares if they wandered as far as the sandbanks, or would be made unholy by people going out there to pry.

My mother and I watched them being carried home. We stood at the stile and could only just make them out, black figures on the streaked shore, while the grey sea licked back to the horizon. Years later I dreamt about them, but in my dream they were Larry and Geraldine, and the funeral procession was also their wedding ceremony. When I woke I cried because it hadn't been.

Days later Larry was found, dumped at last by the tide up near the slipway. He was recognised and claimed by his father, and very quickly removed. My Aunt Bridget, telling us this at the tea table, said that several girls in the village would be in mourning for him now, and quite a few children would never see their father again. I glanced at Geraldine but it seemed that for the day she'd forgotten who he was, and was far more interested in squeezing tomato seeds, which she hated, out through the gaps in her teeth, and picking them out to add to the pyre at the side of her plate.

Explosions on the Sun

MARILYN DUCKWORTH

SOMEONE HAS SAFETY-PINNED a plastic bag inside the bars of Gillian's bottom gate.

A white shawl. Very clean. Crocheted by very clean hands. It flows out of the plastic bag very soft against her sun-browned wrists. She swings it on to her shoulders and dances to the mirror, stroking it. Then thinks to discover where it has come from. A note in the bag explains it has been crocheted for her by a friend of her grandmother who wants her to come to lunch. She doesn't want her grandmother's friends. She has her own. And yet she has danced in front of the mirror and enjoyed the shawl. Madame Truffaut has put out her crochet hook and neatly hooked Gillian into her life. Last time they met she had felt the old woman was shocked by her novitiate's dress. But apparently she has forgiven Gillian her vows to the church. Now that she has renounced them.

She lives, like a witch, at the top of a white palace, at the end of the last corridor. A fat little witch in polyester. She is Belgian.

They eat sponge fingers. They fit Madame's mouth perfectly. She feeds them in greedily, as if she only eats when she has company. Gillian's French limits the conversation. They discuss the weather. She tells Gillian there have been explosions on the sun. This is the explanation for the afternoons of cloud, the phlegm at the back of the sky.

'Explosions,' she repeats. She makes a fat tunnel of her mouth to sound the 'o'. She is very serious. Gillian shudders. She wonders if the world is going to end and how soon. '*They* are responsible, of course.'

Later she realises that what the woman talks of are sunspots, familiar abnormal phenomena after all. But still hears Madame Truffaut's 'explosions' in her head. She looks up at the sky and wonders if a piece of it could fall down and crush her. And who are 'they'? It was much easier when God could be blamed for natural disasters. But Gillian has decided, after much unhappiness, not to believe in God.

She locks the top gate and is inside the cottage taking off her shoes, when she has a strange feeling. There is someone or something outside, watching her. She hasn't locked the lower gate. She sometimes forgets. Tonight it seems important that she should lock it. She runs down quickly and silently in her bare feet. The tunnel of steps is always cool, but tonight it seems cooler than usual. Round the second bend she halts. Her keys rattle as she lowers them behind her. There is a face looking in at the gate and she doesn't want the face to see the keys. Did he hear them? Does he suspect the gate is unlocked?

The face is a man's – ruddy, with curling dark hair and a flash of white teeth. Not a tourist. He looks like a satyr – not young – his cheeks sag. But his eyebrows point upwards. He smiles at Gillian. When she doesn't respond he turns and goes away.

She sits on the steps and waits until she has stopped trembling. The steps are very cold. Then she runs down the last of them and locks the gate. You have to lean on it to get the key to turn. If anyone was waiting there they would have had the gate open while she was struggling with the key. She hates keys. But they're necessary.

That man. She has seen him twice now, she is sure.
She thinks he might be one of them.

She wakes in the still dark and waits for the noise of a
train. Here comes one now. She can count the carriages
from the sound swaying in and out against her window.
When it has gone she gets up to go to the bathroom. The
door is closed and won't give immediately. She turns the
handle a second time and pushes. Rattles the knob. The
door seems to be bolted from the inside. It must have
slammed in the wind, forcing the bolt out of place. What
wind? Not a breath of air. Then she thinks she hears
whispering behind the door. She puts her eye to the crack
but can't see anything. Not even a light. This is absurd.
She will have to go outside and pee under the pittosporum
bush. Who could be in her bathroom at this time of night?
Even for the South of France this is strange. She knocks on
the door.

'Is there anyone there?'

The whispering stops.

She goes outside and squats under the pittosporum bush,
holding her nightie high under her breasts.

As she moves back into the light of the kitchen she
catches sight of the spider. It hasn't had to walk very far to
get there from its web in the bedroom window. The
cottage is only two and a half small rooms. She gets the
feeling the spider knows something about the bathroom
door. Supposing she trod on it now, would these odd
things stop happening? She raises her foot threateningly
and her lower leg begins to shake. She has never killed a
spider in her life. Mosquitoes, ants, even flies – but not a
spider. She puts her hand over the trembling nerve in her
knee and lowers her foot to the floor. The spider plays
dead.

She decides to try the bathroom door again.

It opens. There is a faint flowery smell in the air. Her

grandmother must have come back to have a bath. The whispering would have been her reading Anthony Powell aloud to herself above the steam. Do books have ghosts?

If it wasn't her grandmother, then who was it?

The black-bearded tramp is sitting on a seat overlooking the port. His hair glistens with sweat, his red face is dusty. He is carefully rolling a cigarette from old butts of tobacco. Why does he always wear his coat? Is there nothing underneath? It is more important, of course, for a tramp to be modest than a failed nun on holiday from Scotland. She is walking past him with her Codec plastic bags full of cheese and fish and olives. She must have looked guilty for he invites her again to stop and talk about God. Can he know more about God than Gillian? The tramp is the imaginary badman of little girls. Bluebeard. The real badman is of course disguised – sometimes as the husband they mean to marry. The preacher tramp is kindly and slow. He isn't one of *them*. Nevertheless she is glad she didn't find him in her bathroom last night. It would be like meeting a gorilla.

She assembles lettuce, fish, eggs, olives – on her kitchen bench – and begins hungrily to make herself a *salade Niçoise*. Chopping, whipping and tossing, with her back to the sun. The kitchen is arranged that way. What would it be like to have no sun? If it were totally obscured by Madame Truffaut's explosions, or by something else? She shudders to think of a sunless world. A world without light. Or heat. The eskimo life has never appealed to her. She has poor circulation.

Before she goes to bed she drinks a bottle of good white wine. Blanc de blancs. Twelve per cent. Tonight nothing will disturb her.

It's a fallacy that wine helps you to sleep. It might make you snore and twitch your eyelids, but it keeps the brain awake. Racing in overdrive. She can feel the heat of her body in the mattress and keeps moving to escape it.

At four o'clock she goes to the bathroom. She wishes she didn't have to go. She couldn't bear to find the door locked again. After all, it's her bathroom. Grandmother left it to her in the will. So why does she lock her away from the toilet?

Tonight she takes the few steps across the living room, past the kitchen alcove – and hears the lavatory chain flush. She freezes. A man has come out of the bathroom. Jeans and grubby white shirt. He sees her and sidles with his back to the wall, smiling and waving his hands as if he is trying to wipe her away. These windscreen-wiper movements seem to say – 'Don't touch me. I'm harmless.'

She watches him go, perfectly calm now.

This is very odd, to find a man in her bathroom in the small hours of the morning. She tells herself how odd it is, because in fact it doesn't feel all that odd. It's as if she had put him there herself. But this isn't a dream. She pinches herself, as they used to in books she read as a child. It feels like a real pinch. But what sort of test is that?

She has forgotten to notice if he went down her steps or up into the bushes. The fence is quite high at the back.

She decides to stay awake, sitting at the table, facing the window, and watch the sun come up. If she is here in the morning, that will prove this really happened. Won't it?

Morning, and she is still here sitting at the table. She feels a bit dizzy, from lack of sleep, she decides. She has been reading her grandmother's P. G. Wodehouse books. She hasn't removed any of her things. She is living here as if she were her grandmother, using her crockery, her linen, her books, her view from the window. She moved here for the view. The blue-green mountains, the old ochre bell-tower, the boats. It's like living in an cyric. This reminds her of the dove that flew down across the back of her hand earlier. Was it a real bird? Yes, because she has its feather on the windowsill beside her bible. The odd thing is that she has felt again that same sensation on the back of her hand, as if invisible wings were brushing it. She feels it now, flexing her fingers and watching the movement. There is something there, poised and feathery. She wishes it would fly away. She can hear the doves cooing in the garden above, monotonously, on and on. She feels an emptiness in her chest which is like the emptiness in her mailbox. On bad days people post stones into the emptiness.

She walks to the olive grove past empty houses. Peeling stucco. Wallboards instead of glass behind the barred windows. She peers into the darkness of one but it is so black anyone could be in that room, unseen, watching her. Where does the old tramp sleep in winter?

Still climbing and walking, she finds deep blackberry-bramble steps, going down under shadowy witchy trees. It is like being breathed into the lung of the earth. She hears voices, catches flashes of coloured clothing between branches – but there is no one there. She follows a winding *sentier* between high stone walls. She can't see and has no idea where she is going. She is a white rat in someone's experiment. Who is leading her where? She starts to turn a corner and in the passage ahead of her hears deep heavy breathing. Some large flanked animal is padding towards her. She turns around quickly and finds another path. It is downward. There is smoke blowing across the narrow passage. Some gardener burning rubbish. As she reaches the centre of the smoke she takes a breath, chokes and sits down.

She is helped to her feet immediately. Two men support her, one on each side. The taller one on her left is the young man who had been in her bathroom. When she sees him her knees give way and he trips against her, righting himself with a curse. His hand under her elbow presses her onwards. The older man is the ruddy-faced satyr who was at her gate. They aren't merely helping her up, they are taking her somewhere.

'What are you doing?' She panics. 'Let me go.' And shakes her elbow free.

'I think you were looking for us?'

'What were you doing in my bathroom?' she demands.

The young man starts to laugh and the older man joins him. 'We want to share something with you. It's down here.'

They are back on the witchy steps leading down between scented blackberry bushes. There is a great hole burnt out of the bank. The edges are charred and smoking.

'No!' She pulls back, afraid of the confined entrance. But as they draw closer it becomes larger – large enough for the three of them. Beyond she sees a long glowing passage, red-lit, and at the end of it hears sounds of revelry, music and laughter.

'You didn't have to come in now,' the young man says. 'Do you want to come back some other time?'

'Some other time – yes,' she says. There is a sweetish smell of smoke that is making her sick. 'I know the way.'

'Oh yes.' They laugh together. 'You know the way. You'll find us again.' And they release her. They haven't been holding her with any kind of pressure.

She runs all the way home. On the grass verge an old couple have set up a card table. They are playing euchre, wearing cocked hats made out of French newspapers. 'Peter Sellers is dead. Goodbye Mr Sellers,' a cocked hat calls out to her as she passes by. The Joker is dead.

Her strength is gone. She has difficulty climbing the thirty-eight steps.

After the humid warmth of the day the evening is blissfully cooler. She lies on her garden seat, looking upwards. A bursting green loquat falls out of the loquat tree into her lap. A healthy fruit. This isn't possible. She sits up and examines it, stroking the slightly rough skin. She looks up into the creeper-covered tree. Evil looking fruit, black with disease, peers down at her. The ground is littered with these, and with heavy brown leaves like bits of leather. She pierces the unripe fruit with her thumbnail and it is full of sticky seeds.

They gaze up at her like eyes. Has she killed something living? She digs them into the earth. While she is doing this she notices another dove's feather, very small and pale, lying by the seat. She leaves it there because her hands are dirty.

She dreams of drowned souls. She is leaning on the rail of a ship and sees them in the water. They look like spirals under the waves. Like ammonites. She wakes and her grandmother's bed confronts her. The sculpted footboard is as high as the head. It is wood, not iron, but the curves and pointed chiselled knobs at the corners are like something in a cemetery. Why hasn't she noticed before how like a tomb it is? Of course, she has this notion upside down. The bed is not like a tomb, the tombs have been made to resemble beds. Nevertheless she can't sleep in it tonight. She climbs out and arranges the mattress on the floor.

She is sitting on her mattress, wakeful, spray-can poised like a gun. She can't see the mosquitoes but can hear them dive-bombing in the air, invisibly. At last she grows tired of looking for them in the lamplight – she has decided to leave this on – and shoots at random, away from her nose. The smell creeps back like a fart.

She has decided what to do today. She is going to lift the lid of Grandmother's piano and see if she can remember any of her old tunes. There are music books in the piano stool with pages missing and jumbled. She will sort them into some kind of order and try them out on the yellow keys. She had forgotten the piano. Grandmother had a tablecloth draped over it and clutter parked on both levels. She wants to make a noise.

She makes a noise. This is all it is. Certainly not music. She laughs out loud at herself. She has put her hands down on the keys. They fall automatically into place over the first notes of her 'recital piece'. 'Jesu, Joy of Man's Desiring'. The fingers flutter, hesitate, stumble and go on. It can't simply be that the piano is out of tune. It is her fingers, which have forgotten a remembered sequence which has somehow been jolted askew. How can this have happened? Are there other memories which are distorted like this? Playing over and over in her head, a sharp instead of a flat, a compressed interval? Well, she will have to go back to the beginning. Her first piece. 'Buy a broom. Buy a broom. Buy a broom to sweep your room.'

Some of the lower notes don't sound. She presses them and they thunk tunelessly. She sneaks up on them in a scale, fingering lightly. Still they don't respond. The silences hang like missing rungs in a ladder. She thinks she hears someone laughing outside and bursts on to the verandah, preparing to find one of *them*. Nothing, But someone is making fun of her. She peers up into the sun glare, looking for neighbours in the gardens above. Would laughter carry that far?

Later she thinks she hears somebody whistling at her gate. She is on her way down with her shopping bag, walking very carefully. Whatever or whoever whistled has passed on by the time she has descended the last seventeen steps.

In the grass growing alongside the *raccourci* a small grey snake is sunning itself. As she draws back it shoots off into a hole in the wall. The movement turns over some mechanism in her chest, so that she has to gasp for breath. She runs to get away from the spot and by the time she arrives at the Porte de France she is doubting that she saw the snake. She would prefer to think it was a trick of the light. She slows down and breathes deeply.

★

She has read all her grandmother's books, so decides to visit the English library.

This is housed in a church. How long since she has been in a church? Not long. Three weeks. A lifetime ago. The smell doesn't change.

In the library they are talking very loudly. The library is a social occasion and British voices are raised. Amusing anecdotes, an argument about a book order. An English gentleman gestures with a date stamp. A woman drops a cascade of books. Gillian goes behind a shelf in the small room and blocks her ears. She can't think of the name of an author. All the names have fled out of her head. In ten minutes the library will close. She reaches out for a book. Any book. Her ticket out of this place.

She finds she is walking to the olive park. She has to sit down for a moment on the old tramp's seat, opposite the port. The big olive tree in the corner has crumbled at the base, leaving a deep slotted cavity with decaying edges. Inside she can see litter, drink cans, paper. The tree doesn't seem to mind. Its lacy leaves spread a hazy shadow. She is glad the tramp isn't here. She doesn't want to talk about God. When she is rested she moves on up the *raccourci*, between ochre walls. Blue convolvulus is blooming on a bank above. Something prompts her to turn and look back at the sea. A figure is standing on the sea wall against the sun. From here it looks like him. The young man in jeans. How could she possibly tell? There is something in the angle of his chin. Like a wolf baying at the moon. If he had a beard it would point almost horizontal.

She feels very tired and sits down for a moment on a shallow step. Her skirt trails in the dust. She might as well go down as up.

By the time she reaches the Porte de France she can't see him. Some French people are arguing about a car collision, banging each other's vehicles with fists and shouting. The woman shouts loudest. Gillian goes down the steps to the Café Jardin and orders *thé citron*. The umbrella shade is cool. She stretches her legs under the table and sighs with relief. The second slice of lemon will do for her fish tonight. She wraps it in a paper serviette. Then she remembers she has an invitation to dine out tonight. She looks up past the laundry, the locksmith, to the post-office clock. It is quarter to three, nearly the end of siesta. On a low wall behind the supermarket the checkout girls are lounging in overalls and green aprons. She hears their laughter. A knot of impatient shoppers clusters at the glass doors of the shopfront, wheeling empty trolleys. The girls drift reluctantly towards the back entrance. Their bags of change wait to be collected and tipped into the tills. When Gillian goes home she will have to look for a job. A job like this?

Her dinner invitation has come from a retired Canadian couple who live along the Boulevard – friends of her grandmother. She has to walk past the entrance to the olive park to reach their apartment block.

They sit on a balcony overlooking a blue swimming pool, sipping white wine and *crème de cassis*. From time to time the surface of the pool erupts with an evening bather. She looks beyond a tall canary plain at the glittering port and the blurred sea. Jazz rhythm rises from the park.

When it is time to go she declines her host's offer of a lift. She leaves the marble-floored foyer, walks down the wider path and sees a figure waiting where the Boulevard begins. The young man. Perhaps she expected him to be there? Is this why she preferred to walk? Does she want to get to know the young man?

They are directly opposite the deep blackberry-bramble steps where he had shown her the passage in the bank. She expects him to lead her down there again. Instead he beckons and leads her on along the Boulevard to a roadblock. '*Chantier interdit*'. Beyond the roadblock the way is dusty and uneven. The hillside has eroded and tumbled down. She hangs back.

'It's all right. It's quite safe to walk. I'm taking you to the old cemetery.'

'Why?'

'The view's superb. I thought you'd like to see it.'

There's a full moon so that the sky is milky. Dark cypresses circle the graveyard, black on the moony sky. Inside the gate the graves are shadowy iron cots, like Grandmother's bed, with no space for a ghost to put his feet. Other graves are enclosed dog kennels hewn in stone. She looks for eyes, but there are no eyes looking out.

They move on up to a higher level. On the way they pass crypts with iron doors, like lifts to the Inferno. One of the locks on the double doors has been breached. They swing inwards to a small shadowy room. There are objects in the room – pots of flowers? She leans to look and is suddenly afraid she will be pushed from behind and the doors clang shut on her. She draws back. Now, passing other wrought-iron doors, she imagines prisoners behind the bars, rattling at them, staring out of empty eye sockets. She shudders and runs after the young man to the top level and the breathtaking view. The lights of the port, stringing along the promenade, the town below, the mountains hunched on the bright sky. The view is awe-inspiring. But she can feel death in the soles of her feet.

They look over a wall at the roofs of crypts below. It looks like a small baroque village. With lights inside, these buildings could be inhabited.

'Why did you bring me here? Yes, I know – the view. But why else?'

She is talking to herself for he has gone ahead of her, back down the steps to the lower level. She follows. She doesn't want to be alone. Round a corner he is sitting on a new double grave, like a bed. He runs his hand over the flecked and polished granite. His hand moves up to the headstone, wiping over it, feeling for an inscription. Is that what he's doing?

'There's no inscription!' she notices, following with her own hand.

He reads her thought and laughs. 'That frightens you,

doesn't it? It *is* strange. Here.' He pats the granite. 'It's quite comfortable. Rest.'

She sits. She needs to sit. Her legs are weak and aching.

A moment later he has launched himself upon her, reaching for the neck of her dress, ripping, so that buttons fly like popping corn. Her heel skids on the cold granite as she tries to rise and is forced back.

She screams.

Who will hear?

All these people inscribed on headstones and not a soul to rise and help her. Not even God will hear her now, since he doesn't exist. She struggles, clawing and kicking. And then, quite suddenly he has gone. His weight lifts and his shape melts harmlessly into the shadows.

Another shape materialises, opening a new scream in her throat. The old tramp in his dusty black coat.

Is he about to show her what he wears – or doesn't wear – underneath?

No.

He holds out a hand to help her up. '*Venez.*' He explains that the nasty young fellow has gone, run away. The hand she takes is surprisingly soft, like feathers, and yet she feels safe.

On the way down the hill she asks him to tell her about God.

A Day in the
Life of a Sphere

LUCY ELLMANN

A ROOM THAT has rarely borne the lip of a hoover. A room that like all others in the British Isles is wired for electricity. A room that has been decorated a number of times, painted, wall-papered and stripped in logical cycles. A room with windows, possibly curtains, and a door with handles on each side so that people with things to do in there can enter and exit.

A screw in the upstairs room of a semi–detached in Stevenage, and a personage is born.

A yuletide scene.

We know far too much about people we've only just met. First of all, we know they EXIST. Now, this puts them at an immediate disadvantage, since on the basis of it we can deduce several other embarrassing facts about them.

1.   They have or had two parents. One was able to MEN-STRUATE, etc. The other could EJACULATE, and did.

2.   They themselves have one or other of the two possible sets of GENITALIA, which they have probably used or will use for SEXUAL purposes.

3.   They also have some sort of BUM. One which once wore NAPPIES.

4.   They PISS and SHIT. As did their parents before them.

5.   They may have been BREAST-fed.

6.   At PUBERTY, they sprouted extra bits of CHEST and/or spreads of HAIR.

7.   They have no doubt BURPED during their lifetime, and FARTED.

8.   The ALIMENTARY CANAL in focus: this person one meets at a party or a bus-stop, when they EAT, horrible things happen in their MOUTHS to the FOOD. When they SWALLOW, it all has to squidge past their EPIGLOTIS and down their OESOPHAGUS and then other unmentionably AWFUL things happen to it. And they have indulged in this activity daily for years.

Well! It's enough to keep you indoors – *alone* – all the time, hiding your own EXISTENCE, your somehow slightly more acceptable secrets, these facts, these givens we're all so bored knowing about each other that we try not to mention them much. 'Did you shit satisfactorily this morning, Madam?' or 'Have you *yourself* masturbated lately?' are relatively rare opening gambits.

In fact, we all try to get jobs, careers, vocations, hobbies, allotments, and idiosyncratic tastes in music in order to decorate our lives with proofs of difference, divide our bodies from all the others, to try to forget it's all a mess of atoms anyway and there is no god and, in the end, simply to have something to talk about in polite company (these accomplishments fail with children and animals, who have no shame).

James was having some trouble settling into *his* body. He'd been dreaming about being a sphere, peacefully and happily bobbing around in space, only vaguely and pleasantly aware of other happy spheres near and far, similarly bobbing.

Then he realised he was about to wake up. He much

preferred to be a sphere. But he did feel some curiosity, he took a kindly interest, shall we say, in what sort of person he would turn out to be in his earthly life. A dustman? Well, okay. An artist perhaps, a carpenter, a zoo-keeper? Just in case the body he was about to inhabit was leading a hard life, James began to gear himself up for some amount of trial and tribulation.

The alarm went off. Gone was the sphere dream, only a memory now as James came down to earth and into a woman's bed in a dark room. He was, it seemed, a single mother.

With only a dim hold on her identity and whereabouts, Jamie padded to the bathroom to carry out various functions we've already agreed we can take for granted and are bored by and therefore need not mention. She also got dressed.

She went downstairs to the kitchen and put the kettle on. She opened the blue plastic He-Man lunch-box and dumped most of its contents into the bin. She began to move more adeptly now between fridge and cooker, her bare toes flicking away crumbs and bits of broken glass. She examined the eggs speculatively, but she really didn't see how using up these two old eggs was going to help the 10,000 prematurely slaughtered battery hens, nor their humane and grief-stricken owners. She therefore poured soup from a half-empty tin into a half-empty saucepan, spilling some on her feet, which remained blasé and unruffled.

She went to check out the one envelope the postman had just delivered. One Christmas card, that had the look of Solution all over it: how can I express my seasonal mood to all the millions of people I am vaguely acquainted with, without spending too much money? The creep had evidently managed it. Jamie got the hot soup into the matching He-Man thermos and with dread checked the time.

—8:15—

The hands stretched across the glum white face of the clock like the brow of an insurmountable hill. They were supposed to leave the house at 8:30 and the kid wasn't even up yet. Resisting the impulse to grind her molars together and chip a few points off her canines, Jamie reminded herself that she was a sphere, or at least potentially or essentially one. She proceeded upstairs with a piece of toast on a paper towel.

Alexander's room was festooned with cascades of cloth as if the traditional child-oriented hurricane had struck. He'd been trying to construct a tent (difficult to do in a hurricane). But at least the failed tent covered up the cars and He-Men and transformers and rockets and other toys with sharp pointy bits that lay underneath. Jamie decided on the cheerful approach.

'A is for *Alexander*, B is for *Better*, C is for *Come out of there*, and D, *get Dressed*,' she said in a loud voice, pronouncing the letters phonetically and cheerfully, in accordance with current opinion, and also pointing them each out on the wall where she'd painted the alphabet for him a few years ago AND THE KID STILL COULDN'T READ A DAMN WORD. Except maybe 'Alexander'.

She sat on his feet, which sprang away from her under the blankets. Looking at the tufts of dark hair on the pillow, the only visible sign of her child's existence, she wondered if it was all genes and hormones. Why was she playing at Love? Her willingness to care for this being was simply the delegated will of her genes, who probably laughed their heads off at human attempts to romanticise the business with the term 'emotion'. All that soppy glorification of maternal feeling.

She grabbed a foot and yanked a sock onto it. But how was she going to get him to allow the rest of his clothes to be put on? Given the evident ineffectuality of the Cheerful Educational Mum-Friend, should she allow the Dictatorial Witch Figure to materialise, or inflict the Paralysed - With - Depression - Look - What - You - Do - To - Me -

Everything - Would - Be - A - Lot - Better/Easier/Perfect - You - Know - If - Sometimes - Just - Sometimes - You'd - Do - What - I - Ask one on him? Or maybe either Frantic - With - Worry - Important - Appointment - Today - Can't - Be - Late, or Fire! - Fire! - Fire! - Everybody - Out, would do the trick.

The decision had to be made and then stuck to. Anything would be an effort, though: Jamie's spine had by now assumed the slouching position. She was pretty sick of getting two people dressed every morning. But she was galvanised by the sound of a melancholy bell at 8:30. Bells that sound melancholy really bore you with their sighs. She dragged the kid to school.

He kissed her in nine places before they parted. First her nose, then her chin, her cheeks, three different areas of forehead (which he called her threehead), and on each of her hands as if he were a diminutive but amorous Russian count. But he wasn't. He was only five.

She walked home through the park. Lakes, trees, bushes, birds. Remember birds? You probably heard some when you were a child. Looking down the valley towards Knebworth where she'd met, married and mislaid Alexander's father, Jamie thought she could detect the traces of a great cosmic hand that had made the world – probably a child's. The rivers dug out with a grubby index finger and forced to meander through gratuitous bends, clouds flung into the sky with glad abandon. You could imagine the delight of patting the tops of trees with the palm of your hand like a clump of moss, or flicking them over with a fingernail and blowing them down like birthday-cake candles. Had hands once cupped these hills in lust and smoothed the valley into an abdomen made in heaven? And was there still someone up there, a child grown old and despotic, breathing, panting, farting breezes across the land?

Nope, and it was time to go home and get changed for her heavy date. Who himself had told her that Uncertainty was built into the foundations of the universe – corroborated, he felt, by the fact that people in Papua New Guinea can't make head or tail of Mozart. If Mozart isn't guaranteed, what is?

The date was so heavy she had to take a taxi in order to get to the school in time to pick Alexander up. She chose the wrong taxi. The driver was Maltese and had fought in the war with the British Army he'd signed up right away but what do they do to you after they're finished with you the shits they put him in a military hospital because he'd tried to commit suicide and the other guys told him if you talk to the doctors that's it you'll be in a straitjacket the rest of your bloody life but he'd been rude you see to his Commanding Officer he told him exactly what he thought of the British Army and how they treat you once they've finished with you the British don't know how to sell anything they don't even answer their phones they don't know how to do anything. Jamie wasn't listening after a while, just watching the clock on his dashboard with increasing dismay.

'What time'd you say you had to be there?' he asked impatiently, since she'd been silent.

'Half past three.'

It was 3:45 and they were stuck behind five or six lorries unloading goods to several different establishments, still half a mile from the school.

Out of a proper sense of guilt, the taxi-driver handed her a signed copy of his single, 'Stevenage Is My Town'. Out of a sudden sense of her spirit having been broken by the twenty-five minutes she'd spent in this car, Jamie accepted it, and conjectured that since he was crazy they would no doubt crash.

When she finally arrived at the school, her kid was gone. A man had collected him, the cleaner seemed to remember. Almost everyone else had already gone home – there were just a few stragglers left to watch Jamie begin to cry. 'Stevenage Is My Town' fell to the floor, revealing the 'B' side: 'So Young and Tender'.

She lay on Alexander's bed and looked at the 'W' on the wall, for Who, Why, When and Where, for her Well of Worry, for being Wrong and Wretched. The school was apologetic, the police noncommittal and uninspired. She'd told them to try Knebworth. But apparently her husband didn't live there anymore.

She felt cold. She touched the radiator and it felt cold too. She got the key and started bleeding it. It hissed airily for a while and then fizzed and then spat and then spouted a full stream of steaming water at the wall. She tried to get the key back in then, but the water scalded her. She got a bucket and stood there weeping, wondering what to do.

Images of Alexander lying dead under a hedge led her on to all the times she'd hurt him, yanking him out of bed or onto buses. There'd been that unpleasant disciplinary phase when she'd decided that rather than smack him she would pinch him. How her pinches had made him cry, how sickeningly hard she'd pinched because it was such an unsatisfying outlet for fury. And why, yes why had she not believed him that time he felt sick? She'd yelled at him and slammed his bedroom door shut so he couldn't get out and she'd gone back to bed and not been there when he'd vomited all alone in his own fucking bed you bitch.

The bucket was by now full. She almost slopped it all over herself. She clamped large amounts of Alexander's tent around the radiator and ran downstairs to get rubber gloves and a towel as protection against the scalding water and then tried to get the key in again, but some bit was missing. She found it but couldn't get it and the key to screw into the radiator. Plasticine! That was what she needed. She scrabbled on the floor, flinging the larger toys across the room until she reached the lowest sediment of tiny ones and there she found some old yellow nodules of plasticine. She stuck some in the key and then the screw-pin into the plasticine and enduring the hot key and the hot water as best she could, she stemmed and then stopped the torrent.

She plopped briefly into Alexander's bed again, scalded, appalled, trembling and strangely enlivened, as if she were for once a fully cooperative inhabitant of her body with her rent paid up. She was a mother and she was going to do something if it killed her. She charged to the bus-stop: Action Woman.

Knebworth looked black and empty through the fog, but she was determined to find someone there. No lights shone at the big house where her husband had grown up. The lawn felt thick and wet, unmown. Undaunted, Jamie went straight to the back where there was a cottage, built for a granny that had managed to predecease it somehow.

She rattled the door-handle and found the door was open. And there was Frank, lying on the bed, asleep. Never had she felt like liquidating him more. She shook him for now instead.

'Where is he, where's Alexander? Where *is* he?' she yelled.

'Wha . . . what you mean? What're you . . .'

'You picked him up, didn't you? I know it was you, just *like* you too, to turn up after two years and scare everybody to death. Where the fuck is he?' She started hitting his head. She felt like pounding him into the soft wet granny-soaked ground beneath the cottage.

'Stop hitting me, and I'll tell you,' Frank said rather pathetically. 'You should talk anyway – *you* weren't there to pick 'im up!'

She felt like she'd been flushed through with cold water, like a raw chicken. Could Frank really expect her to play games with him *now*? Must she affect calm in order to avoid a scene in which he tried to apportion blame so that they each had equal shares, NOW? It seemed so.

'Where is Alexander?' she calmly asked.

'Run off when we was in the park. Said he was going home to you. He knows the way . . .' He mumbled on, to the retreating mess of a woman, who had once been his wife.

She waited, weeping, for the bus back to Stevenage. A taxi came by so she stopped it. By standing right in front of it. It turned out to be the same driver with the World War II traumas. He was not pleased by the tirade she gave him all the way back to Stevenage – it would no doubt be added to the annals of injustice with which he would harangue future customers – but he took her where she wanted to go.

She ran across the park calling out for Alexander. At last the length of his name had some use: she uttered it in prolonged cries that woke the birds and bees, the trees, the ducks, and eventually, Alexander himself who was lying on a bench by the duck-pond where they'd daily crumbled bread in his infancy.

'I thought you would be cross with me, Mummy,' was his excuse for sleeping by the duck-pond. She gathered him up, thinking of his duffel-coat with gratitude – the only thing there'd been between him and the fog.

They went home and made another rocket.

'You cut this here and then you glue it there and then you have your round triangle shape,' he informed her. A cone.

They played the record:

> *I stand erect*
> *I deserve respect*
> *In Stevenage, my town.*

And then she got Alexander to allow her to put his pyjamas on him, and she read him a book, his favourite, about a mother who sits on her son's gingerbread man by accident and has to make him four more.

Then Jamie went to bed too, listening to the silence. She used to close her door and play the radio so that she'd only gradually become aware of Alexander's whining, his requests for juice or complaints of monsters formed from the dark shapes in his untidy room. But now she listened with self-satisfaction to his silence, keeping a contented ear cocked for . . . nothing.

She dreamt that night she was a sphere, floating in space. She didn't know who or what she would be when she woke up. It was a short dream, but it felt real. When she awoke, she found she was an old geezer called Jim who lived in a bedsit in Southwark. He had sold his bed long ago to buy cigarettes and given away his dog and needed a complicated heart operation. The room was full of newspapers and cigarette ash.

The Book of Ands

ROBERT GROSSMITH

> In the beginning was the word and.
> St John 1:1

and and and and and and and and and and and and and and and and and and and and and and and and and and and and and and and and and and and and and and and and and and and and and ... I quote from memory the opening words of the *Book of Ands*. In the intervals between the conjunctions lies my story, lie all stories. I'm sorry, this is not the best way to begin. Let me try again.

It is a convention of most stories these days to declare their own fictiveness. Mine, however, is true. I live alone in a top-floor flat in a small university town in a universe expanding at both ands. One more try.

Alone in my flat one afternoon a few months ago (better), I heard a ring at the door. I opened it and a stranger stood there. Dressed in a brightly coloured head-band, a tie-dyed grandad vest and plastic sandals, he had an anachronistic look about him. I asked him what he wanted.

'Got some books to sell,' he said. 'Sci-fi and fantasy

mainly. The guy in the bookshop round the corner said you might be interested.'

I could not restrain a smile. Whenever old Kowalski found himself beleaguered by students trying to unload their books on him for holiday money at the end of the summer term, he always gave them my address, though he knew my tastes were specialised and my funds limited. I would invariably send them on their way unrewarded after examining their wares with a pretence of interest. It was a sort of running joke between us.

'Well, you've come to the right place,' I said. 'I am something of a collector, yes.' I gestured behind me to the sagging bookshelves lining my walls. 'So what rarities do you have to offer me?'

He loosened the drawstring of the duffel bag he carried on his shoulder and emptied its contents on to the mat at my feet. In the cataract of dog-eared paperbacks with garish covers and fanciful titles disgorged for my inspection, my eye fixed on a slim hardback still sporting its glossy white jacket (though somewhat stained and darkened by age), like a dinner guest at the wrong party. The dustflap bore the title *The Book of Ands* and below it in smaller print the author's name, George Lewis Berg. 'What's this?' I said, picking out the volume from the mass grave in which it lay half-buried and opening it at random. The page was filled with regularly spaced columns of the single word 'and'. I thumbed further ahead, then back to the beginning; each page was the same. 'Seems to be some sort of joke, isn't it, a parody?' I said to hide my dismay, thinking of Hemingway and Dickens, those aficionados of the 'and'.

'Sort of, yeah. It was a present from a girl I used to go out with. It's my name, you see. Well, Andy really, but everyone calls me And. I guess she thought it was funny.'

'The flesh made word,' I said.

'Sorry?'

'Nothing.' I had been fingering the book while we

spoke, stroking it, caressing it, rehearsing my proprietary rights. I admit, such curiosities excite me. With feigned indifference I enquired, 'And how much are you asking for this masterpiece, this attack of literary conjunctivitis?'

'I couldn't let it go for less than a quid. Sentimental value. You know.'

I offered him fifty pence and he accepted.

The transaction completed, I invited my visitor in for a coffee. I do not receive many callers and thought it might be agreeable to pass an idle hour or two in bookish conversation. To this end I tried to elicit from my guest his opinion of the British contribution to fantasy literature, with particular reference to Stevenson and the early Wells. Unfortunately he appeared singularly ill-informed about the whole subject – he seemed to be under the impression that Stevenson invented the rocket – and when he had dribbled the last of his coffee into his matted beard I invented an excuse about a dental appointment and saw him to the door. There are so few people these days with whom one can talk about matters that matter.

One such person, perhaps the only person among my own narrow circle of acquaintances, was my friend Kowalski the bookseller, and the following morning I paid him a visit.

'Anything to your liking?'

I didn't understand him at first.

'From that fellow I sent round yesterday?' He had a playful gleam in his eye.

'As a matter of fact I did get one interesting item from him, yes. Something of a surprise. A very odd book. Ever heard of the name George Lewis Berg?'

'Berg, Berg,' he repeated. 'Sounds familiar. So many Bergers and Burgesses these days. But Berg, no, I don't think so. Want me to look in the ELB for you?'

'The Elbe?'

'Encyclopaedia of Literary Biography. Twelve volumes, one volume slightly damaged. Offers invited.'

'Not my line, you know that. My interest is the work, not the life. But yes, look him up for me, will you? B-e-r-g, Berg. I'll keep an eye on the shop for you.'

He laughed. 'Don't worry. No one will come in. People don't buy books any more. Not the sort of books I sell, anyway.'

He wandered off through the dusty stacks crammed with high-quality art books and slim volumes of verse (poetry was his special passion), disappearing through a low arch and round a corner, where I could hear him humming tunelessly to himself as he dragged a stepladder across the wooden floor and mounted it. Some minutes later he returned bearing a weighty folio-sized tome open on his arms, crooked at the spine like a sleeping child.

'Berg, George Lewis,' he read. '1885 to 1949. Novelist and poet. Born Andorra of mixed parentage, German and English. Moved to England aged . . .'

'Where?'

'England.'

'No, where did you say he was born?'

'Andorra. Here, you can read it yourself.' He transferred the volume to my arms and I took it to the window, where the light was better, to read it.

The entry consisted of a two-column biography and a list of Berg's major works – some dozen novels and collections of verse, none of which I had heard of. I learned that he had worked for most of his life as a librarian, until failing eyesight forced him to retire, and had fought against the Fascists in the Spanish Civil War. More to the point as far as I was concerned, I discovered that he had spent the last ten years of his life as a virtual recluse, apparently composing his *magnum opus*. After his death, however, the only manuscript found in his possession was that which came to be published as the *Book of Ands* (a brief description of which was included). Provision had been made in his will for his final work to be privately printed, should he die before completing it, and in the absence of any other manuscript, and out of respect for the dead man's wishes, this was done, thereby producing 'perhaps the most bizarre literary artefact in the history of English letters'. Berg was said to have suffered several bouts of mental instability in his youth, the implication appearing to be that at the end of his life his sanity must finally have deserted him.

I summarised all this for Kowalski and told him how I had purchased a copy of the *Book of Ands* from the student he had sent me the previous day.

'Sounds crazy. Why should anyone want to write a book like that for? Where's the pleasure in such a book?'

'I don't know, it's very strange.' A thought suddenly occurred to me. 'Perhaps, well, perhaps he did write his *magnum opus* and then simply began cutting it.'

'How do you mean?'

'Well, look at the facts. He worked on this novel for ten years, supposedly. How many "ands" can you write in ten years? Enough to fill a whole shelf of books. Yet after his death it seems only a small bundle of pages was found, suggesting he may have written them not long before he died. What did he do for the rest of the time?'

'Are you asking me or telling me?'

'I'm just guessing, but well, perhaps when he'd finished his novel he came to see that any conventional work of fiction – any narrative composed of nouns, verbs, adjectives of the author's choosing – any conventional prose style inevitably limits the reader's imagination, forces him to accept the writer's version of events rather than create his own. Perhaps he began by cutting the odd adjective here and there, as many writers do, and it grew into a passion, a style, or anti-style. Perhaps he cut so much of his original novel that in the end he only had one word left.'

'"And"?'

'Well, perhaps he then threw the manuscript of the novel away and just kept retyping the one word he'd saved, the only word that freed rather than limited the reader's imagination. Perhaps if he'd lived another year the book would have been a couple of thousand pages longer. How can an infinite series be terminated, and all that.'

'Wait a minute, I don't understand. You mean he wanted the reader to sort of . . .'

'Fill in the gaps between the words himself. Yes.'

'In other words . . .'

'Complete the novel himself. Exactly. Supply his own nouns, verbs and adjectives. The perfect collaborative enterprise between reader and writer. Democracy on the page.'

'Sounds crazy,' Kowalski repeated. 'Where's the pleasure in that? Would Byron have written such a book? Would Keats?'

'Perhaps Berg would have regarded Byron and Keats as tyrants. Authorial autocrats, dictators of the *dicht*, imposing their private sensibilities on the reader, stifling the reader's own.'

He shook his head with an expression of pity. 'We can't all be great poets, you know. Some of us are content to sit at the feet of the masters and enjoy the Muse at second-hand. Some of us have no wish to be writers, some of us are happy as readers.' He closed the covers of the unsaleable encyclopaedia and shuffled back with it into the gloom at the rear of the shop. 'If everyone wrote their own books,' he called over his shoulder, 'what would become of the humble bookseller?'

The principle I had hit upon to explain the curious structure of the *Book of Ands* – the reader as writer – intrigued me enormously, and I was keen to put it to the test. Returning home from Kowalski's, I made myself a cup of coffee, lit a cigarette and settled down at my desk with the *Book* opened at page one before me, intending to approach it as I would any other novel, to read each page consecutively, left to right, top to bottom, start to finish. For the first few pages my concentration wavered: the words rang emptily in my ear, an idiot's meaningless stammer echoed to infinity, a beginning never reaching a middle or end. But as I read further I found my attention slowly drifting away from the black blocks of print and drawn instead towards the white spaces between them, as some composers tell us that the silences between the notes in a piece of music are as important as the notes themselves. I recited aloud, louder, thumping out the words with my fist on the desktop, setting up a rhythm, mantra-like, in my brain, till the symbols on the page began to grow dim and diaphanous, as though around them between them, something else was trying to show, struggling to achieve presence. And for no obvious reason I found myself thinking back to my childhood and the day my mother died, and how I happened to find a ten-shilling note, torn and rain-sodden, in a puddle on my way home from school, and the look of pain on my father's face when I burst into the house, singing my good fortune, and the terrible tremor in his voice as he told me of the accident and how my mother had gone to heaven, and the numbness I felt, then the rage, then the grief, and the tears I shed and the nights I lay awake praying to God to take me too, take me too, and how it rained like a monsoon on the day of the funeral, and the relatives stroking my hair and doing their best to comfort me, pity disfiguring their faces, and my father all in black, biting his lip so as not to cry, and the wreath I bought with the ten-shilling note, and how it fell from my hand and dropped in a puddle when I saw the coffin being lowered into the earth, never to re-emerge. And a thousand other more trivial memories, random images from a forgotten past, joining ands, forming a ring, making sense of absence. Reading the *Book* that day, I wrote the story of my own life. I stayed up late into the night to finish it.

Over the next few weeks my obsession with the *Book* deepened. I would walk about the flat with it open in my hands, reading from it like a breviary. I would stand at the window as before a pulpit and declaim its message to the bemused passers-by looking up and exchanging comments in the street below. Each time I opened it I wrote the story of my life anew. How could one life be subject to so many different readings, I wondered. In my more sober moments I reflected on how here was the book predicted by Roland Barthes, the *scriptible* rather than *lisible* novel. I thought of developing my views on the *Book* into a scholarly article and submitting it to one of the literary quarterlies, representing it as a sort of *nouveau roman avant la lettre*, the zero degree of writing, the minimalist text *par excellence*, the literature of exhaustion and silence. I even got as far as a confused and verbose first draft before I started, inevitably, to cut. I considered destroying all my other books, of deleting all but the 'ands'.

I should have understood what was happening sooner, got rid of it sooner. By the time I did, it was too late. I was seated at my desk after a particularly enervating all-night session with the *Book* in which I had again recomposed my life. As I stood up and walked to the window to let in some air and light, I felt myself succumbing to a peculiar sense of dislocation, dispersion, of which I was unable at first to identify the cause. For some moments I stood motionless, gazing dumbly at the curtained window, trying to hold myself together, to grasp what was happening. Then it struck me. If my life could be written or read in so many different ways, if it contained so many different plots, as many plots as readings, did it not follow that it lacked any plot at all? The more I probed this thought, the more alarming it became. What was my life, after all, but a random series of disconnected events, a chaos of discrete impressions strung by memory on a necklace of conjunctions, assigned a spurious structure to create this illusion of a unitary I? Wherein did the order of my life consist but in the momentary arrangement of the fragments of time into a notional pattern of sense, a pattern as arbitrary and ephemeral as the chance constellation of glass beads in a kaleidoscope? What was that famous whimsical definition of a net: a collection of holes held together with string? What was my life, what was the universe, but such a net – a fabric of absences sewn by thought, a chain forged by fancy, the *Book of Ands* made flesh?

Had I possessed a less reverential attitude towards the written word, I might have destroyed the *Book* at once. But I am a true bibliophile: all books for me are holy, sacred texts, scriptures. And I could not bring myself to do it.

I took it instead to Kowalski. 'Here,' I said. 'It's yours. Please.'

'Ah, so this is your famous *Book of Ands.*' He fanned the pages with a practised thumb. 'No,' he said. 'I have no use for this. Who would buy such a book? Keep it.'

'Please!' I insisted. 'Hide it for me. Somewhere no one will find it. High up on a shelf where no one ever looks. Behind another book. Please!'

He gazed at me with curiosity and concern, then shrugged. 'OK,' he said, 'if that's what you want. Crazy, crazy,' I could hear him muttering as he shambled away, though whether he was referring to the book or to me I could not tell.

I left the shop before I could see where he shelved it. But I felt no easier when it was done. I carried the *Book* with me, I knew, and would do so forever, distributing the world between its conjunctions, fitting my thought to its syntax. I understood that the *Book* was a book that had to be written but should never perhaps be read, because once read it could never be forgotten, never be unread. Like the universe itself, infinite but bounded, it would continue, mercilessly, to expand.

Travelling Elsewhere

HOWARD JACOBSON

EVERY GENTILE LIKES to have one Jew he can call a friend. I was Gilbert Massingbird's. He chose me because I stimulated his every dread without posing him a single threat. I *looked* to be in possession of all those qualities which are reputed to explain the awesomeness of Jewish achievement – implacability born of persecution, nervous energy, an insatiable desire for worldly riches, a limitless capacity for disloyalty – but in reality I was passive and impoverished, inert, sentimental, without any surviving marital consolations. I lived in a wet flat in Lower Gornal, waiting for the phone to ring. Whenever a teacher at one of the local comprehensives was assailed, whether by weapons or self-doubt, the Authority rang around a pool of about a dozen replacements. When all the replacements had been assailed the Authority rang me. I was the last resort and the final line of defence. Gilbert, on the other hand, although he wore battle jackets and desert boots and carried his loose change like small arms in a leather powder pouch hanging from his belt, did not even know there was a war on. He took his kids to the country every weekend where he drilled them like boy scouts, and for the rest of the time enjoyed the privileges of academic Oxford, not the least of which being a big house in Summertown, an international reputation for applying religious thought to secular matters, and Iris – apprehensive, artistic, unessayed, and glowing like a girl for Gilbert still, however old she grew. I was just the friend for him.

And for Iris too. They both needed reassuring. I have no proof that I figured in their blackest, their most private domestic fictions, but I know that Gilbert relished the idea of my hankering after Iris and of Iris not hankering after me. Every now and then I would come across one of his stories in the smallest of small magazines, the characters invariably a bearded soldier of the mind who kindled camp-fires at weekends, his unessayed and glowing wife, and an obscurely brilliant Semite with base appetites. The stories always ended the same way, with the wife returning her soft breasts whence they had been briefly, partially, *infinitesimally* removed, and murmuring, 'Dear, dear Elijah' (or Abraham or Mordechai or Judas) 'I do care for you as a friend, but my husband is the only man I will ever permit to possess me. I cleave solely unto him.'

It was out of character for us to go on holiday together. Our intimacy had unspoken rules and stopped short, in actuality at least, of any context in which it might have become necessary for us to disrobe. I had never wanted to see either of them in shorts, and they, I must assume, had never wanted to see me surfing in a prayer shawl. I'm speaking figuratively. The Massingbirds did not in fact take holidays of the undressed kind. Perugia was the sort of place they preferred, somewhere they could do a course as a break from doing the basilicas. On this occasion, though, because the children had grown up and gone, and their own needs had simplified into wanting just to walk and think and sketch, they had picked Cornwall. A cottage had come their way, a couple with whom they had intended to share it had let them down, so they thought of me.

Gilbert rang first, mentioning rambles. I said no. Then

Iris tried me with her apprehensive laugh and inducements of fudge and clotted cream. I heard the familiar distress pretending to be radiance, and measured it against a solitary summer in Lower Gornal. Lower Gornal by a whisker, I decided, but then I remembered that friendship with Gentiles was not meant to be a bed of roses, and I said yes.

We drove down in Gilbert's Skoda, Gilbert logging every mile and every gallon in a notebook. He had gone Eastern European as much for reasons of economy as of principle and felt he had something to prove. Even after we had broken down a third time he was able to show us both, on paper, that we were still doing better than if we'd had a Volvo. 'Better meaning cheaper but not faster,' Iris complained, in an unprecedented outburst of disloyalty. I had noticed before we set out that she was looking tired; now, as we stuttered through those last interminable miles, the skin around her eyes seemed to have splintered into a thousand fragments. It is a heavy price they pay, these wives who would be forever girls, once age discovers the trick that has been played on it.

It must have taken us eighteen hours to get to Tintagel, and about the same number before the Massingbirds decided it was time to leave again. Tintagel was all wrong. More materially, the cottage was all wrong, not being a cottage at all but the rear quarters of a souvenir shop from which it was divided by walls too thin to exclude the commotion of commerce. Iris complained of a till ringing in the night, which I thought implausible; and Gilbert rose furious at having his sleep invaded by the voices of parents telling their children not to touch. 'I wouldn't mind,' he said, 'if they had anything worth touching.'

We stayed just long enough for me to buy a handful of pixie key-rings as presents – I wanted it established early that it was not *my* sensibility that was under strain in Cornwall – then we motored up the coast to Castle Boterel, a village less likely to agitate Iris's neurons, and where Gilbert could more readily accommodate himself to gewgaws, because they were merchandised by the National Trust.

The season was too far advanced for us to hit upon another cottage. We tried six or seven guest houses without success. Either they couldn't take us or we wouldn't take them. For *we*, read the Massingbirds. I would have taken anything, but they were insistent on staying somewhere Cornish, and backed away whenever a person from Hackney or Halesowen answered our enquiries. At last we settled for the one establishment that didn't have a row of toby jugs in its window. Our host wasn't really what we wanted; he affected a Rotarian jocularity ('Call me Jerry, but don't use me like one') and spoke with an Essex whine. But we were weary and grateful for his assurance that his wife at least was Cornish and that his great-grandparents had been born, wed and buried in this self-same village.

I spent the next couple of days walking with the Massingbirds, then left them to it. Gilbert made too much of a virtue of finding mud, it seemed to me, and then of frog-marching us through it. Hedges, bramble, fields with young bulls in them, similarly. If we didn't return to Castle Boterel squelching, with blackthorn in our hair and words of gratitude for Gilbert on our lips, he fell into a sulk. So we got spattered either way.

Back on my own again, I decided against even unaccompanied walks. I had seen what there was to see. Steep cliffs, a wild ocean, and human nature at its most futile. Well and good, I could keep to my room, occasionally look out of a window, and read.

Wrecking was what I read about. Wrecking as it had been perfected here, on this very coast, by the very community Jerry's great-grandparents had belonged to and whose blood flowed still in the veins of Jerry's mocking wife, Vida, with her alert, narrow eyes, and her austere speech-rhythms, blown cold by the same wind that froze every tree for miles around into an attitude of angular submission.

Jerry himself one could not imagine clambering over a heaving deck to make off with a brass bell or the Captain's silver snuff-box; Essex had softened him. But it wasn't at all hard to envisage Vida rampant above the precipices in a howling gale, flashing a delusive torchlight to entice unlucky schooners on to the treacherous rocks below. 'C'mon my loverr,' I could hear her say, as she coaxed the vessel ever nearer. 'That's it, you're almost there, that's my boy, that's my beauty.' And I could readily picture the accompanying play of sardonic laughter on her compressed lips, tinged with orange to match her hair, because I saw it every morning when she served us breakfast.

Apart from the odd hour for darts in one or other of the pubs, I didn't see much of the Massingbirds for the next week. Gilbert tramped, Iris sketched, I read. But from my window I noticed that although they always left together for the cliffs, Gilbert a foot or two ahead as was to be expected, they did not return together. Every afternoon, a little after one, Gilbert slogged it back into the village alone. It was a good four, sometimes even five hours after that before I spotted Iris returning with her sketch-pad underneath her arm and her face set. Had we been living in one of Gilbert's stories I would have gone out and accosted her on the harbour wall, where briefly, partially, *infinitesimally*, I would have put my hands inside the navy blue Guernsey she always wore against the weather, against extravagance, and against me. But in the event it was Gilbert himself who behaved melodramatically, coming to call on me long after I'd gone to bed, and bringing with him a full bottle of whisky and two tumblers from the bathroom.

'Well, lad,' he said, 'I've gone and done it.' Calling me 'lad' was one of the ways he familiarised my outlandishness. I think he'd got the idea of it from Shakespeare. Hal to Falstaff. Only this time the one telling the wild stories wasn't Falstaff.

What had happened was this. On about the third morning of our stay he had gone back to his room to collect a map he'd left behind, and there, to his astonishment, he had found his pyjamas laid out upon the bed; not folded in a square upon his pillow, I was to understand, beneath a clean white towel and a cake of soap, but arranged so as to suggest – well, the form they might have taken had Gilbert still been in them.

The following morning he devised some stratagem whereby he could once more slip back to the room alone. There again, but now with one knee bent and one elbow just a little crooked, lay the empty mummy of himself. And so it did on each succeeding day; except that where at first the sculpture had been rudimentary, suggesting hardly more than a scarecrow or a corpse, the disposition of the figure soon became so subtle that he never knew, when he pushed open his door, whether he would discover himself on his stomach or his side, in an attitude of readiness or repletion, with his buttons fastened or undone.

He gulped at his whisky and wiped his beard with the ears of the little scarf he wore wound tight around his throat, like an urban gipsy. His narration had reached the seventh day. The day God rested, but the day he, Gilbert Massingbird, unlaced his boots at the hotel entrance, ran panting up the creaking staircase to his room, and beheld his pyjama jacket pulled apart, his pyjama trousers removed entirely, and a Cornish pasty placed where his manhood should have been.

I sat very still against my pillows. And raised an eyebrow. 'It was at that point you realised someone in the hotel was interested in you?' I said. His eyes blazed at me.

'Sarah One or Sarah Two?'

Sarah One and Sarah Two were the chambermaids, teenage daughters of 'up country' families. Chambermaiding was a fun thing for them to be doing. There was even a Sarah Three but she was seventy.

Gilbert shook his head. 'I thought of them. But it wasn't.'

'How do you know?'

'I spoke to Vida.'

'And what did she say?'

He accepted there was no point equivocating. 'She said it could hardly have been them seeing as it was her.'

I raised my other eyebrow. I could hear her very words. Something – I hope not mischief – made me mimic her. ''Tweren't they, you daft buggerr, 'twere me.' Gilbert stiffened. Not with anger, it took me a moment or two to realise, but with jealousy. He was suddenly frightened she'd been laying out my pyjamas too. 'You ought to know I'm in love with her,' he said, reminding me what a nakedly territorial assertion that always is.

'You mean you've slept with her?'

'In the sense of sharing her bed, yes.'

'What other sense is there?'

'I haven't *made* love to her, if that's what you mean.' He stressed the wrong word. It was *you* he was really going for. That's to say me. That's to say us. The circumcised ones. The mindless adulterers of Gomorrah. Gilbert had picked me as a friend in anticipation of precisely this conflict. Just as I had picked him precisely to forestall it.

So instead of scoffing at his compunctions I charged him with his responsibilities. I became Iris's champion. How would she feel, I asked him; what would she say?

To my surprise he knew to the last letter what she would say. 'I've done this before, you know,' he told me.

'Slept in the same bed without . . .?'

'I've done it before, that's all.'

'And what did Iris say then?'

He hesitated, overburdened with complications. 'Essentially,' I urged him.

'Essentially she said, "What a waste."'

Two nights later, Iris Massingbird knocked on my door. She was carrying a bottle of red wine and a couple of tumblers from the bathroom. In deference to her distress I didn't throw back my blankets, naked though I was beneath them. I had failed of Jewishness to her husband; I would fail of Jewishness to her.

What had happened was this. Left to herself on the cliffs every afternoon, she had begun to brood. She would soon be fifty. Her children had gone. Gilbert had become so remote she could not remember his face when it was not before her. Her paintings did not hang in famous galleries. Would anyone care, would anyone notice, if she slipped silently into the sea?

'I would, for one.'

She had turned around in alarm, shocked to realise that she had spoken her idlest thoughts aloud, and then to see that it was Jerry — dear, dear Jerry — who had heard and had answered them.

It became a little ritual, an innocuous matter of course, for them to meet after lunch by the pretty white turreted lookout locals called the Coronet. Iris talked about her family and her painting; and Jerry — vulgar, of course, and perhaps even disreputable, but vital, so *vital* — well, Jerry told her about seasonal business and made her laugh. When he suggested one afternoon that she accompany him the next to collect pasties from Liskeard, she agreed, laughing all the while, assuming it was a joke. Who collected pasties from Liskeard?

As it happened, Jerry did. According to Jerry, the best pasties in Cornwall came from Liskeard, and nothing other than the best pasties in Cornwall were served in his hotel. So she went with him, forgetting to mention it to Gilbert, sitting up like a little girl in the front seat of his old Jaguar, which she ticked him off for referring to as his Jew's-canoe. The pasties came frozen in plastic bags and filled the boot and the entire back seat of the car. A couple of boxes of pasties that had not been frozen, that were still smoking hot and smelling unbearably of fresh pastry and onion and swede and seasoning, travelled between them in the front.

And it was those which caused Iris to forget her vows of nearly thirty years.

They had to stop and have one. And the one they had was so good they had to stop and have another. Jerry knew a place on the moor where they could park the Jag by a stream and be approached by curious munching sheep. Their jaws going all the time, the sheep regarded the humans; and *their* jaws going all the time, the humans regarded the sheep. After that, everything seemed to belong to nature. The seats slid back or gave way or vanished altogether, and on a bed of frozen pasties Iris did what she was never allowed to do in any of her husband's fictions.

I smiled at her. My people had danced round graven idols in the desert. A brief binge on Bodmin Moor could not strike me as terrible.

'But I feel so bad about Gilbert,' she explained. 'You see, I do love him.'

'A woman can love her husband and still overdo the pasties once in a while,' I assured her.

'No, not Gilbert. It's Jerry I love.'

'You love Jerry? Already? Do you not feel you should know more about him?'

'What more is there to know? I know he is kind. I know he has a sense of humour. I know he has largesse. Can you imagine Gilbert behaving in that manner in a car full of food? You know his attitude to extravagance. You know what he would have said had he been there.'

'Tell me, Iris.'

'He'd have said, "What a waste."'

When they speak of an adulterer in Castle Boterel, they say, ''Ee travels elsewhere.' The phrase is pleasingly functional, emptying misbehaviour of its excitement, it's true – though travel in a remote county is never without incident – but emptying it at the same time of censure. Methodistical the Cornish may be, made quiescent by superstition and

111

fatalism; but the wrecking instinct is still strong in them also, if no longer for purposes of survival at least as an invigorating pastime.

The Massingbirds returned to Oxford where they pined like mooncalves. Gilbert tried to open up a correspondence with Vida but she wasn't much of a letter-writer. Iris ran back to Castle Boterel for a week, was taken to Liskeard twice, and then sent packing. I assume that if they talk to each other any more, the Massingbirds address the question of waste. I have only just realised what a fearful thing they mean by it. They mean that they have thrown their lives away for nothing if their marriage does not continue; for how can anything be a waste if, in itself and while it's happening, it has provided pleasure?

But I am out of contact with them. I spend more and more of my time in Cornwall now. The place seems to suit my temperament. There's a theory, to which I'm partial, that the Cornish are one of the Lost Tribes of Israel.

The Five
Thousand and One Nights

PENELOPE LIVELY

YOU MAY WELL have wondered about the subsequent marital history of Scheherazade and the Sultan. Did they live happily ever after? Well, of course not – it is only in stories that people do that and Scheherazade was a purveyor of stories. She *was* the story, indeed; the symmetries and resolutions of fiction were not for her. Nor for the Sultan, poor fellow. Poor fellow? With his record? Ah, but he was a reformed character. Tamed by narrative. The sting drawn; the fires banked. He had revised his opinion of women. He loved his wife. He took a benign interest in his children. He hadn't beheaded anyone in years. He was running to fat and looked rather less like Omar Sharif than he had done in his heyday. He drank a lot of coffee and watched videos and paid desultory attention to the family oil business. Sometimes he accompanied his sisters and his old mother to London or to Paris for the shopping season. Life wasn't bad, not bad at all. A little on the quiet side, maybe – once in a while he would feel a twinge of guilty nostalgia for the old days – but agreeable enough. And he was married to the most beautiful and talented woman in the eastern world, was he not?

There was just one problem.

Scheherazade, you will recall, was an accomplished young woman even before her fateful encounter with the Sultan. She had degrees in philosophy, medicine, history and fine arts to which she had now added doctorates in comparative literature and philology. She taught creative writing, she ran crèches and family-planning clinics, she advised governments on women's issues. At forty-two she was as lovely as ever, if not more so, and being a devoted wife she never allowed her commitments to keep her for long away from the Sultan. A night or two occasionally, no more. Their marriage, after all, had its own tradition, its internal structure, its story that could not be interrupted.

For Scheherazade had continued to narrate. After the first thousand nights there had come the second thousand, and the third, and the fourth. Where they were now the Sultan had no idea; he knew only that he was advancing towards old age with Scheherazade's soft and compelling voice still narrating to him across the pillow, night after night after night. There was sometimes an admonitory edge to the mesmeric flow, and he was certainly not allowed to fall asleep; he would jerk himself back to consciousness to find Scheherazade's incomparable eyes staring stonily at him over the embossed satin sheets from Harrods, while her elegant finger tapped irritably at the sleeve of his pyjamas. 'I'm sorry, my dear,' he would say. 'I must have dropped off for a moment. No reflection on you. Marvellous stuff, as ever. Enthralling. It's just that . . .'

'It's just that what?' enquired Scheherazade, icily.

'It's just that I get a bit lost sometimes,' apologised the Sultan. 'You're using some rather confusing words these days, you know. What does sensibility mean? And I get muddled about the settings. Where's Devonshire?'

Scheherazade gave him a freezing look. 'When you've stopped yawning,' she said, 'I'll continue.'

The trouble was that the stories had got longer and

longer and, in the Sultan's opinion, a great deal less gripping. The backgrounds had become more and more exotic and the pace, in his view, slower and slower. The characters bewildered him: all these Elizas and Janes and Catherines. They talked and talked and nothing much happened except that occasionally there was a restrained social event or someone got married. He wondered, secretly, if Scheherazade was losing her touch. The trouble did not lie with him, he felt sure; he'd always been a man for a good yarn. After all, what was it about her that had bewitched him in the first place? Apart, of course, from her physical charms, which were as they had ever been – he had no complaints in that quarter. Except that . . . well, the spirit was willing but the flesh perhaps not quite as game as it had been in its prime.

The Sultan sighed and composed himself to listen. 'It is a truth universally acknowledged,' intoned Scheherazade, 'that a single man in possession of a good fortune must be in want of a wife. And stop *yawning*!' she snapped.

Time passed. The narratives continued. The Sultan was far too much in awe of his wife to complain again. He disliked domestic dissension (this may seem startling, given his past, but remember that we are dealing with a remarkable instance of personality change). And in any case, he did not want the stories to stop, he just wanted to get back to the old days.

He was brooding upon all this one afternoon when Dinarzade paid him a call. Dinarzade, you remember, was Scheherazade's younger sister and indeed had played a crucial role in the events of the wedding night. Latterly, though, the sisters had grown apart somewhat. Dinarzade, who was studying sociology at university, had fallen in with a fundamentalist sect.

Dinarzade settled herself on a heap of cushions at the Sultan's elbow and began to chatter about a party she'd been to, tucking into a box of Turkish delight as she did so. She was almost as lovely as her sister, but very differently turned out. Dinarzade was dressed according to her

115

beliefs (or according to something, at any rate). She wore the chador, and was veiled; her dark and lustrous eyes were all that the Sultan could see of her face. Her body, too, was covered. The general effect, though, was not one of propriety, female reticence and religious piety. Her ankle-length garment was made of cyclamen satin; her pretty feet peeped out from beneath it, shod in high-heeled shrimp-pink silk slippers. Her veil sparkled with sequins and silver beads. She wore pale lilac lace gloves. Quite a lot of her bosom was visible between veil and neckline. The bosom, in Islamic lore, is not a sexually provocative area: it is hair and hands that inflame. The Sultan had always found women's bosoms quite as alluring as any other part and hence had never known whether it was he who was perverted or traditional wisdom that was faulty.

He averted his eyes from the luscious contour of Dinarzade's breasts and sighed. The sigh had in fact nothing to do with frustrated lust but everything to do with the Sultan's more pressing preoccupation.

'What's the matter?' said Dinarzade. 'You're looking down in the mouth?'

'I am feeling a bit low,' confessed the Sultan.

'You poor old thing,' cooed Dinarzade. 'I know what you need – a good cuddle . . .' She moved closer to the Sultan.

'It's very nice of you, my dear,' said the Sultan, with a further sigh. 'But believe it or not I'm even losing heart in that area these days.'

'Can't get it up?' enquired Dinarzade sympathetically.

The Sultan winced. Not for himself but for his sister-in-law. He was old-fashioned where women are concerned (well, we know his track record, don't we?) and he didn't like to hear language like that from a nice girl.

'That's not quite the problem,' he said with dignity. 'It's a spiritual malaise, rather. To be frank, it's the stories. Your sister . . . well, to my mind she's gone right over the top. She's getting more and more experimental. We haven't had a djinn or an ogre or a youngest son or a poor fisherman in years. I never know what's coming next. And they're so long. And the characters are so dull. All these girls agonising about their state of mind.'

'No love interest?'

'There's usually a love interest,' the Sultan admitted. 'But it's all so far-fetched you can't make head nor tail of it. We had one that went on for weeks about people shouting at each other in some place called Yorkshire where they have the most appalling weather. And then no sooner were we through with that than we were off on one about an extraordinarily tiresome young woman who marries a fellow much older than herself and then gives him the run-around. I'm pretty well at the end of my tether. I'll be a nervous wreck before the year's out.'

'Shame . . .' said Dinarzade, taking a bite of Turkish delight. 'She used to be able to do ever such a nice romance.'

'Oh, romance . . .' said the Sultan scornfully. 'It's not the romance I miss. What we never have these days is action. I want some action. Adventure. Feats of daring. Heroism and endurance. Crime. Sex. Violence.'

'I tell you what,' said Dinarzade. 'Why don't you have a go yourself?'

The Sultan turned to stare at her with blank amazement. 'Me? *Me?* What an extraordinary idea! I couldn't do that sort of thing! I mean – that's women's stuff. One isn't . . . well, one is differently equipped. Tell stories!' He laughed lightly.

'Oh, well,' said Dinarzade. 'If you're not capable of it . . .'

The Sultan bridled. 'I imagine that one would be *capable* of it. It just hasn't occurred to one to try.'

It was at this point that Scheherazade walked into the room. The Sultan hastily picked up the newspaper and began to study the oil prices. His wife glanced disapprovingly at her sister and said, 'What's that ridiculous outfit supposed to mean, Dinarzade?' Dinarzade twitched a pink satin slipper and glimmered over the top of her veil.

Scheherazade wore a cream wool Armani suit with a skirt short enough to make the most of her exquisite legs. Her black hair lay in shining waves upon her shoulders. She sat down, kicked off her Kurt Geiger shoes, fished her glasses out of her bag and put them on. She had taken to wearing very large spectacles with light tortoiseshell frames although she was not, so far as the Sultan knew, shortsighted. They were extremely becoming but also intimidating. The Sultan was intimidated right now; he whipped out a calculator and frowned sternly at the oil prices. 'Had a good day, dear?' he enquired.

'Interesting,' said Scheherazade. 'And ultimately productive, I think. I am working on the early stages of an ambitious scheme for setting up creative writing classes in the Sahara. Very exciting. But there are some initial difficulties with literacy that we have to overcome. What have you been doing?'

'Working,' said the Sultan vigorously.

He had, of course, dismissed Dinarzade's absurd suggestion. Indeed, had it come from anyone else he would have felt his manhood to be impugned and would have taken appropriate steps. But Dinarzade . . . the silly girl had always been allowed a certain licence, one could let it pass.

And then matters came to a head. That night Scheherazade began a new story. 'Tonight,' she said, 'we are starting something rather special. It is a narrative which deals with the interior life of a woman. She is not a typical woman but we may perhaps think of her as a quintessential woman, or indeed human being. Her name is Clarissa. You may at first find the ambience and the presentation a little alien, so you will need to pay particular attention. And please . . . you have developed a bad habit of fidgeting. Don't. This style of fiction is extremely cerebral and I need to concentrate in order to do it justice. Are you ready?'

After three nights the Sultan's spirit was broken. He could stand no more, he realised. He had to do something. And it was then that Dinarzade's proposal came back into his head. Well, he thought, I wonder . . . Maybe . . .

All that day he paced the palace gardens, alone. His brow was creased in concentration; his eyes were glazed. From time to time his lips moved. Occasionally he flung himself upon the grass and stared up into the sky. And when the night came he laid his proposal before his wife. With dignity and with firmness.

Scheherazade was thunderstruck. Silenced, indeed. For the first time that he could remember the Sultan saw her at a total loss for words. Then, eventually, she began to laugh.

'Your turn! Well, by all means, if that's what you want ... But ... forgive me ...' – for a moment she was quite overcome with hilarity – '... I mean, it is *too* absurd ... But of course – you must. Please go right ahead.' And Scheherazade propped her head on her elbow and looked across at the Sultan, tolerant and amused.

Two hours later the Sultan ended his tale. He glanced warily at his wife.

Scheherazade stifled a tiny yawn. 'Not bad. It had its moments, I suppose, if you like that kind of thing. Quite good narrative drive. Rather crude characterisation. Far too much rushing about on horseback and waving swords.'

'That was the point,' the Sultan protested. 'It's a war story.'

'Quite,' said Scheherazade. 'Never mind.' And she gave him a kindly little kiss on the cheek, turned over and went to sleep.

The Sultan persisted. Indeed, it was not really persistence that was needed, he found – now that he had got started he was quite carried away. There was more to this than one had thought – it could become quite obsessive. He never knew himself what was coming next. There were so many different ways of doing it. He spoke with tongues, night after night.

'... a Colt .45 looked like a toy pistol in his hand. "Don't nobody try to fancy pants," he said cosily. "Freeze the mitts on the bar."'

Scheherazade gave a little groan. The Sultan broke off. 'What's the matter?'

'*Another* of those . . . There's a certain stylistic panache, I grant you – but what's the point of it?'

'Someone's going to get killed . . .' explained the Sultan.

'Yes, dear, I realise that.'

'. . . and then you have to find out who did it and why.'

'Who cares?' enquired Scheherazade.

The Sultan ignored her. He listened, lovingly, to his own voice: 'The Indian threw me sideways and got a body scissors on me as I fell. He had me in a barrel. His hands went to my neck . . .'

He experimented. He roamed wider and further.

'What's a ray-gun?' said Scheherazade with a sigh. 'And why are they going on about this galaxy?'

'They're in a spaceship. Please don't interrupt.'

'Forgive me. But again, one asks oneself – what is it all *about*?'

'It's allegorical,' said the Sultan with sudden inspiration. He smirked. Scheherazade, thrown, glared at him across the pillow. 'Zap! Vroom! Pow! Gotcha!' continued the Sultan. Scheherazade closed her eyes wearily.

He had taken on a new lease of life. He was filled with a sense of purpose; he felt younger and more vigorous. He thanked heaven that he had realised his potential in time – there would be no more frittering away of his talents on pointless matters of business and finance. Any fool could do that. He went on a diet, had his moustaches trimmed and waxed, discarded his suits and took to wearing flowing robes which, he felt, expressed his artistic temperament rather better.

'How's it going?' asked Dinarzade. 'I love the dressing-gown thing, by the way. Really sexy. Very Clark Gable.' She patted the silken folds of the Sultan's garment.

The Sultan twirled a moustache. 'I think one might say without undue immodesty that it's going rather well. One is into one's stride. One has grasped the essentials.'

'And *whose* idea was it?' purred Dinarzade.

But the Sultan was far beyond giving credit where credit was due. 'The key to it all,' he told Dinarzade, 'is action. Get the action right and the rest follows. You know – shooting things and bullfighting and catching enormous fish and getting drunk and behaving with amazing nonchalance when fatally wounded. I've got some terrific ideas. Marvellous stuff. Can't fail.'

'Sounds great,' said Dinarzade. 'Is there any love?'

'Of course. Doomed love, naturally. To be honest, it brings the tears to my eyes.'

'How does *she* like it?'

'Your sister,' said the Sultan peevishly, 'has a one-track mind. I produce the most stunning piece, a real cliffhanger, and all she does is go on about content and relationships. It's *got* content, I tell her – things are happening, aren't they? And my characters have very interesting relationships – they kill each other and rescue each other from hideous fates and make passionate love. What they don't do is sit around endlessly talking.'

Nevertheless, he was more affected by Scheherazade's strictures than he cared to admit. All right, so she wanted content, did she? Relationships. She wanted depth. Very well, then.

The Sultan flung himself into it. He abandoned himself to his Muse and let fiction flow. He narrated like a man possessed. He unfolded teeming sagas of poverty and social injustice swarming with vibrant characters, lurid with the din and stink of nineteenth-century London. She wanted characterisation, didn't she? Atmosphere? He grew tired of that and summoned up tales of passion, power and betrayal in fields and cow-byres. Inflamed with his own fluency, he was barely aware of his audience. Once or twice, pausing for breath, he noticed Scheherazade, listening now with a rather different look in her eye. 'Good stuff, eh?' said the Sultan.

Scheherazade sniffed. 'I wouldn't try that one about the

man auctioning his wife outside these four walls, if I were you. You'd get ripped apart by the critics.'

The Sultan switched tactics yet again. He plunged into the dark reaches of the human spirit; his men and women seethed and fought and expounded. 'Sex in the head?' said Scheherazade. 'That's a new one on me.' 'Me too,' agreed the Sultan. 'But it's intriguing, don't you think?' He took to the sea in ships; he roamed to the far corners of the earth; he told of love and war and crime and retribution. It was as though he were driven by some irresistible force, and when from time to time he glanced at his wife he saw on her face the pleading look that he knew had once been on his own. But he could not stop; there was no mercy for either of them; he was all set to go on for ever. And then, one dawn, the children came bursting into the room and clustered around the end of the bed. The Sultan broke off. The children clamoured for attention and one of them cried, as children will, 'Tell us a story!'

The Sultan looked at Scheherazade. A strange gleam had come into her eye. 'Very well,' she said. 'Sit down quietly and I'll begin.'

The children sat. The Sultan made himself more comfortable upon the pillows.

'Once upon a time,' said Scheherazade, 'there was a poor fisherman . . .'

Volunteer

TRACEY LLOYD

NOTHING SHOWED IN her face. She did not burn, like so many of them, with the sheer excitement of being in Africa. She was an ordinary-looking girl, slight, not very tall, given a stolid look by a skin which was white and somehow thicker than one was accustomed to, a skin which gave nothing away, showed no angles of bone, no hollows, no blood beating under her cheeks, a skin which wrapped her as a butcher will wrap a joint of lean meat in a covering of white fat. Her lips were colourless, like the fine hair which lay close to her scalp; behind the magnifying lenses of her pale-rimmed spectacles her eyes were an indeterminate blur.

She had never been abroad before. She had scarcely been anywhere, growing up in a quiet little town on the east coast, only child of elderly parents. Her mother died just before Claire finished her training in London, her father within a few weeks of her coming back home to look after him. There was no one else. When she saw the advertisement for a volunteer librarian in East Africa, she wrote off at once.

*

And so she came to Gawani, to live in the house by the lake. It had seen better days, that house. You could just glimpse it from the road, a solid white villa, double-fronted, colonial, imposing. Now the ornamental stone-work was crumbling and the front door was boarded up; a path round the side led past empty crates and bits of a broken motor-bike, and a cabin trunk painted with an address in Rugeley, Staffs.

The kitchen was always full of people. When Claire got home from the library in the evenings she would find them sitting round the table – Sally who worked in the hospital pharmacy, Mike from the vocational school, Scotty the hydrologist, the Australian nurses from the nutrition project, the Dutch boy who was doing rehabilitation work with leprosy patients, and always Jean-Claude, the one they called *mzee* or old man, who had grown up in the Belgian Congo and knew more about Africa than the rest of them put together. Faces would turn briefly to greet her, bodies would shift to make her a space, and all the while the talk would move from one to another like a ball in a children's game.

Claire said very little. They talked about their work, about programmes to sink wells and plant sisal and im-munise babies, about fish-farming and solar power and reafforestation, about adult literacy, rabbit-breeding, ma-laria control, about what they could teach the African and what he could teach them. And Claire listened. She was pale, composed, opaque, seeming to absorb, rather than to radiate, the energy which crackled all round her.

On Saturday nights, when visitors came from miles away and the garden was full of people talking and dancing and blowing smoke up at the stars, she would finish tidying the kitchen before she picked her way along the overgrown path to the seat under the arbour. Jasmine covered the rotting trellis-work with a blanket of delicate, dark green leaves, and beneath it she was almost invisible. She seemed to prefer her own company.

One night as she sat there, mosquitoes whining round her pale ankles, someone came towards her from the lighted house and pulled her to her feet. It was Gary, the Texan from the Peace Corps, who worked right out at the cotton mill and only came to town every three months. He was short-legged and stocky, packed with muscle like one of those ugly little dogs bred to fight; he pressed his hips against her as they danced, rolling the palms of his hands across her shoulder blades and pushing his tongue into her mouth. Later in the bedroom he pushed his penis into her in the same determined way, grunting as he did so, absorbed in a struggle of his own.

She made coffee for him next morning as they all sat around in the kitchen and went to sit on his knee. Resting his hand on the inside of her thigh he shifted his head to the left to see round her and went on arguing with Mike.

'Mwanikuza's a deadhead.' They were talking about the Development Minister. 'If he has such a hang-up about aid workers, why in hell keep hollering for aid?'

'He wants the aid without the workers. And fair enough. You can see his point. I reckon we're a mixed blessing. The blokes out here get demoralised having us standing over them all the time, knowing better. They need to make their own mistakes.'

'Pardon me, Michael.' Gary pulled his coffee towards him and dropped his hand back on Claire's thigh. 'My government's putting half a million dollars' worth of plant into that mill. That may be chicken shit to you but I figure we need to train those guys how to handle it.'

'Fair enough,' said Mike. 'I can see your point of view.'

The next time Gary came to town for the weekend he had a girl with him, a big silent Gawani with the face of a fourteen-year-old and shelf-like buttocks, who spent most of the weekend (when they weren't in bed) painting her toenails with blood-red varnish. The American did not seem to remember his night with Claire.

Mike came to her room a couple of times while Sally was away in England on leave, but he made love to her with the light out and always avoided her eyes the following day.

It was Sally who first brought Didi to the house. She had met him on the plane from the capital and invited him to her welcome-back party. He was a local village boy, a product of the Catholic mission school at Nzumbe, returning after six years at the university to take up a research post in bilharzia control. Sally called him her whizz-kid. He sat in the garden in the late afternoon heat holding a full glass of beer and listening to an argument about Milton Obote, neat and self-contained, with horn-rimmed spectacles which seemed like part of his face.

When the argument was deflated by a joke from Mike, Didi put his glass down beside the crate he was sitting on, tucking it carefully into the side so that no one would stumble over it, and stood up. His jeans were so thoroughly ironed that they shone like polished furniture, and his tennis shirt was as white as a clinical coat.

Claire was in the kitchen, turning the handle of the old-fashioned mincer, when he put his head round the screen door to ask for a little cold water.

'There's some in the fridge. It's filtered.' Her fingers were stiff with shreds of bloodied meat and she had to ask him to help himself, pointing out the glass on the draining-board with an inclination of her forehead.

When he had filled the glass he brought it first to her, and after protesting she drank it down, holding it clumsily between the heels of her hands but still leaving the sides smeared with blood. He washed it carefully and dried it before refilling it.

He sat at the kitchen table and watched her as she chopped the onions, fried the mince, speared tomatoes on the point of a knife and held them in the flame of the gas until the skins blistered and burnt. One by one he opened the little pots of herbs which Sally had brought back from

England and put them to his nose. Claire showed him how to fold spaghetti into boiling water with a fork and later how to fish out one of the slippery strands and test it with his teeth. When they had all eaten, someone took the cassette player outside and he danced with her on the beaten earth of the yard, his head bent towards her, his tight hair now and then touching her face.

He was living out at Butameni with a cousin-brother who worked at the fish-freezing plant and he had to leave before the party was over. Next morning, Claire was in the garden in her nightdress collecting dirty glasses when he came round the side of the house with a loaf of plaited bread from the Arab baker, saying that he had been to Mass and his stomach was empty.

She made coffee and they ate the warm bread together and he warned her that she must never walk in the garden without shoes and explained the life-cycle of the hook worm. Sally came into the kitchen while they were washing up, a *kanga* knotted over her big breasts, and told Didi that it was the first time she had seen an African man with a tea-towel in his hand, but he smiled courteously and went on polishing the glasses.

There was a path behind the house which led to the lake. After a long, late lunch everyone decided, as they did most Sundays, to go for a walk. The sun was beginning to lose its fire but the air still smelled of dried grass. Didi and Claire, a little way behind the others, picked their way across the *shamba*. Trailing stems of purplish-green leaves latticed the banked-up beds of sweet potato, and however carefully they walked small landslides of soil trickled over their feet.

'This is a very important crop,' said Didi. 'In my village they eat it every day. Imagine – every day.'

Beyond the *shamba* the path grew softer, almost spongy; there were reeds on either side and the smell of water. Even so, the little beach came as a surprise. They stood in twos and threes, looking out with a sense of discovery,

127

although the lake here was only an inlet, a horseshoe-shaped bay of shallow green water, hardly part of the real thing. When someone began lobbing in small stones to break up the stillness, Didi drew Claire away, up on to the rocks.

'Bilharzia is very bad here. This is where the snails have their breeding place. Even a splash from the water can be dangerous.'

The rocks were smooth, weathered like giant pebbles, balanced one on the other and looking as though a touch would roll them into the lake. Claire followed Didi as he clambered across them, jumping over gullies, elated by the effort of keeping on her feet. As they climbed higher and higher, further from the beach, the rocks held firm, grew larger, more stable, more rooted in the earth and finally (Claire was gasping for breath) merged into one great smooth plateau, stretching away across the top of the world. Beyond it, so blue that it seemed to have fallen from the sky, lay all the vastness of the lake.

'We call it *bohari*,' said Didi. 'It means sea.'

There was no wind up there, only the mellow warmth of the late-afternoon sun. Inland as it sloped away, the surface of the great rock was puckered with clefts where lichen grew, and it finally dwindled and disappeared into short grass, dry as stubble. Didi found a bush with clusters of fruit, small and round and shiny, and held them out to Claire on the palm of his hand.

When she hesitated he laughed and pressed them into her mouth. They were sweeter than red currants and she burst them one by one on her tongue, as she used to in the garden at home, and felt the juice spurt in her mouth.

There was a moment of awkwardness when he took off his spectacles, and then Claire took hers off, too, and they sat down. She lay back on the rocks and he began to undress her with sure neat movements as though he was peeling a ripe orange, and she closed her eyes and felt the sun on her skin. When she was naked there was a pause; his hands were no longer on her and she thought he must be taking off his own clothes and opened her eyes because she wanted to help him. But he was kneeling beside her gazing at her belly and his face was close enough for her to see the look in his eyes as he said quietly, 'So white.' He leaned forward, and as his soft mouth enclosed hers the rock underneath her buttocks seemed to melt.

A month later, when Mwanikuza made his announcement, Claire and Didi were already married.

Lots of people had tried to talk them out of it. Mike had manoeuvred them back into the kitchen one night, just as everyone was setting off for the hotel, apologetic, diffident, pointing out that Claire was a long way from home and that in a way, though he knew it sounded bloody pompous, he was responsible for her. Sally had come to the library (Didi was living in Claire's room and there was no way to get her on her own in the evenings) and talked in a low, anxious voice about how sex wasn't everything and even she and Mike had their ups and downs and weren't going to decide anything definite until they'd had a year or two to think about it. Father Xavier, when they went to the presbytery to arrange the service, began by making jokes about the bride price and listened sympathetically when Didi said that he wasn't telling his family until it was all over. But when Claire told him that she didn't think she was ready to take instruction, at least not yet, his old face turned sulky and he didn't look at her again.

The ceremony, which he grudgingly agreed to perform, was the perfunctory one reserved for such occasions, and the great open-sided church was almost empty. The cousin-brother from the fish-freezing plant was only told at the last moment and came without his wife and children. Mike and Sally were there, of course, and the Australian girls, and Jean-Claude looking solemn with the nicotine scrubbed off his fingers. One of the Maryknoll sisters from the secondary school, the joky one with the Brooklyn accent, arrived at the last moment, flapping down the aisle in her rubber sandals and genuflecting, as she put it afterwards, 'without breaking my stride'. But most of them reckoned it was against their principles to go to church, even for a wedding, and to be perfectly honest, they felt uncomfortable with Didi. He somehow wasn't African enough.

As if to make up for the service, the party afterwards was one of the biggest they had ever had. Mike and Sally drove out to a village on the lake with a couple of sterilised five-gallon drums from the pharmacy and brought them back full of smoky, home-brewed millet beer. Didi got drunk for the first time in his life and kept hugging everyone and calling them his brothers and sisters, and then fell asleep in the garden and one of the Norwegians had to carry him to bed.

Claire undressed him and he lay on his back, spread-eagled, smiling in his sleep. Music from their wedding party was still drifting in through the fly-screened windows as she bent over him and slowly, gently, so as not to waken him, licked his dark brown skin.

Mwanikuza's announcement blew the household apart. Work permits were cancelled for all aid agency workers and everyone was given forty-eight hours to leave. There was no time to sit around the kitchen table discussing it; they were all too busy packing, arranging flights, salvaging what they could of data they had planned to write up when their contracts ended, queuing outside the post office for calls booked to Trondheim, Brisbane, Fort Worth, Nijmegen. In spite of the chaos, Mike managed to get through to the office in London to arrange that Claire and Didi could take over the house and the following night, when they came back from the airport, they found themselves alone in it.

Hand in hand, they wandered round the abandoned rooms. No one had had time to pack more than their personal effects and there was stuff everywhere. Didi began to tidy up while Claire made supper; later they took the cassette player outside and danced to the old tapes of Dylan and Joan Baez. The music drifted away over the warm garden and lost itself in the darkness.

The following night, after they had eaten the left-over spaghetti, they walked down to the hotel. Jean-Claude was there, eating alone, a cigarette still burning in the ashtray as he forked curry into his mouth. Always a special case, with friends in high places, he had managed to delay his departure.

'We are the last, then,' he said to Claire. Didi was buying drinks.

'I suppose so.' This was the first time he had spoken directly to her.

'It will not last so very long. Mwanikuza is going to lose his job, or perhaps change his mind. You will see. It will be six months, a year, and white faces are coming back. Not the old ones. Not your friends. But white faces. Impossible to do without them.'

'Do you think so?' He was cynical, he had seen so much. She did not know how to argue with him.

'But of course.' He lit another cigarette, the flame of his old-fashioned lighter burning blue behind its perforated metal shield and leaving, as he snapped it shut, a whiff of petrol on the close air. 'For the moment, it will be hard for you.'

He looked round the dining room, at the empty tables laid with white cloths but no cutlery, at the Africans clustering round the bar with Didi in their midst, at Mr Patni smiling with an open bottle in each hand, and finally at Claire. She sat across the table from him, white and crumpled, in a flowered print dress which did not suit her. 'You are the only woman here.'

She laughed. He managed to make the word sound

voluptuous, like something out of Georges Simenon. She had no illusions on that score, knowing herself to be plain, dull and ordinary. It did not matter. What mattered was that Didi wanted her.

She smiled at him as he came towards the table, carrying the drinks. His own glass was half empty.

'I'm sorry. There are men there from my village. They have drunk too much. But it would be discourteous if I did not speak with them.'

'You know what Jean-Claude has just told me?' She could not wait to share it with him. 'Isn't it funny? Me! The only woman in here . . .'

Didi stared. Jean-Claude looked at his plate. There was a trumpet of laughter from the bar and Didi swung round. The drinkers, a dark jostling group, were looking towards them. They turned away when they saw his face.

All the way back along the lake road she tried to reassure him. She reminded him of how little he respected such men. He had often talked to her about them – stupid men, anti-white, anti-progress, who had envied him since they were children together in the village for his brains, his education, his chance to get away; men who kept their own wives at home in subjection and then, when they came to town to waste their money getting drunk, thought that every woman they saw was a prostitute. How could he let such men upset him?

Their feet fell softly on the road. She became aware once again of night sounds she had grown used to – the electric shrilling of cicadas, the steady grunting song of frogs, the insinuating whisper of the reeds.

'Didi? Look, I won't go there again if it upsets you.'

But he said nothing and when they got back to the house she went to bed. She did not know what else to do.

As soon as it was light she got up again. He was sitting in the garden. He had taken one of the patterned cloths Sally bought to cover the cabin trunks and had wound it round his hips. His chest was bare. She put a hand on his shoulder but he did not look up and she felt like an intruder. She went to the kitchen to make coffee, but while she was waiting for the heavy old kettle to boil he crossed behind her on bare feet, went out through the screen door and disappeared round the side of the house.

In the evening when she came home from work he was in the garden and she ran towards him. But it was a stranger who stood up to greet her, smaller and younger, with the same neat head and wide-set eyes, a child of the cousin-brother at the fish plant, come to collect the clothes Didi needed for work.

She packed them slowly, smoothing them with her hands, aware of the same absence of emotion as when her father died. It was as though her feelings had been gathered together in a great net and hauled up somewhere above her head, out of reach, until she was ready for them.

Jean-Claude was right. Within six months white faces began to reappear in town. They were different faces, as he had said: not the scruffy, swashbuckling volunteers with their motor-scooters, shoulder bags, long hair and all-night parties. These were older men (they were all men) with responsible faces, who arrived with wives and children and expensive imported cars.

The wives went round in a group. Claire often saw them in the market, clustered together in their bright dresses. They found out about the Arab baker, and the shop where you could sometimes buy proper toothpaste, and of course they joined the library, but they did not speak to Claire.

She was not surprised. She well understood that scrupulous anti-racism which would never seek help from a white face if a black one was available. Eventually there were seven families in town, all with small children, all friends. She knew them all by sight and she knew where they lived, in the new block of flats on Independence Hill. She sometimes walked up there after work, to get a breath of air, and saw their cars parked under the mango trees. And on Sundays she would watch them from her kitchen window, the whole crowd, crossing the *shamba* to the beach by the lake.

It was the tall woman, the one with frizzy hair and a reader's ticket in the name of P. Thomas, who appeared at the screen door one Sunday afternoon, holding a child in her arms, just as Claire was boiling the kettle.

'He's cut his knee. I'm terribly sorry to bother you, but would you mind frightfully if I just washed it? He slipped over on those rocks by the lake – it's only a graze but what with the flies and bilharzia and everything ... And I absolutely promised my mother. She made such a fuss about us bringing Toby, didn't she, darling? Granny-Mum thought you were going to get all sorts of horrible diseases ...'

They washed him at the kitchen tap and Claire searched through the bottles on the shelf – Tabasco, Sally's Ambre Solaire, Mike's Alka Seltzer – and found some mercuri-chrome. Gary had bought it for his mosquito bites.

The woman dabbed at her son's knee as he sat on the draining board. 'I hope your husband won't mind – me barging in like this – only I knew you lived here – well, we are conspicuous, aren't we, whatever you say ... That's it, Grotbag, you'll live.' She lifted him down. 'Why don't you go and have a look at Claire's garden? Only stay in the shade, darling, and try not to get bitten. I hope you don't mind being called Claire only I wasn't sure how to pronounce ... Akpa ...?'

'Akpwebu.'

'Akpwebu. I saw it on your little thingy – name plate – at the library. Actually I'm really glad to have a chance to meet you. I've been wanting to ask you and your husband to dinner but I wasn't quite sure ... I mean, it's so difficult. We really want to get to know the Africans, as *friends*. I mean, that's why we're here. I haven't come to spend all my time with white people. It doesn't have to be dinner, of course. It could be a drink. Would you ask him? Do you think he'd come?'

'No, I don't think so.'

'Or just, you know, a cup of coffee, one evening. Completely informal.'

'No. Not really.'

'No. Gosh, I'm sorry. I do understand. We must seem awfully frivolous to you, with our parties and everything. And just coming on a short-term contract. Compared with you. I admire you so much. Your commitment. I mean, settling down here.' Hot water began to jerk out of the kettle, splashing with a hiss on top of the stove. 'I'm so sorry to have disturbed you. I must go.'

'We could have a cup of tea if you like.'

They sat at the table, stirring the tea round and round in their mugs. Claire had forgotten how to talk to white people and the woman was tense and embarrassed, looking about her as though she hoped to find a topic of conversation.

Following her gaze, Claire saw the room as though after a long absence. Glue had dried behind the travel posters and they had fallen to the ground like dry leaves. Jam jars where avocado pips had been propped to sprout were stained and empty. A wicker basket held the shrivelled remains of what might once have been guavas. And over everything – books, ashtrays, piled-up copies of airmail newspapers, bottles of olive oil and jars of herbs – there lay a thick dry dust.

Claire's white face was without expression as she said, 'My husband doesn't live here any more.'

The woman hesitated for a moment, and then she gushed with understanding. 'You mean he's left you?'

Claire explained that Didi still came back to the house occasionally and that nothing had been decided. She did not say that he appeared without warning, that he stood in the kitchen looking at her with bewildered eyes, that if she made any move to comfort him he went away.

135

'And otherwise you're on your own here?'

She supposed that she was. Lizards clung to the wall, their bodies greyly transparent (like condoms, thought Claire), their eyes blank. The woman was talking about the British High Commission.

'They ought to know. That you've been deserted. That you're living here like this.' She gestured around the room. 'After all, you're a British national.'

'Not any more. Not since I got married.'

The child in the garden rapped his knuckles against the fly wire and it rattled dully. 'Mum, when are we going?'

She was confident now, in charge, insisting on washing the two mugs and the spoons, drying them, finding an old cloth under the sink and mopping up the splashes on the draining board and the cooker before they went out into the garden.

Her little boy was sitting in the shade under the trellis-work bower. He had broken off sprigs of white jasmine and planted their stalks in the dry ground.

'Darling, you shouldn't have picked the flowers.' She gathered them into a bunch and handed them to Claire. 'They'll revive if you put them in water. Look, I'll be in touch just as soon as I can. I want to talk to Richard – that's my husband. I'm sure there's something we can do to get you back to England. I absolutely refuse to believe that the British government would give you up completely. After all, anyone can make a mistake.'

Claire stood holding the flowers in her pale fingers. Blood beat in her chest and a wave of colour spread slowly over her neck, her cheeks, her forehead, until her face was a deep burning pink.

'It wasn't a mistake,' she said.

A Foreign Dignitary

BERNARD MACLAVERTY

THE VIEW FROM my window at the inn looked outward onto a small courtyard garden where everything seemed to be in bloom at once. The effect was quite, quite lovely. I watched a gardener stooping among the plants weeding, occasionally watering. Like everyone else here, he wore a buff-coloured smock. He had a bag of maroon powder which he was trowelling into the soil around the roots of the more colourful species. It looked like the dried blood fertiliser I use in my own garden at home.

The man raised his head and when he saw me watching him smiled in a gap-toothed manner. I nodded to him, not wanting to seem aloof, and staggered a little as I stepped back from the window. I had been warned about the period of adjustment one must go through at these high altitudes so I sat on a wicker chair until my dizziness passed.

Away from home like this I write a letter to my wife at least once a week, sometimes two if I find time heavy on my hands. The fact that they reach her months later, sometimes even after I have returned, is of little importance to me. After the day-long babble of strange tongues and

137

dialects, in the quiet of my room I establish a communication of a sort with her. In some ways it is a similar activity to prayer and even though there is no hope of a reply I enquire after our daughter, Elgiva. She is a young woman who is ill with a skin complaint which makes her avoid the company of all but her closest female friends. Her condition, which is distressing to look upon, comes and goes for no apparent reason. The skin of her face and throat flares up into a dry angry redness in a patch whose edge is as irregular as a coastline. Her eyes become blood-shot and inflamed. Although she claims the condition is not painful it is pitiful for others to look upon. After her last attack my wife and I decided that it would be best to have all mirrors removed from Elgiva's rooms.

The Director of Prisons, Dak by name, joined me for dinner at the inn. He was a small man with features typical of the region – a large hooked nose, olive skin, an unshaven look. His command of my language was almost perfect. Like everyone else he wore the buff-coloured robe. The only difference was that he had a medallion of some sort hanging on his chest.

He talked about each dish as it was presented, seeming particularly proud of one course containing sea fish. Coming from where I do this did not seem remarkable until I remembered that we were thousands of miles from any coast. And the transport, as I know to my cost, was lamentably slow. I cannot describe the discomfort I endured in getting to this place.

We were in an alcove slightly removed from the others who were eating and drinking. Dak pointed out various men of standing in the community but they all looked alike to me.

'It is a very popular place,' he said. 'All the more so when they know a foreign dignitary is here. They are curious to see you.'

'Dignitary indeed! I am a civil servant – doing my job.'

'A highly placed civil servant.'

'One who carries out others' orders, nonetheless.'

The Director of Prisons leaned towards me and whispered:

'It also means there will be entertainment.'

A small band of musicians began to play while we were having dessert. The sound was thin and, to my ear, quite quite raucous but I applauded loudly when they finished.

It was only when a young girl came out into the space between the tables that I realised she was the sole representative of her sex in that place. She began to dance to the music and again Dak leaned across to me:

'This is for you.'

She was very young, not long out of her childhood, and was dressed in a kind of long white folk costume. The dance consisted mostly of arm movements and girations of the hips – the feet moved but rarely. As she danced her eyes were downcast, which I found very alluring – fixed on the floor some inches in front of where I was sitting. Towards the end of the dance its character changed and the girl stood stock-still with her feet wide apart and began to ruck up her costume finger by finger. Past her shins, past knees, above her thighs until she revealed her tiny dark pubes and buttocks. The men applauded and banged the tables. The girl dropped her costume and bowed to me, then turned and left. Everyone was now looking at me. The Director said:

'She is yours for the night, if you wish it.'

'No, really. It is kind of you to offer but I am a married man. And as you know, that is forbidden in our culture.'

Dak raised an eyebrow and shrugged as if he didn't believe me.

'If it is disease which worries you I can assure you she is a virgin.'

'No, really. Thank you.'

I offered to pay the girl some money lest she be disappointed at my refusal but Dak would not hear of it. He said that already she had been well rewarded.

I spent an uncomfortable night, sleeping only fitfully. I twisted and turned, thinking obsessively about the pleasures I could have had with the child dancer. I knew as a representative of my Government I could not be seen to accept her and yet the child was so attractive. Visions of her little rounded buttocks, her scant hair below the paleness of her belly kept me awake until dawn began to colour the room.

While at breakfast a note was delivered to me from the Director of Prisons informing me that he would meet me before noon. I was amused at the mixture of formality and casualness of these people. When he arrived Dak bowed stiffly, yet apologised because we would have to walk to the prison. Someone had forgotten to arrange transport. I gathered my notebooks and papers and we set off together. As we walked the Director of Prisons insisted on carrying my briefcase.

'I hope you had a comfortable night,' he said.

'Thank you, I did.'

The pavements were in a state of poor repair and the roads rutted and broken. Many beggars sat at street corners but on seeing the man with the medallion did not put their hands out to us. They were emaciated, with the result that their eyes seemed to have grown larger. Our progress was watched by a slow turn of the head.

'Your Government have expressed great interest in our system,' said the Director.

'Indeed. Your crime figures are quite, quite remarkable.'

'The only real crimes are political. Everything else is . . .' He paused for a moment searching for the right word. 'Venial? Misdemeanours which can be forgotten. The man who steals a cow is made to pay it, or its value, back; the murderer usually acts in the heat of the moment and we forgive him provided he makes a contribution to the family of the injured party. I will take you to the Courts tomorrow and you will see the process in action.'

'I very much look forward to that.'

We were moving into a better district. Laburnum trees with their delicate hanging blossoms lined the streets; we proceeded through a wide gateway into a garden of open aspect and thence towards a colonnaded walk.

'The philosophy of imprisonment is one that interests me,' said the Director. 'You can either punish, reform or protect. These are the options. There is no real need for the first one – punishment is very old fashioned. The state should be above such a childish reaction. Although I agree with one of your famous writers: "The power of punishment is to silence, not confute."'

I could not quite place the quotation so allowed him to continue.

'And on the matter of reform, Councillors of the Courts can dissuade most people from committing another crime. Your prisons, I believe, are overflowing with petty criminals who will never change. All this is a great drain on the resources of a State.'

'But what if they offend repeatedly?'

'We have the ultimate threat of imprisonment. It is a great deterrent.'

I was becoming a little breathless and presumed it was the effects of altitude. I tried to hide my panting and asked:

'How far is it to the prison?'

'This is it,' he said. 'We are in it.'

I looked around. Walking through the low colonnade, the place reminded me of a monastery more than anything else. There were two gardeners, one raking the grass he had just scythed, the other working with a hoe in the flower-beds.

'No walls? Not even a gate?'

The Director smiled.

'No.' He seemed to dismiss my incredulity because he went on, 'The one class of offender we have found who is

141

not open to reform is the political animal – the revolutionary. He is a zealot who is . . .' Again he seemed to be searching for a word. '. . . incorrigible, whose sole aim is the overthrow of the whole system and, quite logically, the system needs to protect itself against him more than any other.'

The scraping of our feet sounded in the arches of the cloistered walkway which met just above our heads. I was faintly aware of whispering or scuffling noises but did not want to be impolite and appear to be distracted from what my colleague was saying.

'If a tree is to be attacked by disease where would you afford the most protection? The branches, the bark or at its roots?'

'The roots, of course.'

'Exactly. Then we are of like mind.'

A perfume, as of night-scented stock which I have growing in my garden at home, wafted along between the pillars but there was another smell, not so pleasant, mixed with it like a base note which I couldn't place. The scuffling or whispering became more audible and then I distinctly heard a voice speaking in a language I did not understand. I turned but could see no one. Behind me in a shallow drain I saw what I could only interpret as a piece of human excrement.

We turned at right-angles into another colonnade.

'The cost,' said the Director, 'is what interests your Government most.'

'Indeed.'

'There is a clemency caucus active in government who want the return of the death penalty for political crimes. But I do not agree. What we have here is maximum deterrent along with maximum protection for the minimum cost. Four men can run this whole prison by themselves,' he smiled, 'and still have some time for gardening.'

'Those two men are not prisoners?'

'No, the prisoners are here.' He indicated to my right. I

looked and it was only then that I noticed the uprights which I had, up until that point, taken to be part of the structure of the cloister. They were shaped like tall broom cupboards.

'In here?' I asked. The Director nodded. I stepped forward and by rapping with my knuckle discerned that they were made of metal.

'Iron,' said the Director. 'Treated in such a way that it does not rust.'

I looked at the blank face of the container then examined the side nearest to me.

'Soldered shut,' said the Director, 'and bolted to the stone. That is why we can afford to run the place with only four warders.'

'But how do you feed them?'

'The warders or the prisoners?' The Director smiled.

'The prisoners.'

'Each containment unit has a hole here for food.' The Director pointed to the side furthest from me. I looked at what he indicated and saw a small, square aperture about five feet above the ground. Something moved in the darkness inside. A face stared out at me. Whether it was the face of a horse or a human I could not tell. All I was conscious of was the whiteness of an eye. Dak pointed towards the ground and said:

'And a hole at the bottom for waste.'

'Remarkable. Quite, quite remarkable.'

We turned another corner into a similar colonnade where the flat stones of the floor were shining wet. A man was operating a long jointed bamboo pole which gushed water from its open end. He was guiding the pipe into the upper hole of each containment unit and flushing it out. Soiled water rushed from the hole at floor level and ran down the channel into gratings. He was followed by another man with a wicker basket who was distributing food – what looked like hard balls of dark rice.

We did not like to interrupt this work, so turned yet

another corner. Here I noticed that the containment units were much smaller and remarked on this to the Director.

'Political crimes run in families,' he said. 'In the more extreme cases we find it necessary to confine the whole family. The father may have planted the seed of revolt too deep to be rooted out.'

I asked if I might take some measurements and the Director agreed. I got out my tape and approached the nearest containment unit.

'This is a girl,' said the Director. He pointed to a mark on the metal. My curiosity about who was within was immediately aroused. As I measured I heard small scufflings inside. 'She has only been here since the beginning of the year.' When I came to measure the upper aperture I saw her face. Through the tangle of hair I could see she was pretty – could have been a sister to the girl they had made dance for me the previous night.

'When women commit political crimes,' said the Director, 'they are a hundred times more violent than the men.' Then the prisoner turned to me and did a quite remarkable thing. She spat. I recoiled but the saliva caught on the material of my collar and I dropped my tape while searching for a handkerchief. The Director, apologising profusely, strode down to the corner and called one of his men. Knowing what was liable to be on the floor I picked the tape up with my handkerchief, rolled it all together and put it in my pocket.

The Director came back with the warder who had been scything the grass but who was now carrying a large sledge-hammer. He indicated the girl's containment unit.

'Excuse us,' said the Director. The man raised the hammer, swung it over his shoulder and, with all his strength, crashed it against the metal. There was a thunderous noise, as from the biggest untempered bell I have ever heard. It was deafening for those of us in the confines of the colonnade. What it was like for the creature inside I cannot imagine.

'Proceed,' said the Director and we turned and walked away leaving the man swinging his hammer again and again. As we passed through the gardens back to the inn the sound echoed after us with monotonous regularity.

After lunch at the inn I excused myself to the Director saying that I had to write up my observations and notes. I really wanted a nap because of my previous poor night's rest.

In the quiet of my bedroom I could still hear faintly the continual gong of the sledge-hammer. It occurred to me that the man swinging it must have reached the point of exhaustion and I wondered if someone had relieved him.

Because of the noise, again I was unable to sleep. Instead I began a letter home.

Summer Lightning

ADAM MARS-JONES

YOU ALWAYS WERE fair-skinned, Olive, and giving yourself
to the sun wasn't something you set about lightly. We
went well prepared on our trip to Aberlady Bay. You had
your plastic bottle of tanning milk, with a high factor of
sunscreen, and your sunhat; I carried the big new Thermos
of blue-and-white plastic, whose workings we didn't altogether understand. Each of us, of course, brought a P. G.
Wodehouse paperback along. Yours was *Summer Lightning*.

You were a great admirer of Wodehouse, though I
know it pained your sentimental side that he had so few
good things to say about aunts. The aunt-nephew relationship in Wodehouse is not a tender bond, and there
were times when you found his exploration of its darker
aspects oppressive. So I learnt to take a hint, and if you said
your Wodehouse was getting a bit aunt-heavy, we'd do a
swap, and hope that in my Wodehouse the master was
being less severe about the relationship that gave us our connection.

There are two ways of pronouncing the name Wodehouse, as Wood- or as Woad-. I think it says something
about our relationship that although we said the name of

our hero differently, we pretended not to notice this little parting of the ways. Neither of us tried to prove the other wrong. Possibly it didn't occur to either of us that we might not be right.

It was a beautiful early summer's day, with a faint breeze, but as clear as if clouds had been outlawed or abolished. If we'd been offered a fiver for every cloud we saw before lunchtime, we'd still have had to dig into our pockets for the full cost of our holiday. When you first looked out of the window of our bed-and-breakfast room in Edinburgh, you said it was like the morning after a garden party.

On such a lovely day, we would have liked to take along cold drinks, but our B & B didn't run to the necessary ice. So we used the available amenities to the full, brewing tea with the electric kettle and teabags in our room. We transferred the tea to our Thermos, once we had grasped its basic principle, which seemed to involve thermal pads rather than a vacuum. You had to put boiling water in it for ten minutes, before you filled it with something that needed keeping hot.

We drove out of Edinburgh by way of Portobello and Cockenzie, stopping off at an Italian-run parlour in Mussel-burgh for what turned out to be some of the world's better ice-cream. Aberlady isn't far. The car radio played one of your favourite songs on the way, 'The Lady Is A Tramp', and you sang along for a bit, as if you just wanted to point up the excellence of the lyric, the way people do who don't know whether to be proud or ashamed of their singing voices. You explained that one line in particular haunted you: *'Hate California, it's cold and it's damp . . .'* It haunted you because you could find no sense in it.

We parked the car by a golf course, at the point that looked on the map to be nearest to the beach we wanted. The beaches we want are far from the roads, pretty much by definition, but even by our standards this was a bit of a trek. You promised me that in Scotland there's no such thing as a law of trespass, and I decided to take your word for it. I don't know whether the golf course was technically part of the nature reserve, but certainly there were birds about, singing away when not actually visible, as well as the usual dogged golfers. We passed by them in silence, awed by the equipment and the dedication, above all by the tremendous space that golf opens up, which just hangs there waiting to be filled by something sensible.

By what felt to be the nineteenth hole of fathers standing behind their sons and instructing them in matters of grip and swing, but was probably only the fifth or sixth, you were tired and thirsty. We stopped at a convenient bench, by a water-fountain put up in memory of a local resident. I was all for us staying there until you were fully recovered, but you were back on your feet after only a couple of minutes, and we pressed on past the golf course. The nature reserve contained some sort of sewage plant, but once we were beyond that we could smell the sea. As we climbed the dunes we could catch glimpses of a fine sandy beach, and of tightly curling, self-amused waves. We could also see people standing on top of choice dunes, shading their eyes and peering around, as if they were on top of crow's-nests and not overgrown sandhills. They stepped back from the dunes, formed little groups, and then went back on lookout. They seemed to have borrowed from the nature reserve the watchfulness proper to endangered species.

It didn't take us long to find a dune of our own, one with a dip near its summit which gave us a minimum of privacy without shutting us off from a view of the water. You gave me one of your crinkliest smiles, and you spoke the formula that I've grown so used to: 'Well now, shall we turn this into a naturist event?' And of course I said yes.

How I cringed when I first heard it, the phrase that sounds to me now like Welcome Home! I was sitting in your kitchen, where I had always been so much at my ease, wearing the first grown-up suit I had ever owned. I knew about your new way of life, and I think I even guessed that the couple opposite me at the tea-table were implicated in it. But I was completely unprepared for your summons to nakedness.

I didn't do very well that first time. I had taken my jacket off already, but that was because I was in your kitchen and off my guard. While everyone else undressed without fuss, I loosened the knot of my tie – my fat early-Seventies tie – and I undid the top button of my shirt, but that was as far as I could get. In those days the nearest I could come to the natural was the 'casual', a condition of permanent underlying tension that I wasn't yet willing to release. Being then at a particular peak of self-consciousness, I wasn't prepared even to take my shoes and socks off. I thought I would die if I did. I suppose my reflexive set of values still referred to my mother at that stage – and hers referred to the Royal Family. When I didn't think I had anything as subjective as an opinion at all, all I was doing was reproducing my mother's view of the world.

You were gentle with my refusal. I didn't even realise you were making an exception. Later on, I could see that you were normally strict about the conduct of naturist events, knowing that the clothed pose a threat to the naked, as well as the naked to the clothed. You must have sensed that my refusal was only the leading edge of accept-ance, and that I wouldn't refuse you a second time. I refused only as a horse refuses, at an unfamiliar fence that is well within its power to jump.

All the time that I was trying to be Prince Charles, of course, he was trying to be more like a normal person, and was absolutely longing to be asked to take his shoes and socks off. But we didn't know that back then.

On my second brush with social nakedness, I came much closer. You were having a barbecue, in that little back yard of yours, and you needed my help. For a wild moment I thought that this too might be a naturist event (the fence round your yard was tall enough to make that possible), but I put the idea out of my mind. And of course you were dressed when I arrived, chopping vegetables in your kitchen for a dip, while the charcoal settled to a steady glow in the yard outside. But before your first batch of guests turned up, you undressed, and you persuaded me too from my clothes.

After the first ring came at your front door, when I could hear the amazingly matter-of-fact noise of the new-comers undressing in the hall, I retreated from my naked-ness. I appointed myself cook, a job that in the case of barbecues has no qualifications except willingness, by pick-ing up the big laminated apron from its hook on the back of your kitchen door. By the time you and your party came into the kitchen, I had safely tied its strings round my waist, and had pounced on a big fork and a pair of tongs to give colour to my impersonation. Trembling with tension, I led the way into the yard, and squirted some unnecessary lighter fluid on to the briquettes in the barbecue. A gust of flame leapt up through the grill.

Thanks to the apron, I was labelled a cook and not a person with his own reasons for attending. But there were also elements of martyrdom in the role I played. The design of the apron was much enlarged from the label of a matchbox; I bore the legend 'ENGLAND'S GLORY', and the additional phrases 'Finnish Made' and 'Avge Contents 48'. Behind the apron I felt like a match myself. My head was blazing with metaphysical heat and excitement. I was also exposed, where the apron didn't protect me, to heat from the barbecue on my face and shoulders, and to spitting protests from the meat that I was watching over.

I was closer to nakedness in a social setting than I had been since – I suppose – my christening; but I was set apart by my costume from the true nakedness of my companions. They were in a state of nature, while I looked as if I was stranded halfway through a routine of striptease, my apron an item of would-be allure. Even where we were identical we were marked by differences, so that my buttocks, framed by the apron-edges and dramatised by the apron-strings round my waist, were mysteriously barer than theirs.

As the meat in front of me spat and darkened, the burgers shrinking and the sausages becoming gnarled, I was caught between the shame of being clothed and the shame of going naked. But surrounded by these various flames, something inside me melted and gave way; some final resistance was driven off. When I put on my clothes again at the end of the evening, I remained a naturist beneath them.

I knew there would be trouble when I got home, but my mother gave me only the regulation frosty reception, just as if I'd been out late with a girl. There was none of the extra chill I expected for associating with her so suspect sister. I had thought her anger would at least recognise the magnitude of the change the evening had worked in me. She couldn't have changed my decision, I don't think, but she could have had the satisfaction of greeting what was a turning point in her life, as well as in mine, with emotion on an appropriate scale. But then she was never one, proud as she was of her hard-headedness, to see things as they are.

We weren't like that on our side of the family, were we, Olive? Though if there was 'our side' – me and you – there must have been 'their side' too, and our opponents (I don't say our enemies) never managed to act in concert. My mother and your Joan had the same ideas about what was important, but they could never abide each other. Whenever they were in the same room together, even when your Joan was quite young, there was a great surge of recognition and denial. It was as if each of them was at the same time a cat and a person who hated cats. There was a sustained feline hissing just below the threshold of audibility, and if it was a social occasion people would look down at their drinks, expecting the ice in their glasses to have suddenly melted.

In the long run, your Joan was far more trouble than my mother. At first she bided her time, being too young to translate into action the adult-sized will that had been evident since her cradle days. But she must also have been laying her plans, for what turned out to be a long campaign.

There's a word that naturists use, a term of abuse for everything they despise in the clothed world. You disliked that word, and would never use it of anyone, let alone of your Joan; I'm afraid that doesn't stop it from applying. But then you were a tender naturist, Olive, a naturist without rancour. I salute you. You built up no new defences to make up for the ones you had cast off. Sunhat and sunscreen; that was all. You asked for little, and you managed on a lot less. In my innocence, I thought that all naturists had the same goodness of heart you had, the same robust freshness. I had to learn for myself that there are meannesses of mind and spirit not lodged in folds of clothing or stowed away in pockets. I had to learn that a person can be naked and still be wrapped in bitterness.

The word is 'textile'. The word of abuse. A textile is someone who doesn't exist except as a succession of costumes and I'm afraid your Joan was a textile through and through. She could certainly wear clothes. She could groom like nobody's business, but that was all she could do, and she couldn't groom the whole world to her liking.

She didn't have a lot to object to, I would have thought. Naturist activity in your house was confined to a maximum of two nights a week. On those nights she was under no pressure to stay in. Joan was always a looker, and there was no question of her being short of escorts. Most young women would actually quite appreciate some more or less compulsory nights out, and I suppose even Joan wasn't unwilling. But still she did her best to spoil things. She would come home maddeningly early, flaunting her chastity as if to show up her mother's goings-on (I don't think she ever understood the prudish side of naturism). I imagine her rushing home the moment the credits rolled on the big film, dragging her date behind her, just so she could put a damper on things.

I remember in particular Joan's Grace Kelly phase. Icy Fifties glamour certainly suited her style of beauty, I have to admit that, and I suppose she deserves credit for contriving such a unified look from meagre resources – she haunted charity shops, and she made things herself when she had to. I'm even sure that the magazines she read were promoting just such a look of luscious unavailability. But there was still something perverse about the sheer number of unnecessary items she managed to wear. I seem to remember sashes, shawls, gloves and any number of hats. Your Joan would enter, brazenly covered up, a room from which bodily embarrassment had only recently, and always provisionally, been seen off. She would shake hands all round, sometimes even extending a hand to me, with a raise of her exquisitely plucked eyebrows. She would accept a small drink, sip it demurely but leave it unfinished, shake hands one more time and retire to her room.

I think the only other person who has ever worn gloves and touched me naked has been a doctor. Perhaps that was the key to Joan's power. But she wasn't interested in making anything better. She left a bruise in the evening that took some time to heal.

I imagine her in her room, listening to the social noises below. I imagine her, come to that, outside the front door, saying goodnight to whichever boy it was at the time. Perhaps the magazines she read were advocating Grace Kelly morals (the screen morals, of course, when there's doubt) as well as the costumes. In which case, how odd for her to be crying up the enigma of her body, with a naturist event in full swing just the other side of the door.

But you and I know there was more to it than that.

153

Understanding people is a perfectly valid alternative to liking them, though I'm not sure you ever thought so. But one way or another, it's something we should have discussed. Your Joan was shattered when her father left you, and of course she was very young. I think she was like the traumatised witness to an accident, who confuses the sequence of two impacts. Your husband left you, and a little after that you became a naturist. I think in Joan's mind a primitive scene was constructed, in which it was actually your taking off your clothes that drove him away. So perhaps if she could will you back into your clothes, manipulate you back into your clothes, shame you back into your clothes, her father would come back too, and the whole ensemble of her life would start to match again.

Naturism gave you a new life, Olive. Naturism gave you a new wardrobe, you who had never been a standard size, being built (as you said) for comfort and not for speed. In naturism, as you were fond of remarking, there are only standard sizes. But you were also doing your own bit of superstitious thinking, not so differently from Joan.

Your husband left you, and you never willingly mentioned his name again. You became a naturist, which was something you said you'd always wanted to do. I'm sure it was. But there was a special symbolism involved. When your husband left you, you didn't retreat from the sexual world; you advanced away from it. You entered a nunnery of flesh, a nunnery without habits. And it was as if by the simplification you achieved in your life, you were trying to send the message that getting rid of your husband had been the first part of the same process. You claimed control retrospectively, as if you had shed that man as you now shed your clothes, and the history that clung to them like cigarette smoke at a party.

I never told you my interpretation of your naturism. It would have seemed ungrateful, after everything you had done for me – and everything that naturism had done for me, for that matter. I'm sure you would have been as indulgent of me as you always were. But that wasn't really the way we shared things anyway. We shared holidays, we shared expeditions. We shared things the way we shared the apple we ate in our dune at Aberlady Bay. You took it out of your bag and bit calmly into it, your eyes screwed up against the glare. I asked if I could have the core, you said there wasn't going to be one, and then you handed me a stem still amply, even voluptuously, covered with fruit-flesh.

The beach was certainly a beauty spot, once we'd got the whiff from the sewage plant on the nature reserve out of our nostrils, and provided we half-closed our eyes to avoid seeing Cockenzie power station on the skyline.

I found a piece of driftwood roughly the size of a bedhead in our dune, and wedged it upright in the sand where it would give you some shade once the sun lost a little height.

I wanted a swim, and perhaps you did too, but you had taken too much trouble applying your sunscreen to want to wash it off so soon. You waved me off down the beach, picked up *Summer Lightning*, and lay down on your big towel. The access was steep from our dune to the beach, so I slid down it rather than walked down.

There was a swimmer just leaving the water as I trotted down the beach. 'How warm is it?' I asked, and he shook his head to get the water out of his eyes, before he answered 'About 70 degrees.' I was about to voice my pleasure at this news when I realised his teeth were chattering, and that I wasn't in for any sort of warm swim after all.

I don't know whether the tide was going out or coming in, but as I touched my toes to the freezing shallows I realised that there must be a submerged sand bar a little way out, since the waves came to the point of breaking, and then re-formed. It was as if they had second thoughts, until they were pressed to it a second time, about their moment of foaming disclosure.

I had second thoughts, too, about my swim. I had just reached the point that the body recognises as the point of no return, with ice-cold water inches below my groin, when I found myself, thanks to the sand bar, walking uphill again.

The experience of walking into a cold sea is one of the few in which the genitals – I imagine for both sexes – seem authentically to be at the centre of the universe. Swimming naked makes that moment less bleak: even the most hardened textile can only feel betrayed by a costume that protects the parts from cold and wet for the smallest illusory instant, and then keeps them in contact with cold and wet even after leaving the water.

I found myself walking uphill again. I had to recommit myself to the long slow slope towards immersion. Standing on that sand bar, I turned towards the beach. I lifted an arm to wave, before I had properly located our spot in the dunes, and then I saw you, standing with both arms raised above your head. Just then a wave took me by surprise, a little higher than I expected so that I rose by reflex on tiptoe, and I almost lost my balance. I turned round again, to anticipate any further surprises, and set off away from the false deep and towards the true one.

I've given much thought to those waves since then, to my wave from the sandbank, to what I took to be your wave from the dunes, and yes, to the wave that caught me by surprise and led me to turn my back on you. I encourage myself to be grateful that we parted with what seemed at the time to be a communicative gesture.

I stayed in the water only long enough to duck my head under the surface and take a few token strokes towards the shore. I might not have done even that much if I hadn't been conscious of you watching – as I thought – and of the need, even with the most intimate audience, to meet minimum standards of hardiness.

The water drained promptly from my left ear, but lingered in my right, so I had the irritating sensation, which no amount of finger-wiggling or head-shaking could dislodge, that while the rest of me was in the open air that one ear was enclosed in a small echoing box. Only when I was standing on the wet sand by the shoreline did I look up to the sand-dunes where you were.

Everything was wrong. Your sunhat had fallen off, and though you were still on your towel, your head was downhill from your feet, and you were lying on your front. You never lay like that. I'd offered to rub sunscreen into your back often enough, but you were shy of that contact, oddly so in view of our closeness, and preferred to bear the filtered weight of the sun only on skin that you could efficiently anoint yourself.

I ran. I ran from wet sand on to dry, and from the flat beach to the foothills of the dunes. Then I tried to run up the dune but scrambled instead, stumbled and scrambled. The sand resisted me like the sand in bad dreams, but even if what I had to climb had been a smooth staircase I think I would have felt the same terrible sensation: making no headway, but dreading to arrive. It was an absolutely generic experience of fear, with nothing distinctive about it, nothing that corresponded to the particularity of my love for you.

When I reached you, it didn't take me long to understand that you had yielded to the superior nakedness of death. At that moment, when I expected tears, I heard instead the dismal popping of the membrane of water in my ear being released, and the sound of my own breathing, suddenly further away.

There were other people in the dunes, but they had respected our territorial claim and fallen back a little, though from the sea I had caught glimpses of them on lookout duty. Standing by you, I could see no one, and I had to run back and forth in the long grass for some time before I found someone – who leapt to his feet and started backwards when I invaded his patch of dune. He turned out to be a tourist, and he couldn't help me find a phone. Finally I turned up someone who knew where the nearest phone was, and was even willing to make the call for me. He pulled on his shorts and ran off, warning me that it would be a good long time before anyone came.

I went back and squatted by your side. The sun still had plenty of elevation and power. I know nothing about the posthumous effect of sunlight on flesh; it's not something that interests me in a general way. But it did bother me to see the sun beating down on the unprotected backs of your legs. You would always wince in sympathy when we saw men with flayed shoulders, or girls with sunburned shins and pale calves.

Every few minutes I would hear someone padding into our dune, out of sympathy or maybe just curiosity. I took to humming at those times, humming being the simplest way of conveying without rudeness that I had no immediate needs. After a while people stopped making approaches.

Then I realised that I did have a need after all. Salt from my swim was still on my lips, and I was thirsty. I put it off until I could think of nothing else, and then I picked up our Thermos and unscrewed the lid. But then the tea we had made that morning was so fresh and steaming that I didn't have the heart to drink it. So instead I poured it away. I don't know what gave me the idea, but I walked round you as I did the pouring – I suppose the idea was to surround you with a magic circle of tea. The air was hot and the sand was very dry, so the tea started to evaporate almost immediately, but for the time being it left an emphatic track, edged with splashes, in the sand.

After that it seemed perfectly natural, though I realised at the same time that it was a peculiar inspiration, to take your plastic bottle of tanning milk and squirt that too in a circle round you, this time in the other direction, pointing the nozzle at the middle of the damp track I'd made already. My shoulders and the back of my neck were getting sore from the sun, but it seemed important not to benefit from any protection that you were denied. The bottle made increasingly intimate noises through its nozzle as I came to the end of the tanning milk.

I sat back on my heels for a moment to think. I was looking at the Thermos, so deep, so broad at the neck. It was still damp inside, so I took a handful of sand and dropped it in. The sand stuck to the curved bottom and the sides of the Thermos, as I should have known it would, so I didn't try to empty it out. Instead I poured more handfuls of sand in. Then I took your P. G. Wodehouse and laid it gently on the bed of sand in the Thermos. I added sand until it was fully buried, and then I put in the empty bottle of your tanning milk. I filled the Thermos to the top with sand, and screwed the lid on. The lid squeaked and rasped as I screwed it home, from sand caught up in the thread.

I sat back on my heels to think again. Then I placed the Thermos by your head, just outside the fading circle of tea and tanning milk, and put your sunhat on it.

I sat back and looked at what I had done. There was something baleful about the Thermos with the hat on which I hadn't anticipated, but which placed it in the tradition of grave-ornaments, things intended to watch over the dead and given a small charge of imaginative power for the task. But there was also something Egyptian about what I had done – it was partly the sand that made me think so, but I must also have been thinking when I was putting *Summer Lightning* and the bottle of tanning milk in the Thermos that these were things you might need on your journey. The same applies, I suppose, to the sunhat and the Thermos itself. Anyway, that seemed like an Egyptian thought. It was as if I had an aunt who was a Pharaoh.

★

Then my head cleared and I realised what you would want me to do. What I had done with your things let me express my emotions, but there was something remaining to be done that would express you. I took the edge of your towel – luckily you weren't lying with your full weight on it – and pulled steadily until it came free. Then I used the piece of driftwood, which I had intended as a sunshade, as a clumsy spade instead, and I dug a clumsy hole to bury the towel in. I did this not because it was soiled and I was ashamed of its soiling, but because I didn't want the police to cover you up, to tidy you away as if you had done something wrong by dying.

I kept looking round as I was digging, but people were still being tactful and keeping out of sight. I put our clothes, mine as well as yours, and your bag, in the hole along with the towel, and for the same reasons. It struck me afresh how absurdly sensible your taste in clothes was, when you didn't think clothes, deep down, were sensible at all. I used the piece of driftwood to smooth over the mound I had made, and laid it on top to cover my workings.

It took me a long time, and I had sand under my nails by the time I had finished, but I was satisfied. I still had a long wait before the emergency services arrived. When people from the beach did from time to time pop across to our dune to ask if I was all right – they seemed to leave the dunes on either side empty, as if for reasons of quarantine – I noticed they were wearing their costumes, out of respect. I was keeping mine off, of course, for the same reason. I think there was also a worry in people's minds about whether they had a legal right to be naked, or whether someone had once, way back, misunderstood 'nature reserve' as 'naturist beach'. They weren't going to take any risks, not with the police expected any minute.

I knew that the police, when they arrived, would have body bags or stretchers of some description. I knew I wouldn't be able to defend you for very long. I didn't, I admit, anticipate that the East Lothian police, when their Range Rover appeared at the top of our dune, lights flashing and wheels spinning, would have a maroon-coloured coffin ready in the back, of a plastic that looked like metal. But I was still determined, at that stage, to resist them.

Long before they arrived, the humming I had adopted to keep people at a distance had turned into a peculiar message in its own right. My lips started to move, though I kept my voice right down. But I found that the tune I had chosen, without thinking, to hum was the one you liked so much on the radio that morning – 'The Lady Is A Tramp' – and I found that stupid words of my own were replacing the originals, replacing even the line that had haunted you with its nonsense:

> Lucky Olive Cooper! She died in the sun
> And of her clothing, the po-lice found none
> Lucky Olive Cooper! She died on the beach
> That's why my aunt is out of reach.

Another Time

EDNA O'BRIEN

IT HAPPENS TO one and all. It is given many names, but those who have it know it for what it is — the canker that sets in and makes one crabbed, finding fault with things, complaining, full of secret and not-so-secret spleen. Nelly knew it. She knew she was in trouble after that dream. She dreamed that one of her children had stripped her of everything, even her teeth, and when she wakened she decided that it was time to get away. 'Get away, get away,' she said several times to herself as she hurried up the street to a travel agent's to look at brochures. In a small, unprepossessing office she saw posters of walled cities, all of which were gold-coloured; she saw churches, canals, castles; and each one filled her not with expectations but with doom. It was as bad as that. Suddenly it came to her. She would go home — not to her own people but to a small seaside town about twenty miles from there, a place she had always yearned to go to as a child, a resort where some of the richer people had cottages. It was remote and primitive, on the edge of the Atlantic, the white houses laid out like kerchiefs. She had seen photos of it, and it had for her a touch of mystery, a hidden magic; it was a place where people went when they were happy – newlyweds and those who got legacies. There was a jetty across, so although an island it was not cut off completely, and she was glad of that. The ocean could pound or lap on three sides and yet she had a link with the land, she could get away. Getting away preoccupied her, as if it would lead to redemption.

As she crossed the threshold of the bedroom in her hotel, she saw that it did not bode well. It was a tiny room, with a tiny sagging bed, bits and pieces of tasteless furniture, and a washbasin in one corner with a vein of rust running down from one of the taps. The coat hangers were of metal, and either they were buckled or their hooks were so attenuated that they looked like skewers. A view of the ocean, yes, but it was not an expanse, more a sliver of grey-green sulky sea.

It will get better, she thought, fearing that it wouldn't. She could hear the man in the next room as she hung her clothes. He was coughing. He's lonely, she thought, that's why he's coughing. After she had hung her clothes, she put on a bit of make-up before going down to have a drink with the owners. The owners had welcomed her and asked her to have an early drink before dinner. On impulse, she gave them the bottle of champagne that she had bought at the airport, and now she wished she hadn't. They seemed so taken aback by it – it was too patrician – and it was not chilled.

Opening the champagne took quite a while, because the husband was more interested in telling her about some of his more exotic travels than in wheedling the cork out. The wife was a bit heavy and had a sleepy, sad face with big spaniel eyes. They seemed to have no children, as children were not mentioned. The husband held forth about jobs he had held in Borneo or Karachi or wherever – that was when he was in oil. Then at length he had decided to settle down, and he found himself a wife, and they came back to Ireland, to their roots, and bought this hotel, which was something of a legend. The previous owner was an eccentric and made people do morris dancing and drink mead.

No morris dancing now, Nelly thought as they lifted their glasses. They were tiny glasses – sherry glasses, really – and the champagne was tepid. Just as the cork flew out, a tall boy had come in from the kitchen and stared. He was a simpleton – she could tell by his smile and the way he stared and then had to be told by the wife to go back in to mind the cabbage.

'Go in, Caimin,' she said.

'Yes, ma'am,' he said, coveting the green cork, with its dun-gold paper. The husband was telling Nelly that she had picked a most unfortunate evening for her first dinner. They were overbooked, jam-packed. A party of twelve at one table alone. He himself had not taken the booking; a silly young girl had taken it over the phone. He apologised in advance. Nelly looked around the dismal room, with its checked tablecloths and kitchen chairs, and was not regaled by what she saw. There were empty wine bottles above the sideboard and all along the wall ledge. They were green and dusty and served no purpose whatsoever, and she supposed that the champagne bottle would go up there somewhere and be just as useless. He wasn't pouring fast enough for her. She wanted to drink in great gulps, to forget her surroundings, to be removed from them, to forget the impulse for her coming, and to blot out the admission that she had made a mistake.

'We reserved you that table,' he said, pointing to a table in the corner, close to the window, with a view of the road outside. The road was covered with mist and the summer evening could easily pass for October or November. Suddenly radio music and loud voices came from the kitchen, and then a buxom girl emerged followed by another girl with long plaits. They had come to lay the tables. They were big, strapping girls, and they more or less slung the plates and the cruets onto the tables and made a great clatter with the cutlery box. They eyed Nelly sitting there with the boss and the Mrs, and one of them whispered something to the other – probably about her being a big shot, maybe even someone from the Tourist Board. Occasionally they would laugh, and the simpleton would rush from the kitchen, holding a ladle or a saucepan in his hand, to join in the levity. Soon the wife rose, put her hands to her chest, and said very formally, 'Duty calls.' Then the husband picked up the bottle of champagne and said, 'We'll chill the rest of this for you. You can have it with your meal.'

As she turned the key in her bedroom door, Nelly met her neighbour. He wore a suit and a cap, and it was clear that he was not accustomed to being on holiday. His first remark was how beautiful the hotel was – a palace. A palace! A bit of dark landing with linoleum and off-white doors, like hospital doors, leading to the rooms; a sickly maidenhair fern in a big brass jardinière. He spoke with a clipped Northern accent as he enlarged on the glories of the place, the seashore where he had just been walking, the peace and quiet, and the big feeds. He was on his way to the public house for a few jars before dinner. Would she care to join him? She realised that he had been waiting to pounce, that he must have heard of her arrival – a woman on her own – and that he had assumed they would become friends. She declined. He asked again, thinking she said no only out of courtesy. She declined more firmly. She saw the smile leave his face. She saw the scowl. He could hardly endure this rebuff. His anger was rising. He pulled his key from his pocket and, for no reason, proceeded to open his door again. Anything to withhold his rage. They were from the same country, God damn it; just because she lived abroad was no reason to snub him. She could read his

inner thoughts and guess his outrage by the obsequiousness
of what he then said.

'Aah, thanks a lot,' he said, and repeated it twice over,
when in fact he wanted to strike her. He had reverted to
some shaming moment when he had thanked a superior
whom he really hated.

I have made an enemy, she thought as she entered her
room. She went straight to the washbasin and splashed her
face fiercely with douches of cold water.

Dinner was indeed a boisterous affair. The party of twelve
was mostly children, ranging from teenagers to a baby in a
high chair. The mother addressed each child by name, over
and over, sometimes admonishing, sometimes approving,
so that Nelly soon knew that the baby was called Troy,
short for Troilus, and would have to eat those mashed
potatoes before he got his mashed banana. The mother was
a strong, bossy woman, and without these hordes of children to address she would have been lost; she would have
had no part to play.

'Eat that stew, Kathleen,' she would call, backing it up
with a glare. It was mutton stew, with potatoes and onions
floating in the thickened parsley sauce. Big helpings were
on the plates, and the extra vegetables were piled in white
enamelled dishes, like soap dishes. The champagne on
Nelly's table seemed absurd. Each time she poured, she
looked away, so as not to be seen, and gave her gaze the
benefit of the road in the rain. Most of the other guests
drank soft drinks or milk, but one quiet couple had a
bottle of wine. The man who had invited her to the public
house ate alone and never once looked in her direction. In
fact, when he entered the room he made a show of saluting
one or two other people and deliberately ignored her. He
drank tumbler after tumbler of milk with his stew. The
waitresses, in some show of bravura, had put flowers in
their hair, bits of fuchsia, and it was clear by the way they

giggled that they thought this to be very scandalous. All the guests resented the interlopers who made such a fuss and such demands – asking for more napkins and for orangeade, some begging to be let down from the table, others slapping their food into plump pancakes, others simply whingeing. A German au pair, who sat among the children, occasionally poured from a water jug but otherwise did not pay much attention to their needs. The waitresses dashed about with second helpings and then brought big slabs of rhubarb pie, each decorated with a whorl of cream so whipped that it seemed like an imitation chef's hat. The owner came into the room and went from table to table – except, of course, to the rowdy table – apologising to his guests for the invasion, assuring them that it would not happen again. 'End of story ... end of story,' he kept saying, giving the intruders a stern look. The irate mother, sensing rebuff, ordered a pot of tea and a pot of coffee while telling some of her children to go out and play in the grounds. Meanwhile the whipped cream was leaking into the rectangles of rhubarb pie.

All the guests were given a complimentary glass of port wine, and by the time Nelly had finished hers she was the only one left. The room was almost in darkness and it was dark outside. She kept waiting for the candle stump to sputter out, as if that were to be the signal to go upstairs. Already she was thinking that she had only five more dinners to endure and that she would be going home Saturday. Home now seemed like a nest, with its lamps and its warmth. The simpleton gave her a start as he appeared over her, a big clumsy figure in a sheepskin jacket.

'Will you be here tomorrow?' he asked. He had a muffled voice, and there was a stoppage in his speech. It was as if he had too much saliva.

'I'm afraid I will,' she said, and hoped she didn't sound too peeved.

'I'm glad you'll be here. You're a nice lady,' he said as

he shuffled out, and, rising, she picked her way between the tables, certain that she was about to break down.

In the morning things seemed quite different – sparkling. The sea was bright, like a mirror with the sun dancing on it, and there was nothing to stop her going down there and spending the whole day walking and breathing – getting rid of the cobwebs, as she put it. She would pack a basket and bring down her things. She would write cards to her sons and her friends; she would read, reread, and, after the few days, she would be something of her former self – cheerful, buoyant, out-going.

The sand was a pale, biscuit colour that stretched way ahead of her – to the horizon, it seemed. The people dotted here and there were like figures in a primitive painting. Those in red stood out, both the toddlers and the grown-ups; red was the one splash of colour in this pale-gold, luminous universe. The sea was a baby blue and barely lapped. It seemed so gentle, not like the sea that roared and lashed but like an infinite and glassy terrain that one might scud over. There were dogs, too – the local dogs resenting the dogs that had come with the newcomers, snarling until they got to know them. Some people had erected little tents, obviously intending to settle for the day. Some walked far out to sea, and a few stalwarts were bathing or paddling. Although sunny, it was not yet a hot day. She would walk forever; she would gulp the air with her mouth and her whole being; she would resuscitate herself. Here and there, as she looked down at the sand, she would see empty cans, or seaweed, or little bits of sea holly in clumps – shivering but tenacious.

'I am walking all my bad temper away . . . I am walking my bad temper away,' she said, and thought, How perfect the isolation, the sense of being alone. She loved it – the near-empty seashore, the stretch of sand, the clouds racing so purposefully, and now the sea itself, which had changed colour as if an intemperate painter had just added blue and green and potent violet. The colours were in pockets, they were in patches, and even as she looked there were trans-mutations – actual rainbows in the water, shifting, then dissolving. She would walk forever. There wasn't a boat or a steamer in sight. As she looked back at the town, its cluster of white cottages seemed like little rafts on a sea, on the sea of life, receding. People she met smiled or nodded, to compliment her on her stride, and the good thing was that she always saw them as they came towards her, so that she was not taken by surprise. Yet it was a jolt when a woman ran up to her and took her hand. She recognised Nelly from the short time when she had been a television announcer.

'You disappeared so suddenly,' the woman said, and Nelly nodded. She had given up her glamorous job for a man, even though she knew she was throwing in her lot with a black heart.

'We might see you in the pub tonight. There's a sing-song,' the woman said, and, though smiling, Nelly quivered inwardly. She did not want to meet people, especially those who had known of her in the past; she had put an iron grille over all that, and yet this very encounter was disturbing, as if the weed and bindweed of the past were pushing their way up through the gates of her mind. As she walked on, she found herself remembering her marriage day – two witnesses and a half bottle of cham-pagne. She remembered living in a big, draughty house in the country, and her morning sickness, which at first she did not understand. But it was as if she were recalling a story that had happened to someone else. In a way, she re-membered her divorce far better, because she had had to fight. Once, with a solicitor, she had gone to a suburb of London where she hoped a former housekeeper would testify to her having loved her children; a more recent incumbent had sworn affidavits against her and said she was a wicked woman. In that little sitting room in Tooting, waiting for what was going to be crucial, she sat with the solicitor while the mother put her noisy children to bed. There was a terrible smell, something being cooked.

'Is it a horse they're boiling?' the solicitor said, and she laughed, because she knew he had put himself out of his way to come with her, and that he loved her a little, and that, of course, he would never say so. When the house-keeper came in and kissed her, the kiss itself a guarantee of friendship and loyalty, the solicitor beamed and said, 'We're there . . . we're home and dry.' She got her children in the end. Then there were the years of birthdays and train sets and Christmases and measles and blazers that they grew out of, and then their going away to boarding school and the raw pain of that first rupture, that first farewell. Not for ages had she allowed herself such a glut of memory, such detail.

Yet she was not crushed by these things, and quite gaily she asked aloud what happened to that blue dress with the tulip line, and where was the Georgian claret jug that she had bought for a song. Where, oh where?

Up on the road, there were several cars and a loudspeaker announcing something. Although it was loud, it was sense-less. She was a long way from the hotel but she had her bearings. She knew she could either turn right to head for the one shop and the telephone kiosk or turn left for her hotel and the new chapel beyond it, which had modern stained-glass windows. She felt hot and her throat was parched – she longed for something. She believed that she longed for lemonade. She could taste it again as she had tasted it in childhood, so sweet and yet so tart. The sun shone with a flourish, and the flowers in the cottage gardens – the dahlias, or the devil's pokers, or whatever – seemed to be glistening with life. She stopped by a garden where a yearling calf was letting out a loud lament. He had two wounds where his horns had recently been removed.

They were full of flies. He tried with his head to toss them away, but they had sunk into the wounds, which were covered with some sort of purple ointment. The animal bawled and tossed and even leapt about, and so moved was she to pity that she began to shout, 'Are you there? Are you there?'

Eventually a young man came out, holding a mug of tea. He seemed surprised to have been called.

'He's itchy,' she said, pointing to the yearling.

'He's a devil,' the young man said.

'He's in agony,' she said, and asked if he could do something.

'What can I do?' he said, annoyed that she had summoned him like this.

'I'll help you,' she said, gently, to coax him.

'I have just the thing,' he said, and he ran to the house and came back with a giant canister of wasp repellent.

'Oh, not that,' she said, grabbing it from him and explaining that the flies would wallow in the wounds and dement the poor animal even more. She made him fetch a strip of cardboard, then hold the beast, which bucked and reared while she edged the flies out, pushing them onto the clay and watching them stagger from their somersaults. The man was so impressed by her expertise that he asked if she was a vet.

'Hold him, hold him,' she said, as there was the second wound that she had to tackle. That done, they drove the animal through a side gate, over some cobbles, and into a dark manger. As the man closed the door, the animal yelled to be let out, its cry saying that daylight, even delirious daylight with flies and pain, was preferable to this dark dungeon.

'I told you he was a devil. He never lets up,' the man said, as he motioned her into the house. There was nobody in there, he assured her, his mother being dead. The few flowers in the flower bed, and the gooseberry bushes, had, as she imagined, been sown by his mother. There was also

171

a ridge of flowering potatoes. He went to England for a time, worked in a car factory there, but he always came back in the summer, because he needed the fresh air. He bought a calf or two and sold them when he left.

'Would you marry me?' he said suddenly. She knew that he did not really mean such a thing, that he meant, 'Stay for a bit and talk to me.'

'I am married,' she lied.

'You've no wedding ring,' he said, and she looked down at her hand and smiled, and said she must have forgotten to put it on. Then she excused herself, saying that she had to be back at the hotel, because of a phone call.

Caimin met her at the door. She had had a visitor, a woman. The woman had waited and waited. He handed her a note. It said, 'Hi. Long time no see. I'll call back around four. Gertie.' Who was Gertie? Gertrude. She could only think of Hamlet. Suddenly she was shaking. She could not see anyone. She did not want to meet this Gertie, this stranger.

'Tell her I've gone . . . gone,' she said as she flew up the stairs to her room. Even the disgruntled neighbour, who was on his way out, seemed to sense her disquiet. He smiled, and waved a golf club, proudly. She hated the hotel even more now – the awful washbasin, the stained furniture. She hated it not so much for its own pitiable sake as for what it reminded her of – the rooms and landings of childhood, basins and slop buckets that oozed sadness. It seemed as if the furniture of those times, and her failed marriage, and the flies in the raw wounds, and the several mistakes of her life had got jumbled together and were now hounding her, moving in on her in this place. Various suggestions offered themselves, such as to go back to London to her own house and never leave it again, or to go to the house where she was born and exercise her fury, though she had been back there a few times and was almost indifferent to the sight of it. She saw briars, she saw gates in need of paint, she saw the outside gable wall over which her mother had so lovingly planted a creeper, and she saw the hall door with the padlocks that her brother had put there to keep her and others out. Bastard, she thought, and wished she could scrawl it somewhere for him to see. Her maggot brother.

'This won't do,' she said, sitting on the bed, reliving old hatreds, fresh and vigorous as when first incurred. Coming back had set off this further welter of rage, like a time bomb.

'What is it?' she asked aloud, wondering what particle in the brain is triggered by some smell, or the wind, or a yearling in pain, or a voice sodden with loneliness that says, without meaning it, 'Would you marry me?'

She might have known it: there was a knock on the door, Caimin calling her, saying she had a visitor, saying it with excitement, as if she should be pleased. He had completely misunderstood her instructions, her clamour to be left alone. Out she went, fuming, about to tell him to send the stranger away, but the stranger was standing there beside him – a largish woman in a raincoat, with grey hair drawn back severely in a bun. 'Hay fever,' Nelly heard herself saying, to account for the tears, and for the crumpled handkerchief that she was holding. Caimin left them together on the landing and shuffled off like a dog that knows it has done something wrong.

'You don't remember me,' the woman was saying. She was breathless, as if she had run, so eager was she to be there. Bringing her face closer, she allowed Nelly to scan it, pleased to present this challenge. Nelly realised it must be someone from her nearby home. She tried to recall all her school friends, tried to picture them at their desks, or in the choir on Sundays, or in the school photo that they had all received when they left. This face was not among them.

'No,' she said finally, feeling a little baffled.

'I'm Gertie . . . Mrs Conway's niece. She owned the hotel in your town,' the woman said with a nervous smile. Her excitement was fading and she realised that she was not welcome. She began apologising for barging in, explaining that a woman in the shop said she had seen Nelly Nugent walking on the seashore.

'Mrs Conway's niece,' Nelly said, trying not to bristle. Of course. Gertie's aunt had also owned a house here. They used to come for weekends, had houseparties.

'Gertie,' she whispered, remembering the vivid young girl who had come often to stay at her aunt's hotel. She had served behind the counter like a grownup, and had the opportunity to meet all the men, to flirt with them. Being Gertie, she had snatched the prize of them all.

Yes, she remembered Gertie. She remembered precisely when she had first seen Gertie – unexpectedly, as it happened. She was about to leave her home village, to go to the town to learn shorthand, and an older girl – Eileen, who lived up the country – had promised her a dress that she had become too fat to wear. It was black grosgrain and it had long sleeves – that was all she knew. She walked to Eileen's on a summer's day, after lunch, and twice had to ask the way, as there was more than one family of the same name. She remembered that she had to cross a stream to get to the house, and, yielding to a bit of fancy because of the sunshine and the thought of the dress, she took off her shoes and dipped her feet in the water, which she felt to be like liquid silver washing over her insteps and toes. The dress fitted her perfectly. In fact, it fitted her so well and gave her such allure that Eileen put her arms around her and, almost in tears, said, 'Hold on to your looks, Nell. Whatever you do, hold on to your looks.' That was thirty-odd years ago. Walking down the country road, all alone, she was so sure of herself and her beauty then; she even believed that the trees and the gates and the walls and the brambles partook of it. Along with the dress, Eileen had given her an old handbag, in which there was a little mirror with a tortoiseshell frame tucked inside one of the flaps. From time to time, she ran the looking glass down the length of the dress to see the flair and the grosgrain reflected.

As she neared the town, she decided to do it. It would have been inconceivable on the way up to the country, but now she was a different person – sophisticated, assured – and anyhow she was going away. She decided to seek him out at his lodgings. It was a house not far from the chapel – one of the five or six terraced houses with a tiled hallway and a stained-glass fanlight over the door that shone ruby or blue or green floating patterns on the floor, depending on the position of the sun. The landlady, a thin and inquisitive woman, answered the timid knock, and upon hearing the request said, 'He's having his tea.' Nelly stood her ground; she had come to see him and she was not going away without seeing him. He was the new teacher in the technical college and had many skills. He was swarthy and handsome and he had made an impression on most of the young girls and the women. Many had boasted of having had conversations with him, and promises to learn tennis from him, or woodwork, or the piano accordion. 'I won't keep him long,' she said to the landlady, who was running her tongue all around her teeth, her upper and her lower teeth, before deciding to consider the request.

He sauntered towards her – his red sweater seeming so dashing – with a puzzled smile on his face. The moment he stood in front of her with that look of pleasant enquiry, she registered two things: that his eyes were a dark green that gave the semblance of brown, and that she was not going to be able to say why she had called on him, had him routed from his tea table. She saw, too, that his eyes took in every feature of her, that he knew why she had come, knew that she was smitten, knew that she was

175

embarrassed, and felt a certain animal pleasure, a triumph, in those things, and was not the least bit discomfited. He stood there smiling, studying her face, not in any hurry to break the silence.

'I wondered about your night classes,' she said, even though he, like everybody else, had probably heard the news that she was going to the city to train as a secretary. 'I mean, my mother wondered,' she then said, becoming even clumsier by adding that her mother felt that women should be able to take the woodwork class just the same as men.

'Agreed,' he said with that pleased, tantalising smile. Indeed, one little cautionary part of her recognised him as being rather smug, but it was not enough to dampen the flush of attraction and excitement that she felt towards him. She had felt it for weeks, ever since he came – sighting him on his way to or from Mass, or on his bicycle, or in his tweed jacket with the leather patches on the elbows, or on the hurley pitch in his togs, where he stumbled and fell but always got up again to tackle an opponent. It was obviously time for her to leave, because she had said her piece. Yet she lingered. He put a finger to a tooth where a piece of raisin had stuck. Raisins, he declared, were the bane of his life, as he picked at it assiduously. Then, from the kitchen, she heard his name called: 'Vincent . . . Vince.' It was not the landlady's voice, it was another voice – coyer and younger. Then, in the doorway, Gertie appeared – a girl a bit older than herself – running her hands up and down the jamb, caressing it and smiling at them. She wore trousers that clung to her. They were of a black hairy stuff, like angora. She was like a cat. Like a cat, she stroked the door, ran her fingers along it as if she were running them over his body. He basked for a moment in the excitement of it, poised as he was between two doting creatures – one assured, the other lamentably awkward.

'Your tea is getting cold,' Gertie said.

'How cold?' he asked, amused.
'So-so cold,' she said saucily.

'He always talked about you,' Gertie was saying to her
now, as if she guessed every particle of thought that had
passed in a swoop through Nelly's mind. 'When we had a
card party or a Christmas party, he always boasted that he
knew you. You were a feather in his cap, especially after
you appeared on television.'

'How is he? . . . How are you?' Nelly asked. She remembered hearing about their engagement, their lavish
wedding preparations, and especially their coming to this
very spot for a prolonged honeymoon. In fact, without her
realising it, in some recess of her mind, this place was
always their preserve.

'Oh, he died . . . Didn't you know? He died suddenly . . .'
Gertie said very quietly, her voice trailing off, suggesting
that there were many other things she would have liked to
say, such as what his death had meant to her, and how
happy or unhappy their marriage had been.

'He liked the ladies,' she said then. There was something
so incredibly gentle about it that all of a sudden Nelly
embraced her and invited her to stay and have tea, or a
drink, or whatever.

'I can't,' Gertie said, and explained that a woman friend
had driven over with her for the day, and that the woman
was outside, waiting in the car. 'Another time,' she said.
But they both knew that there would probably not be
another time.

'And you kept the figure,' Gertie said, then drew her
coat open to show her own girth, to pay Nelly a belated
compliment. Then she was gone, hurrying down the stairs,
the belt and buckle of her open raincoat trailing behind
her.

Nelly stood stunned, tears in her eyes. She felt as if doors or windows were swinging open all around her and that she was letting go of some awful affliction. Something had happened. She did not know what it was. But soon she would know. Soon she would feel as she had felt long ago – like a river that winds its way back into its first beloved enclave before finally putting out to sea.

Weeds

RUTH RENDELL

'I AM NOT at all sure,' said Jeremy Flintwine, 'that I would know a weed from whatever the opposite of a weed is.'

The girl looked at him warily. 'A plant.'

'But surely weeds *are* plants.'

Emily Hithe was not prepared to enter into an argument. 'Let me try and explain the game to you again,' she said. 'You have to see if you can find a weed. In the herbaceous borders, in the rosebeds, anywhere. If you find one, all you have to do is show it to my father and he will give you a pound for it. Do you understand now?'

'I thought this was in aid of cancer research. There's not much money to be made that way.'

She smiled rather unpleasantly. 'You won't find any weeds.'

It cost two pounds each to visit the garden. Jeremy, a publisher who lived in Islington, had been brought by the Wragleys with whom he was staying. They had walked here from their house in the village, a very long walk for a Sunday afternoon in summer after a heavy lunch. Nothing had been said about fund-raising or playing games. Jeremy was already wondering how he was going to get back. He very much hoped to catch the twelve minutes past seven train from Diss to London.

The Wragleys and their daughter Penelope, aged eight, had disappeared down one of the paths that led through a shrubbery. People stood about on the lawn drinking tea and eating digestive biscuits which they had had to pay for. Jeremy always found country life amazing. The way everyone knew everyone else, for instance. The extreme eccentricity of almost everybody, so that you suspected people, wrongly, of putting it on. The clothes. Garments he had supposed obsolete, cotton frocks and sports jackets, were everywhere in evidence. He had thought himself suitably dressed but now he wondered. Jeans were not apparently correct wear except on the under-twenties and he was wearing jeans, an old, very clean, pair, selected after long deliberation, with an open-necked shirt and an elegantly shabby Italian silk cardigan. He was also wearing, in the top buttonhole of the cardigan, a scarlet poppy tugged up by its roots from the grass verge by Penelope Wragley.

The gift of this flower had been occasioned by one of George Wragley's literary anecdotes. George, who wrote biographies of poets, was not one of Jeremy's authors but his wife Louise, who produced bestsellers for children and adored her husband, was. Therefore Jeremy found it expedient to listen more or less politely to George going on and on about Francis Thompson and the Meynells. It was during the two-mile-long trudge to the Hithes' garden that George related how one of the Meynell children, with appropriate symbolism, had presented the opium-addicted Thompson with a poppy in a Suffolk field, bidding him, 'Keep this for ever!' Penelope had promptly given Jeremy his buttonhole, which her parents thought a very sweet gesture, though he was neither a poet nor an opium addict.

They had arrived at the gates and paid their entry fee. A lot of people were on the terrace and the lawns. The neatness of the gardens was almost oppressive, some of the flowers looking as if they had been washed and ironed and others as if made of wax. The grass was the green of a billiard table and nearly as smooth. Jeremy asked an elderly woman, one of the tea drinkers, if Rodney Hithe did it all himself.

'He has a man, of course,' she said.

The coolness of her tone was not encouraging but Jeremy tried. 'It must be a lot of work.'

'Oh, old Rod's got that under control,' said the girl with her, a granddaughter perhaps. 'He knows how to crack the whip.'

This Jeremy found easy to believe. Rodney Hithe was a loud man. His voice was loud and he wore a jacket of loud blue and red checked tweed. Though seeming affable enough, calling the women 'darling' and the men 'old boy', Jeremy suspected he was the kind of person it would be troublesome to get on the wrong side of. His raucous voice could be heard from end to end of the garden, and his braying unamused laugh.

'I wouldn't want to find a weed,' said the granddaughter, voicing Jeremy's own feelings. 'Not for a pound. Not at the risk of confronting Rod with it.'

Following the path the Wragleys had taken earlier, Jeremy saw people on their hands and knees, here lifting a blossoming frond, there an umbelliferous stalk, in the forlorn hope of finding treasure underneath. The Wragleys were nowhere to be seen. In a far corner of the garden, where geometric rosebeds were bounded on two sides by flint walls, stood a stone seat. Jeremy thought he would sit down on this seat and have a cigarette. Surely no one could object to his smoking in this remote and secluded spot. There was in any case no one to see him.

He was taking his lighter from his jeans pocket when he heard a sound from the other side of the wall. He listened. It came again, an indrawing of breath and a heavy sigh. Jeremy wondered afterwards why he had not immediately understood what kind of activity would prompt the utterance of these sighs and half-sobs, why he had at first supposed it was pain and not pleasure that gave rise to them. In any case, he was rather an inquisitive man. Not hesitating for long, he hoisted himself up so that he could look over the wall. His experience of the countryside had not prepared him for this. Behind the wall was a smallish enclosed area or farmyard, bounded by buildings of the sty and byre type. Within an aperture in one of these buildings, on a heap of hay, a naked girl could be seen lying in the arms of a man who was not himself naked but dressed in a shirt and a pair of trainers.

'Lying in the arms of' did not accurately express what the girl was doing but it was a euphemism Jeremy much preferred to 'sleeping with' or anything franker. He dropped down off the wall but not before he had noticed that the man was very deeply tanned and had a black beard and that the girl's resemblance to Emily Hithe made it likely this was her sister.

This was no place for a quiet smoke. He walked back through the shrubbery, lighting a cigarette as he went. Weed-hunting was still in progress under the bushes and among the alpines in the rock garden, this latter necessarily being carried out with extreme care, using the fingertips to avoid bruising a petal. He noticed none of the women wore high heels. Rodney Hithe was telling a woman who had brought a Pekingese that the dog must be carried. The Wragleys were on the lawn with a middle-aged couple who both wore straw hats and George Wragley was telling them an anecdote about an old lady who had sat next to P. G. Wodehouse at a dinner party and enthused about his work throughout the meal under the impression he was Edgar Wallace. There was some polite laughter. Jeremy asked Louise what time she thought of leaving.

'Don't you worry, we shan't be late. We'll get you to the station all right. There's always the last train, you know, the eight forty-four.' She went on confidingly, 'I wouldn't want to upset poor old Rod by leaving the minute we arrive. Just between you and me, his marriage hasn't been all it should be of late and I'd hate to add to his troubles.'

This sample of Louise's arrogance rather took Jeremy's breath away. No doubt the woman meant that the presence of anyone as famous as herself in his garden conferred an honour on Rodney Hithe which was ample compensation for his disintegrating home life. He was reflecting on vanity and authors and self-delusion when the subject of Louise's remark came up to them and told Jeremy to put his cigarette out. He spoke in the tone of a prison officer addressing a habitual offender in the area of violent crime. Jeremy, who was not without spirit, decided not to let Hithe cow him.

'It's harmless enough out here, surely.'

'I'd rather you smoked your filthy fags in my wife's drawing room than in my garden.'

Grinding it into the lawn would be an obvious solecism. 'Here,' Jeremy said, 'you can put it out yourself,' and he did his best to meet Hithe's eyes with an equally steady stare. Louise gave a nervous giggle. Holding the cigarette end at arm's length, Hithe went off to find some more suitable extinguishing ground, disappeared in the direction of the house and came back with a gun.

Jeremy was terribly shocked. He was horrified. He re-treated a step or two. Although he quickly understood that Hithe had not returned to wreak vengeance but only to show off his new twelve-bore to the man in the straw hat, he still felt shaken. The ceremony of breaking the gun, he thought it was called, was gone through. The straw-hatted man squinted down the barrel. Jeremy tried to remember if he had ever actually seen a real gun before. This was an aspect of country life he found he disliked rather more than all the other things.

Tea was still being served from a trestle table outside the French windows. He bought himself a cup of tea and several of the more nourishing biscuits. It seemed unlikely that any train passing through north Suffolk on a Sunday evening would have a restaurant or even a buffet car. The time was coming up to six. It was at this point that he noticed the girl he had last seen lying in the arms of the bearded man. She was no longer naked but wearing a T-shirt and a pair of shorts. In spite of these clothes, or perhaps because of them, she looked rather older than when he had previously seen her. Jeremy heard her say to the woman holding the dog, 'He ought to be called a Beijingese, you know,' and give a peal of laughter.

He asked the dog's owner, a woman with a practical air, how far it was to Diss.

'Not far,' she said. 'Two or three miles. Would you say two miles, Deborah, or nearer three?'

Deborah Hithe's opinion on this distance Jeremy was never to learn, for as she opened her mouth to speak, a bellow from Rodney silenced all conversation.

'You didn't find that in this garden!'

He stood in the middle of the lawn, the gun no longer in his hands but passed on for the scrutiny of a girl in riding breeches. Facing him was the young man with the tan and the beard, whom Jeremy knew beyond doubt to be Deborah's lover. He held up, in teasing fashion for the provocation of Hithe, a small plant with a red flower. For a moment the only sound was Louise's giggle, a noise that prior to this weekend he would never have suspected her of so frequently making. A crowd had assembled quite suddenly, surely the whole population of the village, it seemed to Jeremy, which Louise had told him was something over three hundred.

The man with the beard said, 'Certainly I did. You want me to show you where?'

'He should never have pulled it out, of course,' Emily whispered. 'I'm afraid we forgot to put that in the rules, that you're not supposed to pull them out.'

'He's your sister's boyfriend, isn't he?' Jeremy hazarded.

The look he received was one of indignant rage. 'My *sister*? I haven't got a sister.'

Deborah was watching the pair on the lawn. He saw a single tremor shake her. The man who had found the weed made a beckoning gesture to Hithe to follow him along the shrubbery path. George Wragley lifted his shoulders in an exaggerated shrug and began telling the girl in riding breeches a long pointless story about Virginia Woolf. Suddenly Jeremy noticed it had got much colder. It had been a cool, pale grey, still day, a usual English summer day, and now it was growing chilly. He did not know what made him remember the gun, notice its absence.

Penelope Wragley, having ingratiated herself with the woman dispensing tea, was eating up the last of the biscuits. She seemed the best person to ask who Deborah was, the least likely to take immediate inexplicable offence, though he had noticed her looking at him and particularly at his cardigan in a very affronted way. He decided to risk it.

Still staring, she said as if he ought to know, 'Deborah is Mrs Hithe, of course.'

The implications of this would have been enough to occupy Jeremy's thoughts for the duration of his stay in the garden and beyond, if there had not come at this moment a loud report. It was, in his ears, a shattering explosion and it came from the far side of the shrubbery. People began running in the direction of the noise before its reverberations had died away. The lawn emptied. Jeremy was aware that he had begun to shake. He said to the child, who took no notice, 'Don't go!' and then set off himself in pursuit of her.

The man with the beard lay on his back in the rose garden and there was blood on the grass. Deborah knelt beside him, making a loud keening wailing noise, and Hithe stood between two of the geometric rosebeds, holding the gun in his hands. The gun was not exactly smoking but there was a strong smell of gunpowder. A tremendous hubbub arose from the party of weed-hunters, the whole scene observed with a kind of gloating horrified fascination by Penelope Wragley, who had reverted to infantilism and watched with her thumb in her mouth. The weed was nowhere to be seen.

Someone said superfluously, or perhaps not superfluously, 'Of course, it was a particularly tragic kind of accident.'

'In the circumstances.'

The whisper might have come from Louise. Jeremy decided not to stay to confirm this. There was nothing he could do. All he wanted was to get out of this dreadful place as quickly as possible and make his way to Diss and catch a train, any train, possibly the last train. The Wragleys could send his things on.

He retreated the way he had come, surprised to find himself tiptoeing, which was surely unnecessary. Emily went past him, running towards the house and the phone. The Pekingese or Beijingese dog had set up a wild yapping. Jeremy walked quietly around the house, past the drawing room windows, through the open gates and into the lane.

The sound of that shot still rang horribly in his ears, the sight of red blood on green grass was still before his eyes. The unaccustomed walk might be therapeutic. It was a comfort, since a thin rain had begun to fall, to come upon a signpost which told him he was going in the right direction for Diss and it was only a mile and a half away. There was no doubt the country seemed to show people as well as nature in the raw. What a nightmare that whole afternoon had been, culminating in outrageous violence! How horrible, after all, the Wragleys and Penelope were and in a way he had never before suspected! Why were one's authors so awful? Why did they have such appalling spouses and ill-behaved children? Penelope had stared at him when he asked her about Deborah Hithe as disgustedly as if, like that poor man, he had been covered in blood.

And then Jeremy put his hand to his cardigan and felt the front of it, patted it with both hands like a man feeling for his wallet, looked down, saw that the scarlet poppy she had given him was gone. Her indignation was explained.

The poppy must have fallen out when he hoisted himself up and looked over the wall.

It was a moment or two before he understood the cause of his sudden fearful dismay.

Notes of a
Copernican Biographer

PATRICK ROGERS

A NEW BEGINNING, then. A new life.

All this week I have hired a boat to take me up the river, a slow, evil-smelling launch that forces its way down the Thames. My pilot – Ray – knows every nut and bolt of this waterfront. We charged into the grey chop and passed the entrance of West India Dock picking up speed. I never knew this part of town very well but I would never have guessed how riddled with waterways it was here, openings and gangways and catwalks. A lesser Venice.

So, a beginning of new notes. A new life. All else, all that old baggage has been thrown out, and it was left to me to break the mould. Traditional biography has had its day. Truths such as this should perhaps come to us in hallowed places, at the font of the tradition, somewhere like the Bodleian, but no such cinematic setting was granted to me for my revelation.

I was driving back through the brown, smudged Cairo squalor of east London – having wasted all morning with an ancient creature who was supposed to have been a lover of Max Anders, whose biography I was commissioned to write. I had been negotiating my way through the Byzantine clutter of her lies and half-recollected myths. Anders, you ask? He hardly matters now – the painter, deserter who spent the years of the Blitz working on his famous expressionistic canvases. The nudes in the Tate. Death by drowning. I had read eleven thousand letters written by this man, and had been pursuing any minor soul he might have spoken to forty years ago ... Such are the pointless labours of the biographer.

The mould of biography is broken. We construct our elaborate edifice but it remains nothing but a skeleton through which we see only the sky. Now I'm finished with it, that same old obfuscation.

Amongst the drab Victorian edifices, those abandoned wharves and neglected warehouses, the acres of bulldozed rubbish, the council estates and attempted renovations, *there* I have found my new subject. He lives amongst the stink and mud and fish, and centuries-old water, congealed oil, waterlogged timber.

At the helm Ray stood like a dancer with the tiller held between his legs. That high bravado. Late October mornings, and the air at that hour is like ice.

All this I tell Lisbet. I can't remember who referred me to Lisbet, but I went to see her in one of those buildings more suited to merchant bankers or commodity scroungers than a publisher, and with a sense of elation proposed to her nothing short of a revolution in the science of biography. Biography is ready for its Copernicus. She prepared her editorial face and said: 'You don't know who this man is? The man you saw by the docks?'

'Serendipity?'

'That's his name?'

'That's what I call him,' I told her. 'I don't have to know who he is.'

That foxed her; only those in tune with the essential radicalism of my approach could follow me. She wanted to know the other biographies I had written. I told her: Castlereagh, Christopher Marlowe, Marat.

'And what about Anders? Isn't that why you have come to see me – I understood that you'd reached an impasse.'

It was finished, I told her. Abandoned. The line of that tradition had petered out into . . . lies, fictions. You have to hector these publishers. She said that she would read my biographies, but I couldn't see why she should bother. She had a biro at her mercy between crimson-painted nails and was driving the point of it against her note-pad. A nervous gesture. I told her that her office looked across to Serendip's domain, and I could see the sprawl beneath us through the autumn haze; from the floor-to-ceiling windows I could just make out a bend of the river.

Each morning I make my way down the river, past the renovated Isle of Dogs, past the turquoise gas tanks of the north bank, Greenwich, and then we enter silence, a narrow scum-filled canal, that leads to the set of three dull clinker-brick frontages and I am sure that Serendipity lives in one of them. The central one has an open loft and a rust-coloured crane fixed on the landing. Below the central pediment the name HAAG & MENDELSSOHN can be made out in faded white relief.

'Nothing lives round here,' Ray tells me, his motor idling in the channel, kicking up a yellow froth.

On both sides of the warehouses there are clearings behind wire fences, in parts concreted, scattered with bricks, which have been used as a local tip and, contrary to Ray's pronouncement, gangs of birds collected there.

None of the frantic redevelopment has reached this far up the river yet. The canal is a cul-de-sac and a few ditches at the end contribute a sulphurous discharge to the motionless water.

'We're still learning to be his contemporaries,' I told Lisbet. She always waits for me to offer more and rarely passes comment. I can no longer gaze at the panorama beyond the window behind her without feeling a rush of vertigo.

She has read my early biographies. 'They all met violent deaths. And Max Anders, too. Do you feel that this is significant?'

They perplex me, these editors. I had to explain to her again how, coming away from a morning with one of Anders' wartime creatures, I felt it, my revolution, the truth, as clear as day, as I drove down East India Dock Road, and how I turned off and stopped by the river. I was out of breath, panting with the realisation of what I had felt. Do I believe in fate, providence? That wet morning I did. I spotted Serendipity. How I had followed him, watching as he delved into an old paper bag and drew out a chicken leg, and how I lost him near a school. How well he knew his terrain.

'It struck you then?'

'That I had found my subject. Yes. Just as you say: it *struck* me. Now I had the material with which to prove my ideas. The perfect subject! No present, no future, no letters – do you realise how many letters I have read during my career?' Here was the perfect subject. At last that wraith, that fictional enigma that lay at the heart of all conventional biography, of all lives, could be erased. I could tell that she had not completely followed my reasoning. 'I might delve into his past,' I went on, 'scrape up a few anecdotes, an estranged sister, discover his war records, but what would I have uncovered?'

'Nothing,' she conceded. I liked it when she became tractable. 'So you've given up the Anders biography?' She was making notes again. Then she asked me if I understood the concept of *projection*. They never fail to amaze me now, those still rooted to the conventional ways of knowing. 'Don't you feel that your problems might derive from a lack of confidence? In your material? In who you are?' She looked at me as though she had delivered the *coup de grâce* of some monstrous modish therapy, but so as not to hurt her feelings I said nothing.

*

Ray, I feel, has started to enjoy our morning trips.

'What will you do when you find this bloke?'

Invariably now it rains, or a soft windless haze descends, and late in the morning a decaying greenish light covers the docklands. It is always silent amongst the buildings. The occasional seagull, or a loose piece of metal banging somewhere. So many strange things abandoned here. Here you could let go of a past. A purpose no longer understood has fallen into eclipse. Some hung on, others thankfully let go.

'Can I see the notebooks?'

'No.' Lisbet looks almost pleased when I refuse her. I have told her about Serendip's notebooks and she immediately wants to see them.

'Where did you find them?'

'That's unimportant. What is important is the existence of his true voice. These books are the stroke of luck that I've been waiting for – so that I can prove the revolutionary nature of my thesis. You see, everyone else would fall into that old trap – selected quotes, devious extractions. *I don't intend to quote a single word from them!*'

Lisbet waits and scribbles something down. Have I gone too far? Will she refuse to publish?

Instead she says: 'You are separated from your wife. You live . . . in a service flat in Paddington? For the last two years you have been reading the correspondence of this painter, and then suddenly you . . . you feel you've come out into clear air.'

'I'm going bald too!' I laugh. 'What does this have to do with anything?' Does she have a checklist? Must all her authors submit to this inane procedure? With a shot of panic I thought that she had completely failed to appreciate what I am proposing.

Suddenly something moving catches the corner of my eye, something in the bookcase.

'You're recording this!' There is a reel-to-reel tape spool very slowly rotating on a machine.

'Of course.' She is quite calm. 'I told you at the start that I will be recording all our meetings. It's general practice.'

It seemed over-thorough to me, but I said no more.

'You are continuing with your boat trips? But you haven't spotted him yet?'

'It's only a matter of time.'

She taps her biro again, summing something up. She says: 'Freud says somewhere that biographers select their subjects according to a need to enrol them in a list of infantile heroes. What do you say about that?'

'It's – it's a theory.'

'A revivification of the infant's idealised father.' She is doodling now, looking down. 'That as a consequence the biographer blurs and suppresses anything that doesn't fit the image.'

'It sounds like he was describing the biographies written about himself!'

She smiles and changes the subject. For a while we talked about my earlier writings as though they were relevant; it seems that she has quite assiduously consumed them, and then, glancing at her watch, she abruptly announces that the meeting is over.

Of course I'd be a fool to release the notebooks, especially to Lisbet. The temptation to use them in a conventional mode would be too much for the marketing side of any publisher. The mark of a person is what he or she makes of such acts of providence, and the true voice of Serendipity is not a gift that comes every day. *Tuesday. If I start getting some wood up in the loft for winter I can stay there permanent. Dug up a few more potatoes with their bodies like old turds and boiled them up. Scrumptious.* Unmistakably his, the demotic verve. The same vitality that he must invest in his distinctive life. *Down along the gantry and down to the dispatch floor. Thank God I don't have to lug the Dog any more. Buried near the potatoes, the bitch has a purpose now. Maybe that's why they're the shape they are.* These will remain my guide ropes, these old school exercise books with widely spaced lines and a pink margin, their tattered violet blotting-paper covers, and not a word shall appear in my life.

Does she understand that?

Awash these past few years on other people's detritus – and in the modern age these people *live their lives* according to the rules of biography – I had been certain at least of my own biography. Except that it was constructed according to someone else's programme! Important dates, formative experiences, key figures, recurring motifs – all fictions! That's how *I* wrote them. But now the clean slate. My own existence still wore the accretions of that old fiction, which to my amazement Lisbet continued to investigate – the separation from my wife; the noise that comes at night when the refrigerator next door sets up a trembling in the thin wall; when the tall Sikh from downstairs sets out each evening for his temple behind the garage . . . Lisbet wants me to sweep up these elements in the delusion that they have an importance, when I am trying to make it clear to her that the exact opposite is the case: they must be abraded from consciousness. Why speak of me, anyway? I insist. Here we have the first Adam of a new knowledge, an epistemological revolution.

For weeks we'd been cruising past those dead buildings, keeping to the far side on the return leg, but we had spotted nothing. Then, today, Ray suddenly pointed out the stone steps opposite. A man, my size, in an old knee-length Army trench coat.

'Quick!' I shouted. Ray swerved the tiller and accelerated, but the shadow disappeared. We cut the motor and listened. Should I have called out? Called what? It was black in the open loft of the centre building but I was certain that he was in there, watching us. Ray started the motor and as it idled the propeller blades were slowly throwing up bubbles through the murk.

But it was him. The man I had first seen by Limehouse Pier selecting morsels from his paper bag. Faith in my intuition has paid off.

Why get up just because my body wakes? What's a body, anyway? Nights of bliss. With that mattress I got behind the printers in the Tiptree Road.

A week since I spotted Serendipity and nothing since.

'What else can you tell me about him?' Lisbet wants to know. She does not understand how fleeting his appearance had been. 'What clothes was he wearing? Did he look in your direction?' She is almost abnormally fascinated with my impressions of him, yet at times I feel that she does not believe that he exists. Today the sun is a glossy yellow in the haze that covers London. I told her that she must not fall into the old biographer's trap of interpreting appearance as important; that she must accept the contingent. I enjoy lecturing my editors. There are a thousand voices calling you, I tell her. 'Yes – I have that problem,' she says and obviously I have betrayed my surprise. 'It's true,' she went on. 'A myriad theories, a thousand voices. They blow this way and that and I only hear a snatch of one conversation before the wind changes and another drowns it out. I strain to listen. Which one is real?'

I agree with her. 'In my career I have lost count of the lies I have heard.'

'But the lies,' she smiles, 'don't you feel that they sometimes tell you more than the truth?'

Oh yes. As long as you know. That they are lies.

'You're used to biographers, I see,' I laugh.

'Biographers?' She considers this seriously. 'Yes, I suppose you could call them that. *Self*-biographers – *auto*biographers.' She is enjoying some private allusion, I suspect.

'And you are right – they all come to me with their own private programmes.'

Once people used to see me, then just that old cow at the off-licence. Then they did her in and left her in a ditch. To get her house. But no one ever said anything I wanted to hear.

Then Ray surprised me by saying after weeks of these morning trips that he knew of a back waterway. An old bricked canal behind Haag & Mendelssohn's.

The next morning we went past our usual entrance, our small launch kicking up into the brown wake of a tug whose master Ray waved to, and we pushed on through the litter of seagulls. Wharves on the waterfront there had succumbed to rabid redevelopment; others were being razed. Along Greenwich Reach in the falling damp. We approached the entrance to a narrow channel hidden by a row of high metal tanks and once there the landscape changed: a few blank rows of terraces, council blocks, and a pair of inert barge hulks were lashed up to capstans. The waterway split up and empty allotments, building sites, appeared on both sides behind wire fences or black brick walls. There was no sign of activity however. There were two or three odd bits of surviving architecture, a stranded brick chimney or a concrete arch – alien figments, Babylonian or Roman, standing under a North Sea sky – and then Ray entered a channel barely wider than his vessel and we slid along, my head level with the ground. Bald tyres were roped along the sides of the canal.

The waterway came to an end against the weir-gate where all manner of detritus floated on a scummy froth: a Wellington boot, orange peel and flaps of cardboard, skeins of fishing line, a pair of dungarees.

But ahead of us: Serendip's residence. The front, here, was in a much worse state: the concrete yard had given up to weeds and bramble, and an old curve-shouldered refrigerator lay on the remains of a bonfire, its cream sides showing streaks of soot.

We stepped around this rubbish through the open archways. Anarchy: timbers, girders, piles of weed, what looked like shards of smashed toilet bowls. In one place bags of plaster had been ripped open or tossed against the walls: petrified white explosions. I left Ray downstairs and ascended the wide steps to the perilous chapel of Serendip's loft.

With my heart pounding I *knew* I was right.

Looking out from the glassless opening I looked across the canal – and there it was, unnoticed before now: another warehouse, set back, derelict, looking across at this one.

'Find what you're looking for?' Ray shouts from below. Oh yes. I have found that all right.

Roaches here. Encroaching, Serendip puts down in his note-book, scrawling with that broad carpenter's pencil, his words often straying below the line. *You can smell them, smell their noses poking into your business. The Englishman's last privilege, his room, his mattress, turned over. Here I sleep, bastards. Here I try and shut out those dreams. Thin times, poor pickings. Rain. Remember the boots I found near Dagenham Marsh. The girl you foiled in the corner at The Sow's Ear. Remember the half-eaten chicken in the paper bag – how you scoffed it down on Limehouse Pier. Scoured those bones.*

As Christmas approaches and the weather deteriorates I am convinced that my plan makes sense.

'Facts only deepen my incomprehension,' I told Lisbet. 'The less we know the more room there is for self truth.'

She fixed me with that uncommunicative smile of hers.

'I intend to burst through into a new realm of understanding.'

'You make it sound like . . . Zen Biography.'

'Exactly!' I clap my hands so loudly that she starts. 'The beginning of all knowledge is ignorance.'

She touches the glass globule that she uses as a paperweight.

'The only way is to rid ourselves of others' mis-understandings.'

I go home from these meetings with Lisbet in an apprehensive mood these days. Now that I have made my decision I feel like a racer poised on starting blocks. I think of Serendipity in his lair, enjoying the secure knowledge that no one knows of his continued existence, and I sympathise with the anxiousness about being discovered that he has expressed in his notebooks. My own life these last few years has been approaching his state, I see: a downward spiral. Downstairs a door slams and someone turns on a radio. I have thought of my painter, my last subject, who spent his last few years close to where Serendip lives, and wondered if he too had been trying to attain this blessed state.

I remember a day when I must have been only eleven or twelve years old, standing on a grassy knoll with the sun streaking through a broken fence, and all of my playmates must have been called home and I was alone, a warm evening, and with a fit of originality that afflicts you at that age I decided: Yes, that's who I will be. I would not dream of telling Lisbet this. Who was I before deciding that?

'I advise you against pursuing this . . . new subject of yours,' she warned me. She had divined what I had in mind. 'Your boat trips are over. You're not planning anything else?'

I do not answer her.

'You need, we all need, a society that . . . takes note of you.'

From my kitchenette window I see a city, a world, populated by people whom no one sees. The solitary Sikh wheels his bicycle out of the coal shed, but no one sees him; even at the temple his prayers are unacknowledged. The old woman next door, who digs over the narrow trench of clay to plant her vegetables, sits outside in a deckchair whenever there is any sunlight and shows her knees to the sun, certain that no one sees her, no one visits, no one conceives of her existence. The streets, the tube, the buses, are filled with these shadows.

'Sometimes,' Lisbet goes on, 'being ourselves can be a burden, but it's a weight that must be borne. To follow this tramp by the river you can't hope to discover anything.'

'Except myself.'

She paused, sighed. 'Isn't that why you came to me? Why have we had these sessions? After all, Mr Brownlow, you came to me for help.' Her mouth is pursed, tense. She starts again with her usual trickery: 'In opposition to Freud, you know, Jung maintained that we search out our opposites in the other – to complete ourselves. I realise that he was speaking about spouses, but is there much difference between courtship and biographical research?'

I can hardly keep a straight face. I ask you: What have editors ever understood of psychology?

Equipped with sleeping-bag and primus stove I got off the bus on the East India Dock Road and bought a few provisions, some rice and tinned beans, powdered milk, coffee, and made my way to the 'hide'. By walking I had hoped to become acclimatised to the new surroundings, but within minutes I was lost. There were hardly any road names, and the long high wire fences of the docks and building sites prevented any short cuts.

And yet this was the exact state of benighted perplexity I was in search of. I could hear Lisbet: You can't hope to discover anything.

And Serendip in those notebooks that she so greedily wanted to get her hands on: *Day shall come when I will not see myself in the mirror, in the water*.

I skirted around a deserted petrol station and thought I was getting my bearings. By mid-morning, long after I had hoped to be in position, I found a canal I recognised and ran down a lane to the end and clambered over a pile of broken bricks to reach my warehouse opposite Serendipity's.

Although the ground floor was still used for storage — pallet after pallet spread in all directions in the dark — upstairs had all the hallmarks of neglect. In the room at the top I could look across the canal directly into his loft. I used a bit of an old shutter to sweep aside the muck, the bird and rat droppings, then unpacked my rucksack and unrolled my brand-new sleeping-bag. I had thought of bringing a camera, but at the last minute had decided against it: such paraphernalia, along with first drafts, had had their day.

I was soon rewarded.

Early on the second day, stretched out on my stomach and idly watching a storm approach from Holland, I noticed a figure in a greatcoat appear in the doorway opposite; he looked down at the water, sniffed the air, then withdrew into the shadow.

If I could live less then I would eat less. Move less. Come down to this.

I might have written this myself. *See no one for days*, he writes. Or is it *years?* – the writing is unclear. *Feel POSSESSED. That feeling from when I was young centuries ago. Go down to the sea. Go down to the sea for sex. Cockles and mussels. Alive alive-oh.*

I have started a journal of my days here and am loath to leave the loft for long.

Day Four. Now I know how scientists felt when the first coelacanth was netted. Another sighting. He actually came out on the narrow ledge by the channel. It was high tide and the grey water slopped up the steps. He looked towards the river. It has occurred to me that he must be looking out for Ray's boat.

Day Six. About two in the afternoon. Miserable weather. He dangles his feet over the edge of the door opening, eats a pear and tosses the stripped core into the water. How I admire such luxuriousness.

Day Seven. Before it is light in the morning I hear him coughing. Some nights I see the flickering of an open flame against a wall. He must be feeling the cold as well.

Day Eight. Difficult to find clean water. The powdered milk floats like undissolved soap flakes.

And my guess was right. Serendipity has written: *Scraping for firewood. Spend the evening in reverie around the campfire dreaming back. The old boys are here again . . . Tunis, Sicily, Cannae. And that snooping boat hasn't been this way for ten days.*

I have to resist a temptation to shout across the narrow gap that separates us: I am *here*. Over *here*.

When my provisions are low I make a rush to the nearest shop. I know the habitat well now and take a route along the towpath and over a metal footbridge, past a stretch of redevelopment until I reach a pair of stranded bungalows, one alive with Christmas decorations, the other roofless. Most days it rains or turns to sleet. The stout, red-faced woman at the corner shop knows me now, as she knows all her children.

'But you're not from here.'

I'm prepared for this. 'I'm doing some work on the barrier. Tidal variants, that kind of thing.'

She's not interested, though. 'Is that your Christmas dinner?'

A tin of ham. Baked beans. Bread and cheese. I am running out of money.

'Quite a feast, eh?'

She shook her head, but when she thought I wasn't looking she threw in a bar of chocolate.

Back in position I slowly unwrapped the chocolate, peeled back the gold foil and learned to acquire some of Serendip's voluptuousness.

Sometimes he shows himself as if he wants to be seen, looking across the gap that separates us to where I am hidden in the dark. He fixes me with the gaze of a gorilla in a zoo, standing in his Army coat and boots, with woollen mittens and mangy fur cap.

He *has* seen me.

Watching, being watched. Facing each other we crouch squatting like lice over our hoard of memories. Which dwindle.

Day Ten. Very cold. Sleety rain. The only sound: Serendipity's coughing fits. As though he has custard in his lungs.

Lisbet was warning me against abnegation. But she never understood. From the start we were shouting at each other from opposing banks. The beginning of everything will only be when all that dead wood is gone from me, when I no longer wait for the fridge next door to stop its quaking, when my wife's face will mean nothing to me and Lisbet is forgotten – a cell before conception conceiving an undrawn face, an erased past.

Day Twelve. I've calculated that it must be Boxing Day. I meant to phone Lisbet and my wife on Christmas, but anyway I have no money for the phone. Low on fuel. Serendip throws a pot of tea leaves into the canal, to add to the swill. Spent the morning contemplating the cycle the tea must have made from India to the docks, etc. Do the tides here stretch to India?

. . . I glimpse him more and more. His guard down. Can hear him pumping his primus.

I only quote these references as last vestiges of attempts to affirm my existence.

. . . A fire last night. Must be out of fuel for his bloody machine . . .

I must learn to conserve, like him. Must learn to extract blood from the stone.

Lost track of the days. Snow falls. I think it is the new year already – last night I heard shouting miles away and hooting from over the river, Greenwich way. A heavy snowfall in the night, filling all the ledges.

I shovel the bloody stuff off, crack the surface of my bucket with a stick. Cold dark. Once I found a champagne bottle in the gutter. New Year's morning, and the champagne was frozen solid. Remember those trapped bubbles. Dark green glass, the sea.

Went down to the Thames this morning. The first clear day for weeks – but *bitter*. The water still kicks against the canal sides and at high tide the tyres rub down and up endlessly. By the bank I found a fruit bun in a paper bag. The cold and staleness had made it rock hard, but in my mouth it begins to thaw. Rolled those scrumptious currants over the tongue. Eyeing the tide and my threadbare mittens. Can't describe the luxury of freedom these chill, emptied mornings.

Lisbet would say that to abandon oneself to subjectivity neutralises judgement.

I no longer can tell. I barely know who I am. That rare starting point. Only where I am.

And Now This

CARL TIGHE

AND NOW THIS.

I suppose there are advantages to having a criminal brain. If I'd had one I wouldn't be in this mess now. But I was scared. I gave myself up. Phoned them, and they were there in a few minutes.

What galled me, really pissed me off, was that it was a WPC who came for me. I was expecting a man. A real copper. But they sent this hard–hearted bitch in blue . . .

D'you know the difference between a nun on a path and a slag in a bath? Well the nun's got hope in her soul . . . D'you think that's sexist? Does it make any difference if I say it, or if some rugger–bugger makes his mates snigger at it? I've given up worrying about things like that. Given up on a lot of things. Given up on feminism. Given up on women. Not before I gave up on men though. Given up on sex. Well almost. But like the nun on the path.

When the WPC came for me I said if she opened her legs I'd do anything she liked. She just had to say. She slapped the bracelets on. You can't bargain with women police. Too much to prove I suppose. If it had been a proper copper, his trousers would have been round his ankles . . . Never could understand why a woman would want to join up in the first place. Uniforms? Company car? Power?

Ah no. Women aren't into power. Not officially. Nature. Peace. Babies. Creation. Discussion. Isn't that it?

Men. What a word. Men. Starts out all right M: could be mother. Mummy, mama. But it goes wrong. Men. Chopped short. A word like a bullet. Mmmmm. Murder, maelstrom, mayhem, mafia, muscle, me.

Yes all right, I'll come to the point.

I went to the Peace Camp several times. But I had a job, so it was quite a while before I actually took the plunge. I sold all my furniture, even the stereo. Just kept a few books. Piled all my clothes in the back of the car and kissed Mom goodbye. She should have come with me, but she's a bit funny in the head. She's waiting for Dad to come home. He went to Suez in 1956. They never found a body, but she's still waiting. I can hardly remember him.

But that's jumping ahead.

The point is that I was wasting away. My job was in a bank. I wanted to go to Art College. I got 'O' level art and I was good at sketching, but it never worked out. I ended up counting the foreign currency. All grey suits and hushed tones. Long-term prospects, Securities, Bonds. And the hushiest of hushy tones for the word 'Career'. Wankers, the lot of them. The women would totter around in demure skirts and cardies, and not too high heels, and I did too.

Then I met Annie.

I didn't know she was gay. Maybe I was naive, but how can you tell? If they don't want you to know, then you won't.

It got worse and worse at the bank. Dreary and pointless days. Endless. Endless. I'd got a boyfriend: Sebastian. I thought he was OK. Not great, just OK. I thought I could . . . well I . . . he was a way out. If I could marry, I thought, if I could have a baby everything would be all right. Everything would make sense then. I'll have a kid. I'll be a housewife and a mother, and I'll have . . . duties, responsibilities. And I wouldn't have to work at being loved because the kid would love me automatically. So I told Sebastian. He wasn't keen, but he wouldn't give a straight answer. I got desperate and gave him an ultimatum. Baby or Out. I should never have done that, I know now. He was a nice boy and . . . well, he never said a word. Never rang nor nothing. I thought, Oh Hell, he'll be back. Just needs time to adjust. A week, a month maybe. But a month went by and nothing. Then it was nearly a year. And I really liked him, but I couldn't go back on it. I had my pride.

Started going out with blokes – lots of them. They were shits from first to last. Married, or didn't want any commitments beyond a casual fuck. The more I tried, the worse it got. The ones I really fancied – not just the good-looking ones – all belonged to this amateur dramatics society, but they were all gay. It was infuriating because they were the only ones I could sit and talk with. Gay.

Annie said I liked them because I knew they were gay, and they weren't a threat to me. They weren't trying to screw me. Maybe she was right.

I was lonely. I didn't realise how lonely I was until I found I was pregnant. Of course I couldn't put a name to the father. Ridiculous. A year ago all I wanted was a baby, and now all I wanted was an abortion and a shoulder to cry on.

Annie was great. I hardly knew her then, but we talked and talked. I couldn't believe I'd been so stupid. It's always someone else who gets pregnant. But Annie was there, and she helped and . . . she listened. And still I didn't realise.

She took me to the clinic. Bought me fruit, flowers. Went to see my mom and told her some cock-and-bull story . . . bad choice of phrase that . . . about me having inflamed tubes. Of course Mom took it all in, and then when she came to see me she kept on asking about my tubes and I had to try and keep a straight face. Annie said I could stay with her for a few days. She thought it would be better than going home to Mom. So . . . we used to sit up until all hours just talking. Annie would cook, and we'd open a bottle of vino, and then Annie would light a candle and we'd just talk and talk.

Mostly we talked about sex. Even when we talked about other things we always came back to sex. And slowly I began to realise that Annie was gay. She led me round to the idea very gently. And the more I thought about it, the more it made sense. Perfect sense. I'd just never considered it before. Who could understand a woman as well as another woman? Certainly not men. Men just want something warm and wet to come into. Shoot their love snot and make a fast getaway, and that's the end of it. Annie said there was no way men would ever understand women, and that there was no reason for women to ever want to understand men. She was very quiet, and gentle and sensible and rational about it all . . . and just kind. I let it happen. And it was great. I felt warm and cosy and secure with Annie. For the first time in years. We started going to women's discos together, and just cut men out altogether. Annie wouldn't even go into a shop if there was a male assistant. And we started visiting the Peace Camp at weekends. We camped out in the warm glow of what women could achieve by themselves.

I started dressing differently too. Once . . . just once . . . I went to the bank in dungarees and a sweater. All clean and new, mind. No tat. The manager called me into his office and said he didn't mind how I dressed outside bank hours, but that while I was at work I must wear a bra because I was upsetting the staff. Then he said I had to wear a skirt as well and adhere to the dress-code. He didn't want any of the big brown bum brigade in his bank. I asked him what he meant by that and he said: 'Lesbians. I don't want any lezzies here.'

I resigned. Told him on the spot, then went home to

Annie and cried my eyes out. It was something of a relief though. I felt like a person, at least. Annie said that 'The first dim outlines of an identity were being formed . . .'

Annie said responsibility for yourself is not a thing you can share. That's the first real shock of being a person. I'm not sure it was true in my case. Thinking back I see that really I just wanted to surrender responsibility to someone else. Anyone. I never wanted to share responsibility. I wanted to avoid it altogether. It didn't matter a damn in the end whether it was a man or a woman.

It was great living with Annie. At first, anyway. After a couple of weeks we started getting into roles. One of us was butch and the other had to be all coy and yielding. Annie said I had to give up meat because it was 'masculine'. And she expected me to hate men. This went on for months, and then slowly it grew on me that what Annie was doing was building a society without men. But we weren't just getting rid of them, or even replacing them with women: we were replacing them with women who behaved like men. Annie took up weight lifting, and said that as she was the one with the job I should do the housework and the cleaning and shopping. I began to feel . . . leached. Drained. Bled out.

And I still fancied men. Annie could never forgive me for that. If she saw me looking at some guy's bum she'd go into a real rage.

So I thought: Oh fuck it. And I packed up and went back to my mom's. I don't think Mom even realised that I'd been away. She just asked if I'd seen Dad on the way in.

By this time my job prospects were absolutely buggered. I went to London and got a job clearing tables in a restaurant, but couldn't afford a place to stay on the money. After three weeks sleeping in the back of the car I came home again. Then the Job Centre called me in.

It's what comes of having 'O' level art, I suppose. Do you know DOC POTTER'S ALL-NITE TATTOO PARLOUR? Filthy little hole jammed in under the railway arches. Unhygienic, disgusting tip of a place. Suits the customers. The real Doc Potter's dead. He sold out when he retired, and the guy everybody thinks is Doc Potter is actually a dismal old shit called Finkelbaum. Hungarian or something. Said he learnt tattooing in the war.

Pissed all day, Finkelbaum. Pickled in Alcohol. Most of the time he was incapable of working and he just sat there nodding. He did have his sober moments though, and he taught me tattooing. Strictly illegal, but he didn't give a shit, and neither did I. He even did a couple of tattoos on me. Love and Hate on the knuckles. It seemed like a good idea at the time, but I wear gloves now.

He kept this huge catalogue of sketches and designs. The customers could look through it. The big stuff was too expensive for most people so mostly we just did little stuff. If anybody asked for an Indian Chief, or a Pirate Galleon, or a Spread Eagle, then Doc would suddenly come alive. But mostly it was just Mom & Dad, Love & Hate, Brenda . . .

We did most business just after the Falklands. There was a queue. And they all wanted badges and daggers and parachutes. Crap like that. Death or Glory, Gotcha . . . Doc couldn't face it so I did most of them. I sent them out with this bright scab blossoming up their arms, marked for life, and they loved it. Mostly they got some thrill out of being tattooed by a woman.

I was there for a long time, and slowly things began to shape up into something like a life. Well a routine at least. And I got on OK with Doc Potter too. Then one day, just as I was changing the ink bottles, I heard someone come into the shop, and when I went out to see, there was this Hell's Angel type. Blond, blue eyes, leather jacket. Built like a brick shit house, with muscles rippling under his T-shirt like cats in a sack. He just stood there looking at me and I could feel my crotch just melt away. He handed me a pattern; a dolphin. A leaping dolphin. This hunko wanted a dolphin tattooed on him. I hadn't seen the Doc for a couple of days, so I thought I'd do it. This one was all mine.

He lay on the table, face down, and I started. Four hours, and not a sound out of him. Not a grunt, nothing. Just the sound of sweat pattering onto the table from his arm pits. I could smell him, hot and strong. When it was finished he stood up and looked in the mirror. He smiled at me, and I lay down on the table. He stood over me for a moment, and then he just slipped inside me. He didn't have to do anything, I just came and came and came. And then I cried. And he tumbled out of me, zipped up and just walked off as if it was the most natural thing in the world. Normal. And I lay there like some dead fish, gutted, belly up.

Two weeks later I had to take time off to go to the women's clinic and they told me he'd given me a dose of the pox. They gave me tablets and advice, but it all went by in a daze. Nothing mattered any more. I didn't struggle. After a while they said I was clear. I'd already made up my mind. Doc Potter had to go into a home for a while, to dry out. That left me in charge. I decided to close up shop. I thought: 'Fuck it, I'll go off on my own for a while, be myself.' At least I wasn't pregnant, and I had some savings, even though I'd made some heavy dope investments.

I don't remember going to the Peace Camp. It must have been a couple of weeks later, but there's a lot of things I don't remember. I have a hazy recollection of the Camp Committee telling me I'd frightened one of the young girls by 'making advances'. Very coy, that 'making advances'. Don't remember what I did though.

Everything round then is hazy. I have images of the camp. The benders, the smoke, the endless bloody rain, the smell of sweaty bodies, and the stink of shit. And I remember the hard, tight faces of the police on the main gate. I remember the soldiers at the wire too. And I remember singing and singing. We sang as if it was a weapon, as if our lives depended on it. Somebody tied ribbons on the main gate.

I didn't get on too well with anybody in the camp. They were all so goody-goody girls together. Wives of university lecturers mostly. Not many counter assistants from Woolies there. And there were the radicals and the brown rice and dungaree brigade. You've seen them on the telly – non-violent, sentimental. You know what they say: the future is female.

I do remember my first arrest.

I was queuing at the stand-pipe for water. I'd been waiting in line for a while, and all of a sudden this white Rolls-Royce drove up to the main gate. We all watched. Then the door opened and out stepped this woman. She had on a really fabulous calf length white fur coat and she looked wonderful. The lot of us just stood there with our mouths open, completely gob-smacked. We just gawped at her, and then we looked at each other, covered in mud, smelly, cold. Another van drove up, and a couple of cars. It was TV News and some reporters. And then this woman started parading about like a film star or something, and the cameras started clicking and whirring. She posed in front of the main gate and walked along the wire. One of the girls asked who she was, and the reporters said she was a beauty queen, all set to become the next Miss World or Miss Universe or something. All the soldiers gathered along the wire, and she took off her coat. Underneath it she had a bikini. And then she really began to perform, wriggling her bum, bouncing her tits, pouting, spreading her legs, sticking her bum out . . . She drove the soldiers wild, and then she fondled their guns through the wire. And like a troop of baboons they whistled and cheered. They loved it. And I remember this line of red, sweaty faces: they looked at her, and they looked at us. And we felt like lumps of dog shit.

I was furious. I dropped my bucket and ran full pelt at the beauty queen. I wanted to knock her over, to roll her in the dirt, but one of my wellies came off in the mud just as I got to her, and she just turned and looked at me. She was absolutely beautiful. Stunning. Deep blue eyes. Black hair. A smooth, clear forehead. Lips . . . I wanted to hit her, to kiss her, talk with her, trample her in the mud. I couldn't speak for rage and lust. I hopped about on one foot with a wet sock and my wellie in my hand, then some paratrooper kicked the legs out from under me and there I was sprawling in the dirt. Fitting really. I felt like filth.

They booked me with threatening behaviour and attempted assault with a deadly weapon.

The women stood bail for me. Against their better judgements, they made that quite clear. So I was out next day. That was when I saw the newspapers. There I was splashed across the front page. Me and the beauty queen. But instead of me trying to keep my balance in the mud, they made it look as if I was leaping at her, like my arm was about to smash her with the wellie, and the wellie looked more like a boot. The headline ran: 'Ban the Bomb Beast attacks Brave Beauty!'

I sat in a café for a while. I didn't know whether I could go back to the camp. Or if I wanted to. I sat in the café waiting for someone to recognise me. My teeth chattered, and I remember thinking I should go to the swimming baths to get cleaned up. I was still filthy from the previous day. But . . . I don't think I went to the baths though. I think I must have got the name of the motel from the newspaper because the next thing, I was standing at a door. Knocking. The door opened and there she was. It took her a moment to realise who I was and then she opened her mouth to scream. I whacked her with the flat of my hand and pushed past her. I didn't mean to hit her, but it felt good and she passed out, right on the spot. It can't have been my strength. It must have been fear. She hadn't been frightened of me at the camp, but perhaps she'd read the papers that morning.

I stood around wondering what to do. I thought I should take her to the hospital so I bundled her onto the back seat of my car. I wasn't panicked or anything. On the contrary, I was very calm. Anyway she just lay there and once or twice she moaned. I stopped to see if she was all right, but she'd thrown up all over the place and just lay there sucking her thumb. That made me really mad.

Doc Potter was drying out still so I took her to the Tattoo parlour. I don't know why. It just seemed right. I parked round the back and carried her inside. She lay where I put her, sucking her thumb. So, there we were: beauty and the beast in the palace of painted pricks. I made some tea on the old gas ring and sat down for a think. It was just beginning to dawn on me what I'd done. Technically it was kidnapping, and that left me in deep, deep shit. All the same Beauty just lay there. She didn't do anything, and I realised I was stuck with her.

The old place was just the same. Ink bottles, machinery, the table, the catalogue, the dirt. My stash was still in place behind the medicine cupboard. The more I thought about it the more it seemed like the only solution. So I slipped her a dose of the first thing that came to hand. She cried when she felt the needle, but she didn't struggle, and then just slid away to sleep. I thought I might have overdone it, but she was breathing all right. And then I could say to myself, well it's just to keep her quiet. It's only until you get yourself sorted out. It's for her own good, in case she runs out into the road or something. I'll just keep her quiet. Easy.

I eased her onto the table.

I had no plans. I hadn't intended any of this. I finished my tea and checked she was still breathing. I stood looking at her. It was the first time I'd had time to really look at her. She really was as good as my first glimpse at the camp gates. She was so beautiful it hurt to look, and it hurt to look away. And afterwards I knew it would hurt to look in a mirror. I drank her in.

Everything hurt so that my head buzzed and roared. Everything hurt. It hurt.

I stripped her. I had never realised how beautiful a body could be. How perfect. It was ages before I got up the nerve to touch her. And then I touched and felt. I squeezed and stroked. I ran my hands over her face, her shoulders, touched her nipples, her navel, her knees; combed my fingers through her hair and breathed in her smell. And before I knew it I was kissing her. Licking her. Sucking her. Not abuse. Not worship . . . there's no word for it. Sugar and spice and all things nice, that's what little girls are made of. Strange that we all taste of anchovies.

I cried. Tasted my salt on her body. She lay there and I wanted something more from her.

I still can't find the word. Lust. Joy. Rage. Desire. Maybe. But no. I wanted to . . . No, possess is too masculine. Penetrate, even more masculine. Defile? Deflower? No. But there is something about those words . . . Get inside her . . . Did I want to get inside her? Live inside her? Be her? It wasn't enough to have her in my control. That wasn't it at all. I wanted to walk around in that beautiful body and be loved for it. It was so easy for her. If I couldn't . . .

And there she lay. Oblivious. Calm. Complacent. Secure. And it made me mad. I thought: It really makes no difference whether she's awake or not. She's the same. Untouchable. I can't make her love me. That's next best to being her. Inside this body there's a mind that doesn't give a toss about me! Untouched and untouchable in that perfect body. No reason ever to think, or worry.

I took down the ink gun.

Do you know how many words there are to describe tattooing? Doc Potter had a Thesaurus with all the words underlined: Bedizen, prick, stigmatise, perforate, inscribe, incise . . . Americans say Cosmetologise. He must have learned them all when he first came here.

I've seen the police photographs. But that's not what it looked like at first. I took the blue ink and wrote 'Fresh Milk' on her tits. I put 'Navel Patrol' on her belly button, and 'squeeze here'. I was going to put 'Made in England' on her arse, but I didn't. That wasn't it. They were just words. The wrong words. It wasn't what I wanted. I wanted more. I wanted different. So I got down the catalogue and set to work again.

Three days. Every so often I'd stop and make us both a cup of tea. Force her to drink some. Then it was finished. Hard work; I was exhausted, but I knew it was good. I'd given my best. Flowers, beasts, scrolls, fluting, tracery, fretwork, arabesques, French knots, Celtic beltwork, heraldry. She was a sort of living cathedral.

I washed her down with disinfectant solution, covered her with a sheet to keep the light off her, then went to the phone box on the corner. I called an ambulance and then the police. I was finished. I wanted to die. I lay down on Doc's smelly little cot to wait.

A Merican

JONATHAN TREITEL

'ME SPEAKEE NO English,' I say to the hairy men with sour smells who say rude words to me on the street or in the mall, or to the heavy breaths on the phone. Then they stroll away or ring off.

It's not true. I speak English fluently. Maybe I upset an idiom sometimes but this is California where everything is new and nothing is perfect. Even as a girl, I knew *basu kontoreru* (which is how we pronounced 'birth control'), and *jiruba* ('jitterbug': try saying it out loud like a GI sidling up and pressing against you at a dance), and a host of new guest-words: *Hershey bar* and *Mickey Mouse*. And there was one half-English word that had been in our language a long time, ever since Admiral Perry had sailed victorious into Yokohama a century earlier: *merican* (it means: a hard punch on the jaw).

The GIs smelled like cheese or slightly rotten meat. The cocktail cherries at the Manhattan Club in downtown Tokyo were pierced with Stars and Stripes made of a toothpick and tissue paper, and some of the other girls would delicately tear two strips off a flag and stuff one in each nostril, but I never did: I reckoned it was my duty to sniff the foreigners to the full. They bounced towards me in a long skipping stride, leaned against the shiny bar and breathed in my face, offered a cigarette (I didn't say no; I stored it in my pocket), pointed at themselves (at their broad corn-fed belly) and mouthed the four syllables of 'America'; I scraped my finger across my neck and murmured, 'Japan'. And then we danced.

Then, during the slow cheek-to-cheeks, they used to tell me about their folks back in Iowa or Brooklyn, about their mom baking apple pie in the stoop on the prairie, about their pop stuffing his corn-cob pipe with pastrami harvested on the Greenwich Village ranch, and their girlfriend, pouting her crimson lips all across the States. And if they were kind and generous, I told them in return about my hometown: a friendly but fictional place named *Usa* (pronounced in two syllables), somewhere in the black middle of Japan, where folks hang out at the soda joint, sip long cool ones through plastic straws, and mutter soporific lists of baseball statistics.

But if they were rough, and squeezed my thigh through the thin sequined dress so hard that five bruises grew like mushrooms, I told them the truth. 'I come from Nagasaki.' Then they would leave me, and find another girl. Maybe they thought radiation sickness, or something, was infectious.

I selected the kindest foreigner, came to America with him, and here I still am.

Well, I do come from Nagasaki. I left in 1940, though, when I was eight, so I don't remember it a whole lot. My father was an official in the Defence Ministry; we moved around like crazy. At the end, we were in Tokyo. A thousand-bomber raid caused a firestorm which killed my father and mother – such a huge weight of explosives and incendiary devices for two medium-sized people. I was in a shelter at school, and survived. I have a photo of my parents, taken long before the War: my mother is young and plump, wearing a kimono with a peony design, and sliding one foot against the opposite leg to scratch some minor itch; my father has on pince-nez (I don't remember him ever wearing this, but he must have); I am not yet born.

I dream about my parents; I speak to them words of love and reconciliation; but I speak in English and they don't understand one word.

My husband, George, is a civil engineer on the faculty at Stanford University. He works late often. He comes home, takes off his glasses and rests them on the bedside table; slides in beside me. I rub the red v-mark high on his nose-ridge. Then (after making love, sometimes) we sleep. My daughter, Carolyn, is a sophomore at U.C. Berkeley, getting on fine there, I guess. There are some young Japanese here on campus, students and post-docs, but I don't speak the language fluently any more, and we don't have much in common. Mostly I socialise with the other faculty wives; we have a little group that meets for coffee mornings. We all gossip about 'relationships' and swap mildly lewd anecdotes about somebody else's husband. I giggle with accuracy. When one of the other ladies, new at Stanford, asks me what I am (and they do, they all do, within half an hour of declaring, 'Hi!'), I'm up front about it; I say straight out: 'I'm an ethnic. The Japanese kind.' They ask my advice about Japanese food, and I tell them, you can get plenty of authentic cuisine round here, now. There's a teriyaki fast-food place in the mall, and a new sushi bar just opened up in Palo Alto. But when I was in Tokyo in the days after, all we ever ate (or so I remember) was rice and Hershey bars.

Of the years between 1940 and 1947, between Nagasaki and California, I recall only scraps. Bombs, shelters, blazes, cinders, Imperial boy-soldiers, GIs . . . *There* I was, a school-girl in a quiet classroom, manipulating the fine-haired brush to inscribe ideograms on creamy paper. And *there* I was, a young bride in San Francisco, crying minutely when a fragment of confetti fluttered on my left eyeball.

Nagasaki was cool and pale green. Bridges everywhere, in a criss-cross pattern. The sea was constructed from short diagonal strokes. People were gentle; they bowed with politeness or to pat the head of a little girl: myself. Even the longshoremen by the waterfront, drunk on sake and male comradeship, crooned sweet, moody songs. I passed happy hours at school, learning the complexity of Japanese calligraphy (I've forgotten almost all of it). But I left Nagasaki behind when I was only a sophomore in Junior High. (Yes, I know this last phrase sounds absurdly American: but how else can I say it? Yes, I *know*.)

My best friend was Tama, which means *jewel*. I remember her hunched over the low desk, drawing the ideogram for her own name in a neat circling stroke. Her calligraphy was beautiful and rapid. We told each other we would never part, though of course we did, when my father was transferred. We always shared our food in the lunch recess. I would dip my chopsticks into her lunch box and pick out a few grains of rice; she would peer into my box and pluck a dark sliver of seaweed. (I remember the appearance of the food, but not its taste.) While she ate, she always tucked her writing brush behind her left ear.

As part of some cultural exchange deal three years back, the Japanese government sent over an exhibition about present-day Hiroshima and Nagasaki. It was on display at the Asian Museum in San Francisco. George said, 'Let's go on August ninth' (which is the anniversary of the death of Nagasaki) but I said, 'No, it'll be too crowded.' So we went on the tenth. There were huge blow-up photos, big as the wall of a Japanese house, of steelworks and sewage plants in modern Nagasaki. George, who's into engineering, just loved to stab the photo with his index finger and point out details. Also the famous Cloud. (A pair of them, in fact, one for each city.) A memory jumped: Tama, at school, sketching on my palm with her brush a rapid picture of a cloud and somebody atop it. Then she murmured (I translate approximately), 'The count is seated

219

on the cloud, alas.' The Japanese language is rich in puns; these syllables could also mean something silly and sexy. We giggled together till our mouths filled with saliva which trickled down the windpipe; then we began to choke.

Also, near the entrance to the exhibition, a rectangular wooden frame holding a fraction of ground-level Nagasaki: cement and scorched earth; and on it, in the form of lighter patches against the dark, were the shadows of two people vaporised by the flash. One of them had a brush (or something) tucked behind her left ear. I decided this must be Tama. (I had to know, or make up, *something* about her fate.) Then we had to leave the exhibition, because I was going to the mall to help my daughter buy a ball gown for her Junior Prom.

A year ago, on a humid cloudy day, at some reception for foreign visitors at the International Center here on campus, I met a young Japanese post-doc. He was doing research on the electron properties of ceramic composites, as he explained at formidable length. I fought back with a detailed analysis of the American electoral system. He was tall and stooping and carried his textbooks in a yellow Minnie Mouse backpack. He came from Nagasaki. We got to chatting – in my broken Japanese and then in his broken English – about the city. He produced from his backpack a Japanese paperback entitled (I translate) *An Anthology Of Memoirs Of Nagasaki: They Who Have Survived*. I glanced down the list of authors: one of them was the familiar circling ideogram. Tama. He offered to lend me the book, and I said, sure.

It was only when I got home that I remembered I can't read Japanese; I know this sounds ridiculous. Well, I know the two syllabic alphabets (used, for instance, for transliterating English; I can always read the labels on the packaging of electronics – things like: 'Toshiba Computer 512 Kilobyte External Disk Drive'), plus some of the commoner ideograms. Dictionaries are tough to use, because you have to know the ideograms well in order to find where a strange one is located. Laboriously, I managed to translate the blurb. It said – among much else – that here were excerpts from a journal written by Tama in the war years, and that she died of radiation sickness in 1946. I shut the book and sent it back to the post-doc. I enclosed a thankyou note, and a cutting from the *San Jose Mercury* elucidating the US electoral system with greater clarity than I had done. I bowed to my memory of Tama, and said, 'Thank you.'

A few weeks ago, I read that a small press in Berkeley had just published an English translation of the book, so I ordered a copy through the Printers Inc Bookstore. It arrived this morning. The English title is *We Remember*. I went out on the sundeck of our house to read in privacy. I sat cross-legged on the planks near the edge. The San Francisco Bay was on my left, the Pacific on my right; green foothills stretched ahead. On the patio below, Carolyn was partying with some boyfriend of hers, dunking each other in the pool. The Grateful Dead was playing on the outdoor speakers; I shouted down to my daughter to turn the volume low; she replied, 'Mom!' in a long, pitying whine, but did as I had asked. I opened the book and began scouting down the index for Tama's name in English transliteration. Fingers scraped up my cheeks and tugged my hair back behind my ears. Hands pressed over my eyes like blindfolds. A voice: 'Guess who?'

'George,' I said. 'Yup. Want to dance?' 'No, I want to read.' 'C'mon. Come *on*.' He detached the headphones of a walkman from his own head and fastened it on mine. I heard furious Forties dance music crackling. George began to budge in rhythmic kicks and jumps; I was tethered to him by the cord of the walkman. 'Dance,' he said. 'No, I can't.' 'Jitterbug?' 'No, I can't remember.' But I was forced to move as he moved. We swayed to and fro across the sundeck, nearer and farther from the edge. I saw blue splashes, in the distance, of Ocean and Bay. Over the music, I heard my daughter and her friend: ambivalent shrieks. I tripped over the walkman cord – my husband and I tumbled on the springy duckboards.

George lay on top of me. 'Remember how we made love?' he whispered, 'in Japan, in '46, in the tiny room with the slats?' 'No,' I answered, 'I don't remember how to jitterbug.'

He rolled over onto *We Remember*. 'What's this,' he asked, 'that's pressing in my back?' I told him. He opened the book at random, and began to read. I tried not to listen to him: just to the music on the walkman, and the Grateful Dead below, and the teasing voices of Carolyn and her friend. I remembered my GI acquaintances at the Manhattan Club, and their sour smell. They each used to keep a packet of Trojans in their wallet, behind the photo of girlfriend or Mom. There was a latex shortage in Japan, so I used to beg or steal a few condoms and trade them on the black market. I couldn't help hearing George. He was reading out the journal entry by Tama, written on the penultimate day of Nagasaki:

Whoopee! Today is only twenty-three days till I graduate, and Mr Hiromoto-san, my homeroom teacher, says I will probably be valedictorian of the senior year! Today, in Civics . . . George's voice droned on and on.

Yes, the translation is clumsy and annoyingly free – but that is not the point. Translated into American English, what else could Tama be but an American kid? I can't hear or imagine a Japanese girl in those words; no, it sounds as if it is all happening to someone like Carolyn, here in California, now.

I confess to George, 'I always used to pierce the condoms with my fingernail. I wanted to become pregnant so you'd take me to America. I didn't, but you did anyhow.' He slaps me a hard punch on the jaw. I yell, 'A *merican*!'

I look out across the hills to San Francisco, and then in the other direction, to the Pacific. A Flying Fortress, specially modified to bear its load, is approaching at high altitude. It speeds overhead; the bomb doors open; the plane bobs and banks steeply, turns back towards the ocean. A heavy lone object borne by a white parachute drifts over California. It will soon descend.

Children of
the Headmaster

WILLIAM TREVOR

THE GREATER PART of the house was shabby from use. The
white paintwork of the corridors and the rooms had been
chipped and soiled. Generations of feet had clattered against
skirting-boards; fingers had darkened an area around door-
handles; shoulders had worn patches on walls. The part of
the house known as 'private side' was in better decorative
repair, this being the wing occupied by the Headmaster's
family – six people in contrast to the hundred and twenty-
odd boys who comprised the boarding-school. In the holidays the house regained its unity, and the Headmaster's
children were together again. Jonathan returned to his own
room from whichever dormitory he had occupied during
the term, and was glad to do so. Margery, Georgina and
Harriet explored the forbidden territory of the last few
months.

Mr Arbuary, the children's father, had bought the house
with money left to his wife in a will. On learning about
the legacy, the Arbuarys returned to England from Hong
Kong, where Mr Arbuary had been a police officer. The
legacy allowed them the first chance in their married life to
'do something', as they put it privately to one another. In

those days Mrs Arbuary was on for anything, but had since developed a nervous condition that drained her energy. Only the two older children were born before the family's return to England, Jonathan and Margery.

Mr Arbuary was a tall, bespectacled man with a sandy moustache, increasing in stoutness as the years advanced, and balding at about the same rate. His wife, once stout herself, was skin and bone due to her nervous complaint, with lank fair hair and eyes as darting as a rabbit's. The combination had produced children who were physically like neither of them except that they were blue-eyed and were not sallow-skinned or black-haired. Yet among the children there was a distinct family resemblance: a longish face in which the features were cut with a precision that lent them an aristocratic air, a tendency to stare. Margery and Georgina, when they were ten and nine respectively, were pretty. Harriet, at eight, gave little indication of how she would be in the future. Jonathan, the oldest, had already been told by the Classics master, Old Mudger, that he was not without good looks.

The house that was both school and home was on the outskirts of a seaside town, at the end of a brief, hydrangea-laden drive. In purchasing it and deciding to start a boarding-school, Mr Arbuary did his homework carefully. He recalled his own schooldays and all that had gone with them in the name of education and 'older values'. He believed in older values. At a time when the country he returned to appeared to be in the hands of football hooligans and trade unionists such values surely needed to be re-established, and when he thought about them Mr Arbuary was glad he had decided to invest his wife's legacy in a preparatory school rather than an hotel, which had been an alternative. He sought the assistance of an old school-fellow who had spent the intervening years in the preparatory-school world and was familiar with the ropes. This was the Classics master whom generations of boys came to know as Old Mudger when Mr Arbuary had enticed him to the new establishment. Mrs Arbuary – presenting in those days a motherly front – took on the responsibility of catering and care of the boys' health. The boarding-school began with three pupils, increasing its intake slowly at first, later accelerating.

'Now,' Georgina prompted on the first afternoon of the Easter holidays in 1988. 'Anything good?'

The furniture-room, in the attics above the private part of the house, was the children's secret place. They crouched among the stored furniture that, ten years ago, their mother had inherited with the legacy. That morning the boys had gone, by car mostly, a few by train. In contrast to the bustle and the rush there'd been, the house was as silent as a tomb.

'Nothing much,' Jonathan said. 'Really.'

'Must have been *something*,' Harriet insisted.

Jonathan said that the winter term in the other side of the house had been bitterly cold. Everyone had chilblains. He recounted the itching of his own, and the huddling around the coke boiler, and his poor showing at algebra, geometry and Latin. His sisters were not much impressed. He said: 'Half Starving got hauled up. He nearly got the sack.'

Three times a year Jonathan brought to his sisters the excitement of the world they were protected from, for it was one of the Headmaster's rules that family life and school life should in no way impinge upon one another. The girls heard the great waves of noise and silence that came whenever the whole school congregated, a burst of general laughter sometimes, a master's voice raised to address the ranks of boys at hand-inspection times in the hall, the chatter at milk-and-biscuits time. They saw, from the high windows of the house, the boys in their games clothes setting off for the playing-fields. Sometimes, when an emergency arose, a senior boy would cross to private side to summon their father. He would glance at the three girls with curiosity, and they at him. On Sundays the girls came closer to the school, walking with their mother and the undermatron, Miss Mainwaring, behind the long crocodile of boys to church, and sitting five pews behind them.

'Why did Half Starving get hauled up?' Georgina asked.

Half Starving was the sobriquet the current junior master had earned because of his unhealthily pallid appearance. As such, he had been known to the girls ever since their brother had passed the nickname on. By now they'd forgotten his real name.

'Because of something he said to Haxby,' Jonathan said. At lunch one day Half Starving had asked Haxby what the joke was, since the whole table had begun to snigger. 'No joke, sir,' Haxby replied, and Half Starving said: 'What age are you, Haxby?' When Haxby said nine, Half Starving said he'd never seen a boy of nine with grey hair before.

Georgina giggled, and so did Harriet. Margery said: 'What happened then?'

'Another boy said that wasn't a very nice thing to say because Haxby couldn't help his hair. The boy – Temple, I think it was – said it was a personal remark, and Half Starving said he hadn't meant to make a personal remark. Then he asked Haxby if he'd ever heard of the Elephant Man.'

'The *what*?' Harriet stared at Jonathan with her mouth open, the way her father said she never in any circumstances whatsoever should.

'A man in a peepshow, who looked like an elephant. Someone asked Half Starving if Haxby reminded him of this elephant person and Half Starving said the elephant person had had grey hair when he was a boy also. Then someone said Haxby might be good in a peepshow and Half Starving asked Haxby if travelling about sounded like a life he'd enjoy. Everyone laughed and afterwards Cuthbert hauled Half Starving up because of the noise.'

Cuthbert was the school's nickname for the children's father. Jonathan had felt embarrassed about using it to his sisters at first, but he'd got over that years ago. For his own part, Mr Arbuary liked simply to be known as 'the Head-master'.

'I think I know which Haxby is,' Margery said. 'Funny looking fish. All the same, I doubt anyone would pay to see him in a peepshow. Anything else?'

'Spence II puked in the dorm, first night of term. All the mint chocs he brought back and something that looked like turnips. Mange-coloured.'

'Ugh!' Harriet said.

Baddle, Thompson-Wright and Wardle had been caned for giving cheek. Thompson-Wright had blubbed, the others hadn't. The piano master had been seen on the promenade with one of the maids, Reene.

Jonathan's sisters were interested in that. The piano master's head sloped at an angle from his shoulders. He dressed like an undertaker and did not strike the girls as the kind to take women on to the promenade.

'Who saw them?' Georgina asked.

'Pomeroy when he was going for Old Mudger's tobac-co.'

'I don't like to think of it,' Margery said. 'Isn't the piano master meant to smell?'

Jonathan said the piano master himself didn't smell: more likely it was his clothes. 'Something gets singed when it's ironed.'

'A vest,' Harriet suggested.

'I don't know what it is.'

'I think a vest probably.'

Soon after that the children left the furniture-room. There was tea in the dining-room then, a daily ritual in the holidays, the long mahogany table with carved ends laid for six. The Headmaster liked it to be so. He liked Mrs Arbuary to make sandwiches: sardine and egg in winter, in summer cucumber and tomato. The Headmaster's favourite cake was fruitcake, so there was fruitcake as well.

The dining-room was a darkish room, wallpaper in crimson and black stripes combining with two sets of curtains – velvet, in crimson also, and net – to set this sombre tone. The grained paintwork was the same deep brown as the curlicued sideboard, on which were arrayed the silver teapots and water-jugs, the gravy boats and loving cups, that Mrs Arbuary had inherited at the same time as the furniture and her legacy. It was an aunt who had died.

The children took their places at the table. Mrs Arbuary poured tea. The maid who had been observed in the piano master's company brought in a plate of buttered toast. She and the other domestic staff – Monica and Mrs Hodge and Mrs Hodge's husband, who was the general handyman – continued to come daily to the school during the holidays, but for much shorter hours. That was the only way the Arbuarys could keep them.

'Thank you, Reene,' the Headmaster said, and the girls began to giggle, thinking about the piano master. He was a man who had never earned a nickname, and it was a tradition at the school not ever to employ his surname. Since Jonathan had passed that fact on to his sisters they had not, even in their thoughts, done so either.

'Well,' the Headmaster said next. 'We are *en famille*.'

Mrs Arbuary, who rarely instigated conversations and only occasionally contributed to them, did not do so now. She smeared raspberry jam on a finger of toast and raised it to her lips. The school was a triumph for her husband after a lustreless career in Hong Kong, but it had brought her low. Being answerable to often grumpy parents, organising a kitchen and taking responsibility during epidemics did not suit her nature. She had been happier before.

'A good term,' the Headmaster said. 'I think we might compliment ourselves on a successful term. Eh, Jonathan?'

'I suppose so.' The tone was less ungracious than the sentiment. Jonathan drummed as much cheeriness into it as he could muster, yet felt the opinion must be expressed honestly in those words. He had no idea if the term had been successful or not; he supposed so if his father claimed so.

'A single defeat on the hockey field,' the Headmaster reminded him. 'And your own report's not half bad, old chap.'

'Georgina got a frightful one,' Harriet said.

The girls attended a day school in the town, St Agnes's. When the time came they would be sent away to boarding-school, but at the preparatory stage funds could not be stretched. Once, years ago, his wife had suggested that the girls might receive their preparatory education at her husband's school, but this was before she appreciated that the older values would not permit this.

'Georgina', Mr Arbuary said, in his headmaster's rather than his father's voice, 'has much to mend this holidays. So, too, has Harriet.'

'My report wasn't too awful,' Harriet insisted in an unconvincing mutter meant mainly for herself.

'Speak clearly if you wish to be heard, Harriet. Reports are written to be assessed by parents. I would remind you of that.'

'I only meant –'

'You are a chatterbox, Harriet. What should be placed on chatterboxes?'

'Lids.'

'Precisely so.'

A silence fell around the table. Mrs Arbuary cut the fruitcake. The Headmaster passed his cup for more tea. Eventually he said: 'It is always a pity, I think, when Easter is as early as it is this year.'

He gave no reason for this view, but elicited nonetheless a general response – murmurs of agreement, nods. Neither Mrs Arbuary nor the children minded when Easter fell, but the dining-room responses were required.

Increasingly, there was much that Jonathan did not pass on to his sisters. Mrs Arbuary's nickname, for instance, was the Hen because a boy called McAtters had said she was like a

hen whose feathers had been drenched in a shower of rain
– a reference to what McAtters, and others, considered to be
a feeble manner. It had been noticed that Mrs Arbuary
feared, not just her husband, but Miss Mainwaring the
undermatron and most of the assistant masters. It had been
noticed that she played obsessively with one of her fore-
fingers whenever parents engaged in conversation. A boy
called Windercrank said that once when she looked up
from a flowerbed she was weeding there were soil-stained
tears on her cheeks.

Jonathan had not passed on to his sisters the news that
their father was generally despised. It had been easier to tell
them about Old Mudger, how he sometimes came into the
dorm if a boy had been sent to bed before prep because
Miss Mainwaring thought he was looking peaky. 'Well,
friendly, I suppose,' Jonathan had explained to Georgina
and Harriet. 'Anyway, that's what we call it. Friendly.'
Margery had an inkling: he'd seen it in her eyes. All three
of them had laughed over the Mudger being friendly,
Georgina and Harriet knowing it was funny because no
one would particularly want to be friendly with their
father's old school-fellow. But they wouldn't laugh – nor
would he – if he told them their mother was called the
Hen. They wouldn't laugh if he told them their father was
scorned for his pomposity, and mocked behind his back as
a fearsome figure of fun.

And now – this Easter holidays – there was something else.
A boy Jonathan did not like, who was a year older than he
was, called Tottle, had sent a message to Margery. All term
he had been bothering Jonathan with his messages, and
Jonathan had explained that because of the Headmaster's
rules he would have no opportunity to deliver one until
the holidays. Tottle had doubted his trustworthiness in the
matter, and two days before the term ended he pushed
him into a corner of the lavatories and rammed his

fist into Jonathan's stomach. He kept it there, pressing very hard, until Jonathan promised that he would deliver the message to Margery as soon as possible in the holidays. When Jonathan had first been a pupil in his father's school, when he was seven, no one had even seemed to notice his sisters, but during the last year or so – because they were older, he supposed – all that had changed. Boys he wasn't friends with asked questions about them, boys who'd never spoken to him before. Once, at lunch, Half Starving had warned a boy not to speak like that about the Headmaster's daughters. 'Fancy them yourself, sir?' someone else shouted down the table, and Half Starving went red, the way he always did when matters got out of hand.

'Tell her to meet me, first night of term,' Tottle's message was. 'Round by the carpentry hut. Seven.'

Tottle had looked round and smiled at Margery in church, he claimed. The third Sunday he'd done it she'd smiled back. Without any evidence to the contrary, Jonathan had denied that. 'You bloody little tit,' Tottle snapped, driving his fist further into Jonathan's stomach, hurting him considerably.

Tottle was due to leave at the end of next term, but Jonathan guessed that after Tottle there would be someone else, and that soon there would be messages for Georgina as well as Margery, and later for Harriet. He wouldn't have to be involved in that because he'd have left himself by then, but some other means of communication would be found, through Reene or Mrs Hodge or Hodge. Jonathan hated the thought of that; he hated his sisters being at the receiving end of dormitory coarseness. In the darkness there'd been guffaws when the unclothing of Reene by the piano master had been mooted – and sly tittering which he'd easily joined in himself. Not that he'd even believed Pomeroy when he said he'd seen them on the promenade. Pomeroy didn't often tell the truth.

But it wasn't the pursuit of his sisters that worried Jonathan most: it was what they would learn by the carpentry shed or in the seclusion of the hydrangeas. It stood to reason that their pursuers would let things slip. 'Cuthbert,' Tottle would say, and Margery would laugh, saying she knew her father was called Cuthbert. Then, bit by bit, on similar occasions, all the rest of it would tumble out. You giggled when the Hen was imitated, the stutter she'd developed, her agitated playing with a forefinger. Cuthbert's walk was imitated, his catchphrases concerning the older values repeated in self-important tones. 'Bad taste' another catchphrase was. When the pomposity was laid aside and severity took its place he punished ruthlessly, his own appointed source of justice. When the rules were broken he showed no mercy. Other people's fathers were businessmen or doctors, Bakinghouse's was a deep-sea sal-vage operator. No one mentioned what they were like; no one knew.

'Margery,' Jonathan said in the furniture-room when Georgina and Harriet were receiving tuition from their father. 'Margery, do you know what a boy called Tottle looks like?'

Margery went pink. 'Tottle?' she said.

'He's one of the first three leading into church. There's Reece and Greated, then usually Tottle.'

'Yes, I know Tottle,' Margery admitted, and Jonathan knew from her casual tone that what Tottle had said about Margery smiling back was true.

'Tottle sent you a message,' Jonathan said.

'What kind of a message?' She turned her head away, trying to get her face into the shadows.

'He said to meet him by the carpentry shed next term. Seven o'clock the first evening.'

'Blooming cheek!'

'You won't, will you, Margery? He made me promise I'd tell you, otherwise I wouldn't have.'

'Of course I won't.'

'Tottle's not all that nice.'

'He's not bad-looking if he's the one I'm thinking of.'

233

Jonathan didn't say anything. Bakinghouse's father might turn into some kind of predator when he was at the bottom of the sea, quite different from the person Bakinghouse knew. A businessman mightn't be much liked by office people, but his family wouldn't know that either.

'Why d'you think Mummy's so nervy, Margery?'

'Nervy?'

'You know what I mean.'

Margery nodded. She didn't know, she said, sounding surprised. 'When did Tottle give you the message, Jonathan?'

'Two days before the end of term.'

Lying in bed the night before, he had made up his mind that he would pass the message on when Georgina and Harriet were occupied in one of the classrooms the next day. Best to get it over, he'd thought, and it was then that he began to wonder about their mother. He never had before, and clearly Margery hadn't either. He remembered someone saying that the Hen was probably the way she was because of Cuthbert. 'Poor old Hen,' a voice in the dorm had sympathised.

'Don't tell the others,' Margery pleaded. 'Please.'

'Of course not.'

Their mother overheard things in the laundry room when boys came for next week's sheets and clean pyjamas, and in the hall when she gave out the milk. As someone once said, it was easy to forget the poor old Hen was there.

'Don't meet him, Margery.'

'I told you I wouldn't.'

'Tottle's got a thing on you.'

Again Margery reddened. She told her brother not to be silly. Else why would Tottle want to meet her by the carpentry shed? he replied; it stood to reason. Tottle wasn't a prefect; he hadn't been made a prefect even though he was one of the oldest boys in the school. Had he been a prefect he wouldn't have been the third boy to enter the church on Sundays; he'd have led a battalion, as the five houses into which the school was divided were called. He wasn't a prefect because the Headmaster didn't consider him worthy and made no secret of the fact.

'It's nothing like that,' Margery persisted.

Jonathan didn't want to argue. He didn't even want to think about Tottle now that the message had been delivered. He changed the conversation; he asked Margery about Miss Mole, one of the mistresses who taught her, and about whom Margery was sometimes funny. But he hardly listened when she told him. It hadn't occurred to him before that Tottle was in some way attempting to avenge himself.

There was roast lamb for lunch. The Headmaster carved it. There was mint sauce, and carrots and mashed potatoes.

'I think we learned a thing or two this morning,' the Headmaster said. 'I hope we can compliment ourselves on that.'

Was he as bad as they said? Jonathan wondered. It was ridiculous to say he was like Mussolini, yet it had been said. 'Bully-boys are always a bit comic,' a boy called Piercey had said. 'Hitler, Mussolini, Cromwell. The Reverend Ian Paisley.'

'Jonathan.' His mother smiled at him, indicating that he should pass a dish to Harriet. By the end of the holidays she would be far less taut; that was always so. She and Mrs Hodge and Monica would launder blankets and clean the dormitory windows and polish the linoleum and wash down the walls where it was necessary. Then all the beds had to be made and the dining-hall given a cleaning, the tables scrubbed and the serving range gone over with steel-wool. Hodge would clean the dining-hall windows because they were awkwardly placed. Crockery that had been broken during the term would be replaced.

'Sorry,' Jonathan said, moving the dish of carrots towards his youngest sister. By the end of the holidays, though still subdued and jumpy, Mrs Arbuary would be more inclined to take part in mealtime conversation. Her hands would not quiver so much.

'Mrs Salkind telephoned in the middle of our labours,' the Headmaster reported. 'Apparently the Salkinds are being posted abroad. Did you know this, Jonathan? Did Salkind say?'

Jonathan shook his head.

'Apparently to Egypt. Some business thing.'

'Did Mrs Salkind give notice?' The hopeful note in his mother's tone caught in Jonathan's imagination. With a bit of luck all the other parents might give notice also. Again and again, that very afternoon, the telephone might ring and the news would be that father after father had been posted to distant parts. The school would close.

'On the contrary,' the Headmaster replied. 'No, quite the contrary. Our Master Salkind will be flown back and forth at the expense of some manufacturing company. Heavy-duty vehicle springs, I believe it is, that pay the piper where Salkind senior is concerned. I recall correctly, Jonathan?'

'I'm afraid I don't know.'

'No cause for fear, old chap. Heavy-duty vehicle springs, if I am not wildly astray, featured long in a conversation with the senior Salkind. Buses, lorries, military transports. Now, it seems, the good man is to instruct the Egyptians in their manufacture, or else to set up a factory, or generally to liaise. The good Mrs Salkind did not reveal.'

While speaking, the Headmaster cut the meat on his plate, adding potatoes and carrots to each forkful. He paused to eat between sentences, so that what he said came slowly from him. When the children were younger they had fidgeted during their father's mealtime dissertations. They had since learned not to.

'No, the reason for the good lady's telephone call was to enquire if Master Salkind might have extra French.'

Not wishing to listen, Jonathan thought of Tottle again.

The older boy's rather big, handsome face appeared clearly in his mind, a smile slung lazily across it. He glanced at Margery, seated opposite him. Was she, too, thinking about her admirer, visualising him also? Was she wondering what it would be like to meet him as he'd suggested, what he'd say, how he'd act?

'French, apparently, is commercially *de rigueur* in Egypt, or at least in the Salkinds' corner of it.'

In the darkness of the dormitory there were confessions of desire. When one voice left off another began. Tales were told of what had been seen or heard. Intentions were declared, pretences aired.

'Though, truth to tell, I can hardly think of a reason why French should feature in any way whatsoever since the Egyptians have a perfectly good language of their own.'

The confessions of desire had to do with film stars usually, occasionally with Lady Di or Fergie, less often with Reene or Monica.

'Were you aware of that, old chap? French in Egypt?'

'No.'

'I think, you know, the good lady may have got it wrong.'

Tottle intended to try it on, and then to laugh in that way he had. He would put his big face close to Margery's, he'd put his big lips on to hers, and his hands would go all over her, just as though it wasn't real, just as though he was pretending. And later on, with someone else, it would be the same for Georgina, and for Harriet.

'But since Master Salkind's French is shaky an extra hour a week will hardly come amiss, eh?'

Everyone agreed.

The days of that Easter holiday went similarly by. The children of the Headmaster spent long afternoons on the grey sands that stretched beyond the shingle and the sea-front promenade. They sat in the Yew Tree Café sipping Coca-Cola and nibbling cheap biscuits. When their week's pocket-money ran out they crouched instead among the furniture of the furniture-room. Every morning Georgina and Harriet were given tuition by their father, and Jonathan and Margery read, alone in their rooms.

Tottle was not again mentioned, but as the weeks passed Jonathan found himself more and more dismayed by all that his imagination threw at him. It felt like that: as though heavy lumps of information were being lobbed in his direction, relentlessly and slowly. They dropped into the pond of his consciousness, creating little pictures. They nagged him, and the intensity of colour in the pictures increased, and faces and expressions acquired greater distinctness.

Two nights before the holidays ended, restlessly awake, Jonathan arrived at a decision. The next afternoon he did not accompany his sisters to the sea-front and the Yew Tree Café, presenting them with the unlikely excuse that he had some history to read. He watched them set off from the window of his bedroom, delayed another twenty minutes, and then went slowly downstairs. He paused again, in doubt and trepidation, before he found the courage to knock on his father's study door. He had no idea how he might express himself.

'Yes?' the Headmaster responded.

Jonathan closed the door behind him. The study smelt, as always, of his father's pipe tobacco and a mustiness that could not be identified. Glass-paned cupboards were full of text-books. There were supplies of chalk and geometrical instruments, globes of the world, cartridges for fountain-pens, stacks of new exercise-books, blotting-paper, pencils. His father sat behind his desk, a pipe in his mouth, the new term's timetables spread about before him.

'Well, old chap? Come to lend a hand?'

Beyond the geniality lay the ghost of the Headmaster's termtime self, of severity and suspicion. Pomposity wasn't what mattered most; talk of 'older values' and 'bad taste' was only tedious on its own. 'Cruel bloody hypocrite,' some boy — neither Tottle nor Piercey — had said once. 'Nasty brute.'

'Always tricky, the summer timetables.'

Jonathan nodded.

'Cricket's greedy,' the Headmaster said. 'Where time's concerned.'

'Yes, it is.'

His father knocked the ashes out of his pipe and drew a tin of tobacco towards him. All his life, Jonathan had been familiar with these tins: Three Nuns the tobacco was called, orange lettering on a creamy ground. He watched his father pressing the coiled shreds into the bowl of his pipe. His father knew: that was what Jonathan had at length deduced. His father had so determinedly separated private side from the school because he knew the girls must not be exposed to crudities. His father knew, but he didn't know enough. You couldn't insist there was a shutter that came down just because you pretended it did. You couldn't insist Old Mudger was a Mr Chips just because he looked like one.

'Girls out somewhere?' his father said.

'I think so.'

A match was struck, the tobacco caught. Jonathan watched it reddening, and smoke streaming from between his father's tightly clenched teeth. There was no conversation they could have. He could not mention the voices in the darkness of the dormitory, the confessions of desire, the declarations of intention. He could not tell his father he was despised for being the person he was, that boys were sorry for a woman they had likened to a hen. He could not warn him of Tottle's revenge, nor suggest what lay ahead for Georgina and Harriet. Lying awake the night before, he had wanted to protect his sisters, and his mother also, because they were not to blame. And in a way he had even wanted to protect his father because he didn't know enough, because he blustered and was oppressive, and went about things stupidly.

'Well, I'd best get on, old chap,' his father said, applying himself once more to the sheets of paper that constituted the summer timetables. The balding head was bent again. Smoke eddied about it complacently.

Jonathan went away, softly closing the study door behind him. He ran through the empty corridors of the school, and down the hydrangea drive. He ran along the sea-front, looking for his sisters.

The Scenic Railway

EDWARD UPWARD

THE EARLY AFTERNOON was warmly bright, the grey-white autumnal clematis was profuse on the roadside hedges, the views of sea and country became more extensive as the car went up the hill, and the tones of the voices of the five disabled passengers who were being driven by Leslie Brellis to the Happiland Amusement Park were cheerfully expectant; but Leslie began to suspect he might not have fully recovered yet from the attack of giddiness he'd had soon after getting out of bed this morning. When the trees of the Park, with the red-and-white-striped dome of the Pleasure Palace conspicuous among them, came into sight not far ahead in a valley descending steeply to the coastline below the hill, he noticed that the dome appeared to sway slightly as if shaken by a minor earth tremor, though the high cedars around it were quite unmoved. The appearance might be due to a trick of the afternoon sunlight on the spirally twisted stripes of the dome. But if the swaying he seemed to see had no objective reality at all, not even the reality of an externally caused deceptive appearance, and was due solely to the distortion of his seeing by a dizzy shakiness in himself, he ought not to be driving these disabled

241

people in this car. Perhaps he ought to stop at once.

He thought of asking Willie Tyler, who sat beside him staring raptly ahead through the windscreen of the car, some not too particularised question which would lead Willie to reveal whether he too had noticed an apparent swaying of the dome. But Willie was an inveterate romancer and quite capable, if he guessed what Leslie was trying to find out, of saying he was sure the dome was moving up and down as well as from side to side. Also an answer of any kind from Willie would take time to get, because he had a speech defect, a stammer which every now and then when he seemed to be speaking almost easily would bring him to a dead stop, with his mouth open, agonisingly trying to utter a next word and absolutely unable to say anything more until someone else spoke the word for him and he was gratefully able to go on again. And Leslie in any case did not really need to ask Willie about the dome. He was becoming all too certain that its swaying was an illusion produced by his own physical state. But he knew that if he stopped his large estate car anywhere here on this narrow curving road along the hillside it would be a hazard to other traffic.

He drove on, much more slowly than before. He realised how right his wife Lana had been at breakfast to warn him that his vertigo this morning, like his similar attack last month, was mainly caused by his putting extra pressure on himself recently and that he must give up this weekly driving he had volunteered to do for a local 'caring' organisation, or else he would become incapable of going on any longer with the political activities which had mattered more than anything else to him and to her ever since their retirement to the South Coast fifteen years before. But by the end of breakfast, though he had promised her he would not drive for the organisation again after today, he had told her he mustn't fail to transport his disabled group this afternoon, because their outing to the Happiland Park was the one they looked forward to above every other in the year. And now on this narrow road along the hillside he might at any moment, owing to an optical misjudgement, steer the car over the edge of the road and plunge it with himself and his group inside it to the bottom of the hill. However, the road in front of him did not appear to sway, nor did he feel at all dizzy. He decided to drive carefully on for as long as he felt no worse.

The Park was quite near at last. He was seeing it from above, looking down even on the high dome of the Pleasure Palace. The spirally twisted red and white stripes were reassuringly steady, and so was the minaret-like top of a helter-skelter tower just beyond the Palace, and so were the hugely elongated grey neck and disproportionately small head of a perhaps life-size model of a dinosaur whose body was hidden behind low trees beyond the helter-skelter. He began to feel safer, almost as if he had already brought the car to within a few hundred yards of the turnstiles at the Park entrance. But he remembered that in the road ahead there was a steep double zigzag he would have to steer the car down before it would be on the same level as the entrance. Surprisingly soon the road began to dip and in a moment the car was on the zigzag and more surprisingly still he had so little doubt of his ability to steer successfully that he even accelerated slightly when rounding the zigzag's final bend.

He brought the car safely to a stop in one of the few remaining empty spaces at the far end of the large asphalt-surfaced car park opposite the turnstiles. He quickly opened the door beside his driving seat with the intention of going round immediately to open the other three doors for his disabled passengers. At the instant when he stood fully upright after leaving his seat he felt the same kind of preliminary giddiness that had come upon him this morning just before he had fallen strengthlessly backwards flat on to the carpeted bedroom floor; but now a panic fear of hitting the back of his head on the hard ground surged up in him and gave him the strength to remain standing. He managed to walk round the bonnet of the car with hardly any unsteadiness, though he felt an extreme acceleration in the beating of his heart. Fortunately only one of his passengers needed to be helped out of the car, Miss Bilston, whose legs were abnormally short, and he found he could lift her without difficulty gently down from the front seat. The others – Miss Dover, who had a heart condition, Mr Unwin, a sufferer from Parkinson's Disease, Mrs Unwin with rheumatoid arthritis, though they were slow in getting out (Mrs Unwin slid out backwards) – did not expect or want a steadying hand from Leslie; and Willie Tyler, giving no outward sign of disability at all, was almost running as he came round the car from the driver's door, which he could reach because the front seat was a long undivided one made for three people including the driver. Soon they were all walking at the pace of the slowest, Miss Bilston, towards the turnstiles across the asphalt, and Leslie succeeded in willing himself to begin talking with simulated enthusiasm about the Scenic Railway they would be going on this afternoon. He told them he was greatly looking forward to it, as he knew it had been wonderfully changed since he had last been on it ten years before and it was now said to be the most remarkable of its kind anywhere in the world. Wanting to make amends to them for his long silence during the drive, he persevered in forcing himself to be cheerfully talkative until, with a little relief, he was aware of having arrived within a few yards of the entrance of the Happiland Park, inside which he would before long be meeting other drivers for the organisation who would already have got there with their groups, and his responsibility for his own group would be shared, or if necessary the main organiser, Nigel Crowbridge, could take over from him altogether.

Under the barkless and highly varnished criss-crossing tree branches of the big rustic entrance arch Crowbridge was standing near the thatch-roofed hut from which the turnstiles were controlled. At the sight of him, unshakily upright in spite of being in his middle eighties, Leslie knew it would not be easy to complain to him of feeling shaky himself, and it would be even less easy to suggest to him that some of the other drivers should be asked to make room in their cars for Mr and Mrs Unwin and Miss Dover and Miss Bilston and Willie when the time came to take all the disabled people home again. But though Leslie did not feel unsteady on his feet now, this might be only because fear of falling was still keeping him tensely upright; and for how much longer would his fear, even if it were to rise to the level of panic again, have power to suppress the extreme vertigo that might be lurking in him? He might be more seriously unwell than he had yet suspected. He would be guilty of criminal irresponsibility if, out of shame at the thought of having to reveal his weakness to Crowbridge, he failed to tell him anything about it and took the risk of driving his own group back to their homes. Undoubtedly the revelation would come as a shock to Crowbridge, who looked all too pleased to see Leslie's group approaching (perhaps they were late and he'd been wondering whether Leslie's car had broken down). 'The Scenic Train is waiting for you in the station,' he told them as he welcomingly waved them on through the turnstile nearest to the hut – he must have arranged beforehand that they, and Leslie, should go through without having to buy entrance tickets – and, while Crowbridge stayed behind at the hut to pay the ticket man there, Leslie's group began to move off on their own, Mrs Unwin holding Miss Bilston's hand, towards the glass-roofed and glass-walled station less than a hundred yards away across a gravelled open space. Leslie lingered until Crowbridge joined him, but before he could bring himself to say anything about his giddiness, Crowbridge said, 'A ride on the Scenic Railway is the ideal Amusement for them here – quite exciting without being at all bumpy or alarming.'

He spoke in the confidential tone of one public school man talking to another about people he did not regard as their social equals. For a moment this antagonised Leslie so acutely that it could have spurred him to say immediately that he wouldn't be driving his disabled group back home today, but he noticed that Willie Tyler had lagged behind the others and was still within earshot. He did not want Willie to hear something which could spoil his enjoyment of the Happiland Park from the start.

The reason for Willie's lagging behind was most probably that he was keen to continue being near Leslie, who, unlike any of the other drivers for the organisation, including Crowbridge, did not treat him as a compulsive fibber to be tolerantly humoured but accepted his exaggerations and inventions with something of the kind of interest and willing suspension of disbelief required by serious works of fiction. Leslie decided, as he and Crowbridge caught up with Willie on their way to the Scenic Train, that he would not tell Crowbridge about his giddiness till after the whole party of the disabled people and their drivers had finished the 'high tea' Crowbridge had ordered for them at the terminus restaurant, and that he would make the telling easier by offering to pay for a taxi to take his own group back to their homes. But even before he and Crowbridge and Willie caught up with the rest of his group the slight feeling of relief his decision gave him was followed by a sudden new premonitory dizziness which in turn, almost instantly, was countered by a powerful renewal of fear in him. He wasn't diverted at all from this fear when he saw, just outside the station and jutting up from the steep valley beyond, the head and shoulders of a gigantic glossily coloured plastic effigy of a famous film-cartoon character, a sailorman whose name Leslie could not at once remember, with puckered-up cheeks indicating a hidden clenching of toothless gums and with a short-stemmed clay pipe stuffed so far into his pursed-up mouth that the clay bowl almost touched his bulbous nose – an effigy which helped to intensify Leslie's fear because in its hugeness it was strange enough to have been a hallucination produced by a dizzy derangement of his eyesight, though he was as sure as he could be that it was objectively real. And when he came with Crowbridge and Willie and the rest of his group into the station, the green-tailed and vermilion-mouthed dragon train waiting at the platform seemed similarly sinister.

The small roofless darkly shiny carriages, linked closely together like green-painted vertebrae of a monstrous snake, were mostly occupied already by other disabled groups in the organisation, and while Crowbridge went forward to speak to and sit beside one of the other drivers – Colonel Disley – Leslie's group got into the last carriage in the train. When Leslie carefully lifted Miss Bilston on to a seat beside Mrs Unwin he was again conscious of the violent beating of his heart, and this did not at once become any less violent after he had quickly sat down next to Willie who had chosen to sit with an empty seat beside him no doubt in the hope that Leslie would take it.

Their seats were the rearmost ones in the train. The tail of the dragon, with what appeared to be a large metal arrowhead at the tip of it, curved up over their heads from behind them. Willie was pointing up at this and trying to say something, but he was unable to enunciate a single word. He got no help from Leslie who, soon after sitting down securely on this seat that had a high outer side designed presumably to hinder anyone from falling out of the carriage accidentally, felt a new dread which for a while distracted his attention from everything other than itself. It supplanted his fear of falling and it had misery in it combined with a different fear. It was a dread that he might not succeed in avoiding attacks of vertigo after today merely by giving up his work for the disabled, and that the extra pressure he had been putting on himself for two months now might already have done him an injury severe and lasting enough to force him to give up his political activities too. At a time when the anti-capitalist cause, which for so many years had been more important to him and Lana than anything else in their lives, was at its lowest ebb yet in the advanced capitalist countries of the world and needed the utmost help its supporters could give it, he had in all probability made himself permanently useless to it. This thought depressed him so deeply that he lost all awareness of Willie sitting beside him, and he hardly noticed the train starting to move and the scenery coming into view just outside the station.

Or was it the scenery, not the train, that was moving? Certainly he felt a vibration which could have been transmitted to his uncushioned wooden seat from wheels turning on rails beneath the carriage. But the high grass alongside the track was passing at a speed impossible for the train itself to have achieved so soon, except at a rate of acceleration that would have brought excessive discomfort to its passengers. Yes, relatively to the track, the scenery was moving – and so was the train, but much more slowly – and the grass beside the track was moving faster than the more distant scenery, though this too seemed to move less slowly backwards than the train moved forwards. The difference in speed between the passing of the trackside grass and of the bluish romantic-looking hills in the background must have been intended by the designer of the railway to create an illusion that the hills were at a distance of many miles from the train, whereas actually they were unlikely to be as much as twenty yards away and had possibly been painted on the canvas of a long high horizontal backdrop which was kept moving by vertical rollers revolving behind it. How ridiculous the bluish hills seemed, and how inferior to the reality they were hiding – the real tree'd valley descending steeply to the sea. For a while he stared at the backward-moving artificial scenery, though without clearly focusing it, because now almost everything in his immediate surroundings was becoming excluded from his consciousness again, this time by a misery which was less about the unlikelihood of his being able to continue his political activities than about the present state of the cause whose triumph he and Lana had once so confidently hoped would extend all over the world before they died. Yet, as he half-unseeingly stared, an imaginary scene based partly on the actual artificial one, though much more alerting and substantial-seeming, became visible in his mind.

The bluish hills were replaced by a wide mud-coloured treeless and grassless landscape sloping downwards from the foreground on the right and rising again to a horizon not less than a mile away in the background on the left, and two parallel military trenches that had been dug a hundred yards or so apart went down the slope and then up to and over the horizon. He remained well aware that none of this was being shown actually by the moving backdrop he was staring towards, but the imagined scene was incomparably more vivid and significant than the actual external one which was still visible to him, though faintly, beneath it. From along the whole viewable length of the trenches unarmed soldiers began to emerge, only a few at first but soon many, who met in the no-man's-land between the trenches. He was seeing the beginning of the fraternisation of British and German troops on the first Christmas Day of the First World War, and he was seeing it because it had always been for him and Lana one of the guarantees history had given that the ordinary people of all nations would eventually join together against the rulers in whose interests they had been tricked into killing one another. He watched the British and German soldiers exchange helmets, show family photographs to each other, visit each other's trenches, start playing a game of football in no-man's-land. But a feeling which might have become elation was quickly aborted in him by his foreknowledge, as he watched these men, that the generals on both sides would soon regain control of them and mutual slaughter would be resumed and would be continued through three more Christmases without any further fraternising breaks, and that he would live on into and through a Second World War brought about like the First by imperialistic capitalism, which would survive it to prepare for a Third.

However, the misery reviving in him now was checked

by his awareness of a change that was coming over the imagined scene. He was still looking at a wide treeless, houseless, and hedgeless stretch of land, but here the ground was dark to the point of being black, and instead of trenches there were innumerable parallel plough-furrows in it which reached from the railway uninterruptedly up to the horizon. It was apparently boundless in all directions like the sea, or like a landscape in another world. It was a Ukrainian field he had seen from a train when he had been on a visit to the Soviet Union during the spring of 1932, in ignorance of the famine that had followed the peasants' resistance to Stalin's forced collectivisation policy and before the assassination of Kirov and the beginning of Stalin's pre-Second World War political purges. It had been all the more impressive and exhilarating because he had seen it as a field in a vast country where for the first time anywhere the domination of the capitalist class had been broken and power had been taken over by a government which had proclaimed solidarity with the workers everywhere in the world. But he was seeing it now as a field in a country where great-nation patriotism had for too long been more evident than Leninist internationalism. The thought of this, and of the decline of international working-class support for the Soviet Union that the retreat from Leninism there had both caused and been prolonged by, renewed the misery Leslie had been feeling just before the Christmas Day trenches began to change to the furrows of the ploughed field. That imagined field was fading now, making him aware again of the actual dragon train he seemed to have been travelling in for quite a long while already with Willie beside him, and of the continuously moving artificial scenery showing at present an assemblage of holiday motor-coaches parked under palm trees on a Mediterranean-like seafront, though before long his imagination was once again transforming the scenery.

He was looking at an expanse of rough countryside with low hills gorse-covered except where the slopes had been cleared to make way for vineyards and for groves of olive trees. A motor-coach which came up along a valley road stopped in the foreground. As its passengers got out of it almost the only thing to distinguish them immediately from an ordinary random group of mainly elderly late-summer-holiday tourists was that there were more men among them than women, but he knew that he was seeing in his imagination a party of British veterans of the International Brigade who with a few of their relatives were able at last, after the death of the Spanish fascist dictator Franco, to revisit the Jarama valley where forty years earlier the British battalion had taken part in halting the fascist offensive against the vital road linking Valencia with Madrid, and on the first day of going into action had lost three hundred men out of six hundred. He saw they were singing now as they and the few women with them walked up the valley away from the motor-coach, and in his mind he heard the tune and the words of their song, the words of the original version of the famous Jarama song they had first sung during the three months they had been ordered to stay on in the valley after the fascist offensive had been checked – 'For 'tis here that we wasted our manhood/And most of our old age as well.' They came to a stop in front of a single tree on an open space of higher ground, and standing in a semicircle they sang a verse of the Internationale. One of the men stepped forward towards the tree, then turned to face the rest of the group. He was holding with both his hands a small oblong packet which was tightly sheathed in a covering of thick plastic. He had difficulty in opening the packet but he persisted without awkwardness and drew out a small wooden casket and scattered the ashes it contained. Leslie knew that these were the ashes of a veteran who had wanted to join the others here but had died in England only a few days before their coach tour had begun. The feelings of the veterans watching the scattering of the ashes did not plainly show in their faces – until suddenly a tall man standing at the far side of the semicircle bowed his head and bitterly wept. He was grieving, Leslie knew, not only for the comrade they were commemorating here, nor only for the many comrades who had been killed during the war against fascism in Spain, but also for the cause of working-class internationalism that had suffered a defeat then from which, after more than forty years, it had not yet recovered.

Leslie realised that he too was weeping, and at the same time he was aware that the dragon train in which he was riding was drawing into the terminus station of the Scenic Railway. He was sure that Willie must have seen him weeping, but he hoped that the other four members of his group occupying the seats immediately in front of him had not seen. With difficulty he pretended to be about to sneeze, and bringing out a handkerchief from his pocket as if to blow his nose he wiped his eyes and his cheeks. By the time the train came to a stop at the terminus platform his eyes and cheeks were dry, and he was able to assume a look which he hoped was at least unmiserable if not actually cheerful as he helped Miss Bilston down from her seat in the train. He got the impression that neither she nor Miss Dover nor the Unwins had seen his tears; possibly their attention had been hypnotically held by the artificial scenery they had been staring at. Walking with them along the platform he was surprised to find himself free both from any premonition of vertigo and from the intense fear of falling that had kept him upright on his way to the train. And now he saw something that inexplicably freed him also from the grief he had been feeling in the train.

It was a tree. Not one depicted on the artificial scenery, nor one created by his imagination, but a real tree rooted in the steep slope of the real valley and visible through the high glass side-wall of the station. He saw it only for a moment as he followed his own group and the other disabled groups out of the station on their way to the Aviary, famous especially for its birds of prey, which was to be the first of several other exciting though not too alarming or physically risky Amusements they were to be treated to before they had their 'high tea' at the terminus restaurant. He could not understand why the tree had affected him in the way it had, and a need to understand this grew strong in him before he reached the entrance to the Aviary where Colonel Disley stood waiting for him. Broadly short, hatless, large-spectacled, and with a face like Rudyard Kipling's though there was nothing else literary about him (Leslie had discovered that he had never heard of D. H. Lawrence), Disley was about to say something to Leslie, who however got in first with, 'Do you mind keeping an eye on my group for a short while? I want to go and pay a visit back at the station.' Leslie hadn't noticed whether or not there was a Gents at the station but if there wasn't Disley luckily didn't seem to know there wasn't. 'See you later,' he said, 'and perhaps you'll drop in at my house for a drink when this jaunt's over.' Leslie, putting on a look of urgency which he hoped would be taken as a convincing excuse for his not answering this invitation, hurried away from Disley in the direction of the station.

The tree was a sycamore, autumnal, with the wings of its seeds showing clearly among its not yet fallen leaves, a very tall tree rising from a projecting grassy ledge many feet below in the steeply sloping side of the valley and reaching up as high as the top of the glass roof of the glass-walled terminus. It reminded him of a tree that had been outside the railway station of his home town, the town where he had been born, though the tree there had not been a sycamore but an ash and had grown out of the side of the high embankment on which the station had been built, and at the bottom of the embankment a road had led to a taxi-cab rank, whereas at the bottom of the valley here and almost directly below the sycamore was a pond, a surprisingly large one with reeds growing round it and with birds – could they be ducks? – swimming on it. Its water was too high above sea-level to be sea water and must have accumulated gradually in an impermeable

hollow created by a landslide some while ago. He
remembered the reedy pond in the public park of his home
town. He noticed quite near the terminus entrance a narrow
path leading down along the side of the valley to the foot
of the sycamore and then curving on down to the pond.
He decided to go a little way along this path to get a better
view of the pond. He felt sure that neither Disley nor
Crowbridge would take it amiss if he left his group in their
charge rather longer than he had given Disley to expect.

Disley, who was greatly interested in birds of prey, did not
notice that Leslie at least ten minutes after leaving him to
'pay a visit' at the station had not yet returned; but Willie
did notice, and his curiosity about what Leslie might be doing
overcame the keen interest he too had in condors and vul-
tures and eagles. He was able to walk out of the Aviary without being immediately missed by Disley or Crowbridge or
by any of his disabled friends – somewhat like a little boy
who gets lost in a Zoo when the attention of his parents
and his siblings is monopolised for a moment too long by
the antics of one of the animals – though Willie was away for
so short a time that only the sight of him running as fast as
he was capable of when he came in again through the Aviary
entrance made Disley aware that he had been away at all.

He was desperately trying to say something, and totally
failing. Disley, who prided himself on his skill in helping
Willie to talk, experimentally suggested various words to
him to get him started, such as 'money', 'pocket', 'train',
but Willie shook his head each time until Disley said 'Mr
Brellis', and then he vigorously nodded. Eventually Disley
got out of him that Mr Brellis was paddling, not in the sea
but in a pond with ducks on it, and that the pond was halfway down the side of the valley. Disley repeated this story,
with an ill-disguised wink, to Crowbridge who had come up
to him to propose that they should take the party on to see
the Smugglers' Cave and also the Aquarium before taking
them to the restaurant. Then Disley said to Willie, 'Mr Brellis would have had to look pretty slippy to get down there

in the short time since he was with us here.' 'He did slip,' Willie said, enunciating the words very clearly. Disley and Crowbridge exchanged inconspicuous smiles. But they didn't feel inclined to go on humouring Willie, who was unsuccessfully and agonisingly trying to add something to his story.

Leslie knew that he did slip, at the top of the path leading downwards to the foot of the sycamore. With astonishing velocity he sat down on a hard surface somewhere below the path, jarring his spine. His legs dangled into a softness as of high grass. He was surprised to feel no pain, and the ease with which he was able after a minute or two to stand up again seemed to prove that he had not injured himself at all. On the contrary he felt strangely invigorated, and not only physically. His imagination became even more strongly alive than when he had watched the artificial scenery from the dragon train, and the scene he began to imagine now was so vivid that it completely replaced in his consciousness the real sycamore and the real valley.

He was standing at the top of a long covered footway that sloped down from the station platform-exit towards the side road leading leftward to the taxi-cab rank and rightward to the main street of his home town. The unwalled gaps between the iron pillars that upheld the curved roof over the footway gave a high clear view of the brewery tower and the church spire and even of the short bridge under which flowed (though he couldn't yet see it) the small river whose course through the town, whether briefly in the open or more often concealed in culverts, he remembered so well that he could almost have sketched a rapid map of it in his notebook as he stood here now. But sketching anything at all would have been made impossible for him by his emotion at the sight of his home town.

He felt gladness, and he felt sorrow, and above all he felt love – not only his own love for this town he had been too long away from but its love (which seemed to emanate from everything he saw now) for him. Yet when he walked down the footway and came out on to the side road, the love he felt began to have anxiety in it. He was afraid that during all the years since he had last been here the town might have changed too much for him to find his way back to those places he most of all needed to revisit.

For a while nothing appeared unfamiliar to him. He crossed the main street near where it went beneath the brown-brick railway bridge, and after turning away from the bridge to walk along the pavement towards the town centre he soon reached Southern Road which ran parallel to the railway and looked entirely unchanged, with the trees all along both sides of it and even up to the far end of it easily recognisable as London planes by the light-coloured patches where the bark had flaked off from their trunks. The plane trees helped to assure him, as he crossed the entrance to Southern Road and walked on along the main street, that he was taking the right route to find what he first of all wanted to find, and the assurance they gave him was strengthened as he passed the house of Dr Woodcote and the old Corn Exchange building, which were exactly where they used to be. For a moment he was alarmed when, staring ahead along the main street towards the town centre, he discovered that the market-place which should have been just beyond the crossroads had disappeared and that the whole scene had become unrecognisable. But in the next moment he found he had reached the entrance to the road he had not allowed himself till now to be fully conscious of yearning to reach: Northern Road – and looking along this he could see on one side the wicket gate, as he had privately and romantically named it in his boyhood, which led into a market garden by the back way, and on the opposite side the small convent school which even some Anglican parents (middle-class ones for whom the lower-class local Church of England elementary school would have been unthinkable as an alternative) sent their girl children to until they were old enough for the High School, but he could not yet see the house he longed to see.

The street lamps came on soon after he had started

walking up Northern Road. He had not realised how late the afternoon had become. There was still no sign of darkness in the air when he passed the convent and reached the first of a group of identical-looking houses, one of which used to be named Braemar. He walked more and more slowly, unable to remember where it had been positioned among the other houses and increasingly apprehensive that he would not be able to recognise it if its name had been changed. But its name had not been changed, was inscribed just as formerly in gilded cursive lettering on the glass above its front door. He dared to stop soon after having very slowly passed the house, and then he turned back and stopped again, this time within a few paces of the gate which he would have to open if he were to decide to walk up the short tiled path to the door.

He stood looking towards the bay window of the front sitting-room. The curtains had not yet been drawn across, nor had the light been switched on inside. In his boyhood more than fifty years before he would never have had the courage even to linger for a moment or two here, far less to stand staring as he was now. At most he would have walked or more probably bicycled slowly past the house – but not so slowly that his slowness would have been obvious – hoping that he might get at least a glimpse of Elizabeth, or even that she might see him passing, though he was afraid this could make her think worse rather than better of him if he appeared to her to be merely on his way along Northern Road to somewhere else. He was never able to overcome the awed timidity that was caused by the very intensity of his love for her and led him at last to write her the letter which put an end for ever to his hope of being loved by her in return. Standing here near the gate outside her house this evening half a century afterwards he could not forget the final shameful fortnight that had begun when he had dared to post to her, anonymously, a book of poems by Rupert Brooke, bound in brown suede leather, which within a few days had brought him a brief letter from her saying, sarcastically as it seemed to him, that someone had sent her a beautiful book but unfortunately had 'omitted to enclose their name', and he had written her a panicking answer improbably explaining that he had sent her the book because he had thought she had sent him one but he had realised later that the book he had received must have come from Mr Hobson, an old friend of his family. He never saw or heard from her again. Yet now as he continued staring at the window the memory of this unhappy ending became incomparably less important to him than the scene his imagination soon took him to see inside the room: Elizabeth smiling with the lit candles of the Christmas tree behind her when he had arrived for the party where he had met her again for the first time since their childhood at kindergarten together ten years earlier, and before the evening of dancing had been over he had known he was utterly in love with her. How insignificant his miserable timidity was made to seem now by that remembered happiness.

He took a step towards the front gate. He hadn't the least expectation that Elizabeth would still be living in this house. Yet if he were to open the gate and go up the path and ring the front-door bell, someone who knew something about her might come to the door. He did not open the gate. He remembered that her house had not been the ultimate destination he had aimed to reach when he had set out from the station into the town. He must move on. He could come back here later, perhaps tomorrow. The evening was getting darker and, though he was confident as he began walking again that he was taking the right route, he wanted to see clearly any changes that might have been made to the houses that had once been familiar to him along it. He came to the end of Northern Road and saw on the far side of the T-junction there a large square-shaped yellow-brick house recognisable to him immediately as the one where Mr Hobson had lived. He walked towards it across a road which meant more to him than any other in this town – Junction Road, at the end of which his own home had been. In the lower rooms of Mr Hobson's house the lights were on. It might not be impossible, he thought, that in these times when more people than formerly reached a very advanced age Mr Hobson was still alive. Leslie did not stop to stare at the windows here but walking on he remembered Mr Hobson's offer to him long ago of a job which could have led eventually to a partnership in Mr Hobson's prosperous and by bourgeois standards reputable firm. If he had accepted that offer he might have become a success, highly respected in the town, though even supposing the prospect of that success might have persuaded Elizabeth to forgive him and to marry him he was as certain still as he had been then that he would have found such a job unbearable. And Elizabeth could never have been what Lana had been to him. But as he continued walking, he thought with gratitude and warmth of Mr Hobson who, childless, had at one time seemed to regard him almost as a son and had genuinely wanted to help him.

From the moment when he got a first glimpse of his own home ahead at the corner of Junction Road he could no longer think of Mr Hobson or even of Elizabeth. Nor could he think about his home: he could only feel, and his feeling was of fear as well as of yearning. He was not, or would not let himself be, fully aware of what he was afraid of. The exterior of the house, so far as he could see by the light of nearby street lamps when he reached the corner of the road, had suffered no hideous change since he had last seen it. The Virginia creeper at its red autumnal best now was still thick on the house walls, and where the wide gravel path leading from the double front gate to the front door narrowed as it went on beyond the bow-window of the drawing-room he saw that the two privet hedges were still densely there hiding the sunken garden which the path zigzaggingly reached through the gap between their overlapping ends. How often in his childhood he had trickily steered his pedal motor-car at speed down that zigzag and how often the chain had slipped off the cogs as he had struggled to pedal it up again. The remembrance helped him temporarily to forget his fear as he opened the customarily used righthand half of the double gate – (had the other half ever been used?) – and went along the very short gravel 'drive' to the front door. But when he stood in the porch and was facing the door his fear returned.

The light visible through the thick wavy semi-transparent glass panels of the door was as dim almost as it had been during black-out hours in the Second World War (though it had never been really bright even when he had lived here before the war). Like a stranger now he had to press the bell-push beside the door instead of being able to let himself into the house with his latch key. He did not hear the bell ring and no one came to the door. He found just above the door-handle the familiar unpolished bronze knocker, shaped like the head of an Egyptian pharaoh, blacker than ever, and he knocked twice with this, not too loudly. Soon he saw someone moving slowly in the hall who loomed up towards the glass panels and at last reached the door. He did not instantly recognise his mother when she opened the door, because he had hardly had the remotest hope that she would still be here, but she knew him at once. 'Oh Leslie,' she said, and she put her arms round his shoulders and kissed him. 'I'm so glad.'

'I wish I could have let you know beforehand that I would be coming,' he said.

She seemed not to hear this. 'I'm so glad,' she said again, and then she called out into the hall, 'Arthur, it's Leslie.'

His father came out from the morning-room at the back of the hall. He shook hands with Leslie. Long ago Leslie had felt hurt that after he had reached the age of thirteen his father when welcoming him home from boarding-school or saying goodbye at the end of the holidays had taken to shaking hands with him instead of kissing him, but the warmth of his father's handshake now did away finally with Leslie's fear. His parents were both of them not only still alive but looked not so very much older than when he had last seen them.

'You are just in time for tea,' his mother said, leading the way into the large room which she had long ago named the south room. The light here was a little less dim than in the hall. There was a teapot covered with a knitted woollen cosy on the antique small round table in the middle of the room. His mother went to the dark-oak corner cupboard at the end of the room to fetch an extra tea cup and saucer and a plate. He sat down in the brown-leather armchair he so well remembered. His father sat down opposite him in an almost identical chair, though with an inflated rubber ring for a cushion just as formerly. Leslie had a feeling of safety such as he believed would not have been possible for him anywhere else than here.

The things he had especially wanted to tell his parents began to seem less urgent as he rested so comfortably in this chair. He must not let himself forget what these things were, however. He wanted to say how sorry he was that because of the work he had been doing he had not been able to come home before today. He wanted to say how sorry he was that he had disappointed them long ago by not taking the job Mr Hobson had offered him, and to explain that he could not have endured it and that the life he had chosen had been the only tolerable one for him. He wanted to admit that this work he had given his best energies to had not been a success, nor had the cause he had worked for, though also he would tell them he had never doubted – and was more convinced than ever – that it would triumph in the end. But why should he risk upsetting his parents by saying any of these things? Their happiness at having him here with them again was so evident. And why should he risk disturbing his own happy drowsiness which was increasing in him every moment as he sat here? 'Home is a place where I am well thought of,' he said to himself as he sank into the comfort of his armchair, as he slid more deeply, more and more deeply, downwards into its safety.

Ind Aff

or Out of Love in Sarajevo

FAY WELDON

THIS IS A sad story. It has to be. It rained in Sarajevo, and we had expected fine weather.

The rain filled up Sarajevo's pride, two footprints set into a pavement which mark the spot where the young assassin Princip stood to shoot the Archduke Franz Ferdinand and his wife. (Don't forget his wife: everyone forgets his wife, the archduchess.) That was in the summer of 1914. Sarajevo is a pretty town, Balkan style, mountain-rimmed. A broad, swift, shallow river runs through its centre, carrying the mountain snow away, arched by many bridges. The one nearest the two footprints has been named the Princip Bridge. The young man is a hero in these parts. Not only does he bring in the tourists – look, look, the spot, the very spot! – but by his action, as everyone knows, he lit a spark which fired the timber which caused World War 1 which crumbled the Austro-Hungarian Empire, the crumbling of which made modern Yugoslavia possible. Forty million dead (or was it thirty?) but who cares? So long as he loved his country.

The river, they say, can run so shallow in the summer it's known derisively as 'the wet road'. Today, from what I could see through the sheets of falling rain, it seemed full enough. Yugoslavian streets are always busy – no one stays home if they can help it (thus can an indecent shortage of housing space create a sociable nation) and it seemed as if by common consent a shield of bobbing umbrellas had been erected two metres high to keep the rain off the streets. It just hadn't worked around Princip's corner.

'Come all this way,' said Peter, who was a professor of classical history, 'and you can't even see the footprints properly, just two undistinguished puddles.' Ah, but I loved him. I shivered for his disappointment. He was supervising my thesis on varying concepts of morality and duty in the early Greek States as evidenced in their poetry and drama. I was dependent upon him for my academic future. He said I had a good mind but not a first-class mind and somehow I didn't take it as an insult. I had a feeling first-class minds weren't all that good in bed.

Sarajevo is in Bosnia, in the centre of Yugoslavia, that grouping of unlikely states, that distillation of languages into the phonetic reasonableness of Serbo-Croatian. We'd sheltered from the rain in an ancient mosque in Serbian Belgrade; done the same in a monastery in Croatia; now we spent a wet couple of days in Sarajevo beneath other people's umbrellas. We planned to go on to Montenegro, on the coast, where the fish and the artists come from, to swim and lie in the sun, and recover from the exhaustion caused by the sexual and moral torments of the last year. It couldn't possibly go on raining forever. Could it? Satellite pictures showed black clouds swishing gently all over Europe, over the Balkans, into Asia – practically all the way from Moscow to London, in fact. It wasn't that Peter and myself were being singled out. No. It was raining on his wife, too, back in Cambridge.

Peter was trying to decide, as he had been for the past year, between his wife and myself as his permanent life partner. To this end we had gone away, off the beaten track, for a holiday; if not with his wife's blessing, at least with her knowledge. Were we really, truly suited? We had to be sure, you see, that this was more than just any old professor-student romance; that it was the Real Thing, because the longer the indecision went on the longer Mrs Piper would be left dangling in uncertainty and distress. They had been married for twenty-four years; they had stopped loving each other a long time ago, of course – but there would be a fearful personal and practical upheaval entailed if he decided to leave permanently and shack up, as he put it, with me. Which I certainly wanted him to do. I loved him. And so far I was winning hands down. It didn't seem much of a contest at all, in fact. I'd been cool and thin and informed on the seat next to him in a Zagreb theatre (Mrs Piper was sweaty and only liked telly); was now eager and anxious for social and political instruction in Sarajevo (Mrs Piper spat in the face of knowledge, he'd once told me); and planned to be lissom (and I thought topless but I hadn't quite decided: this might be the area where the age difference showed) while I splashed and shrieked like a bathing belle in the shallows of the Monte-negrin coast. (Mrs Piper was a swimming coach: I imagined she smelt permanently of chlorine.)

In fact so far as I could see, it was no contest at all between his wife and myself. But Peter liked to luxuriate in guilt and indecision. And I loved him with an inordinate affection.

Princip's prints are a metre apart, placed as a modern cop on a training shoot-out would place his feet – the left in front at a slight outward angle, the right behind, facing forward. There seemed great energy focused here. Both hands on the gun, run, stop, plant the feet, aim, fire! I could see the footprints well enough, in spite of Peter's complaint. They were clear enough to me.

We went to a restaurant for lunch, since it was too wet to do what we loved to do: that is, buy bread, cheese, sausage, wine, and go off somewhere in our hired car, into the woods or the hills, and picnic and make love. It was a private restaurant – Yugoslavia went over to a mixed capitalist-communist economy years back, so you get either the best or worst of both systems, depending on your mood – that is to say, we knew we would pay more but be given a choice. We chose the wild boar.

'Probably ordinary pork soaked in red cabbage water to darken it,' said Peter. He was not in a good mood.

Cucumber salad was served first.

'Everything in this country comes with cucumber salad,' complained Peter. I noticed I had become used to his complaining. I supposed that when you had been married a little you simply wouldn't hear it. He was forty-six and I was twenty-five.

'They grow a lot of cucumber,' I said.

'If they can grow cucumbers,' Peter then asked, 'why can't they grow *mange-tout*?' It seemed a why-can't-they-eat-cake sort of argument to me, but not knowing enough about horticulture not to be outflanked if I debated the point, I moved the subject on to safer ground.

'I suppose Princip's action couldn't really have started World War 1,' I remarked. 'Otherwise, what a thing to have on your conscience! One little shot and the deaths of thirty million.'

'Forty,' he corrected me. Though how they reckon these things and get them right I can't imagine. 'Of course he didn't start the war. That's just a simple tale to keep the children quiet. It takes more than an assassination to start a war. What happened was that the build-up of political and economic tensions in the Balkans was such that it had to find some release.'

'So it was merely the shot that lit the spark that fired the timber that started the war, etcetera?'

'Quite,' he said. 'World War 1 would have had to have started sooner or later.'

'A bit later or a bit sooner,' I said, 'might have made the

265

difference of a million or so; if it was you on the battlefield in the mud and the rain you'd notice; exactly when they fired the starting-pistol; exactly when they blew the final whistle. Is that what they do when a war ends; blow a whistle? So that everyone just comes in from the trenches.'

But he wasn't listening. He was parting the flesh of the soft collapsed orangey-red pepper which sat in the middle of his cucumber salad; he was carefully extracting the pips. His nan had once told him they could never be digested, would stick inside and do terrible damage. I loved him for his dexterity and patience with his knife and fork. I'd finished my salad yonks ago, pips and all. I was hungry. I wanted my wild boar.

Peter might be forty-six, but he was six foot two and grizzled and muscled with it, in a dark-eyed, intelligent, broad-jawed kind of way. I adored him. I loved to be seen with him. 'Muscular academic, not weedy academic' as my younger sister Clare once said. 'Muscular academic is just a generally superior human being: everything works well from the brain to the toes. Weedy academic is when there isn't enough vital energy in the person, and the brain drains all the strength from the other parts.' Well, Clare should know. Clare is only twenty-three, but of the superior human variety kind herself, vividly pretty, bright and competent – somewhere behind a heavy curtain of vibrant red hair, which she only parts for effect. She had her first degree at twenty. Now she's married to a Harvard professor of economics seconded to the United Nations. She can even cook. I gave up competing yonks ago. Though she too is capable of self-deception. I would say her husband was definitely of the weedy academic rather than the muscular academic type. And they have to live in Brussels.

The archduke's chauffeur had lost his way, and was parked on the corner trying to recover his nerve when Princip came running out of a café, planted his feet, aimed, and fired. Princip was nineteen – too young to hang. But they sent him to prison for life and, since he had TB to begin with, he only lasted three years. He died in 1918, in an Austrian prison. Or perhaps it was more than TB: perhaps they gave him a hard time, not learning till later, when the Austro-Hungarian Empire collapsed, that he was a hero. Poor Princip, too young to die – like so many other millions. Dying for love of a country.

'I love you,' I said to Peter, my living man, progenitor already of three children by his chlorinated, swimming-coach wife.

'How much do you love me?'

'Inordinately! I love you with inordinate affection.' It was a joke between us. Ind Aff!

'Inordinate affection is a sin,' he'd told me. 'According to the Wesleyans. John Wesley himself worried about it to such a degree he ended up abbreviating it in his diaries. Ind Aff. He maintained that what he felt for young Sophy, the eighteen-year-old in his congregation, was not Ind Aff, which bears the spirit away from God towards the flesh: he insisted that what he felt was a pure and spiritual, if passionate, concern for her soul.'

Peter said now, as we waited for our wild boar, and he picked over his pepper, 'Your Ind Aff is my wife's sorrow, that's the trouble.' He wanted, I knew, one of the long half-wrangles, half soul-sharings that we could keep going for hours, and led to piercing pains in the heart which could only be made better in bed. But our bedroom at the Hotel Europa was small and dark and looked out into the well of the building – a punishment room if ever there was one. (Reception staff did sometimes take against us.) When Peter had tried to change it in his quasi-Serbo-Croatian, they'd shrugged their Bosnian shoulders and pretended not to understand, so we'd decided to put up with it. I did not fancy pushing hard single beds together – it seemed easier not to have the pain in the heart in the first place. 'Look,' I said, 'this holiday is supposed to be just the two of us, not Mrs Piper as well. Shall we talk about something else?'

*

Do not think that the archduke's chauffeur was merely careless, an inefficient chauffeur, when he took the wrong turning. He was, I imagine, in a state of shock, fright, and confusion. There had been two previous attempts on the archduke's life since the cavalcade had entered town. The first was a bomb which got the car in front and killed its driver. The second was a shot fired by none other than young Princip, which had missed. Princip had vanished into the crowd and gone to sit down in a corner café and ordered coffee to calm his nerves. I expect his hand trembled at the best of times – he did have TB. (Not the best choice of assassin, but no doubt those who arrange these things have to make do with what they can get.) The archduke's chauffeur panicked, took the wrong road, realised what he'd done, and stopped to await rescue and instructions just outside the café where Princip sat drinking his coffee.

'What shall we talk about?' asked Peter, in even less of a good mood.

'The collapse of the Austro-Hungarian Empire?' I suggested. 'How does an empire collapse? Is there no money to pay the military or the police, so everyone goes home? Or what?' He liked to be asked questions.

'The Hungro-Austrarian Empire,' said Peter to me, 'didn't so much collapse as fail to exist any more. War destroys social organisations. The same thing happened after World War 2. There being no organised bodies left between Moscow and London – and for London read Washington, then as now – it was left to these two to put in their own puppet governments. Yalta, 1944. It's taken the best part of forty-five years for nations of West and East Europe to remember who they are.'

'Austro-Hungarian,' I said, 'not Hungro-Austrarian.'

'I didn't say Hungro-Austrarian,' he said.

'You did,' I said.

'Didn't,' he said. 'What the hell are they doing about our wild boar? Are they out in the hills shooting it?'

My sister Clare had been surprisingly understanding about Peter. When I worried about him being older, she pooh-poohed it; when I worried about him being married, she said, 'Just go for it, sister. If you can unhinge a marriage, it's ripe for unhinging, it would happen sooner or later, it might as well be you. See a catch, go ahead and catch! Go for it!'

Princip saw the archduke's car parked outside, and went for it. Second chances are rare in life: they must be responded to. Except perhaps his second chance was missing in the first place? Should he have taken his cue from fate, and just sat and finished his coffee, and gone home to his mother? But what's a man to do when he loves his country? Fate delivered the archduke into his hands: how could he resist it? A parked car, a uniformed and medalled chest, the persecutor of his country – how could Princip not, believing God to be on his side, but see this as His intervention, push his coffee aside and leap to his feet?

Two waiters stood idly by and watched us waiting for our wild boar. One was young and handsome in a mountainous Bosnian way – flashing eyes, hooked nose, luxuriant black hair, sensuous mouth. He was about my age. He smiled. His teeth were even and white. I smiled back, and instead of the pain in the heart I'd become accustomed to as an erotic sensation, now felt, quite violently, an associated yet different pang which got my lower stomach. The true, the real pain of Ind Aff!

'Fancy him?' asked Peter.

'No,' I said. 'I just thought if I smiled the wild boar might come quicker.'

The other waiter was older and gentler: his eyes were soft and kind. I thought he looked at me reproachfully. I could see why. In a world which for once, after centuries of savagery, was finally full of young men, unslaughtered, what was I doing with this man with thinning hair?

'What are you thinking of?' Professor Piper asked me. He liked to be in my head.

'How much I love you,' I said automatically, and was finally aware how much I lied. 'And about the archduke's assassination,' I went on, to cover the kind of tremble in my head as I came to my senses, 'and let's not forget his wife, she died too – how can you say World War 1 would have happened anyway. If Princip hadn't shot the archduke, something else, some undisclosed, unsuspected variable, might have come along and defused the whole political/ military situation, and neither World War 1 nor 2 ever happened. We'll just never know, will we?'

I had my passport and my travellers' cheques with me. (Peter felt it was less confusing if we each paid our own way.) I stood up, and took my raincoat from the peg.

'Where are you going?' he asked, startled.

'Home,' I said. I kissed the top of his head, where it was balding. It smelt gently of chlorine, which may have come from thinking about his wife so much, but might merely have been that he'd taken a shower that morning. ('The water all over Yugoslavia, though safe to drink, is unusually chlorinated': Guide Book.) As I left to catch a taxi to the airport the younger of the two waiters emerged from the kitchen with two piled plates of roasted wild boar, potatoes duchesse, and stewed peppers. ('Yugoslavian diet is un-usually rich in proteins and fats': Guide Book.) I could tell from the glisten of oil that the food was no longer hot, and I was not tempted to stay, hungry though I was. Thus fate – or was it Bosnian wilfulness? – confirmed the wisdom of my intent.

And that was how I fell out of love with my professor, in Sarajevo, a city to which I am grateful to this day, though I never got to see very much of it, because of the rain.

It was a silly sad thing to do, in the first place, to confuse mere passing academic ambition with love: to try and outdo my sister Clare. (Professor Piper was spiteful, as it happened, and did his best to have my thesis refused, but I went to appeal, which he never thought I'd dare, and won.

I had a first-class mind after all.) A silly sad episode, which I regret. As silly and sad as Princip, poor young man, with his feverish mind, his bright tubercular cheeks, and his inordinate affection for his country, pushing aside his cup of coffee, leaping to his feet, taking his gun in both hands, planting his feet, aiming, and firing – one, two, three shots – and starting World War 1. The first one missed, the second got the wife (never forget the wife), and the third got the archduke and a whole generation, and their children, and their children's children, and on and on forever. If he'd just hung on a bit, there in Sarajevo, that June day, he might have come to his senses. People do, sometimes quite quickly.

Just Like Stone's Hotel

KIT WRIGHT

WHEN MAURICE UNEXPECTEDLY met us, he banged his cane on the ground, then held it up in both hands like a mace. He seemed delighted.

'You rascals,' he said, 'you rascals!'

He stood in the middle of the Knightsbridge pavement while crowds hurtled past him, the December night wind hacking at the tails of his ancient camel-hair coat.

'Where the devil have you sprung from?'

We had, in fact, just emerged from the Underground, two of his former drinking friends from nights in Stone's Hotel.

'You young buggers. It must be years.'

However long it had been Maurice looked much the same. The large vinous features were aubergine in the raw wind, the sunk eyes watering strongly. He was clearly bucked by the meeting; nothing would do but we all go back to the house for a drink, 'though not', he added, 'as I shall explain, in my case'.

The idea of a house was a wholly new aspect of Maurice who had lived for years in the seedy decayed grandeur of Stone's. Peter and I had worked next door and often used its bar where Maurice nightly held loud and omniscient court.

'Had to leave Stone's,' he said as he fumbled his key in a nearby mews cottage lock. 'One thing and another. Ah. Come in. Mine and the ex's, this is. Renée.'

We edged through a beige hall and turned into a tiny living room crammed with dwarf furniture and trinkets.

'I've been here some time. Very convenient. *Well*,' he said, wheezing and turning to us, 'what an extraordinary thing. How nice to see you chaps.'

'And you too, Maurice,' I said. 'It really is.'

'Now. What'll you have to drink? I have to tell you,' he said, lowering his voice as though undesirables might hear, 'that I myself have knocked the boozing on the head. Enough was enough. And I can only say that *I've never felt better in my life*.' Then heartily: 'Sit down on anything you think won't break.'

My colleague Peter was a large, square man and he lowered himself gingerly on to a *pouffe*.

Maurice was groping in the cabinet. 'Whisky do?'

'That'd be splendid,' I said.

Peter said: 'Fine, Maurice.'

'For God's sake sit down, you other great bugger. I don't give it a thought these days. Therapy and so on. Clinic, dry-out, the whole shebang – in with the druggies, mutual help. And it has. Water?'

'Yes please,' we said.

But Maurice breathily heaved himself down with only a bottle of Johnny Walker Red Label and, we were surprised to see, three glasses. He placed them loudly and separately on the hideous little table.

'Yes.' He unscrewed the top. '*Oh* yes. Virtually twice the man. When I was on the sauce I don't think I really had any conception of what life was.'

He leaned forward to emphasise:

'*Or what I am.* Well, bloody different now.'

He poured two largish whiskies for us, then a giant

measure into his own glass. He took a long draught and regarded us foxily.

'I bet you buggers would chuckle.'

We sipped.

'I mean me. Navy and the whole damn thing – sixty-six and these addicts. Well, you'd be wrong, you clever young buggers. Very nice to see you.'

He lit a cigarette and inhaled deeply.

'*Very* nice to see you. Not a drop. They showed me the way. And of course I showed them a thing or two. But it all has to come from here.'

He tapped his head.

'If you're going to give anything up, you have to have something up here to replace it. With, or whatever. I mean, Jesus Christ wasn't born in a day.'

There seemed no answer to the silence that followed this insight. Maurice drained his glass and refilled it.

'Help yourselves, by the way. It's a matter of inner resources. Could one of you chaps get some water? It's out there.'

He fluttered a vague arm. Peter uncoiled himself from the *pouffe*, went out to the kitchen and returned with a filled-up milk jug.

'*Inner resources*. To tell you the truth, never thought I had all that much in the way of them. At sea, of course, you're often on your tod, watches and so on, but generally anything but. When it comes to beating the sherbet, self's the man. Good old self.'

He took a deep swig. Peter said, 'But Maurice, you seem to be actually drinking *now*.'

'What? I've had help, of course, my God I've had help. Couldn't have managed without it. These junkies at the old clinics, poor devils. Bloody nice fellows and girls, most of them. And they were damned interested to hear about *my* life and times, I can tell you. Drink up, the bottle's there. Then Renée, of course – I can only say that she's been an absolute pillar. Taking me back till I get on my feet, won't be long. A Christian woman in the deepest sense – I don't think I'd necessarily have put it like that in all those years we were together, but that's what she is all right. I mean, she may not go to church and so on but what the hell's *that* got to do with anything?'

Peter said he thought he'd better be going.

'Must you? Well, very nice to see you. Shan't get up if you don't mind. Know your way.'

Peter's exit collided with someone's entry for a shrill voice cried from the front doorway, 'Who the hell are you?' and a small furious woman of late middle-age bounced into the living room. Her fur coat, flecked with snow, seemed several sizes too large and her vividly painted lips were spread in a feral snarl at Maurice.

'*How* did you get in? You stole the key, you bastard! Get out of my house, *get . . . out . . . of my . . . fucking . . . house!*'

On the street Maurice seemed philosophical.

'Temperamental, of course, Renée, always has been. You can't be married for all those years without knowing that. Still . . . didn't think she'd mind, somehow. Well, well,' he sighed, viewing the sky with distaste. 'Bloody snowing now, of course.'

We moved off up the cobbles. At the archway to the mews he stopped, as though arrested by some new and important idea.

'I expect you probably want another drink,' he said, eyeing me sternly.

The pub, filled with crop-haired soldiers from the barracks, was already hung with tinsel and Maurice's cane snagged a fairy-lit Christmas tree on our way to the bar. A Musak tape played varnished carols.

'I'm expecting good things of 1974,' he said when I'd got the whiskies.

'Have you plans?'

'Not particularly.' He took a cigarette from my packet on the table. 'Not particularly. In control now, however,

275

that's the difference. Command of the road wherever it leads.'

'Where,' I said, 'does it lead tonight?'

'I was coming to that. Naturally there are several options.' He laughed harshly. 'You know us sailors, girls in every port!' He drank towards the bottom of his glass.

'Friends in many quarters of the metropolis.'

'Where *have* you been staying? I mean last night, for instance?'

'Not really on the cards, old man. A misunderstanding, ridiculous really, you know the sort of thing that happens. And I was the bastard's best man,' he added bitterly. 'Still, plenty of chinas. But it might be just as well.'

'All right,' I said. 'But it's a bit sticky at home at the moment. So just tonight, eh?'

He looked offended.

'My dear chap. You know me. Is it closing time?'

'Not quite.'

'You could do with another,' he said, 'I imagine.'

So I got two more, we sank them and, both quite drunk, shuffled out into the night.

'Bloody snowing,' said Maurice. 'Cab?'

I said: 'Sorry, Maurice. No money. We've just about enough for the tube.'

'Very well,' he said reproachfully. 'I suppose that'll have to be it.'

The snow was in fact sleetish, thin and unsettling, but persistent as we edged towards the Underground.

'I suppose it'll be a sodding White Christmas,' said Maurice, gesturing peevishly with his cane. He wheezed, slowed and halted from time to time on our journey to Knightsbridge station but we caught a late train and he sank in deeply, hefting the cane across his knees.

'Do we have to change on this damned thing?'

'No. Caledonian Road. We're just outside.'

'Thank God for that. You rascal,' he said. 'Tell you what, let's have a drink.'

'I'm sorry, Maurice,' I said, 'but I don't think we've got a drop of anything at home.'

'No no no. Now.'

'How?'

'Here's how,' he said, delved into a wide inner pocket of the camel-hair coat and produced a silver hip-flask. 'Quite a bit here. I very rarely touch the stuff. Very rarely indeed. Just memory, I suppose.'

He drained it and went to sleep, clasping it to his heart and snoring. When I hauled him awake at Caledonian Road, he was outraged by the violation and for several seconds didn't know me. Finally home, there was scant welcome for either of us.

At dawn my wife was wide awake, staring at the ceiling. She said: 'I'm not getting up till he's gone.'

'It's all right,' I said, 'he's in the spare room. We made him a bed up.'

'I made him a bed up. And I'm not getting up till he's gone.'

I lumbered blearily into the kitchen. Maurice was sitting at the table in the clothes he'd slept in, drinking a glass of sherry and smoking a cigar.

'Morning, old man,' he said cheerily. 'Quite wrong about the booze, as you see. Found a bottle in one of those cupboards there.'

'Oh yes,' I said. 'Cyprus or something. Where on earth did you get that cigar?'

'God knows. It was in my top pocket. Somebody must have given it me.'

I put on the kettle. 'Maurice,' I said, 'do you have any plans for today?'

'Not particularly.' He let out a gust of foul cigar smoke. 'Why? Thought I'd hang about here for a bit if it's all the same with you. Make a few phone calls. One or two things to check up on.'

He finished his glass of sherry and poured himself another.

'Give me ten minutes,' I said.

'Long as you like,' said Maurice.

I prepared myself for the day, took my wife a cup of tea which she accepted sightlessly with an outstretched arm, and returned to the kitchen.

'Now,' I said.

'Now what?' said Maurice, each broken vein already alert with alcoholic interest.

'What we'll do is we'll go into town. To the office.'

'Very kind thought. But I think I'd –'

'Office. Get your coat on.'

He grumbled through the slush to the tube. At work he took the chair on the other side of my desk, ordered coffee from my secretary, laid his cane on the floor and was soon snoring gently.

Peter put his head round the door. 'How did you get on with old – Oh. By the way, are you going to do anything about Rawsthorne?'

At a quarter-past ten Mr E. J. Rawsthorne rang in person to say he was withdrawing the account. The next call was from my wife with the news that she was leaving.

'I don't know for how long. I don't know whether I'm coming back. I don't plan to. It doesn't work.'

'Where are you going?'

'I've left my key on the dresser. Your very dear old friend seems to have the other one – how long have you invited him for?'

'What? I told you, it was just last night.'

'Well, the spare key's not in the jug. You must have given it to another great old chum, mustn't you? Or left it in a pub. Have a nice Christmas,' she said, and put the phone down.

Maurice's snores had changed to a thin whistling. I went round my desk, lifted him to his feet by both camel-hair shoulders and shook him.

'What the hell are you –'

'Give me that key.'

'Get your hands off me!' he shouted with surprising force. 'What on *earth* are you talking about?'

'Have you or have you not got the key?'

'Of course I've got the bloody key.'

I dropped my hands and he staggered against the desk, wheezing heavily.

'Give it here.'

'Why? It's not yours.'

I stared at him. 'It's not mine?'

'Of course it isn't.'

'Then who the hell's is it?'

'Renée's, you idiot. Who happens to be,' he said, squaring his shoulders, 'my ex-wife. And as far as I can see, the matter is no concern whatever of yours. Would you mind handing me that cane? I have no wish to stay here a moment longer.'

And he made a haughty exit. When I went to the bank at lunchtime, the same pub tape of carols was playing, as though my life had somehow been looped in its spool. That night I wanted to walk home. There was no snow but it was very cold and my footsteps rang as I moved through the black winter limes in the park and the sharp metallic outlines of hedges. All the way round to Great Portland Street and up, and east, tacking through the little lit back-streets to my door. Which I looked at, remembering, before I let myself in.

A light was on in the kitchen. Maurice was sitting there, drinking a glass of sherry and smoking a cigar.

He said: 'It's just like Stone's Hotel.'

Biographical
Notes on the Authors

J. G. BALLARD was born in 1930 in Shanghai. After internment by the Japanese (on which experience his best-known novel *Empire of the Sun* is based) he read medicine at Cambridge. He then became a copywriter, a Covent Garden porter and an RAF pilot. He has contributed to all the leading science fiction magazines and published ten novels. He is a widower, with three children.

PETER CAREY was shortlisted for the 1985 Booker Prize for *Illywhacker* and won it three years later with *Oscar and Lucinda*. His career began with an acclaimed volume of short stories, *The Fat Man in History*. He lives in Sydney, Australia.

ANGELA CARTER was born in 1940. She has published eight novels, the most recent being *Nights at the Circus* (1984); three collections of short stories, including *Black Venus* (1985); and two works of non-fiction. She has done a considerable amount of work for radio and, together with Neil Jordan, she wrote the film script of her story 'The Company of Wolves'. Her journalism has appeared in almost every major British publication and her poetry has been published in the *Listener* and the *London Magazine*. Her work has been translated into many languages. She lives in London.

ADRIAN DANNATT, who is 27, has been described in the *Guardian* as 'a name to look out for in the future'. His poetry has appeared in various magazines and *PEN New Poetry II*; his stories in *Square Peg*, *Over 21* and *Encounter*.

BERLIE DOHERTY has lived in Sheffield since her student days at Durham. Her novels for children are serialised on *Jackanory* and Radio 4, and in 1987 her teenage novel *Granny was a Buffer Girl* was awarded the Carnegie Medal and an American prize. Her poems and stories (for both adults and children) are included in anthologies and such magazines as *Stand* and *Critical Quarterly*.

MARILYN DUCKWORTH is a New Zealand novelist and short-story writer, who spent her childhood in England. Her first novels, *A Gap in the Spectrum* and *The Matchbox House*, were recently reissued by the OUP in their NZ classics series. In 1984 her fifth novel, *Disorderly Conduct,* won the New Zealand Book Award. A collection of stories was published in autumn 1989.

LUCY ELLMANN was born in 1956 and educated at Falmouth and Canterbury art schools, the Courtauld Institute of Art and Essex University. Her first novel, *Sweet Desserts*, was published by Virago in 1988 and won the *Guardian* award for the best first novel. She lives in London with her small daughter.

ROBERT GROSSMITH, born in Dagenham in 1954, took a degree in Philosophy and Psychology at Keele. After community theatre work in Dorset he moved to Sweden as a translator, then spent a year in the USA, where he published some fiction in magazines. His first novel will be published in autumn 1990.

BIOGRAPHICAL NOTES ON THE AUTHORS

HOWARD JACOBSON was born in Manchester in 1942 and educated at Cambridge, where he studied English under F. R. Leavis. He has taught at Sydney University, Cambridge and the Wolverhampton Polytechnic, which last institution inspired his first novel, *Coming From Behind*, in 1983. His other novels are *Peeping Tom* and *Redback*. Now a full-time writer and broadcaster, he lives in London with his Australian wife.

PENELOPE LIVELY grew up in Egypt but settled in England after the war and took a degree in Modern History at Oxford. She is a popular children's writer and has won both the Carnegie Medal and the Whitbread Award. Her first adult novel in 1977, *The Road to Lichfield*, was shortlisted for the Booker Prize, as was *According to Mark* in 1984. Three years later *Moon Tiger* won it.

TRACEY LLOYD, who was born in Suffolk, began her career as an actress before starting to write for theatre and television. Several of her stories are based on her experiences of living in East Africa and Papua New Guinea, where she ran a touring theatre company. Currently working on a radio play, she lives in Oxford.

BERNARD MACLAVERTY was born in Belfast where he lived until 1975. He has been a medical laboratory technician, a mature student, a teacher and for two years writer-in-residence at the University of Aberdeen. He has published three collections of short stories – *Secrets*, *A Time to Dance*, *The Great Profundo* – and two novels, *Lamb* and *Cal*, plus versions of these fictions for radio, television and film. He lives in Glasgow.

ADAM MARS-JONES was born in London in 1954 and educated at Westminster, Cambridge and Virginia. His first book of fiction, *Lantern Lecture*, won the Somerset Maugham Award in 1982. His most recent book of stories, in collaboration with Edmund White, is *The Darker Proof* (1987, enlarged 1988). He reviews films for the *Independent*.

BIOGRAPHICAL NOTES ON THE AUTHORS

EDNA O'BRIEN was born in County Clare, Ireland. She is the author of three plays, five collections of short stories and ten novels. She now lives in London. A new collection of stories will be published in spring 1990.

RUTH RENDELL has been writing suspense fiction and detective stories for the past twenty-five years. She has thrice won the Crime Writers' Gold Dagger Award. Her Chief Inspector Wexford has appeared in fourteen novels and is now the subject of television serials. Her books have been translated into sixteen languages. She also writes under the name of Barbara Vine. A Fellow of the Royal Society of Literature, she is married, has one grown-up son and lives with her husband in a sixteenth-century farmhouse in Suffolk.

PATRICK ROGERS was born in 1955 in the United Kingdom, emigrated to Australia at the age of ten, and has alternated between the two countries since he was twenty. He writes radio and television drama as well as fiction. He now lives in Victoria, Australia.

CARL TIGHE was born in Handsworth, Birmingham, in 1950 and was educated at Swansea and Leeds University. After working as a lavatory cleaner, bread roundsman and toy salesman, he taught in Poland for three years. He was awarded the All-London Drama prize in 1988 and his first book, *Gdansk: The Unauthorised Biography*, is due in 1990. He is currently working on a volume of short stories.

JONATHAN TREITEL was born in London in 1959. He has worked as a physicist in California. He has a doctorate in philosophy of science from Stanford University. His poems are included in Faber's *Poetry Introduction* 7.

WILLIAM TREVOR was born in Cork in 1928, was educated at

Trinity College, Dublin, and has spent a great part of his life in Ireland. Since his first novel, *The Old Boys*, was awarded the Hawthornden Prize in 1964, his work has received many honours including the Whitbread Prize for Fiction. He is a member of the Irish Academy of Letters and has been awarded an honorary CBE.

EDWARD UPWARD was born in 1903 in Romford, Essex. As an undergraduate at Cambridge, he invented with Christopher Isherwood the imaginary village of Mortmere. He became a schoolmaster and was for sixteen years a member of the Communist Party, but left in 1948, believing it had ceased to be Marxist. His first novel, *Journey to the Border*, is regarded as a key book of the 1930s. Since retirement to the Isle of Wight, his trilogy *The Spiral Ascent* has appeared, as well as two books of stories.

FAY WELDON was born and brought up in New Zealand and went to St Andrews University, where she graduated in Economics and Psychology. After a decade of odd jobs and hard times, she started writing and now, though primarily a novelist (*Praxis, Puffball, The Life and Loves of a She-Devil, The Shrapnel Academy, Leader of the Band* and *The Cloning of Joanna May*), she has also had two collections of short stories published (*Polaris* and *Watching Me, Watching You*) and writes radio and television plays.

KIT WRIGHT was born in Kent in 1944 and educated at Berkhamstead and New College, Oxford. He taught briefly in schools and for three years at Brock University, Ontario. He was Education Secretary to the Poetry Society for a spell, since when he has been a freelance writer. His collections of poetry include *Bump-Starting the Hearse*. He also writes and edits books of poetry for children, most recently *Cat Among the Pigeons*. He lives in North London.

Acknowledgements

'The Secret History of World War 3', copyright © J. G. Ballard 1988, was first published in *Ambit* 114, 1988, and is reprinted by permission of the author and Margaret Hanbury, 27 Walcot Square, London SE11 4UB.

'A Letter to Our Son', copyright © Peter Carey 1988, was first published in *Granta* 24, summer 1988, and is reprinted by permission of the author and Rogers, Coleridge & White, 20 Powis Mews, London W11 1JN.

''Tis Pity She's a Whore', copyright © Angela Carter 1988, was first published in *Granta* 25, autumn 1988, and is reprinted by permission of the author and Rogers, Coleridge & White, 20 Powis Mews, London W11 1JN.

'Card Trick with Hearts', copyright © Adrian Dannatt 1988, was first published in the *London Magazine*, October/November 1988 and is reprinted by permission of the author.

'The Bad Boy', copyright © Berlie Doherty 1988, was first published in the *Critical Quarterly*, summer 1988, and is reprinted by permission of the author.

'Explosions on the Sun', copyright © Marilyn Duckworth 1986, was first published in *Landfall*, New Zealand; first British publication in the *Critical Quarterly*, winter 1988; reprinted by permission of the author.

ACKNOWLEDGEMENTS

'A Day in the Life of a Sphere', copyright © Lucy Ellmann 1988, was first published in the *New Statesman*, 23/30 December 1988, and is reprinted by permission of the author and Rogers, Coleridge & White, 20 Powis Mews, London W11 1JN.

'The Book of Ands', copyright © Robert Grossmith 1988, was first published in the *Critical Quarterly*, autumn 1988, and is reprinted by permission of the author.

'Travelling Elsewhere', copyright © Howard Jacobson 1988, was first published in the *Observer* magazine, 2 October 1988, and is reprinted by permission of the author and Peters, Fraser & Dunlop, 5th Floor, The Chambers, Chelsea Harbour, Lots Road, London SW10 0XF.

'The Five Thousand and One Nights', copyright © Penelope Lively 1988, was first published in the *Observer* magazine, 28 August 1988, and is reprinted by permission of the author and Murray Pollinger, 4 Garrick Street, London WC2E 9BH.

'Volunteer', copyright © Tracey Lloyd 1988, was first published in *Woman's Journal*, July 1988, and is reprinted by permission of the author and Maggie Noach, 21 Redan Street, London W14 0AB.

'Summer Lightning', copyright © Adam Mars-Jones 1988, was first published in the *Observer* magazine, 14 August 1988, and is reprinted by permission of the author and Peters, Fraser & Dunlop, 5th Floor, The Chambers, Chelsea Harbour, Lots Road, London SW10 0XF.

'A Foreign Dignitary', copyright © Bernard MacLaverty 1988, was first published in the *New Statesman*, 15 January 1988, and is reprinted by permission of the author.

'Another Time', copyright © Edna O'Brien 1988, was first published in the *New Yorker*, 14 November 1988, and is reprinted by permission of the author and Duncan Heath Associates, Paramount House, 162–170 Wardour Street, London W1V 3AT.

'Weeds', copyright © Ruth Rendell 1988, was first published in the *Observer* magazine, 4 September 1988, and is reprinted by permission of the author and Peters, Fraser & Dunlop, 5th Floor, The Chambers, Chelsea Harbour, Lots Road, London SW10 0XF.

'Notes of a Copernican Biographer', copyright © Patrick Rogers 1988, was first published in *Panurge* 8, April 1988, and is reprinted by permission of the author.

'And Now This', copyright © Carl Tighe 1988, was first published in

Ambit 113, 1988, and is reprinted by permission of the author.

'Children of the Headmaster', copyright © William Trevor 1988, was first published in the *Spectator*, 24/31 December 1988, and is reprinted by permission of the author and Peters, Fraser & Dunlop, 5th Floor, The Chambers, Chelsea Harbour, Lots Road, London SW10 0XF.

'A merican', copyright © Jonathan Treitel 1988, was first published in the *Critical Quarterly*, autumn 1988, and is reprinted by permission of the author.

'The Scenic Railway', copyright © Edward Upward 1988, was first published in the *London Magazine*, June 1988, and is reprinted by permission of the author.

'Ind Aff – or Out of Love in Sarajevo', copyright © Fay Weldon 1988, was first published in the *Observer* magazine, 7 August 1988, and is reprinted by permission of the author and Anthony Sheil Associates, 43 Doughty Street, London WC1N 2LF.

'Just Like Stone's Hotel', copyright © Kit Wright 1988, was first published in the *London Magazine*, August/September 1988, and is reprinted by permission of the author.

We are grateful to the editors of the publications in which the stories first appeared for permission to reprint them in this book.

Also available in Minerva

Giles Gordon & David Hughes

THE MINERVA
BOOK OF SHORT STORIES 1

The Minerva Book of Short Stories 1 is the first in a series of paperback anthologies taken from William Heinemann's *Best Short Stories* series. It combines the short fictions of leading writers with those of an exciting wealth of new talent. Varied, illuminating and enjoyable, this volume is a remarkable tribute to the current richness of the form.

'Stories from masters like William Trevor and newcomers like Hanif Kureishi. It is a selection with an all-round assurance of tone. Outstanding is Nadine Gordimer's *Spoils*, an ambitious account of Africa's balance of terror' *Daily Telegraph*

'A wide-ranging and impressive collection' *Independent*

Christopher Burns · Patrice Chaplin · Jim Clarke
Richard Crawford · Ronald Frame · Sophie Frank
Penelope Gilliatt · Nadine Gordimer · Georgina
Hammick
Hanif Kureishi · Jim Mangnall · Adam Mars-Jones
Deborah Moggach · Salman Rushdie · Graham Seal
Lionel Seepaul · Helen Simpson · William Trevor
Guy Vanderhaeghe · Marina Warner

A NEW BOOK OF DUBLINERS

Edited by Ben Forkner

This collection of stories set in Dublin in this century, apart from containing James Joyce's story 'Ivy Day in the Committee Room' taken from his celebrated collection of stories, *Dubliners,* contains stories by fourteen other writers. The editor's aim in this collection was to search out stories in which the special qualities of Dublin life enter into the narrative as an active force. Most of the writers in the collection were not Dubliners but came to Dublin from other regions and other cities of Ireland.

As the editor writes: 'Dublin is surpassingly prodigal of public theatre of all sorts and there is far more than one type of stage in these stories . . . Whatever else binds these brilliantly varied stories together, they are bound most of all by the success with which they extend Joyce's achievement in *Dubliners* through almost a century of creative association between a single city and a single literary genre.'

Christopher Hope

LEARNING TO FLY

This astonishingly subversive collection of tales about South Africa by the author of *A Separate Development* and *My Chocolate Redeemer* is based on his award-winning collection *Private Parts* but contain a large element of new material. We meet Colonel Rocco 'Window Jumpin'' du Preez and Colonel Jake 'Dancin'' Mphalele, both top-flight security interrogators. Then there is Hilton, the student radical who out-radicalises them all including, eventually, himself in a surprising resurrection; and, most movingly, Ndbele, who has to create his own world in order to abide by the rules of a racially obsessed society.

Christopher Hope's vivid, humorous vision of both sides of South African life wickedly lays bare the absurdities of apartheid in a series of stories which is at once wry, savage, ironic and elegant.

'Not until the end of *Private Parts* can one fully appreciate the care, the skill, with which these ten short stories were assembled . . . The effect is insidious and devastating – a total flaying of the rationale with which apartheid is veiled. Beneath it, there is exposed so monstrous a travesty of reason that anyone (of whatever colour) attempting to live by its rules must themselves become mad in order to feel themselves sane . . . Other South African writers have said this, but none with such ferocious humour, creative imagination or style'   *New Statesman*

Moy McCrory

BLEEDING SINNERS

'*Bleeding Sinners* deals with women's fertility; its pain
and pleasure; its consequences in a world fettered by
ignorance and fear. Its eleven short stories range from
the frankly fantastic – as when a bored wife wakes up
to find her husband has turned into a giant sprouting
potato – to the naturalistic Belfast setting of the title
piece . . . This is an extraordinary book about ordinary
experience, beautifully written and observed'
Time Out

'Moy McCrory has a laser-sharp eye and knife-like pen
. . . the story "Drop Stars Fall in Unmarked Places" is
a consciously literary poetic gem . . . by itself it makes
Bleeding Sinners worth the price and marks Moy
McCrory as a writer to watch'   *Scotland on Sunday*

'Her prose style is taut and muscular, her narrative skill
tackles complex interwoven time-scapes with deceptive
ease . . . this is a book which demands to be read'
Spare Rib

'McCrory writes revealingly about a raw world that
cannot settle cosily into sistership. She can also be very
witty'   *Guardian*

'Generous and compassionate, and to coin a phrase,
bloody marvellous'   *Irish Times*

Christopher Hope

MY CHOCOLATE REDEEMER

'Bella is a teenage chocolate addict who listens to heavy metal music on her Walkman and is given to fits of praying and prying . . . Bella lives in a gossipy village by an idyllic lake in France with her aristocratic grandmother who adores the charismatic leader of a fascist political party dedicated to ridding France of its black citizens; and her uncle, a mad scientist who is attempting to duplicate the birth of the universe in his laboratory.

'This rather perverse, eccentric society is shaken by the appearance of a deposed African leader, an urbane man with a reputation for intense cruelty and cannibalism. Perhaps his unusual diet is what makes him so delectable, for he is Bella's chocolate daddy, his skin so dark and lustrous that she imagines eating him . . .

'A fantasy with realistic trappings . . . beautifully written with angry irony surging through the narrative'
Listener

'A clever, wry and beautifully written novel about self-deception and the origins of despotism'   *Guardian*

'Unholy, stylish and very funny'
Elaine Feinstein, *Times*

'Curious, alarming and exceptionally original'
Hermione Lee, *Irish Times*

A Selected List of Titles Available from Minerva

While every effort is made to keep prices low, it is sometimes necessary to increase prices at short notice. Mandarin Paperbacks reserves the right to show new retail prices on covers which may differ from those previously advertised in the text or elsewhere.

The prices shown below were correct at the time of going to press.

Fiction

☐	7493 9026 3	**I Pass Like Night**	Jonathan Ames	£3.99 BX
☐	7493 9006 9	**The Tidewater Tales**	John Bath	£4.99 BX
☐	7493 9004 2	**A Casual Brutality**	Neil Blessondath	£4.50 BX
☐	7493 9028 2	**Interior**	Justin Cartwright	£3.99 BC
☐	7493 9002 6	**No Telephone to Heaven**	Michelle Cliff	£3.99 BX
☐	7493 9028 X	**Not Not While the Giro**	James Kelman	£4.50 BX
☐	7493 9011 5	**Parable of the Blind**	Gert Hofmann	£3.99 BC
☐	7493 9010 7	**The Inventor**	Jakov Lind	£3.99 BC
☐	7493 9003 4	**Fall of the Imam**	Nawal El Saadewi	£3.99 BC

Non-Fiction

☐	7493 9012 3	**Days in the Life**	Jonathon Green	£4.99 BC
☐	7493 9019 0	**In Search of J D Salinger**	Ian Hamilton	£4.99 BX
☐	7493 9023 9	**Stealing from a Deep Place**	Brian Hall	£3.99 BX
☐	7493 9005 0	**The Orton Diaries**	John Lahr	£5.99 BC
☐	7493 9014 X	**Nora**	Brenda Maddox	£6.99 BC

All these books are available at your bookshop or newsagent, or can be ordered direct from the publisher. Just tick the titles you want and fill in the form below. Available in:
BX: British Commonwealth excluding Canada
BC: British Commonwealth including Canada

Mandarin Paperbacks, Cash Sales Department, PO Box 11, Falmouth, Cornwall TR10 9EN.

Please send cheque or postal order, no currency, for purchase price quoted and allow the following for postage and packing:

UK	80p for the first book, 20p for each additional book ordered to a maximum charge of £2.00.
BFPO	80p for the first book, 20p for each additional book.
Overseas including Eire	£1.50 for the first book, £1.00 for the second and 30p for each additional book thereafter.

NAME (Block letters) ....

ADDRESS ....

....

....